NOVELS BY EDITH PATTOU

East

West

Hero's Song: The First Song of Eirren

Fire Arrow: The Second Song of Eirren

Ghosting

WEST

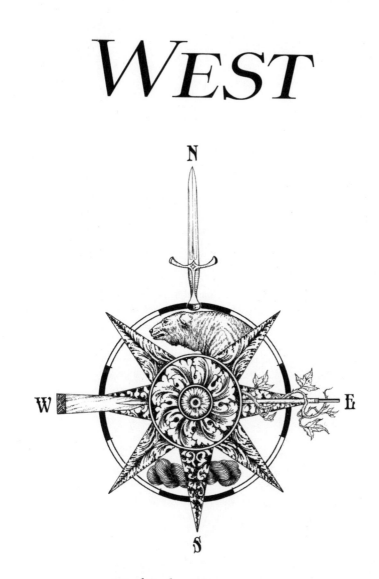

Edith Pattou

HOUGHTON MIFFLIN HARCOURT

BOSTON   NEW YORK

hmhco.com

The text was set in ITC Legacy Serif Std.

Library of Congress Cataloging-in-Publication Data
Names: Pattou, Edith, author.
Title: West / Edith Pattou.
Description: Boston ; New York : HMH Books for Young Readers, 2018. |
Sequel to: East. | Summary: When a sudden storm destroys Charles' ship
and he is presumed dead, Rose believes something sinister is at work
and she sets off on a perilous journey, with the fate of
the entire world at stake.
Identifiers: LCCN 2018007162 | ISBN 9781328773937 (hardback)
Subjects: | CYAC: Fairy tales.
Classification: LCC PZ8.P2815 Wes 2018 | DDC [Fic—dc23
LC record available at https://lccn.loc.gov/2018007162

Printed in the United States of America
DOC 10 9 8 7 6 5 4 3 2 1
4500729106

For Vita and
for all the Roses in this world,
who are brave, who are warriors,
and who persevere,
no matter what

PROLOGUE

I HAD PLACED THE BOX, the one etched with runes that contained the story of Rose and her white bear, in a quiet corner of my library. There was a woven cloth on top where my cat would often nap in the late afternoon sun. It was a handsome box with the look of an antique and would get the occasional compliment from visitors.

"From Norway," I'd say. "It has been in the family for a very long time."

One afternoon in September, I was seized with a desire to open the box. It had been some time since I had revisited Rose's story. My cat was ill-pleased to have her nap interrupted and watched me with an annoyed expression as I rummaged through, taking things out and examining them all over again. The maps with their elaborate wind roses, the sheaves of music tied with ribbon, the mouthpiece of a flute, and those impossibly small soft leather boots.

They all told the story of Rose and her journey to the land that lay east of the sun and west of the moon.

The tale began on a desperately poor farmhold in Norway, or Njord as it was called back then, with a daughter who lay on the verge of death. An enormous white bear appeared in the doorway, promising healing as well as riches to the family, if the youngest daughter would come away with him.

This daughter was Rose, a north-born child with a wild and wandering spirit. For just short of a year, Rose lived in a castle carved into a mountain where she wove gowns the color of silver, gold, and moonglow, and fell a little bit in love with the white bear.

But then all was lost, because of trickery and Rose's own powerful curiosity. And so she set out on that odds-defying journey to make right the wrong she had done.

As she traveled to the land that lay east of the sun and west of the moon, Rose encountered those who helped her—a mother and daughter from France, a drunken sea captain, a wise Inuit shaman, and a young boy troll named Tuki—as well as those who wished to destroy her—a powerful Troll Queen with an all-consuming, destructive love.

When I opened the box, I did not hear the music I'd heard the first time I opened it, which was both a relief and a disappointment.

But I found something new, something I had not noticed before. It was a key, ivory colored and just larger than a child's finger. It was sewn, securely and with even stitches, onto a crumpled piece of paper. The paper bore no writing and was brown with age, and the thread seemed ancient and gossamer thin, but it held fast.

I found the key jammed into a bottom corner of the box and, when I pulled it loose, was astonished to discover a false bottom to the wooden box. Yes, a false bottom. I had thought such things only existed in dime novels. But there it was, and what I found inside was that Rose's story had not ended where I thought it had. Not by a long shot.

Of course stories never do. There are always thousands of details, small and meaningful, that follow a happy ending, or what one believes to be a happy ending.

Rose herself said much the same thing, but she said it better.

I have already told the story of my white bear and me. I told it in words, which didn't come easily, and also in cloth, which did. If I had to do it again, I think I would make a map of it. I am not a mapmaker like my father, but it runs deep in my blood.

And these are the bearings of that story, the north, south, east, and west of it:

A meadow in Fransk where a prince played with a red ball. A farmhold in Njord where a girl learned about the lies parents will tell to keep their children safe. A doorway in that farmhold where an enchanted white bear asked the girl to come away with him to save her family. Njord-sjoen, the sea under which that same girl was carried, swaddled in sealskin and enchantment. A castle carved into a mountain where all was lost because of a candle, and then, because of a name written in a book of music, all was gained. An ice ballroom where a girl wearing a mask and a moon dress had her heart broken. Kentta murha, *the killing field of the trolls, where they sent their human servants to freeze and die. Tatke Fjord where the ship called* Rose *came and rescued those "softskin" servants who had survived. And finally the front parlor of the farmhold where the enchanted white bear, no longer a prince but human once again, finally slipped the Valois ring onto the girl's thumb and made her his wife.*

That is the map of what came before, the map of then.

But now there is a different map, with different bearings.

Stories often end with a marriage and those expected words happily ever after. *Stories should be like that perhaps, but life is not. In truth, my story with the white bear was very far from being over after we got married.*

A new map, with new bearings.

There were times when I wished I somehow could have frozen that day, the day in the front parlor when Charles and I were married. That we could have stayed in that moment forever. Or even better, the moments afterward, when we snuck off, just the two of us, finding a quiet spot overlooking the Trondheim harbor. We drank fresh apple juice, ate warm brown bread, and watched stars flickering in the not quite dark summer sky. And we both knew we were where we truly belonged, with each other.

But of course if we had stayed frozen in that moment, I would not have known the joy of bringing a bairn into the world, that squalling, red-faced, miraculous being who completed my heart.

I don't know why we had trouble naming our bairn, but we did. First we thought we would name him after Tuki, the brave young troll who died so that we might survive. But then we thought that our firstborn should be named Charles, should be given the name his father had reclaimed after so long an ordeal.

We went back and forth.

One day Estelle, a dear and much loved part of our family, cried out that when the bairn was squalling he looked exactly like the West Wind in a drawing in one of her storybooks. She called him vent de l'ouest, and from that point on we took to calling him Winn, short for wind. We thought of it as a temporary name, that his true name would come clear to us as he grew older.

And so it was we had a new map, a map of now. A map of home and love and music and family.

Then it all changed. And all of our north, south, east, and west bearings were gone. In the blink of an eye.

BOOK ONE

OEST

They were lost in the waves, on wind-tossed ship.

—*The Edda*

MOTHER

I HAD NEVER BEEN ONE TO DREAM. This irked me much in my youth because dreams were rich with portents and guideposts for one's life. I sorely envied those who dreamed, even though Arne always said it was for the best, that I was far too susceptible to being swayed by superstitions as it was.

At any rate, I had resigned myself to the fact that I was the dreamless kind and would always remain so, until that night in late spring when I had the dream about Rose.

I woke up drenched with sweat, clutching Arne's arm so hard that he had marks on his forearm for days afterward.

"Eugenia!" he was saying, half in pain and half in concern. He told me later that my eyes had been crazed, wide with terror.

"Arne," I gasped, barely able to breathe.

"What was it, my dear? A nightmare?" Arne asked, reaching out his arms to pull me to him, to comfort me, but I jerked back, holding him away with a hand on his chest.

"It was horrible. Horrible," I moaned, and began to shake.

"Tell me," Arne said.

"It was Rose," I cried. "I dreamed . . . Oh, Arne!" And with that, I began to sob.

He held me and kept me close until the tears eased and I could breathe again.

Rose was the youngest of our seven children, and she was always the one who had given me the most anguish over the years. Indeed, little more than three years earlier, we had come close to losing her forever when she set out on her quest to find Charles after he had been taken by the Troll Queen.

"'Twas only a dream," Arne said softly, trying to comfort me. But all I could do was shake my head in despair.

He led me into the kitchen and made me a cup of chamomile tea. While it cooled, I tried to sort myself out. Part of me did not want to tell Arne the dream. I worried that giving it voice might somehow make it come true.

Arne tried his best to reassure me, pointing out that the night before I had eaten rather more onions than usual with the roasted beef, which wasn't a bit true.

Finally he said, "Tell me the dream, Eugenia." And I did. I could not keep it bottled up inside me any longer.

"The dream began," I said, "with Rose wandering alone through a forest. And I was there too, following behind, but she could not see me. As Rose wended her way through the trees, she came upon an overlarge gray raven perched on a low-hanging branch. Instead of giving it a wide berth, as

I would have had her do, Rose made straight for it. And the raven swooped toward her. She froze in place, and as the bird hurtled at her, cawing loudly, Rose suddenly faded to a dull gray color, and I realized with horror that she had turned to ash."

"Ash?" Arne said, making sure he had heard me correctly.

"Yes, ash," I said, "and then the bird flew up into the sky, its powerful wings beating the air, which caused the ash-Rose to fly up as well. But all at once, she was no longer recognizable as a person, was instead a swirling, spiraling pattern of gray. Abruptly the bird disappeared and the air was still. The ashes dispersed and separated and fell softly to the ground, blanketing the forest floor, as if with a dusting of gray snow."

Arne was staring at me, his mouth slightly open.

"Something terrible is going to happen to Rose," I cried out, my voice shrill.

We had not seen Rose and Charles for more than a year, but they were due to visit us in two weeks' time. Rose was coming with her bairn from their home near La Rochelle in Fransk, while Charles was returning from a recent stay in Stockholm, Sverige, where he had been commissioned by King Gustav himself to play his flauto in the royal orchestra and to share his expertise and refinements on the orchestra's wind instruments.

Arne shut his mouth and sat up straighter. "Nonsense," he said briskly. "'Twas only the onions you ate."

"But Arne—" I cried.

"There are no ravens on ships," he said. "You'll see, Eugenia. Rose and her bairn will be with us soon, safe and sound."

I prayed that he was right.

ROSE

") T IS A NORTH WIND," came a voice beside me.

"Is it?" I said.

"Yes," said Sib, "with a bit of west mixed in."

I turned to smile at Sib, who had come to stand beside me at the ship's railing. Sib was one of the so-called "softskin" servants who had escaped Niflheim after the destruction of the Troll Queen's ice palace. Three years had passed since she came to live with Charles and me in Fransk. We had become fast friends, and in many ways, I was closer to her than to any of my siblings, except my brother Neddy, of course. Her true name was Sibhoirdeas, but she said that most who had known her called her Sib.

"That's Neddy's direction," I said with a smile. "North-west."

Sib returned my smile, for she knew all about the unusual birth direction superstition of my mother's family, which had been so much a part of my growing up in Njord, that the direction a woman faced when giving birth shaped the personality of the child. My mother never wanted a north-facing bairn, who would be wild and headstrong with a love for adventuring, but that's exactly what I had been. Mother, however, had refused to accept this and was determined that I should be an east-born child. I didn't learn of my true north nature until I was older.

"This northwest wind suits you," Sib said. "Though perhaps not as well as a pure north wind. But you look happy, Rose."

I nodded. It was our sixth day on the ship called *Guillemot*, which was taking us to Trondheim. It was my first visit home since Winn's birth and only the second since Charles and I had been married.

"I will be seeing my family soon," I said. "And Winn will meet his grandparents, aunts, uncles, and cousins."

I smiled down on the sleeping face of my bairn, who was swaddled in a sling over my shoulders. It still made me catch my breath, looking at those almost translucent eyelids lined with golden lashes.

I gazed out over the expanse of Njordsjoen again. It was choppy, a deep blue almost to blackness, but this too made me catch my breath. The open sea. I had missed it, the salty wind in my face, the call of the gulls.

These past three years had been happy ones for my white bear and me, carving out a life for ourselves in Fransk. Yet there were moments now and then when that old restlessness would overtake me, and I would be driven to strap on my boots and go wandering through the countryside.

Charles understood. "If it wasn't for your wild nature, I would still be a white bear. Or worse," he once said to me, when I had finished apologizing for being gone overlong.

Even after the birth of Winn, my white bear accepted my wanderlust. He would just brush my forehead with his lips and say, "Off with you."

I loved our bairn with all my heart, knew from the moment I kissed that wrinkled, damp face for the first time that I would have given my life for him. But at the same time, it was perhaps the hardest test I had ever faced, balancing my wild, northern nature with that love. Because that is the truth of a bairn, that they need you, body and soul, and I was tethered to him in a way I had never known.

Charles felt the same way, but for him being tethered was exactly what he wanted. Having roots, a home he could call his own, after almost one hundred and fifty years of roaming the world as a white bear, was all the happiness he desired.

It was odd, I suppose, that I still sometimes called him White Bear, but I did. Charles didn't come easily to my tongue. It was as if that person taken from his life by the Troll Queen so long ago was something of a stranger to me, and in some deep down way, I would always think of him as a white bear.

I would occasionally slip. The first time I actually called him White Bear after we were wed, he flinched. But then he smiled.

"So be it," he said, pulling me to him. "After all, it was as a white bear that I first loved you."

"And I you," I whispered into his shoulder.

I'm embarrassed to say, however, that most often I called him such things as "my love" and "dear." Hardly words I would ever have imagined myself saying back when I was young and wild, climbing trees and falling into ponds.

Sib broke into my thoughts, telling me that she had just checked on Estelle and that the herbal remedies Sib had given her had done nothing to relieve the girl's seasickness.

"Poor Estelle," I said. And indeed Estelle had had a rough time this past year. When her mother, Sofi, had died unexpectedly of a wasting sickness, there were no relatives left to care for her, her uncle Serge having emigrated to Spania. Charles and I were happy to bring her into our family. We loved her dearly, and she was a resilient girl. Still, the loss of her mother had been hard.

We thought a journey to Njord would be a welcome distraction, and because she had always longed to see the world, Estelle was thrilled at the prospect. Until we boarded the *Guillemot*. With the first roll of the ship, she had been laid low by seasickness.

ESTELLE

I THOUGHT I WAS GOING TO DIE. I wished to die. The ship felt like a giant hand holding me and shaking me as if I was a pair of dice in some horrible game meant to kill me.

I missed my *maman*. I missed Fransk. I missed land under my feet that didn't heave and bounce around. Tante Sib said I must drink water and eat hard crackers, but if I did, I only threw them up.

I had wanted to journey to see the wide world, but the moment I stepped onto the miserable ship, I wished I had not. I would have traded my favorite dress, the sky blue one Maman made for me before she died, to be back on solid land.

Even though I loved Rose like I loved my *maman*, I could not help being most unpleasant to her and to Tante Sib.

Rose said they understood and that I must have courage, that we would be in Trondheim soon. She even promised to make me a new dress or perhaps buy me one from a nice shop in town. That made me feel better for a moment, but then the ship lurched and I threw up again even though there was nothing left to throw up.

Mon Dieu, s'il te plaît, sauve-moi!

ROSE

A S SIB AND I STOOD at the ship's railing, I noticed that the wind had quickened and that the surface of Njordsjoen had grown choppier. I glanced sideways at Sib, whose silver hair was flying around her face. She wore an abstracted, faraway expression, one I'd seen many times before. And for the first time, I impulsively asked the question I'd always wanted to ask.

"Where do you go, Sib?"

She turned to gaze at me, surprised.

"I mean, when your face is like that, where do you go?" I said.

She hesitated for a moment, then said, "I'm listening to the wind."

I must have looked confused, for she gave a little laugh.

"It's true. Did you know that there are many winds, Rose? Many more than just the north, south, east, and west winds."

"How many?" I asked.

"More than can be counted. And each land has its own names for their winds."

"Tell me," I said.

She smiled and said, "All right. For example, the wind, the gentle one that was just playing on your skin a few minutes ago, before the direction changed, that was the *ciuin* wind, as we call it in Skottland. It is a favorite of mine."

"And you know the names of all these winds?"

"Many," she said.

"How do you know so much about wind, Sib?" And despite our close bond, I was struck, not for the first time, by how little I knew of her past, before coming to the ice palace in Niflheim. I had asked, but she always seemed to deflect my questions, and I was left with the vague impression of a life spent in many different places, with no family still living.

"I had a teacher, and I paid attention," she answered briefly. I was about to ask more, but she changed the subject to Estelle.

"I wish there was something I could do to make her feel better," said Sib.

I nodded. I was lucky that I had never been prone to seasickness, and Winn, too, seemed to love being on board the ship, his bright blue eyes taking it all in. After those first few months of endless squalling, he had turned out to be a good-natured, easy bairn. He slept well on the ship, lulled by the roll of the waves.

The sky had darkened, and the ship suddenly gave a sharp pitch.

Sib looked out at the sea, a puzzled look on her face. "I

don't know this wind," she said. "It doesn't feel right to me. 'Tis a good thing we are almost to Trondheim."

"Poor Estelle," I murmured, trying to steady myself on the rolling deck. "She will be glad to be back on land again."

One of the sailors shouted out that all passengers should go below, and Sib, Winn, and I went to join Estelle in our cabin.

NEDDY

I BEGAN TO BE VERY TIRED of hearing about Mother's dream, and her incessant picking apart of the portents of ravens and forests covered with falling ash.

"Onions," Father kept saying. And another time he said that he had it on good authority that ashes were a portent of birth. "Perhaps Rose and Charles are planning another bairn," he suggested cheerfully.

But even that didn't make Mother hold her tongue. Quite the contrary.

Still I had to confess that when the *Guillemot* sailed into the Trondheim harbor and we saw Rose at the rail waving to us, I was much relieved.

She was carrying the bairn they called Winn in her arms. On one side of her was the silver-haired Sib, and on the other was the girl Estelle, whom they had adopted into their family when her mother died. Even at a distance I could see the young girl was not feeling well.

When they disembarked, we all greeted them with hugs and tears of joy. Mother held out her arms to Winn, who went to her straightaway. She began to quiz Rose about his birth direction, but Rose just shook her head with a smile, refusing to be drawn.

The girl Estelle, whom I had met during one of my visits to Fransk, made us all laugh when she got down on her knees, saying, "*Mon Dieu*, how I love you, ground that does not heave and roll beneath me."

I turned to greet Sib, and the most extraordinary and unexpected thing happened. A breeze coming off the water had blown her silver hair across her face, and as she brushed it away, our eyes met. In that moment, my heart did a most unusual flip-flopping inside my chest and suddenly began to hammer as if I had just done a tremendous sprint around the harbor.

I must have looked a little stunned, for she said in her sweet, low voice, "Is something wrong, Neddy? You do remember me, don't you?"

"Of course," I stuttered.

And in truth I remembered Sib well, even from the very first time I had seen her, one of the ragtag group of survivors cresting the top of the ridge of Tatke Fjord. Though she had been quiet, she had stood out with her pale skin and silver hair. Then, and even now, I was not able to guess her age. Her skin was unlined, even luminous, but there was the silver hair, and occasionally she would have an expression on her face of the sort you'd see on a very old woman, one who had lived through a lifetime of joys as well as hardships.

But none of this accounted for the odd hammering of my heart.

Winn let out a cry, and Rose said, "Someone is hungry!" And we grabbed up their luggage and began to head for home.

A brisk wind had kicked up, and as we passed a group of sailors, we heard them talking loudly about the rough seas and how they'd heard there were violent storms to the east. A thread of uneasiness went through me. Charles was headed here from the east. I fervently hoped that his ship was not affected by the storms.

WHITE BEAR

E VEN THOUGH MY STAY in Stockholm in the court of King
Gustav had only lasted a fortnight, it had felt an eternity.
I couldn't wait to be done with the gossip, the intrigue, the
sheer artificiality of court life.

The only pleasant moments for me were when I was playing my flauto with the orchestra and could hear the soaring
music all around me.

King Gustav had an immense love of music, had put
together what I believed to be the very first true orchestra in
all of Europa, perhaps the entire world. It was called Kungliga
Hovkapellet and featured some of the finest musicians it had
been my privilege to play alongside. King Gustav spared no
expense when it came to his orchestra, and he was an extremely
generous and charming patron. But I quickly became aware
that he also had a sly and ruthless side, and a terrible temper
that could erupt at any moment.

There was a good deal of political intrigue in the court,
and King Gustav showed signs of paranoia, to the point that
he even took me aside one day, asking if I thought the treble
viol player had the look of a poisoner about him.

But the hardest thing about it all was being away from home, separated from Rose and our bairn, as well as Estelle, whom I now thought of as a daughter, and Sib. I couldn't wait to be reunited with them.

I had placed the silver Valois ring on Rose's thumb a little more than three years ago. It was the ring I had given her just before I was taken away by the Troll Queen to the land that lay east of the sun and west of the moon, the ring Rose had worn on her thumb throughout the long and difficult journey to find me. Valois was the title of the line of royalty from which I was descended, though I had known nothing of my past until Neddy helped me piece it together.

During these past three years, I have felt like the luckiest man in all the land to be able to wake up and look into those violet eyes every morning.

Still, I would be lying if I were to say I had not thought about the great *what if* of my life. *What if* the Troll Queen had never spotted me that day, playing on the hillside with other children near the castle where I lived as prince of Fransk? What if I had not forgotten that cursed red ball and instead had gone inside earlier, with the other children? What if the Troll Queen had not kidnapped me, if her father had not then cursed me to be a white bear?

If those "what-if"s had not happened, I would have grown up to be king of Fransk.

King.

Unfathomable.

I thought of King Gustav, of his fine robes and resplendent palace, of the orchestra he had created. But I also thought of his three successive wives and a host of children he seemed barely to know, of the backbiting courtiers and the air of distrust and intrigue that seemed to surround him.

No. It was true that one hundred fifty years enchanted as a white bear had almost destroyed me. But at the end of it there was Rose. My heart-mate.

*What if*s be damned. All that mattered was my life with Rose and our family.

The seas were rough, and there was talk of high winds from the east. All the better, I thought, for it would carry me that much faster to Trondheim.

MOTHER

ROSE EXPLAINED TO ME how she and Charles had been undecided about what to name their bairn and that while they were making up their minds, they had taken to calling him Winn.

I seized on that, for I quickly sensed that the bairn was a west child through and through.

"Nonsense," Rose had replied when I told her my feeling. "He is called Winn only because of Estelle and the illustration in a book. I already told you I have no idea what direction I was facing when I gave birth."

I did not believe her, but could tell by the stubborn set of her chin, one I knew so well, that she would admit to nothing further on the subject.

So I shifted my attention to Sib. Finding her alone in the back garden, I asked her about the circumstances of Winn's birth.

"A wonderful day it was," she said.

"Where was Rose, when she birthed him?"

"In her bed, in the room she and Charles share," Sib replied.

"And does the bed face the doorway?" I had not been to

Rose and Charles's home in Fransk. Neddy was the only one of us who had.

"Yes," said Sib.

"And which direction does that door lie?" I asked, leaning forward.

She smiled at me in such a way that I knew Rose had told her of our family's birth direction superstition.

"I can't say exactly," she said slowly. "But there was a lovely wind that day."

"What wind?" I asked.

She smiled again, and said, "Did you know that in some places in the world, there is something quite similar to your birth direction lore? It has to do with the winds."

"There is?" I said, much interested.

"Yes," she said. "In those places, they believe that the direction the wind is blowing when a child is born will be a determining factor in its life."

I gaped at her. "What places?"

"Oh, I believe in pockets of Skottland, and a few others, less well known."

I found this fascinating but wanted to get back to the subject at hand. "You never did answer me, Sib. What is the wind that was blowing when Winn was born?"

She laughed. "Very well. It was Zephyrus."

"And in what direction does Zephyrus blow?" I asked eagerly.

"Is that Winn I hear?" she said, looking toward the bedroom where he was napping. "Sounds like his hunger cry." And she hurried away.

I quickly went to look for Neddy and found him at his worktable.

"Do you know the names of the winds, Neddy?" I asked.

"A few," he said. "They are sometimes named in stories I have read."

"I was just wondering if you were familiar with the wind called Zephyrus?"

"Oh, yes," he said. "That is one that is much spoken of by the old Gresk poets. In fact, it is featured in the tale about Psyche. Zephyrus is the wind that blows her to the god known as Eros."

"Yes, fine," I said, impatient. "But in what direction does Zephyrus blow?"

"I believe it is a gentle west wind," Neddy said. "But why—"

"Aha!" I said in triumph. "It is just as I thought."

I then left Neddy, who wore a look of abject confusion.

ESTELLE

T HINGS WERE DIFFERENT IN NJORD. Some of it was very nice, like the cloudberries with fresh cream, and the *kjottboller*, the tender little balls of meat that tasted so good. And I loved the bluebells and ladyslipper flowers that bloomed all over. But some of it was not so nice, like the slimy pickled herring Rose's *maman,* Eugenia, loved so well, and how chilly it was, so that even though it was summer, the air still felt cold, especially at night, and I had to stay by the fire to keep my fingers from going numb. And the sun stayed out so much longer. I missed the moon.

But I liked the town of Trondheim very much, and it was so close to walk there, not like living out in the farmlands as I had in Fransk first with my *maman* and later with Rose and Charles. It reminded me of visits to La Rochelle, all the shops and people, but in Trondheim the buildings were painted in bright colors and there were different kinds of shops than in La Rochelle. People were nice too, smiling at me when I passed them, especially when I had Winn in the sling around my shoulders. It faced forward so his big, toothless smile always caught people's eyes.

I liked Rose's many nieces and nephews. Her brother Willem and sister Sara had three children each, and I especially liked Gudrun, who was Willem's eldest daughter. She had two blond braids and laughed a lot. The only thing I didn't like was when she told me scary stories about the Nokken who lived under the bridge that went over the Nidelva River, the bridge I crossed every day when I went into town. She and the other children warned me that the Nokken could shape-shift and turn himself into a white horse who would offer children rides and then plunge into the water, carrying them to their deaths.

Gudrun's brother, Anders, also told me of the hideous old ghost witch named Pesta, who carried a broom and a rake. She had been around since the terrible plague hundreds of years ago and would travel from farm to farm. If she carried the rake, only some of the people living in the farm would die, but if she carried a broom, everyone in the family would die. They said she had been seen lately, in the distance.

Rose caught Anders telling me about Pesta and scolded him. She told me later that these were just imaginary stories, like the ones I used to make up when I was young, the ones about ghost-wolves and troll-witches.

I knew she wanted to comfort me, but because I knew that the story of Rose's journey to the land that lay east of the sun and west of the moon was a true story, I knew there really were evil creatures in the world like trolls, or Huldre, as Rose said they called themselves.

When I was younger, I did love stories of derring-do and longed to be out in the world having adventures. But after my *maman* died, I was not so sure. And now that I have been on a ship and thought I would die of the *mal de mer*, I realized I was happier staying in one place, especially one with shops and nice people smiling at me on the street.

NEDDY

CHARLES'S SHIP WAS LATE by two days. All of us, except perhaps Rose, were worried. And in fact it was not unusual for ships to be a day or two late, since so much depended on the prevailing winds. But there had been much talk about the fearsome storms in the east.

I went down to the harbor as I had the previous days and was in time to see a tall ship docking. It was not Charles's ship but looked as if it had been through stormy weather, with sails tattered and one of the midmasts partly broken off.

I approached one of the sailors as he disembarked and asked if there had been any news of the ship called *Hynde* bound from Sverige. He appeared to be exhausted, but looked me in the eye, a grim expression on his face.

"The tidings are ill," he said. "We heard that the *Hynde*, along with several others traveling in that part of the sea, sailed straight into the center of the storm. It is said that it was wrecked, with very few survivors."

A cold feeling spread through me. "Where did it founder?" I asked.

"Off the coast of Fransk, near a town called Etretat."

"So far west?" I said in surprise, thinking hopefully that perhaps it was not the same ship.

"The winds were immense," the sailor said. "No one had ever seen their like before. Many, many ships were blown off course. Our ship caught only the tail end of it, and I hope I never live through winds like that again. No, I'm afraid it was definitely the *Hynde* that was wrecked off Etretat."

I closed my eyes. *Charles,* I thought.

MOTHER

W HEN NEDDY RETURNED from the harbor, I saw at once something was very wrong.

"It is Charles," Neddy said, his voice cracking. "His ship was wrecked. Off the coast of Fransk."

"Fransk?" Arne said in disbelief. "But—"

"Yes, I know," Neddy said. "I thought the same. But I checked with one of the sailors whom had weathered some of the same storm, and the word up and down the coasts is that this was a most unusual storm and that it pushed the *Hynde* through the southern end of Njordsjoen down into the straits of Dover. There are said to be very few survivors."

"My dream," I whispered. "Not Rose, but Charles."

"Eugenia," Arne said, his tone firm.

Just then Rose, Sib, and Estelle all came into the house. Estelle was chattering about the delicious *solskinnskringle* pastries they had gotten from the *boulangerie* they had visited in Trondheim, but Rose stopped abruptly when she saw us huddled in the great room.

"What is it?" she asked.

Neddy went to her. "It's Charles. We've just learned the ship he was traveling on was wrecked."

Rose went pale. She handed Winn, who was half asleep, to Estelle, asking her please to take the bairn upstairs and put him down for a nap.

Estelle looked frightened, but she did as Rose asked.

"Go on," Rose said to Neddy, and he recounted to her all he had learned.

She listened closely, then said, "He is not dead."

"I hope he was one of the survivors," Neddy said, "but—"

"No, I know he is not dead," she said. "We must go to him, to Etretat."

"Rose," I said, rising and going to her, putting my arm around her shoulders.

"Yes, Mother," she said calmly.

"It may be that . . ." I started, faltering. "You must prepare yourself."

She looked at me straight on, her eyes bright. "Mother, I would know. Here," she said, laying her hand over her heart. "I would know if my white bear were gone."

ROSE

I WENT TO MY ROOM TO PACK. Opening the cupboard where I had stored some of my old cherished belongings, I pulled out the cloak with the wind rose design, the one I had made what seemed a lifetime ago on Widow Hautzig's old loom.

The cloak was fraying at the hem and some of the stitching had come loose, but the wind rose design that I had copied from Father's artwork was still easy to make out. It was also easy for me now to see the lie as well as the truth in the design.

Because I had been born to replace my sister Elise, an east-born, it had been imperative to my mother that I too be born facing east. But the circumstances of my birth during a violent storm in Askoy Forest were such that I wound up being born north. My father told me that was the reason he had always called me Nyamh in his heart, though Mother insisted I was in fact east-born and would be Ebba Rose. Father at least prevailed when he said I would go by the name Rose, for the center of the wind rose.

When he designed my wind rose, something he did for each of his eight children, he mostly used the symbols of the east direction (hourglass, bees, herbs), but he had also slipped in one representing the north, hidden in the clouds. It was a white bear. And little did he know as he drew the lines, that one day a white bear would become the latitude and longitude of my life.

In the cupboard I also found the candle Mother had given me, the candle I had used to light the unlightable darkness of my bedchamber when I was in the castle in the mountain, the candle that had led to such a catastrophic outcome. There was a time I had thought to get rid of it because of all the unhappiness it had brought about, but the practical side of me reasoned that such a candle might well come in handy. I also had the flint, and I packed both in my knapsack.

At the bottom of the cupboard, I found Sofi's map, the one she had given me at the beginning of my journey to the land that lay east of the sun and west of the moon. It was much the worse for wear, torn and frayed and water-stained, but still mostly decipherable. And I also found the *leidarstein* that Thor had given me. These I put into my pack as well.

And last, I lifted out the story knife, the beautifully carved blade that Malmo had given me, with which we passed the long days telling stories inside the ice house we built, the blizzard Negea raging outside. I had also used it in the ice palace to tell my story finally to Tuki, to ask his help in freeing my white bear from the Troll Queen. I shivered, thinking of the terrible moment when Tuki had been destroyed by the queen's rage.

I already had with me the *echecs* piece called Queen Maraboo that Estelle had given me back when I first set out on my journey to the land that lay east of the sun and west of the moon. Unlike my mother, I did not have many superstitions, but Maraboo was my one lucky talisman, and I always carried it with me on my wanderings. As I stowed it in the pocket of the cloak, I realized that by taking with me the story knife, the map, the *leidarstein,* and Queen Maraboo, I would have something from each of the friends who had helped me on my last journey.

I was dismayed when I learned we could not book passage to Fransk for more than a week. The shipping lines had been much disrupted by the storm.

"It will give us time to prepare," said Neddy, seeking to comfort me. But I would not be comforted until I had gotten to Etretat and found my white bear.

NEDDY

ROSE WAS IN AN AGONY of restlessness, which I well understood.

Unlike her, however, I was not optimistic about the outcome of our journey, but I believed she must see for herself. And it would give us the opportunity to honor Charles there in the place where I felt almost sure he had lost his life. A marker or grave of some kind.

Of course I confided none of these feelings to Rose, but Father and I discussed it several times, and he said that both he and Mother were in agreement with me.

It was a difficult time. Only Estelle, and of course little Winn, seemed unaffected.

Then our departure got pushed back even further, and I thought Rose was going to explode with impatience. She threatened to find a boat of her own and paddle herself to Fransk. She asked our sister Sara's husband, Harald Soren, who was a merchant, if he could help, if he had a ship to spare, but much as it saddened him, he could come up with no ship that would get us there any sooner than the one we already had booked our passage on. His small fleet of ships had also been badly affected by the storms.

One afternoon, five days before we were due to sail for Fransk, a ship came into harbor. It had come from Le Havre, but I learned that it had made a stop near the town of Etretat to see if it could provide any aid to the town and any survivors of the wreck of the *Hynde*. I was closely questioning one of the sailors of that ship when the captain himself approached me.

"I understand you are the son of Arne the mapmaker?" he said, and I nodded. "I have a packet here addressed to him."

My breath caught in my throat, and I took the packet with trembling hands. I did not recognize the handwriting on the outside, but was fairly certain it was not Charles's.

I was sorely tempted to open it, but holding myself in check, I hurried home as fast as I could.

When I got there, I found Father and Mother in the kitchen. Rose had gone for a walk with Winn and Sib. Estelle was with Gudrun at Willem's home.

Father hesitated a moment, but opened the packet. When he pulled out the paper inside, a small silver ring fell out. It landed on the kitchen table with a ping, spinning around until it fell on its side. I reached for it, my heart pounding. It looked exactly like the ring Rose had worn for so long, while she journeyed to find the white bear in the land that lay east of the sun and west of the moon. The Valois ring that Charles had put on her finger when they wed. But that made no sense, since I had seen that ring on Rose's finger just this morning.

And then I remembered. Rose told me that she had had an identical ring made for Charles, which she gave him after the birth of Winn. It also had the word *Valois* inscribed inside.

Father was reading the paper that had come in the packet, and his face had gone very pale.

"What is it?" Mother asked.

He looked up at us, tears pooling in his eyes. "It is from a friend of mine, a mapmaker who lives in Fransk. He used to reside in Paris but had retired and is now living in the countryside near Etretat. He had heard of the wreck and traveled there to see if he could offer assistance. When he arrived in town, he learned that Rose's husband had been one of the passengers.

"He tracked down all the survivors," Father continued, "but could not locate Charles. Finally he found a badly injured man, a soldier by the name of Julien, who had been with Charles on the ship and was with him when he . . ." Father's voice broke.

I took the letter from Father and began to read out loud the words of the soldier who had been with Charles.

". . . a mortal wound to the head. I tried to stanch the blood, but I knew he was dying. He knew it too, and he pulled a ring off his finger and handed it to me. 'Give this to my wife, Rose, from Charles,' he said. He made me swear an inviolable oath. Then he died."

"No," came a voice loudly from the doorway. It was Rose.

ROSE

I WENT TO THE KITCHEN TABLE.

I had recognized the ring from across the room, but I picked it up anyway, my eyes searching for the word *Valois*.

I found it, and my mind was flooded with the memory of the smile Charles had given me when I put it on his finger. Radiant, matching my own.

"Thank you, Rose," he had said. "I will wear it always," he added, his voice solemn. "Until I die."

I didn't remember any superstitious shiver at those words, only joy. Because it mirrored exactly the way I felt about the ring he had given me.

"Rose?" came Neddy's voice, gentle.

I looked down at my hand. I had been clutching the ring so tightly that it had left a mark in my palm. A half circle. If what the letter said was true, then the half circle was me. If Charles was gone, I was half, and would never be whole again.

A shudder went through me, but I straightened. "No," I said again, even louder. Because in spite of all I had heard, despite the ring I held in my hand, I could not accept that Charles was gone. I *would* not accept it.

"Show me the letter," I said.

Neddy passed me the page, his face etched in grief.

I read it through closely. It was signed by the soldier Julien. The words sounded true, plausible. But there was something about it that didn't seem right to me. Why would he have called himself Charles? I rarely called him that. He would have said, *Give this to Rose, from her white bear.* I was sure of it.

But there was something else, something I could not put my finger on, that bothered me about the letter. It had to do with the wording, the language used. It sounded stilted somehow.

"What nationality is this soldier?" I asked suddenly. "Does it say in the cover letter, from Father's friend?"

Neddy looked down at the first page of the document. "He describes the soldier as Spanien."

Maybe that's it, I thought. *It was stilted because he was communicating in Njorden, which isn't his language.*

"Though it also says here that he spoke Njorden quite fluently," said Neddy.

I read through the letter again. I could feel everyone's eyes on me. I could also feel their pity, their belief that I was clutching at straws.

And then it came to me. It was the formality of the language.

It was the kind of language the Troll Queen used, at least as Charles described it. I remembered him telling me of the conditions the Troll Queen's father had set when he turned Charles into a white bear, the Troll King had called them "inviolable."

But both the Troll Queen and her father were dead.

I got a prickling feeling along my skin. And I knew. The letter was a fake. It had been written by a troll. The queen might have been dead, but it was likely that not all the members of the Huldre race had perished in Niflheim.

And one of them had written that letter.

 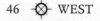

MOTHER

ROSE WAS DETERMINED to go to Fransk, especially once she was convinced the letter was not real. And as much as Arne tried to convince her that his mapmaker friend would not be fooled, that events must have happened as this soldier described, Rose would not listen.

I was glad when Neddy insisted on going with her, along with Sib.

Arne and I were happy to watch over Winn and Estelle, and Willem and Sara both offered to help as well. Estelle and Gudrun, Willem's middle daughter, had become close friends, and Sara's youngest was the same age as Winn, so she was well prepared to care for a bairn.

Rose, Neddy, and Sib were to leave two days after Midsummer, and I think the solstice celebration provided a welcome distraction from the looming journey, as well as what all of us, except perhaps Sib, who was hard to read, believed to be Rose's stubborn and mistaken belief that Charles was not dead.

I knew that my dream of the ash-Rose and the raven had portended ill and hoped that Neddy was right, that seeing the wrecked ship and speaking to the soldier who had been with Charles when he died would finally convince Rose. And though the pain would be immense, in time I prayed that she would heal.

Estelle was very excited about Midsummer. She said they did not celebrate the solstice in Fransk as we did in Njord. She had brought a dress with her that her mother had made for her before she died, which Estelle said was *parfait* for dancing.

She was not disappointed. The weather that night was perfect, with a soft, fresh breeze blowing off the sea. The women and girls wore flower wreaths in their hair and everyone danced around the *maistongen*, a tall pole with a crossbar that had been draped in wreaths and flowers.

When it was finally dark and Winn was fast asleep in Rose's arms, I smiled to see the awestruck expression on Estelle's face as the bonfires all along the Nidelva River were lit. They burned fiercely, dazzling our eyes and leaping high into the night sky with orange-yellow flames. The reflections of the bonfires in the water made the sight doubly beautiful.

"C'est magnifique!" Estelle said, her eyes aglow.

Winn woke up just as the fires were beginning to flicker and flare out. He fussed a little, but I quickly passed around our traditional Midsummer pancakes spread with sweet butter and sprinkled with sugar, and all was well again.

I thought of my dream and of Charles, of the terrible way he had perished. I thought too of Rose heading off on this fool's journey to find him, and for a moment I worried that nothing would ever be well again.

Then Winn let out one of his sweet laughs, reaching happily for another pancake. Someone started singing the traditional "Sma Frosker" song, and Estelle got up and started acting it out, pretending to be a little frog, which made Winn laugh even louder. I exchanged a smile with Arne.

It was Midsummer, and there were pancakes and songs and dancing. In this moment we could set aside our troubles and be content.

ROSE

FOR JUST A FEW MOMENTS during the Midsummer bonfires, I was able to forget about the journey that lay ahead. But as I gazed down at Winn's sweet face laughing at Estelle's capers, his chin shiny with butter, I remembered. I couldn't bear the thought of leaving them both behind.

But I must find my white bear.

Once before, I had journeyed to find him, and I had succeeded at great odds. I refused to believe that I could not do it again.

Unless, a small voice in my head whispered, *unless your family is right, that the letter is real and your white bear truly is in the land of the dead.* In stories you could journey to that land. But in real life there was no such pathway.

I shook my head fiercely. No. It was not true. The letter was a fake, and Charles still lived. Somewhere. And I would find him.

I wore both rings now. Charles's original ring, which had been my wedding ring, and the one I had given him. I had tied silver thread around it so it would not slip off my finger. I wore one on each of my thumbs.

NEDDY

A S I WATCHED ROSE BID FAREWELL to Winn, I saw that
her eyes were bright with tears. She kissed him on the
forehead and reluctantly handed him to Mother. Both Mother
and Sara assured her that they would take good care of him,
and even Estelle piped up, saying she too would help watch
over the *bébé*.

Rose hugged the young Fransk girl tightly, saying how
much she would miss her. Tears ran freely down Estelle's
cheeks as she hugged Rose back. Then, as Rose went to board
the ship, Estelle ran up to her and hugged her one last time,
and I could hear her say something about Queen Maraboo.
Rose smiled and reached into the inner pocket of her cloak,
pulling out the game piece Estelle had given her years before,
the last time Rose set off to find the white bear. Tears stung
my own eyes as I thought how this time she was setting off to
bury him.

"It is my good luck," Rose said, holding up Queen Maraboo.

I had been surprised and secretly pleased that Sib had
wanted to accompany Rose and me. The news of Charles had
distracted me, made me notice it less, but the sensation of that

strange flipping of my heart had lingered. It was an extraordinary thing. Part of me wanted to be near her all the time, yet I also felt awkward, worried perhaps that she would hear that noisy heart of mine.

In the past both Sara and Rose had teased me about finding a wife, wondering why I was the only one of us who remained unwed. Sara had certainly tried matching me up with local maidens, but for whatever reason, I found I had little interest in pursuing a friendship with any of them. I had certainly never experienced this strange heart-thumping feeling before.

Another odd thing was that all of a sudden I had developed a strong urge to write poetry, which seemed related to Sib and my unruly heart. I hadn't thought about writing a poem since I was a young boy, and those early efforts had been so bad that I was sure anyone who remembered them would have been quite alarmed at the thought of me taking it up again. Especially Rose. I remembered that when I read her the poem I'd written about a white bear, she had fallen into paroxysms of laughter so severe that she developed a case of hiccups lasting several hours. That was the last poem I ever wrote.

No, perhaps it would be better to forget the whole poem writing idea, I told myself.

Our sea journey to Etretat would take roughly five days. On the second afternoon, I had a conversation with a man from Anglia. He was a friendly sort but was preoccupied with disturbing news of a spreading sickness that had struck many in the city of London as well as the outlying countryside of Anglia. He said it was called the Sweating Sickness. After his business in Fransk, he was due to go back to London and was concerned about what he might find there.

In my historical researches over the years, I had learned of such deadly illnesses that spread quickly through cities and towns, of course none worse than the horrific plague that almost cut the population of Europa by half back in the fourteenth century.

And of course it had been just such an epidemic of influenza that had killed my mother's parents, as well as many inhabitants of Trondheim, leading to the collapse of my grandfather Esbjorn's mapmaking business. That in turn had led my father to become a farmer, with all the disastrous turns of events that followed for our family.

Thus I was sympathetic to the man's concerns and was uneasy to learn about the disturbing news from Anglia. So many ships sailed back and forth between that country and Njord.

ROSE

I WAS SITTING IN A SUNNY SPOT on deck, working on mending my old cloak. I had to use quite a large needle to baste the lining around both the collar and hem, which were much frayed. As I sewed, I thought about Charles, about the ship he had been on and the soldier named Julien to whom he had given the ring. If there really was such a person and he wasn't a troll as I suspected, Julien must have been mistaken about the severity of Charles's wound. The soldier had survived the shipwreck, and so had Charles.

Sib appeared and sat beside me. I asked where Neddy was, and she said he was with his new friend from Anglia. I continued my sewing while Sib gazed out at the horizon.

"Why did you come with us, Sib?" I asked, suddenly breaking our silence.

She looked startled.

"Is it that you believe as the rest do," I said, "that Charles is dead? And you wanted to be with me when I learned the news?"

"No." She shook her head slowly. "That's not why."

"Then why? Does it have to do with Neddy?" I asked. I had

noticed in Neddy an odd awkwardness around Sib during the previous days and wondered what was going on between them.

"Neddy?" She looked genuinely surprised.

I worried that I had said something out of turn, but her mind was clearly elsewhere.

"No," she said again, then turned to look me in the eyes. "Rose, I do not know if Charles still lives or not, though I believe it is possible. But in either event, I wanted to be with you, to help you in whatever way I can." She turned away from me then, her eyes again focused on a distant point of the horizon. "There is another smaller reason, and it will perhaps sound odd, but I also came because of the wind, or rather the winds, they spoke of, like none ever seen before."

"What do you mean?"

"They puzzle me. I felt them, a little, on our journey to Trondheim. I wanted to come where they were worst, to see for myself."

"But they are long gone," I said. Indeed the weather had been fine, a light brisk breeze just right for propelling the ship toward Fransk.

"I can still feel them," she said with a little shrug. "Smell them even."

"How do you know so much about wind, Sib?" I asked.

"You asked me that before."

"And as I recall, I got a very unsatisfactory answer," I replied with a smile.

"As I said then, I had a teacher, long ago. I was a good student," she said.

"How do you learn the winds?" I asked.

"Each person learns the winds in their own way," she said, her eyes far away again. "Some experience them as songs, some as stories. It depends on the kind of person you are."

"How do *you* feel them?" I asked.

"Songs," she said. "I hear the music in them." She paused, fiddling with a strand of her silver hair, then spoke again, her voice low and serious. "And when you know the wind well, when you can sing its song or tell its story, you can affect it. Bend it."

I looked at her in astonishment. "Are you saying you can do that?"

Sib gazed at me, at my expression of disbelief, and laughed gently. "There. I've said too much. Now you think I'm crazy. Never mind. My ma always said I had a rich imagination," Sib said with a smile.

Neddy joined us, saying it was time to go below deck for the evening meal. I quickly stowed my mending, which I hadn't quite finished, and as I walked with Neddy and Sib, I thought about what she had said. I couldn't recall her ever mentioning her mother before, but more, I couldn't fathom the idea of someone being able to bend the wind. The only magic I'd ever seen had been done by the Troll Queen or was a result of troll arts, which I thought of as evil.

NEDDY

THE FIRST GLIMPSE WE HAD of Etretat was its massive chalk cliffs gleaming alabaster in the morning sun. I had never seen anything like it.

The coastline was jagged with many outcropping of rocks that jutted out of the water. A challenge for a ship's captain, even in calm waters. A chill went through me as I pictured those fearsome winds that had driven Charles's ship across a roiling sea, with this deadly honeycomb of pale rock to navigate through. When the white needle, or *aiguille blanche* as the Fransk sailors called it, came into sight, I wondered if perhaps it marked the spot where Charles's ship had foundered. I learned later that the wreck had occurred several leagues south of town and was no longer visible, as the sea and winds had broken it up. What was left was submerged, lying on the sea floor.

We found lodging at an inn and began our inquiries there. We knew that Father's mapmaker friend was no longer in Etretat, having gone back to his home inland. But we hoped, Rose especially, that the soldier Julien would still be in town, recuperating from his injuries.

The horrific shipwreck was still much on people's minds. The innkeeper said that he had done a brisk business providing lodging for grieving relatives of those who had lost their lives.

He told us the little he knew about the survivors, only four or five by his reckoning, and he believed they were still in town, because of their extensive injuries. He thought that perhaps one had died in the past few days.

A house owned by a local woman with skill in herbs and healing had been used as a makeshift hospital, and as far as the innkeeper knew, at least two of the survivors were still there.

Many bodies had washed up and were buried in a meadow some distance from town. It was thought that a number of them would never be recovered at all, as there was a strong tide that would have carried them out to sea.

I volunteered to take on the unhappy task of reviewing the recorded list of the bodies that had been found and identified, while Rose was determined to go to the house where the survivors were being cared for. Sib said she wanted to go down to the beach near the *aiguille blanche.*

"The wind?" Rose said softly to her as we all parted.

Sib nodded with a smile, and I wondered what they were talking about.

ROSE

T HE WOMAN WHO HAD OPENED her home as a temporary
hospital had gingerbread-colored hair and a kind smile.
Her name was Hannah, and she looked exhausted but had
clearly encountered many others like me.

She shook her head sadly as I described Charles to her. "I'm
sorry," she said, her voice gentle.

Hannah said she had only two remaining patients, a griz-
zled older man who had been the ship's cook and a middle-
aged woman who had been traveling to Njord to meet her first
grandchild. Hannah said she feared the poor lady would not
get the chance to meet the new bairn.

I asked about the soldier named Julien who had survived.
She brightened a little, saying that he had left her house several days ago.

"Quite a recovery he had," she said. "When he first came
to me, I was certain he wouldn't survive. But he rebounded
in an extraordinary way. Indeed, I thought surely his leg was
badly broken, but I must have been mistaken, for he was able
to leave, with no splint or crutch or anything except a bit of a
limp."

She went on to say that he clearly had a strong will and a very appealing way about him, and that he had told her he was taking a room at an inn near the harbor. He was planning to return to his home in Spania as soon as he could book passage.

She gave me the name of the inn and I turned to go, thanking her profusely, but, on a hunch, turned back.

"By chance," I asked, "did this soldier Julien have any visitors while he was here?"

"Oh, yes, he did," Hannah replied. "He came early on, shortly after the wreck. Very distinctive man he was. Hard to forget." She gave an involuntary shudder. "I don't think I heard his name . . ." She paused, thinking.

I waited, trying to be patient.

"No, can't remember. But he stayed some time with Master Julien. And seeing family must have done him good, because I swear that it was after he left that Julien seemed different. Stronger. He even sat up a bit, which he hadn't been able to do before. I think he said the fellow was a distant cousin. Though I have to say, they didn't look a bit alike. Master Julien is quite a nice-looking young man. The cousin—" She cleared her throat. "Well, he had bad skin, scarred I think, and very pale. He was thin, too, like a skeleton."

"What was his voice like?" I asked, my heart beating a little faster.

"Awful sounding, now that you mention it, like he'd had a bad cold or even damage to his throat. Raspy."

I had a prickling feeling all along my skin, but I took a deep breath, and after thanking Hannah again, I headed back to town.

I walked in a daze, barely aware of the path beneath my feet. Pale, rough skin. Raspy voice. Those were the characteristics I remembered so vividly from Urda and Tuki and the Troll Queen herself. Troll characteristics.

I had been right. If the soldier Julien was not a troll himself, he was clearly in league with at least one of the Huldre people.

MOTHER

ROSE AND NEDDY HAD BEEN GONE a week when Neddy's good friend Havamal came by to inquire after our family. He had heard the news about Charles and the shipwreck and was wondering if we had heard anything further. I told him it was too soon, but that we weren't optimistic. He nodded, saying that he had heard the storms had been unprecedented in their ferocity. Havamal was a historian and told us that the last storm to have caused so much damage and loss of life had occurred some seventy years ago.

Before he left, Havamal also told us the sad news that Farmer Magnus had recently and quite suddenly passed away. Farmer Magnus was a neighbor of Havamal's, as well as being a prominent resident of Trondheim.

"How did he die?" I asked.

"Some kind of influenza," he said. "Everyone was surprised because he'd always been such a healthy, strong fellow."

I nodded agreement. Farmer Magnus had been only a little older than Arne and me. I felt a tremor of unease. Arne said I worried too much, especially when it came to influenza, but he knew that I came by it honestly, since I had lost both my parents in an epidemic back when Arne and I were first married.

When Havamal was gone, I quickly collected a few acorns and laid one on each of the windowsills of our house.

Later in the afternoon, Arne found one of them and brought it to me with a suspicious look on his face.

"What have you gotten in your head now, Eugenia?" he said.

"'Tis nothing," I said. "Just a bit of good luck for the home."

I'm not sure he believed me, but he just shook his head and put the acorn back where he found it.

"Is Estelle out walking?" he asked. I nodded.

Estelle had gotten into the habit of taking Winn out for a walk during the hour before dinner. I suspected part of her reason was to avoid kitchen duty, but I encouraged her, seeing that it made her feel important, and I'll admit it was a relief to have the two of them out from underfoot while I was cooking.

"Dinner will be ready soon," I said.

But before going back to the kitchen, I went to fetch two sprigs of mugwort from the garden shed. Tying them together with red thread, I nailed the bundle to the top of our front doorway.

I knew Arne would shake his head at me, but I have always believed it is better to err on the side of caution.

ROSE

I LOOKED CALM ON THE OUTSIDE, but my mind was reeling. If it was true that the man who claimed to have seen my white bear die had had a troll visitor, what did it mean?

When the pale queen destroyed the ice palace, I had seen all those trolls die with my own eyes. Charles later told me he understood that nearly all the trolls in the Huldre kingdom had been assembled to see their queen wed.

These past years, we had thought they were all gone, perished when the Troll Queen unleashed her rage at Tuki and obliterated her beautiful palace.

We two alone had survived, along with a number of softskin slaves who had been shut up in the servants' quarters, far away from the main building of the palace. We had found no sign of surviving trolls in the quiet desolation of the ruins.

But were there trolls who still lived? Who either had not been at the wedding or had somehow escaped? And who perhaps sought revenge on the softskin prince who had chosen me above their queen?

I had thought the Troll Queen's arts were without equal,

but now I wondered if there were other trolls who had similar power, strong enough to cause a storm on the sea unlike any seen before.

Could the soldier Julien in fact be a troll that had shape-shifted into the guise of a human?

I found the inn where Hannah said Julien was staying. It was near the docks, in a different, rougher part of Etretat than the lodgings we had found. When I inquired of a tired-looking woman who was sweeping the front stoop about the soldier, Julien, who was staying there, she told me he wasn't in, but that I'd most likely find him at the public house down the road.

I found the establishment she described and entered. The room was dark and smelled of burnt malt. It was mostly empty at this early hour, and I approached a man who stood behind the bar, drying and stacking tankards.

"Is there a soldier by the name of Julien here?" I asked.

He frowned at me, then gestured with a nod to a table in the far corner of the room. A man was sitting there, leaning back in his chair, looking like he was dozing. A half-empty pint of lager sat in front of him.

Cautiously, I approached. "Excuse me?" I said, coming up to the table.

His eyes blinked open. In the dim light I could see that he was still a young man, though he bore scars on his face that looked old. The scars made his skin look ridged.

"Are you the soldier called Julien?" I asked, keeping my voice as steady as I could.

"*Si*," he replied with a grin. "*Quién es esta hermosa dama con ojos de color violeta?*"

I took a deep breath. His voice was normal, no hint of the raspy cadence of a troll. And he did indeed seem to be from Spania.

"I'm sorry," I said. "I don't know much Spanien. Do you speak Njorden or Fransk?"

"Both," he said in Njorden. "And yes, I am the soldier Julien. Unless you have come to conscript me back into the army. If that is the case, lovely lady with the violet eyes, I am someone else entirely," he went on, his grin growing broader.

"You are the man who was with my husband when he died?" I said, deliberately, my eyes locked on his.

His face froze, the grin still in place but its previous warmth had disappeared. He reached for his pint and drained the remaining lager. Then he set it down, swallowing hard, and took a deep breath. "Please, sit," he said. "Would you like something to drink? Or eat? Their boiled beef stew isn't entirely inedible."

"No, thank you," I said. But I did take a seat in the chair opposite him.

He was studying my face closely. "I am very sorry for your loss," he said, his voice deep and solemn. I saw his eyes take in the two rings on my thumbs, and he seemed to flinch a little.

"Tell me," I said.

"It is hard . . ." he started.

"Hard to remember? Or hard to tell me?" I asked bluntly.

"Both," he said. "I have seen much of death, but this was . . ." Again he trailed off. He was looking down at his hands.

"I want to hear it. Don't worry. I am strong."

He looked up at me briefly. "I can see that," he said.

And so he launched into the story I had heard Neddy read from the letter. The words were much the same as those I'd heard in my parents' great room. Except for the word *inviolable*. He didn't use that word.

"You are sure he said 'from Charles'?" I asked.

His eyes were on his empty tankard, as if he wished it were full again.

"Yes," he said.

"Thank you for keeping the ring and seeing that it was sent to me," I said, touching the ring on my right thumb.

He nodded, still staring down at his tankard.

It was a plausible story. There was nothing in his manner, other than not always meeting my eyes, to indicate he was lying.

"I am deeply sorry," he said again. And his voice broke a little, almost as if he meant it.

"Thank you," I replied. "You have been through a rough time yourself," I went on. "It must have been comforting to see your cousin."

"Cousin?" he said, puzzled. But then his expression shifted, and he quickly added, "Yes, yes indeed. It was good of him to travel here." He rose abruptly. I thought for a moment I detected fear in his eyes, which unnerved me. It was so at odds with his reckless air of bravado.

"I am sorry to rush off," he said, "but I have an appointment down at the harbor regarding a place on a ship heading back home to Spania. You can find me here later if you have any further questions, or if there is anything at all I can do for you." He stood and limped across the room and out the door.

NEDDY

Rose was not yet back from her errand, so I went to look for Sib. Though I had not found Charles's name in the lists of identified bodies, I was still feeling low in spirits. All those lost lives, all the grieving families—mothers, fathers, wives, children—left behind.

I came upon Sib sitting on a large rock near the shoreline. She welcomed me with a smile and made room for me next to her.

"You found nothing?" she asked softly.

"Nothing," I replied.

"That could be a good thing," she said.

I didn't answer. Sib saw that I was downcast, and she laid a hand on my arm. At the touch of her warm fingers, my heart began that overloud pounding and I could feel myself flush. She did not seem to notice, her gaze now directed toward the blue expanse of the sea.

As she looked outward to the water, I studied her profile, the pale, ageless skin, the clear brown, farseeing eyes. And I wondered as I had so many times before how old she was, all the life she had lived before coming to be connected to our family.

She never spoke of her past except in vague generalities, and she would always evade the questions that Rose in particular was not shy about asking. But the few times she did speak of her family, it was with love, not bitterness. I wondered what had happened to them, why there had been no one to return to after leaving Niflheim.

"Have you ever been married, Sib?" The words came out of my mouth almost unbidden, and I immediately regretted them.

She looked startled and turned to me.

"Why do you ask?" she said.

I cast about for a reason that might make sense and came up with a half-true but feeble statement about how seeing the names of the dead had made me think of all the widows left behind.

"I wondered if you have had a similar loss," I said.

She nodded slightly. "Yes, I have," she said. "But not a husband. My father was lost to the sea when I was only a bairn. And I lost my mother as well, many years ago."

"I'm sorry," I said, laying my hand on hers. I thought there was no way she could not be aware of my hammering heart. She did turn to look at me, and I could have sworn the look that passed across her face was one of sorrow.

But then she smiled her sweet smile, squeezed my hand,

and stood, saying, "Perhaps we'd better see what Rose is doing? She has been gone long."

I nodded dumbly and rose to my feet. As we walked back toward our lodging place, I was pleased that Sib laced her arm through mine.

ROSE

I FOUND IT VERY DIFFICULT following the soldier Julien without him being aware of me, but somehow I managed it. Fortunately he didn't move swiftly due to his limp.

He did not go to the harbor as he had said, but instead to the inn near the docks where I had first gone looking for him. He went inside, and as I stood in the shadow of a shop, trying to decide what to do next, he emerged again, carrying a large pack.

I shadowed him to the harbor. He stopped in front of a ship docked there, set his pack down, and stood still, seemingly waiting for someone. I tried to look inconspicuous, sheltering near a large pile of barrels. Shortly Julien was approached by a tall, thin man in a black coat. They appeared to be arguing, but I was too far away to hear what they said.

Abruptly the soldier Julien turned and headed up the gangway of the nearby ship. The man in the black coat watched for a moment, then turned and headed in the opposite direction.

I stood still, my heart beating fast. Should I board the ship and confront Julien, or should I follow the man in the black coat? I decided all at once to follow the man in the black coat. The one I was convinced was a troll.

ESTELLE

G RAND-MÈRE EUGENIA INSISTED that I tie a pouch containing garlic and angelica root to my bedpost.

Quelle odeur!

I asked Grand-père Arne why I must have it there, and he told me that for now it would be best if I was patient with Grand-mère Eugenia. He said it was just her superstitious way. He said that she was upset about a recent death in town, but more important, the family was going through a hard time because of not knowing what had happened to Charles.

I knew everyone thought he was dead. Except Rose.

But I believed in Rose and was sure she would find him and bring him back to us, safe and sound.

Then Grand-père Arne said he would draw me my own wind rose! I was *très* excited.

ROSE

I ALMOST LOST THE TALL DARK FIGURE several times but managed to keep him in sight. Just beyond the harbor, there was a path leading up and above the chalk cliffs. It wound along the coastline, and he followed it for several miles until the town was left behind. We passed the distinctive white arch that jutted into the sea right beside the *aiguille blanche*.

Abruptly he veered right, away from the sea, and came to a small house. I saw him open the front door and enter, closing the door behind him.

I stood for several minutes, not sure what to do next. If he was a troll with arts, it would no doubt be foolish to confront him. Should I go back and ask for help from Neddy and Sib?

I couldn't wait, though. I had to know. I went up to the door and knocked.

There was no response, so I rapped again. Still nothing. I reached down and tried the handle. It turned easily, and I opened the door.

It was one big room, with a fireplace, a rough table and chairs, and a pallet in the corner for sleeping. Light came in through the windows, and it was immediately clear that no one was there.

The furnishings were simple and impersonal, and it looked to be a place rented out for short-term lodging. It did not in any way resemble my idea of a troll dwelling. Certainly it had none of the grandeur of the ice palace in Niflheim, nor the rich furnishings of the castle in the mountain.

I had noticed there was a shed attached to the back, and cautiously I crossed to the small door at the far end of the room. Opening it slowly, I leaned forward. It was darker in the shed, but it too was clearly empty.

Had he slipped through the shed and out the back? I walked to the far door, tripping over something that pro- truded from the floor. I opened the door and peered out into the sunshine. I could see no sign of anybody.

Backing up, I went to see what I had tripped over. I knelt down and discovered what looked to be a handle of some kind. Curious, I pulled on it. It was a trapdoor and swung up easily. I peered down into the opening, but it was too dark to see anything. I had my pack with me and dug into it for the candle and flint I had brought. Lighting the wick, I held the candle over the opening and saw what appeared to be a short ladder. My pulse quickened. It was not a simple wooden lad- der that you might expect in the cellar of a plain house like this, but rather it was a finely wrought, ornate ladder made of gleaming metal, decorated with scrollwork and patterns of leaves.

This is definitely more troll-like, I thought. The flickering light of the candle only revealed so much, but I thought I could see where the ladder ended, on a shelf of rock not too far below. Blowing the candle out, I slung my pack on my back and began to climb down the ladder, feeling my way in the dark.

When I reached the bottom, I stepped off onto the rock surface. I relit the candle and held it up, surveying my surroundings. I was in a small cave, and at the other end I could see an opening. It looked to be the entrance to a tunnel, so I crossed to it and peered in. I could see it had been carved by skilled hands; the walls were smooth, and there were decorative patterns etched around the entrance.

I had to bend low to enter and couldn't walk upright most of the way. In fact, it kept getting lower and narrower, so that by the time I reached the end, I was nearly doubled over.

Finally the tunnel ended and I stepped out onto a broad ledge. There was a dim light coming from somewhere, though I could not find its source. But it gave enough light for me to make out that I was standing on a cliff, overlooking an enormous cavern.

I walked to the edge and peered over, but the dim light didn't penetrate all the way down, so I couldn't see the bottom.

A few feet away, I noticed a pile of what was clearly coiled-up rope. I went over to examine it and saw that it was very long and attached at one end to a large metal ring, which was in turn bolted to the rock ledge.

This seemed to be the only way to get down into the cavern. I knew that it was reckless and that Neddy would be horrified, but I decided I would climb down to find out what lay below.

I lifted the heavy coils of rope and threw it over the side. I listened closely to see if I could hear it hit the ground, but I heard nothing. Either the rope wasn't long enough and hadn't hit the bottom at all or the bottom was too far away for the sound to carry.

It didn't matter. If there was a possibility, however small, that my white bear was somewhere near the bottom of that cavern, I had to go there.

I took a deep breath and gripped the rope firmly. Letting myself over the edge, I squeezed my legs around it and began to descend, hand under hand. As I went, I instinctively clenched the rope between my feet to keep myself from sliding down too quickly.

When I was a child, Father had made me a perch up in a tree near our home. It was not quite a treehouse, more like a wide shelf, and it could be reached only by climbing a long rope. It was one of the many ploys my parents had come up with over the years to keep me close at home rather than wandering far and wide and falling into ravines and ponds. Such ploys didn't work of course, but I did love that tree perch, and Father described my ability to climb the rope at an early age as something miraculous, since I took to climbing as if I were part squirrel.

Still, I had not climbed a rope in many years, either up or down, and it didn't help that the light grew dimmer as I descended into the cavern and that I had no idea what lay at the bottom.

Climbing down a rope wasn't as hard as climbing up, but this was a very long rope. My muscles began to ache, and my hands were getting raw from clutching the scratchy material. One of my legs began to cramp. And I still couldn't see the bottom.

I can do this, I said to myself. *It can't be that much longer.* I looked down again and thought I saw a glimmer of something almost shiny. Water maybe. A little hope flared in me. If the water was deep enough, it might break my fall if my hands and legs gave out. I continued to descend, hand under hand, my trembling legs clinging.

Suddenly my foot came to a place in the rope that felt different, thinner, and when my hands reached it, I realized with horror that the rope was badly frayed. It began to come apart in my fingers. And then it split and I was falling.

I'm not sure how far I fell. It seemed like time slowed and I was hanging in the air, my arms and legs flailing.

I landed, hard, splashing into cold water. I thudded onto my backside on the rocky bottom of the pool of water. Pain shuddered through my tailbone, and water splashed up into my eyes and mouth. Spluttering, I pulled myself into a sitting position, discovering that the water only came up to my chest.

I got shakily to my feet. Nothing felt broken, just a sore backside, and I was already shivering from the cold water.

I splashed out of the pool onto a dry rocky surface. There was still light, but it was very dim, so I retrieved my candle, which fortunately had only gotten slightly damp. I was able to light it, and holding it up, I gazed around me. It was a high, vaulted cavern, large in width, with the pool of water in the center.

I spotted a faint circle of light on the far side of the cavern. I cautiously crossed to it and saw that it was the entrance to another tunnel. I could see that it was a larger version of the tunnel I had gone through to get to the top of this cavern, the same polished surface and similar carvings. And a brighter light shone from within.

Taking a deep breath, I entered, holding my candle in front of me.

MOTHER

I T WAS THE MORNING of the fifth day after the death of Farmer Magnus when word came that Havamal's wife had fallen ill. She was dead by evening.

I felt a chill of foreboding. I prayed that this was not the beginning of a full-blown epidemic of influenza, but I very much feared that it was.

Arne insisted we send word to Neddy and Rose in Etretat, since Havamal was one of Neddy's closest friends. I briefly argued against it, saying there was nothing they could do, and if there was trouble ahead, they were better off staying away. But I knew Arne was right. Neddy would want to know.

I put Estelle to work gathering acorns, and soon our windowsills were lined with them. And now all of us had garlic and angelica root tied to our bedposts.

ROSE

T HE FARTHER I WENT, the lighter it got, and I no longer needed my candle. As I blew it out, I noticed that it
wasn't any smaller than when I packed it back in Trondheim.
Troll wax was clearly different from ours.

The tunnel took a sharp right turn and emptied into a
large, well-lit room with walls and floor and ceiling all made
of the same polished white stone. It was different from troll
domiciles I'd been in before. Nonetheless, I was sure it was
Huldre made. And it was the first real proof to me that I had
been right, that trolls were involved with what had happened
to my white bear.

It was grand but also austere, and still I could not find a
source for the light. It was almost as if the pale stone itself was
glowing.

There wasn't much furniture, mostly tables of the same
white stone that lined the edges of the room and one large
table in the middle with white stone chairs around it.

There were objects on the tables that lined the walls. One
table had a grouping of ornate metal boxes; another had an

imposing *echecs* set laid out with delicately carved game pieces made of white and gray marble.

My eye was caught by the table next to it, which held a collection of swords. They ranged from small to large, each one different, but all were unlike swords I had seen before, certainly not like the one the soldier Julien had worn at his hip. Most were elaborate, made of light-colored metal, and were encased in scabbards that bore swirling designs embellished with jewels. But at the far end of the table was a small sword that stood out because it was so plain and battered. While the others were gleaming and new, this one looked old and well-used, and for some reason, I was drawn to it. It was encased in a beaten-up leather scabbard, and the scrollwork on the pommel was so worn down I couldn't make out the design. I picked it up, and it felt good in my hand.

"An excellent selection." A grating voice came from behind me, echoing harshly in the large room. "But it is poor manners to take what is not yours."

I jumped, then spun around. A tall figure stood not ten feet from me. The man in the black coat. He was skeletally thin, and his skin was grayish white. The texture was rough, and I could see why Hannah had called it scarred, but I immediately recognized it as the whorled tree-bark skin of a troll. He had the fine, beautiful features of trolls, but the gray cast of his white skin and his skeletal frame made it a repellent beauty. He wore black clothing, and his eyes were black as well.

"She said you were resourceful, though I doubted her. A softskin girl," he said with disdain. "Still, my queen is sparing in her compliments."

My mind whirled. *My queen?* Was it possible? No, it could not be. I had seen her die.

"No, she did not die," he said, with a smile that made my stomach contract. "My queen is very much alive."

Alive. My heart started beating high and fast. The Troll Queen was alive.

BOOK TWO

SUND

Whence does the wind blow o'er the waves, yet is never seen itself?
—*The Edda*

TROLL QUEEN

THE ROAD BACK HAS BEEN LONG, and it has been slow. But I am very close to being whole again. And I am stronger even than before; my arts blaze hot and terrible.

When the ice palace was destroyed and I fell into the abyss, the troll prince Jaaloki found me and helped me to heal. He and his fellow Under Huldre.

But it was Urda who kept me alive until they came. I would not have survived without her. And the same is true for her. We were both mortally wounded, and we depended on each other, fed on each other, blended our arts. At first she blamed me for her son Tuki's death, but in time, she came to see that he deserved to die. His betrayal was too immense.

My hate has fueled me during the long recovery, giving me strength when I weakened. For I did hate. I do hate. I hate them all. I hate all softskins, their pasty, doughy skin, their artless, messy ways.

The time has come to rid the earth of softskins.

Especially the softskin girl. But first I will amuse myself. Make her suffer.

She has jumped ahead in the game. I knew it was a

possibility, and it matters not. All that is lost by her going to Etretat and finding Jaaloki is that she will not witness first-hand the painful deaths of those family members she loves most. She will only hear the news of it instead.

And now, as I have instructed him, Prince Jaaloki shall make the first move.

ROSE

I AM JAALOKI," THE SKELETAL TROLL SAID, his black eyes
staring at me. "Prince of the Under Huldre. I was a wedding guest. I saw you wash the shirt. I saw my queen fall. But
she was strong, and she survived. I helped her, along with
others of the Under Huldre."

I dimly remembered Charles telling me of the different
races of trolls. There were trolls who lived up in the farthest
regions of the Arktisk in the kingdom called Niflheim, as well
as those at the bottom of the world, the Southern Huldre. And
then there were the Under Huldre who lived below the earth's
surface.

"She has healed, softskin girl," he went on. "And you should
know that her arts are stronger than before. She has moved to
her favorite aerie at the top of the softskin world. And she pre-
pares for Aagnorak."

"Aagnorak?" I said.

All he did was smile, and again my stomach knotted.

He let out a hissing sound that I took to be a laugh and
said, "She is weary of softskins. It is time to be done with you."

"Where is Charles?" I said.

"The one who was a white bear?" he said. "Ah yes, he is easily found. At least what remains of him."

My skin went cold. "What do you mean? Is he alive?" I asked.

He let out that hissing laugh again. "You can discover this for yourself. Because he is in a place you know well, where you spent a year of your life." He paused, giving me an appraising look, and added, "Though you may not know that place as well as you thought you did."

"But Charles," I stuttered out, my brain whirling, "what has—"

He interrupted me sharply. "The one who was a white bear no longer matters to my queen. He is not important. It is the bairn who matters now."

He smiled his evil, sick-making smile. "My queen plays with you, softskin girl. Like a game of *skac*." His eyes went briefly to the *echecs* set on the nearby table. "You made a lucky guess, jumping ahead in the game. But it will not prevent the inevitable. And now it is my move."

He let out his hissing laugh, then spoke one last time. "You must not take what is not yours. You softskins may lack respect, but that is an inviolable rule in the Huldre world." His eyes went to the sword, which I still held in my hand. I glanced down at it, having forgotten that I even had it.

I felt a flickering of outrage. The Huldre had no trouble stealing softskins to use as slaves and then discard. Perhaps this "inviolable" Huldre rule, not taking what was not yours, applied only to precious objects, not to people.

I heard a rustling sound and looked back up in time to see him throw off his black cloak and his body begin to change.

NEDDY

S IB AND I WAITED FOR ROSE a while longer, then decided to go to the home of the healing woman named Hannah, the last place we knew Rose was headed. Hannah told us that she had directed Rose to the lodging of the soldier Julien, whom she described to us, and so we made our way there.

When we got to the inn near the docks, a woman sitting on the outside stoop said that as far as she knew, the soldier named Julien had just boarded a ship bound for Spania. She also told us that earlier in the day, she had directed Rose to a local public house where she would be likely to find him.

We made our way to the public house, where the innkeeper confirmed seeing a girl talking to the Spanien soldier earlier that day. They'd both left at around the same time, though not together.

"Where could she be?" I asked Sib as we left the public house.

Sib shook her head. "I don't know, Neddy. But she will turn up. She always does."

ROSE

IN THE COURSE OF MY JOURNEY to the land that lay east of the sun and west of the moon, there had been much that was magic, events that could not be explained by the natural way of things. But only a few times had they happened right in front of my eyes. Like the Troll Queen using her white-hot arts to turn Tuki into a smear on the floor of the ice palace.

But this was different. The troll called Jaaloki was shifting, changing. It wasn't a sudden thing but a steady progression. His features began to blur, his black eyes becoming smaller while his head grew larger. His whole body was growing, elongating, and as he thickened, the rest of his black clothing fell off, landing in a heap at his feet, or where his feet used to be.

A hissing sound emanated from his mouth, which was now lipless, and he had no nose that I could see, except two long slits.

He was down on the floor, his head upraised, and I realized that he had changed into a very large white snake.

There are those who are terrified of snakes, like Estelle, who was much relieved to hear that there were fewer snakes in Njord than Fransk, but I was not one. I have always found them fascinating and beautiful in their own way. But no matter how beautiful, being faced with a snake that was larger than me was terrifying, especially as he began to slide forward.

I grasped the handle of the sword tightly, thinking to somehow use it to defend myself, but before I could even react, he lunged at me. Beginning at my feet, he swiftly began coiling himself around me, first my legs, then my torso. Instinctively I raised my arms so they wouldn't be bound to my sides, but he thrust his head sharply at my right arm, dislodging the sword from my hand. It clattered to the floor and I reached down to try to grab it, but in a flash he had wound around me, pinning my sword hand tightly to my side.

He tightened his body around me, and I wondered if he was planning to squeeze me to death.

He raised his head up, so that his small black eyes were looking directly into mine, and let out that hissing sound that I knew to be a laugh. His breath smelled of hidden dark places under the earth, and I saw that he didn't have fangs like the adders we have in Njord, but instead two rows of small sharp teeth.

Keeping his black eyes fixed on me, he began to tighten his coils around me. I felt my chest constricting, my ribs bending inward, and my breath grew labored.

I suddenly remembered the needle I had stuck in my cloak from the mending I was doing on board the ship. I had never gotten to finish it and had left the needle where it was.

Grabbing hold of the long needle hidden in the collar of my cloak, I reached up and instinctively thrust it at his face. I was aiming for one of those small black eyes, but at the last minute, he moved slightly, and instead the needle went straight into one of the nose slits and stuck there.

His body jerked, and letting out a shrill, hissing scream, he struck at my face, his teeth bared.

I felt a searing pain just next to my eye. I cried out. He pulled his head back, and I could see my blood on his teeth. My lungs were heaving, and the pain on my face was almost unbearable, but I raised my arm again, and with the flat of my hand, I pushed the needle farther up his nose.

He let out another shriek, and his body abruptly loosened, enough for me to wriggle free.

I ran, grabbing up the sword at my feet, and headed toward the arched entrance. The sibilant screaming went on behind me, and I heard a dragging, sliding sound that I was sure meant he was coming after me.

ESTELLE

I WAS VERY CROSS WITH GRAND-MÈRE EUGENIA. She said that I could no longer walk with Winn before dinner. I didn't understand it. Grand-père Arne said it was because of her fears of an influenza epidemic. He said she lost both her mother and father that way, and I guess I understood that. After my *maman* died, I was very worried every time Rose, and Charles too, started to cough.

But still. Only two people had died in Trondheim. It seemed unfair. And it didn't help that Gudrun had gone off to the countryside for a visit with a school friend for several weeks.

I missed Rose and Sib and Charles. I missed Gudrun. I missed my walks with Winn. I had just started to explore an area I hadn't seen before, a little-used pathway down by the Nidelva River. The view there was *magnifique*. And now I was stuck in the kitchen every evening helping to chop onions and carrots.

But then Grand-père Arne showed me the wind rose he was working on, the one he was designing for me. And it was beautiful! He said that Grand-mère Eugenia had guessed that

I was a west child because I had many qualities that fit, but he said he saw a little north in me.

"Seasickness notwithstanding, I believe you have a streak of the explorer in you," he said with a twinkle in his eye.

He showed me the symbols for west (a heart and a harp, among others) and the one for north he had drawn in. A lion. It made my heart swell with happiness.

He said he hoped to have it finished in a week.

ROSE

I RAN AS FAST AS I COULD, retracing my steps through the polished tunnel, emerging into the large cavern. I stopped and listened. No sound came from the tunnel.

Blood was running down my face, and the pain was searing. I felt lightheaded too, my heart racing. I wondered if there had been venom in the troll-snake's bite.

Keeping an eye on the tunnel entrance, I moved over to the shallow pool I had fallen into when the rope broke. Setting down the sword, which I still clutched in my right hand, I found a cloth in my pack and wet it in the water, using it to wipe the blood off my face. I held it against the wound.

No snake appeared at the tunnel entrance, and I wondered if perhaps he had been too hurt by my needle to follow. Or more likely, he knew there was no need because he had poisoned me with his bite.

I tried to push the fear away and instead focused on looking up at the frayed rope that hung far above me. Much too high for me to reach. I walked all around the periphery of the cavern, looking for any other way out. There was none, only the tunnel leading back to the troll-snake.

My legs were shaking by the time I came back to the pool and the rope dangling high above it. I sank to a sitting position and gazed up and around the cavern, studying the craggy walls.

I was a good climber, not only of ropes, but trees and cliffs and rocky walls as well. There seemed to be plenty of crags and ledges to provide hand- and footholds, and I spotted what looked to be a decent-size ledge, several feet above the bottom of the rope. If I could make it up to that ledge, it looked as if I would not have to jump too far to grab the rope.

But the light was dim and the pain of the troll-snake bite was searing. I willed myself to breathe slowly, to relax, but my heart was still beating fast and my skin felt cold and clammy. *Maybe it's just my wet clothing,* I tried to tell myself. But when I stood, the rocky surface of the cavern tilted and I almost fell. I managed to stay on my feet somehow, and the ground below me steadied.

I took several deep breaths, trying hard to keep the dizziness at bay. Then I cautiously began to walk over to the rockface directly below the ledge I had spotted. With shaking hands, I pulled the candle out of my pack and lit it. It gave me a little more light, and I gazed closely at the rockface, making note of the places in the surface where I could gain hand- and footholds. I couldn't see clearly all the way to the ledge, but what I could see was sufficient. As long as my strength held out, I was confident I could make it to the ledge.

My mouth was dry, but I had heard that one shouldn't drink or eat after being bitten by a snake, so I refrained from drinking from my skin bag. I stowed the candle in my pack, along with the sword, and I began to climb.

I made it up about ten feet before the first wave of dizziness hit me. I clung tightly, resting my clammy cheek against the rough rockface. I concentrated on breathing evenly.

I gazed up, my vision blurring, and spotted my next hand-and foothold. I moved slowly upward.

It took all my concentration, finding those little edges for my fingertips, wider places for my feet.

I came to a more difficult stretch with fewer holds. In one place, there was only a shallow crack, and I had to put my toe in and twist it, hard. The higher I climbed, the more aware I became of the empty air under my feet.

When I reached it, I discovered the ledge was narrower than it had looked from below. There was barely room for both my feet, and I had to hold myself onto it by clutching a rock crag that stuck out about shoulder level. I longed to sit or, even better, lie down, but there was no space for that.

I gingerly turned myself around on the narrow ledge so I was facing forward, still holding tightly to the rock at my shoulder. I could dimly see the rope that dangled there, just out of reach. My breathing was short, and my head was swimming. And even worse, the palms of my hands were wet with sweat and kept slipping on the handhold.

I stared fixedly at the rope. I guessed it was about four feet distant from me. Another wave of dizziness hit me, and my fingers slipped on the rock I was holding. I just barely kept my grip on it.

I stared at the rope, and a sob closed my throat. I wasn't going to be able to do it, to propel myself off the narrow ledge and grab the rope. My hands were too weak and slick with sweat, my legs rubbery.

Despair filled me. I thought about what the creature Jaaloki had said about my white bear. *He is easily found. At least what remains of him.*

What did it mean? Where was Charles? And if I did find him, what would I find? A corpse? A pile of bones? A dying white bear?

My fingers slipped a little. My heart pounded. I was higher than I had been when the rope broke, and I knew that if I fell from this ledge, the water would offer little protection and I would be badly hurt. Between that and the venom that I was now convinced the troll-snake had poisoned me with, I would almost certainly die.

I could climb back down somehow, but there was no way out except perhaps through the lair of the troll-snake.

As I clung there, fighting off the dizziness, I thought about how it was I had ended up here on this ledge in a dim cavern with a bleeding snakebite on my face and poison beginning to trickle through my veins. What was the beginning moment?

Was it my own violent birth on the stormy afternoon in Askoy Forest, or was it the lie when Nyamh became Ebba Rose? Or was it Charles's beginning, his birth as prince of Fransk and the day he went to play with a red ball?

It was all of these, I realized. But more, it was the moment when my life wove together with the life of an enchanted white bear.

But where was my white bear now? And *what* was he? Nothing but a hollowed-out body, battered by the storm, left to die?

And if he was gone, if he no longer lived, maybe it was easier just to let go. To stop fighting against the dizziness, stop scrabbling with weakening hands to hold on to the crag. My muscles ached; my head felt heavy.

An image of my bairn's face came to me. Winn. He was laughing as Estelle made silly faces at him, his tiny hands with pink fingers curling toward her.

No. I must at least try to grab the rope.

But then I heard a noise. The troll-snake finally slithering after me? I didn't think so. It sounded more like a voice, calling out. It was faint through the roaring in my ears. For a second, I thought I was hallucinating. But it came again.

"*Violeta Ojos*? Are you there?"

It was the soldier Julien, naming me for my purple eyes as he had done in the public house. He was calling from the top of the cavern, where the rope was fastened. For a moment I didn't know if I should respond. He had been working with

Jaaloki and had lied about Charles. How could I trust him? But another wave of dizziness hit, and I realized I had no choice.

"Yes, it is Rose," I croaked. "Rose," I said again, trying to make my voice louder.

"Hello? Is someone there?" he yelled.

"I'm here," I called out as loudly as I could. "I'm hurt," I added.

"I'm coming." The rope moved, and I could hear him grunting as he began to descend.

After long moments filled with the sound of grunting, the creaking of the rope, and my own hammering heart, he came into sight.

"Here," I called.

He lowered himself until we were at eye level. I was breathing heavily and didn't think I could hold on to the rock much longer. But how was he going to be able to help me?

He began a rocking motion so that the rope started swaying.

"When I get close enough, I'm going to grab you. Are you strong enough to hold tight to me once I've got you?"

"Yes," I said, though I was fairly sure I was lying. I blinked hard against the blur in my eyes and brain.

"Here we go." He gave a great heave, and I felt his strong arm grab me around the waist. I fell onto him and wrapped my shaking arms around his neck, trying desperately to hold on.

He let out a loud grunt, and we slipped down the rope a few inches. *Now we are both going to fall,* I thought dully. But we didn't. He let out a string of what I guessed to be Spanien curse words, and painstakingly, laboriously, he began to climb up the rope.

It was slow going, and I almost lost consciousness once or twice, but somehow I didn't, and he got us to the top.

"You're going to need to grab hold of the ledge," he said. "Violeta?"

I dimly heard his voice and tried to answer, but my mouth was dry and I couldn't form the words.

"Can you pull yourself up? I'll try pushing," he gasped out.

Taking a deep breath, I reached for the top of the cliff just above me. I could feel one of his hands on my back.

"I can't," I said, faltering, my eyesight blurring again.

"Yes, you can," he said.

And I did. My hands scrabbled on the rough rocks, and I could feel him pushing, and finally I was off Julien, off the rope, lying on the rock surface.

He fell next to me, wheezing. We lay there a few moments side by side. All I wanted to do was sleep. Some voice told me I shouldn't, not yet, but a grayness filled my head. I was drifting off.

"Violeta!"

I became aware of him crouching beside me. "Rose," I whispered.

"Where are you . . ." he started, then said, "Your face." He must have spotted the blood. I could feel him press something against my wound. I let out a cry of pain.

Everything was spinning. I felt like I was being pulled down into a deep dark hole in the ground.

"It was a snake . . . bite," I said thickly.

"*Infierno*," he said.

I felt his hands on my face and a wrenching pain where I had been bitten. It stopped, and I heard what sounded like spitting, then the pain again, then spitting. It lasted a few minutes, and I think I screamed.

I could hear him breathing heavily, and more sounds of spitting.

More breathing.

Suddenly he stood and gathered me up in his arms, and it was then that I lost consciousness.

NEDDY

S IB AND I WERE SITTING in the public room of the inn where we were lodging, half-eaten plates of food in front of us. Every time the door opened, we both immediately looked to see who had entered. But it was never Rose.

"I'm worried, Sib," I said for perhaps the hundredth time.

"I know," she replied, her voice calm, but I could tell she was just as concerned as I was.

We began to get meaningful glances from the innkeeper, who clearly wanted to close for the night.

"I won't be able to sleep," I said.

"Nor will I," she said.

A man limped through the door. His eyes briefly searched the room, and when he saw us, he immediately made his way to our table.

"You'll be the brother of Vio—I mean, Rose?" he asked, his expression grim.

"Yes," I said in some alarm.

"I am the soldier, Julien," he said.

"The one who was with Charles when—" I began, but he cut me off.

"No, in fact," he said. "But that is a story for another time. Your sister is ailing. I've taken her to the house run by the woman Hannah. You will want to come straight away."

He turned to leave and waited for us by the door while we settled our bill with the innkeeper.

As we walked, the soldier gave a terse account of what had happened. He said he'd found Rose in one of the caves that lie underground along the coast of Etretat and that she was suffering from a snakebite to her face.

"Oh, no!" I cried.

"What kind of snake?" asked Sib.

"We don't know. She lost consciousness before she could describe it. Hannah is puzzled by the bite mark. It is large and doesn't look like any snake she has encountered before. And the symptoms are different as well."

"I have some experience with snakebites," said Sib. "Perhaps I can be of help."

When we got to Rose, Sib was also perplexed. But she was able to suggest a supplemental theriac—a paste made of castor oil, cassia wood, aristolochia, anise seed, and pepper—to put on the wound.

For the next twenty-four hours, Rose was in and out of consciousness. She was feverish, and yet her skin was damp and cold to the touch. Her breathing was rapid and shallow. One of us was always by her side, sometimes both of us, and the soldier Julien stayed nearby as well.

The wound across her upper left cheekbone was inflamed and jagged, and based on the little I had seen of snakebites, it certainly did not seem typical. It looked like it was made by a creature with many sharp teeth that were all the same size, with no fangs.

Hannah said that Julien may have saved Rose's life by sucking out whatever poison was still in the wound.

As it was, I was very worried, watching her pale face with the livid wound, but on the morning of the second day, the worst seemed to pass. She blinked her eyes rapidly, and when she saw me, she said, "Neddy?" in a whispery voice.

Several hours later, she was able to sit up and even swallow some beef broth.

"There is much I must tell you, Neddy," she said between spoonfuls, her eyes bright. "But the main thing is, I believe I know where Charles is. And I must go there as soon as possible."

ROSE

I T TOOK TIME TO FULLY RECOVER from the venom of the troll-snake's bite, which gave me time to think.

I had much to think about—all that the troll Jaaloki had said. Some of it made little sense, and some was terrifying.

I knew one thing was certain. The Troll Queen lived. And she meant great harm to both me and the "softskin" world. I was certain she had caused the winds that wrecked Charles's ship. But whether she had meant to kill him or only to make me believe he was dead, I didn't know.

The words *what remains of him* kept spinning in my head until I thought I would go mad. But it was clear that the place Jaaloki referred to, the one where I had spent almost a year and that he said I "know well," was the castle in the mountain. It was indeed a place I knew well. During my year there, living with the white bear and the two trolls, Urda and Tuki, I had explored it from top to bottom.

But what had he meant by saying I might not know it as well as I thought I did? Was there some part of it I had not discovered, or had he or the Troll Queen changed it somehow? Turned it into a prison for Charles? Or a graveyard? I didn't know. All I knew was that I must go there as soon as I was strong enough to travel.

And then there was the horrifying thing Jaaloki had said about "the bairn," that it was not Charles who mattered now. Only the bairn.

Was he talking about Winn? Did the Troll Queen intend to do harm to our son? If revenge was her aim, there would be none greater than to harm our bairn.

If Winn was in danger, should I not go to Trondheim to watch over him, keep him safe? But I had to go to the castle in the mountain, to find Charles.

My head spun, the room tilted, and I lay back down. No, the first thing I had to do was to heal so I could leave this sickbed.

NEDDY

WHEN ROSE TOLD SIB AND ME the whole story of what had happened to her in the underground cavern—about the troll prince Jaaloki, who turned into a white snake, and all he had said to her—I could hardly take it in.

That the Troll Queen was still alive and bent on some kind of revenge on Rose and Charles was terrifying. That it had spilled over into our world, with ships full of innocent people being destroyed, was the stuff of nightmares.

Unlike me, Sib showed no surprise.

"I knew there was something wrong about those winds. Evil," she said with a shudder.

None of us could guess what Jaaloki had meant by the ominous words *what remains of him,* but I was very much afraid that our journey would end with the outcome I had expected here in Etretat, a grave for Charles.

"Neddy," Rose said, "and Sib, I have a very great favor to ask of you both."

"What is it?" I asked.

"I must go look for my white bear at the castle in the mountain. But I fear for Winn, back in Trondheim."

I agreed that the words the troll Jaaloki had said about "the bairn" were indeed sinister.

"Would you be willing to return to Trondheim, to watch over Winn, while I journey to the castle?" Rose asked, her voice urgent.

I was silent. I didn't like the idea of letting Rose go off alone to the castle in the mountain.

"Please, Neddy," she implored. "It will give me some measure of comfort to know you and Sib are there, looking out for him."

Still I didn't speak. Rose's eyes were fastened on me.

"Very well," I said reluctantly.

"I will go too," said Sib. And I was glad.

"But, Rose," Sib went on, "what is this I see in your pack? Is it a sword?"

I too had noticed it sticking out of the top of Rose's pack.

Rose nodded. "I had just picked it up when the troll Jaaloki first came into the room. And I was holding it when he attacked me. Much good it did me," she said. "He did not want me to take it, though it does not look valuable."

"May I see it?" I asked.

"Of course," Rose said.

It was a small sword and looked well worn. I pulled it out of its scabbard, and the blade itself was tarnished. Sib came beside me and peered closely at it. Wordlessly she held out her hand, and I put the sword handle in it.

She bent over it. I thought she was looking more closely at the worn designs, but then I saw that her eyes were closed.

She straightened after a few moments. There was a look of wonder in her eyes.

"Remarkable," she said.

"What?" asked Rose.

"It is . . ." She hesitated with a sidelong glance at me. "I think it is some kind of wind sword. I can hear"—again she darted a look at me—"many winds."

"What are you talking about?" I asked, mystified.

"Sib knows a lot about wind, Neddy," Rose said.

"I will explain later," Sib said to me. "But whoever crafted it, Rose, knows of wind music. Further, I am sure it is not troll made."

"How do you know? And if not troll, then . . ." Rose asked.

"I can't tell you that."

We both looked at Sib questioningly.

She shook her head and would say no more, putting the sword back in Rose's pack.

Rose changed the subject to the soldier Julien.

During her sickness from the snakebite, he had been ever present, clearly as worried about her as we were, and both Sib and I had grown to like him very much. I had forgotten his briefly muttered words about not in fact being with Charles when he died and was dismayed to hear what Rose had to say about him.

"You believe he was in league with the troll Jaaloki?" I asked in surprise.

"I know he was," Rose responded. "And I must speak with him immediately. Can you please send him to me?"

I agreed.

ROSE

THE SOLDIER JULIEN ENTERED THE ROOM. He looked a little wary, but said, "It is good to see you much recovered, Violeta."

"Rose," I said.

He smiled. "As you say, Rose."

I did not smile back. "Thank you for saving my life," I said stiffly.

It was the first time we had been face-to-face since he dragged me up that rope out of the cavern.

He nodded and seemed to want to say something, but I stopped him.

"Who are you?" I asked. "And what is your true relation to the one called Jaaloki?"

He gazed at me, and I saw again that hint of fear that had unnerved me before.

Then he appeared to make up his mind and began to speak.

"I will tell you the truth," he said. "All of it." And he lowered himself into a chair across from me.

"First I must say to you that what I did was wrong, and for

that I apologize. There can be no excuse, but I will tell you how it happened.

"I was a passenger on the *Hynde*," he began. "The storm hit, and it was like something straight out of hell, a horrific churning and roiling sea, with those fearsome winds. Death and terror all around me. I was certain it was the end, for me and for everyone on that ship. But somehow I grabbed hold of a piece of splintered deck, and more dead than alive, I clung to it.

"I lost consciousness at some point, but was found washed up on the shore and taken to the healing woman called Hannah. Even then, I knew death was close. I drifted in and out, but there was a moment when I came wide awake to find a man sitting beside me. He had his hand on my leg, which was shattered.

"He stared me in the eye, this *diablo* man, and his eyes were horrible—flat and of the deepest black. When he spoke, his voice was grating and at first hard to understand, but finally I heard him say that there was infection in my leg and so much blood lost that I would be dead by morning. But, he said, if I chose to live, he had the arts to pull me back from death. If he did this, however, I must agree to do him a favor in return. I will tell you the truth, Violeta, I believed myself to be hallucinating or dreaming at that point, but I said, 'Yes, of course, I choose to live, if it is truly possible.'

"'Oh yes, it is possible,' he said to me with a stomach-turning smile, and all of a sudden I felt warmth and energy coursing through my body. It was almost as if I could feel torn things in my leg, and then in my whole body, knitting together. I cried out in wonder, and the *diablo* man just kept smiling.

"'Rest now,' he said. 'I will be back to complete our bargain.' When the morning came, the woman Hannah arrived to check on me, and she was stunned to find me not only alive but sitting up, with color in my face.

"'Quite a miracle!' she said. And it was. Over the next few days, as I continued to improve, I thought I must have hallucinated the *diablo* man, that my body had miraculously healed on its own. But on the fourth day, he came back.

"He said he was pleased to see me so much recovered and that now was the time for me to complete my side of the bargain. He told me of a man who died on the *Hynde* and that I was to tell anyone who asked that I had been with him when he died. I was also to write a note, which he would dictate, to that effect, enclosing a ring, which he would give me.

"I had no idea why he would want me to do this dishonest thing, and I opened my mouth to protest, but he cut me off, reminding me that he had brought me back from death. And he went on to say that if that was not incentive enough, he himself would go to Spania, to the farm where my family lives in a village at the foot of the Pyrennes. He knew the name of the village, and more, he knew the names of my family members. And he said that if I did not do what he asked, my young brother and sister, Fredo and Denora, who are twins, would die.

"I almost leapt out of the bed I lay in, but I suddenly felt my breath go short. And even though he did not leave his seat, or touch me in any way, I knew that he was causing my breath to stop. I lost consciousness, and when I came to, I saw him sitting there, still smiling. I was terrified, not just for myself, but for my brother and sister. For I knew he had the power and the will to kill them.

"So I agreed to do as he said," Julien said.

I understood then the fear I had seen in his eyes. And even if I could not forgive him for the lies he had told about Charles, I could also understand why he had done it.

He leaned forward, his eyes bright. "Yes, I was frightened. I am still. And I knew it was wrong to go along with him, but I told myself, to assuage my conscience, that the story I was to tell was most likely a true story. I was on that ship, people dying all around me. I should have died too. I reasoned that if this man named Charles was on the ship, he had surely perished, and what did it matter if I told a false version of it?"

He looked me in the eyes and said, "I was wrong. I know. But Vio . . . Rose, if your husband was on that ship, there is no other truth. He did not survive. He could not have survived."

"Did you not wonder why the *diablo* man would ask you to do this thing, have you tell this lie?" I asked.

"I did. But I could think of no answer that made sense. Perhaps you can tell me?"

I shook my head.

"Will you at least tell me what happened to you down in the cavern, Violeta? Was it the *diablo* man who hurt you?" he asked, leaning forward, his eyes glittering.

I ignored his question. "Tell me how it was you came back for me? I saw you board the ship for Spania."

"I meant to leave, to get back to my family, make sure they were safe. But I couldn't. I felt remorse. Lying to one who had lost her husband as you had. I turned around and got off the ship. I tracked you down. A sailor had spotted you following the *diablo*, and a boy tending sheep in the pasture above saw you go into the hut."

I was silent for a few moments. "I am grateful that you came after me," I said. "And I hope that doing so has not endangered your family. It is possible that the *diablo* man does not know."

He nodded, and then his eyes went to my pack.

"What are your plans?" he asked.

"That is not your concern."

He sighed, but smiled at me again. "Well, perhaps, my lovely Violeta"—and he laid emphasis on the name—"our paths will cross again, under different circumstances, and you will allow me to make amends."

"Rose," I said with equal emphasis. "And you already have. You saved my life. We are even."

He nodded, saying, "*Buen viaje*, Rose. Safe journey."

"The same to you," I said.

NEDDY

I WENT DOWN TO THE DOCKS and booked passage on a ship to Trondheim for Sib and me that would be leaving in two days' time. I found one for Rose that was scheduled to depart for La Rochelle the day after that. Rose would then either travel by foot or buy a horse to get from there to the castle in the mountain. Her journey would take her near her home, the one she and Charles had lived in since they married, the house where Winn was born. But Rose had already said she would not stop there, wanting to get to the castle in the mountain as soon as possible. I wondered too if the sight of their home would be painful to her with so much still unknown about Charles's fate.

Upon returning from the harbor, I discovered that Sib had gone to her favorite inlet, and I found Rose at the inn, in the room she and Sib shared.

"What do you think you will find at the castle in the mountain, Rose?" I asked.

She shook her head, closing her eyes. "I don't know."

"Do you think the Troll Queen will be there?" I asked, trying to keep the worry out of my voice.

"No, I don't," she replied, opening her eyes. "The troll Jaaloki said she was somewhere else, her favorite aerie above the softskin world. Preparing for Aagnorak, whatever that may be."

"But you think it means ill for our world?"

"I do."

We fell silent.

I studied my sister. She had unwrapped the wound on her face, and it was still livid and inflamed, though better than when I had first seen it.

"Does Sib's balm help with the pain of your bite?"

"It does," Rose answered. "And she said, too, that it would lessen the scarring. Sib has been wonderful through all this. I am ever astounded at all the things she knows about, the skills she possesses."

I nodded. "Sometimes it is puzzling, almost impossible to fathom in one so young. Although I don't know her age. Have you been able to find it out?"

She shook her head, then said gently, "Neddy, what are your feelings for Sib?"

I shifted in my chair, trying to act natural. "What do you mean? She is a friend."

"Is she perhaps more than that?" Rose asked.

My heart beat a little faster. I had always told Rose everything, but this time I felt constrained, not sure how to express what my feelings were since I barely understood them myself.

"You are blushing, Neddy!" she said, smiling. "I haven't seen you blush since you were a boy."

"I'm not," I protested. "The room is warm—"

"Neddy, what is wrong with you? I love Sib. We all love Sib. If you have feelings for her, make them known. It is high time you were married."

"I don't know what you are talking about," I said stiffly.

"Oh, Neddy," Rose said. "You are as stubborn as I am. But you should say something to her. I know what you can do! Why don't you write her a poem?"

Rose was teasing me, referring to my long-ago efforts at writing poetry. I refrained from telling her I had had the urge to write a poem about Sib and, wisely, abandoned the idea.

"You always were terrible at giving advice, Rose," I said, teasing back.

"All right, I'll stop meddling. But"—and her face grew serious—"one thing I have learned, Neddy, is that life is short. You must not waste time."

I smiled absently, thinking about Rose's words. Perhaps she was right.

ROSE

I FELT WELL ENOUGH THAT AFTERNOON to join Sib at her favorite inlet.

"A good spot for wind-listening?" I asked, teasing.

"In fact, it is," she responded with a smile. But her smile quickly faded. "The winds that caused the shipwreck, Rose, as I said before, they had a dark music to them. They were all wrong. At first it seemed as if they had come from no specific direction. But then I found that they were mostly southern and yet had a mountainous feel to them, which is an unusual combination. I decided they must have come from the highest peaks of the mountains that run along the border between Fransk and Sveitsland."

"The Alpes?" I asked.

"I think so."

The Troll Queen's aerie, high above the softskin world. Could it be in the Alpes?

"I have never been there," Sib said. "They are said to be breathtaking."

"One of the few places you haven't been," I said with a

smile. "I swear you are as much of a wanderer as I am. Perhaps even more so."

She smiled, her gaze on the horizon.

"Sib, can I ask," I said suddenly. "What do you feel for Neddy?" So much for my vow not to meddle.

She gave me a startled look and fell silent, as if deciding whether or not to give me a direct answer. She closed her eyes for a long moment and when she opened them again, they were soft with feeling.

"He is dear to me."

"As friend or brother or more?" I asked.

Again she hesitated. "There are reasons, Rose, that I . . ." She paused and then began again. "My past has things in it that make it difficult, perhaps impossible for me to ever think of having a husband."

I stared at her in wonder. "What things?" I asked.

"I have never spoken of them, to anyone. Do you recognize this wind, Rose?"

I thought she was trying to change the subject and shook my head impatiently. "No —" I began, but she interrupted.

"This is *ciuin*. I introduced you to it once before, and it is one I know well, for it blows through Anglia and Skottland." She closed her eyes and breathed it in, and I saw both her lips and her fingers move almost imperceptibly. And I don't know how else to describe it, but the wind seemed to curl around us, as if it were a pair of arms.

"Listen," she said.

And I did.

Just for a moment, I heard a soft, laughing sort of music. I got a queer feeling in my heart and looked at Sib as if she had become a stranger all of a sudden. I remembered our talk of winds before, about how knowing the winds allows you to bend them. And how she had identified my sword as a wind sword, not troll made.

"Do you have arts, Sib?" I whispered.

"Not arts, not like the Troll Queen," she said. "I call it music. Wind music."

"Is this wind music the reason you can't marry?" I said, looking her directly in the eyes.

"No," she said, unblinking. "But it is related, the *why* of it."

I gazed at her, mystified.

Sib let out a sigh, looking unbearably sad. "You have to believe me, Rose. It is better for Neddy that he seek a wife elsewhere."

And she stood and began to move away from me, taking her curling wind with her.

"Sib!" I called after her.

She turned and looked at me.

"Can you teach it to me?" I asked. "This wind music?"

She smiled and said, "Yes."

"Now?"

She laughed. "I can try. A beginning, anyway."

She came back and sat beside me and started telling me about the wind. How, according to an early belief, the only two things the creator did not make were water and air.

"I told you already that all the winds have names," she said.

"Yes," I said, "and that you know many of them."

She nodded. And in a lilting voice, she began to list them. I knew I would never remember them all, so I just listened, entranced by the poetry of their names and the remarkable variety. They ranged from the gentle, *kaiaulu*, a soft trade wind from the tropics, to the moderate, *williwaw*, a sudden blast of wind descending from the mountains to the sea, to the vast, *jufeng*, a violent wind blowing from all four directions.

When she was done naming the winds, Sib had me close my eyes. She said to just listen. When I said I couldn't hear anything, she said to try listening in a different way.

"Listen with your ears, but also with your skin, your nose, your fingers, your heart."

With my eyes shut all I could hear was the sound of the waves breaking on the shore, the piercing cries of seabirds calling to each other. But I tried to focus harder, to make my whole body aware of the air around me, the feel of it on my skin.

"There is a different wind now, one that blew *ciuin* away. Listen," Sib said.

And this time I heard it. It was similar to the soft music of *ciuin*, but clearer and brighter. It was very direct, not shy at all.

"You hear it," said Sib.

I nodded, my eyes still closed.

"That wind is *deasiar*, a southwesterly wind from Anglia."

"I like it," I said, opening my eyes.

"Yes," agreed Sib, "it is a good wind. But I find that most winds are good. There are only a few I do not like, that frighten me. The powerful, unpredictable, killing ones."

"Like the one from the Alpes," I said.

"Yes," Sib replied with a slight shiver.

We were interrupted then by Neddy, who was calling to us.

"Thank you," I said to Sib.

She smiled at me. "It is nice, even sort of a relief, to share this with someone. With you," she said.

And arm in arm, we went to join Neddy.

NEDDY

WHEN WE WERE PREPARING TO BOARD our ship for Trondheim, I was approached by the first mate, who told me the ship had stopped in Trondheim on its way south to Fransk, and that he bore a letter for me. It was from Father.

Tearing it open, heart pounding, I quickly scanned the contents. I was relieved to learn that there were no ill tidings of the family, especially Winn, but was devastated to hear the news of Havamal's wife, as well as the death of Farmer Magnus. I thought back to what I had learned of the Sweating Sickness from the Anglian man on our voyage to Etretat and felt uneasy.

When I told the news to Rose and Sib, they too were alarmed.

"I hope it is not the beginning of an epidemic there," said Rose.

"I also hope that," said Sib gravely. "But I am glad I am going with you, Neddy." She went on to say that she once lived through an epidemic of the Sweating Sickness, that she knew how to treat it, and more important, how to prevent getting it.

I saw the fear in Rose's face and could tell that for a

moment she was wavering in her decision not to come with us. But abruptly she straightened her back.

"Look after them," she said to us both. "And, if you are able, send word to La Rochelle with news. I will go there after the castle in the mountain." She gave us both a fierce hug and stood watching as we boarded the ship.

ROSE

I T WAS DIFFICULT SAYING GOODBYE to Neddy and Sib. I watched their ship set sail and then, walking away, felt an unexpected stab of loneliness. I had gotten used to having Neddy and Sib as traveling companions. I would miss them.

Impatient, I shook the feeling off. I had traveled solo most of my life, even after marrying Charles. It was in my nature to journey alone.

I directed my steps to the dock where the ship I would be taking to La Rochelle was due to arrive, wanting to find out the departure time the next day. I was stunned to learn that the ship had canceled its stop in Etretat. The next ship headed for La Rochelle wouldn't arrive for a fortnight.

I could almost walk there in that time, I thought furiously. I checked my coin purse. Because of the uncertainty of what I would find in Etretat, I had brought a fairly large amount of money with me.

Counting what I had left, I thought I had enough to purchase a horse, though it would leave me with little left over.

But I must get to the castle in the mountain. I could not bear any more delays.

My landlord referred me to a horse trader in town, and I made my way there. His name was Tomas, and he had two horses for sale. When he told me the price for the smaller horse, I was dismayed. It was much higher than I had anticipated, and I wondered if he was trying to cheat me. I had heard rumors that there were a few unscrupulous tradespeople in town who had deliberately raised their prices on goods, preying on the relatives of shipwreck victims.

I named a lower sum, one that was still more than fair, but he merely turned away as if I wasn't worth his time.

"Please," I said. "I must get to La Rochelle, and there is no ship until—"

He interrupted me with a Fransk curse word. I stood still, anger filling me.

"Perhaps," I said, a tight smile on my face, "I ought to pay a visit to the mayor of this town before I depart. The healer Hannah told me he is an honorable man and would be dismayed to learn there are tradespeople in Etretat who are taking advantage of the victims of the terrible tragedy that happened here."

"Now, see here—" began Tomas, looking uneasy.

"On the other hand," I went on, "if you will accept my previous offer, I might be persuaded to change my plans and leave Etretat without paying my respects to the mayor."

Tomas was silent for a moment, then stuck out his hand. "*Je suis d'accord,*" he said gruffly.

I shook his hand and paid the sum I had offered.

That afternoon I left Etretat on horseback to go in search of my white bear.

MOTHER

S EVERAL DAYS WENT BY with no news of any other sickness, and I began to breathe a little easier. Perhaps, as Arne kept saying, they truly had been isolated cases.

But on the sixth day, word came that two children in the family of the farmhold down the road from Havamal had fallen ill.

I had seen the whole family at the marketplace just two days prior, and a sense of horror came over me. How many had come into contact with those children? And how soon would the parents be affected?

All I could do was pray.

NEDDY

A FTER A STOP IN THE CITY OF AMSTERDAM in Hollande, we arrived in our first Njorden port of Stavanger.

Before we departed Stavanger, the captain informed the passengers that it had been confirmed that the Sweating Sickness had come to northern Njord and that as a result, the ship would go no farther than Kristiansund.

I was dismayed. Kristiansund was many leagues from Trondheim.

"Is Trondheim hard hit?" I asked, dread filling me.

"There is no word yet that it is, but we aren't taking any chances," the captain replied.

Later Sib and I stood by the railing, watching Stavanger recede into the distance.

"Is it a long journey between Kristiansund and Trondheim?" she asked.

I nodded, frowning. "And with the Sweating Sickness, it may be difficult to find conveyance."

"Then we will walk," she said, taking my arm.

ROSE

T HE EFFECT OF THE TROLL-SNAKE VENOM had not entirely
left me. Sometimes, out of the blue, I would feel dizzy,
the sky and ground tilting all around me, and I had to lay my
head on my horse's neck. It usually passed fairly quickly, and
fortunately I never actually fell off my horse. She was a gentle
filly I named Ciuin, after that gentle wind of Sib's, and was all
white except for her muzzle and her two back legs, which were
dark brown. She took my dizzy spells in stride.

But worse than the lightheadedness was the fact that I had
begun to have nightmares.

Like my mother, I had never been prone to dreaming. The
one exception to this was while I was living in the castle in the
mountain and had a series of horrific nightmares about my
mysterious night visitor, one of the reasons I disastrously lit
the candle and saw Charles's face for the first time. Of course I
hadn't known then that if I had only kept my fear and curiosity under control for one more cycle of the moon, had not used
the troll candle supplied by my mother to see who my nighttime visitor was, Charles would have been released from his
enchantment. There would have been no impossible journey

to a land that lay east of the sun and west of the moon. But that was not to be.

My first nightmare was about the troll-snake himself. Jaaloki. Except in the dream, he was half troll, half snake. He was coiled around me, but his face and upper body were Jaaloki's. He reached out his skeletal hands and wrapped them around my throat, choking me. I woke up dizzy, my breath coming in gasps.

I laid my palm on my chest, trying to calm my rapidly beating heart. I decided that tomorrow I would start practicing with the sword in case I had to face the troll-snake again.

The next day, at my first stop for the midday meal in a grove of poplar trees, after I had finished eating, I took the sword from my pack.

It was heavier than I remembered. I held it awkwardly in front of me, and feeling slightly foolish, I made a halfhearted thrust forward. The weight of the sword threw me off balance, and I almost fell on my face.

Planting my feet firmly on the ground and taking a deep breath, I cast my mind back to my childhood. The only time I had been exposed to swordplay was with my oldest brother, Nils Erlend. Because he had left home at a young age, I had barely known Nils. His visits home were few and far between. Mother liked to point out that he had the most north in him, which explained his wandering ways. He had had a series of occupations, including sailor, traveling merchant, and once, for a brief time, soldier.

It was during his stint as a soldier that he came home for one of his rare visits. I had idolized Nils Erlend from afar, and seeing him in his soldier garb, with the sword buckled at his hip, increased my admiration tenfold. I was very young at the time, and after Nils's visit, I became fascinated by swords. My brother Willem agreed to whittle me a small wooden sword and even helped me fashion a belt with a loop where the small wooden sword could be carried. How I had loved that sword.

I recalled that during his visit, Nils had given Neddy and me a brief demonstration of swordplay. I was the most interested, with Neddy soon wandering off to read a book. If only I could remember the details.

I closed my eyes, concentrating. Nils had said something about how to grip the sword, how you should hold it lightly, delicately. And I remembered that he had laid great emphasis on how you stood in relation to your opponent—sideways was best—and that you must also be light on your feet. "Like you are dancing," he had said.

I remembered giggling at that. Dancing was something you did with flowers in your hair on Midsummer. Sword fighting was a serious business. But Nils had frowned at me and said to stop laughing and listen.

So in that grove of poplar trees, I held the sword lightly in my hand and began to move. I imagined Nils Erlend before me. And an odd thing happened. As I lifted the sword, it unexpectedly felt lighter, moving easily, almost of its own accord. I held it high above me and stared up at the tarnished blade. The sun's rays glanced off it, making it gleam in the afternoon light.

I remembered what Sib had said about it being a wind sword. What did that mean? I wondered again.

I continued to move around the grove, thrusting and swinging the sword, imagining dueling with an imaginary foe. I quick-stepped forward and then back, and indeed I discovered Nils Erlend was right. It was like dancing.

I thought back to the dances I had shared with Charles. The first, that horrible awkward troll dance at the ice palace. But a few times after we were married, we'd gone to fairs at a nearby village, and there was usually dancing. Those had been happy moments. I felt a piercing stab of missing my white bear. But I pushed those thoughts away and concentrated on the sword, on my feet, and on my imaginary foe.

The feeling that the sword moved of its own accord did not last, and I thought I must have imagined it. If anything, the sword felt heavier and heavier as time went on, and practicing with it was hard work. All the muscles in my body began to ache, and sweat was dripping off me.

Finally I sank, exhausted, into a sitting position, dropping the sword beside me, and reached for my skin bag of water.

Then I remembered Nils Erlend telling me that a good soldier always took care of his weapon before himself. As I'd watched him pantomime wiping the blood of his slain enemies off the blade of his sword, I had felt a thrill of horror.

I set down the skin bag and sheathed my sword. I sat there breathing hard, wondering if I really did want to learn how to use a sword after all. Then I thought of my encounter with Jaaloki and all that stood between my white bear and me. I was going to find him. I *had* to. And I had to learn to use the sword because of the danger I almost certainly would face along the way. It was well to be prepared.

NEDDY

I T WAS A STRANGE, IN-BETWEEN TIME, the sea journey from Stavanger to Kristiansund.

There was much talk of the Sweating Sickness; many on board worried about loved ones in northern Njord. The captain told us that if there was sickness in Kristiansund, he would not land there. A system of flags would be in place to warn approaching ships of unsafe conditions.

Sib shared with me her own experience of the Sweating Sickness. At that time, it had been called the Anglian Sweate, and she gave me advice on how best to keep from contracting it. She even spent some of the voyage sewing muslin cloth masks that she said we must wear over our noses and mouths while tending to the sick.

As before, I was puzzled by her account of the Anglian Sweate. I had read much of Anglia's history and thought I remembered that the last such epidemic had occurred in the 1400s, well before Sib could have been born. Perhaps there had been a small later outbreak in her village that had gone unrecorded in the history books.

At any rate, I fervently hoped that this current outbreak in

Njord would end up being equally insignificant, not one that would be recorded in the historical records of this time.

As we approached the harbor of Kristiansund, all the passengers were on deck. The captain had told us that if there was a solid black flag flying, he would turn the ship around and make for the nearest southern port.

Sib and I were standing side by side, and I found myself thinking of Rose's words to me about life being short. We did not know what we were going to find when we got to Trondheim. Maybe Rose was right. I should make my feelings known.

"Sib," I said quickly, before I could change my mind.

She turned to look at me. Her eyes held mine, intent, full of feeling, but when I opened my mouth to speak, she raised a finger and placed it across my lips.

"No, Neddy," she said softly. "Not now."

I stared at her, mutely.

"Not now," she repeated.

I closed my eyes, breathing deeply. Why not now? I wondered. But a voice inside told me I should trust Sib.

Just then, I heard a shout go up. There was no black flag. It was safe to disembark at Kristiansund.

When we disembarked, the captain told us that local officials were strongly advising against traveling to Trondheim, as it had been hard hit by the Sweating Sickness. And as I had feared, we were unable to find any kind of transport, and so we set out on foot.

The weather was unusually hot for this time of year, the air damp and oppressive.

ROSE

I T TOOK ME THREE DAYS to get to the outskirts of the *hanté* forest, the impenetrable, expansive woodland the trolls had caused to grow up around the castle in the mountain. At every meal break during those three days of travel, I practiced swordplay, and I seemed to be getting stronger and more adept at swinging the blade.

I didn't like the idea of entering the *hanté* forest at night, so I made camp nearby. Before I went to sleep, I had one more practice session and decided that my sword arm was definitely getting stronger.

The next morning, I entered the forest, leading my horse, Ciuin, behind me. I found it just as dense and impenetrable as it had been the times before when I had journeyed through it. Perhaps even worse now. The going was so slow that I finally took the sword out of my pack and began using it to hack my way through the tangle of trees and undergrowth. At first it was awkward, but as I grew used to wielding it, I found the wind sword to be surprisingly effective. In fact, a few times when I swung it, I thought I heard a sort of whooshing sound, and I once again had the feeling that it could move on its own.

When I stopped in a small clearing for a rest and a draft of water, I tested the sword, swinging it in a large arc above my head. And I definitely heard and felt the whoosh then. It was like a sudden rush of wind.

Ciuin nickered, looking a little apprehensive. I went to comfort her, and as I fed her a ration of oats, I wondered about the sword. What made it a wind sword, and why had Sib been so sure it was not Huldre made?

It took an entire day to get through the forest, but finally we emerged. There was still a day's journey to go, past the deserted farm that had once grown the food for the inhabitants of the castle in the mountain.

But at last Ciuin and I arrived at the base of the mountain.

NEDDY

I KNEW THE ROAD BETWEEN KRISTIANSUND and Trondheim well. I had helped Father remap it some years back when someone found a faster route around one of the higher ridges through a previously undiscovered valley.

In spite of that improvement, it remained a difficult journey to tackle by foot; there was a series of small mountains, as well as a number of rivers and streams that needed to be crossed. I knew it would take us a solid four days of walking to get there.

The steamy heat, so unnatural for September, continued. We met no travelers on the road, either coming or going, but in the late afternoon of our first day, we came across an abandoned cart. It was filled with household belongings, but there was no sign of a horse or any other living beings.

Suddenly Sib gave a little gasp and hurried across the road and down an incline to a small stream. I followed her and found her crouched over the bodies of a young woman and a bairn. Both were clearly dead. Sib gestured for me to come no closer, and I watched in horror as she gently pulled the mother's cloak up so it covered both their faces.

"Should we not bury them?" I asked as she came back up the incline, her cheeks pale.

She shook her head. "I know it feels wrong, but I fear this is just the beginning," she said grimly. "We should limit our contact with those infected. Also, if we stopped to bury them all, we would be much delayed in our journey to Trondheim. And we must get there as quickly as we can, Neddy. Rose trusted us to keep Winn safe."

I nodded, and silently we resumed our walking.

Sib was right. We must have come across three more carts, each bearing one or more victims of the Sweating Sickness. The bodies were usually either in or beside the carts, though like the first ones, we did find them close to a nearby stream. We did not see any horses with the carts and thought they must either have run off or been stolen. Each time, Sib made me stay back, and she donned one of her muslin masks and checked to make sure no one was still alive.

It was a horrific, bone-chilling journey, and my fear of what we would find when we got to Trondheim heightened with each step we took.

Back in Kristiansund we had found a ferryman who was willing to carry us across the Kvernesfjord—one of the widest fjords in this part of Njord. He had charged us an exorbitant price and practically shoved us off the boat when we got to the other side. But when we came to the ferry at Kanestraum, to cross the Halsfjord, we were not so lucky.

The ferry was shut down, with no sign of anyone attending it. We were surprised by this because we were still leagues away from Trondheim. Clearly people weren't taking any chances.

"We'll have to go by Sunndalsora, and climb Trollheimen," I said bleakly, knowing it would add at least two days to our journey.

Sib was looking out at the fjord, her eyes scanning the shoreline nearest us.

"I see a boat," she said. "The wind is good. Come," she added, taking my hand.

We made our way down to a small currach pulled up on the rocky shore. It didn't look particularly seaworthy, with weathered wood and a stained, waterlogged sail lying in the bottom, but there were no obvious holes in the hull. Sib was determined, so I helped her climb aboard and pushed us off into the fjord. We raised the sodden sail with difficulty, then, holding the rope to the boom, Sib sat on a rickety bench, gesturing for me to take the tiller.

She was very still, and I noticed that her eyes had that unfocused faraway look I had seen before. As we gently bobbed on the water, I told Sib I couldn't feel the wind she had mentioned, but she ignored me. I began to look for oars, since it seemed likely we'd have to row across Halsfjord, which would be no easy task. But perhaps no worse than climbing Trollheimen.

Unexpectedly I felt a gust of wind across my face. Sib was sitting as before, eyes still unfocused, the rope to the sail lying limp in her hand. The soggy fabric began to flap, at first just a little and then more energetically. I took the rope from Sib, pulling it taut.

The wind caught the sail, and the currach lurched forward.

"You were right," I called to Sib.

"I am always right when it comes to wind," Sib called back, smiling.

And the breeze propelled us swiftly across the fjord.

We made landfall on a small patch of rocky beach, and as we got out of the boat, Sib staggered slightly. I noticed, too, that her cheeks were paler than usual.

"Just tired," she murmured in response to my concerned query.

As we climbed a hill to rejoin the road to Trondheim, we spied another abandoned cart, not far from the ferry dock on this side of the fjord. Sprawled next to it was the lifeless body of a middle-aged man, who looked as if he had died only recently. And there was a horse harnessed to the cart. The horse looked edgy and also seemed hot and thirsty in the sultry weather.

I unhitched the animal while Sib found some oats and fresh water in the cart.

"I think we should take the horse," I said to Sib.

"I was thinking the same," she replied. And she looked exhausted, like she could barely put one foot ahead of the other.

Taking the horse didn't feel like stealing, not in these dire times.

We didn't ride the horse at first, not until it had regained its strength, after a goodly share of oats and water. But the animal, a big, sturdy chestnut with graying hair around the eyes, turned out to have a docile temperament and a good deal of stamina. Our journey went much more quickly.

We passed through several small villages, each seeming almost deserted, though I occasionally caught a flicker of movement at cottage windows.

People in Njord were terrified, and rightly so.

ROSE

WHEN CHARLES AND I LEFT the castle in the mountain three years ago for what we thought was the last time, we had decided to drag several large rocks in front of the doorway. Because it was located in such a remote spot surrounded by a virtually impenetrable forest, we thought it unlikely anyone would come across it, but it seemed best to ensure that no unsuspecting person should be exposed to the world of the Huldre and their arts.

The rocks were still there, and no one would suspect that a castle was hidden inside that small mountain.

I tethered Ciuin at a nearby copse of trees, leaving her a supply of oats and water, and approached the door. It took a little time and sweat to remove the rocks, but by late afternoon, I had succeeded.

I straightened and, taking a deep breath, entered the castle.

There was no light coming from inside, but I quickly found the sconces holding the oil lamps that lined the halls. I fashioned a makeshift torch and lit the lamps as I traveled down the front hallway.

The castle was just as it had been before. The layout of the rooms, which I had come to know by heart when I lived there for a year, was exactly the same.

The memories began to wash over me with each flickering glimpse of a remembered chair or fireplace. The deeper into the castle I went, the more I saw—the room with the musical instruments, the library, the chamber I had slept in. I couldn't bear the sight of the bed, the bed where I had leaned over the white bear with my candle and destroyed everything. A happier sight was my weaving room, and I closed my eyes, thinking of the white bear lying on the rug as I wove and told him stories.

I felt surrounded by ghosts, the whispered footsteps of a white bear's paws, Tuki's rough, eager voice, his mother Urda's severe expression when she discovered our language game. And more recently, Charles's reassuring hand on my back as we walked through these halls that last time.

There was a pretty room I had called the "game room" in my head, though it was a room I had spent little time in. I called it that because there were various games set up, most especially a handsome *echecs* set. I had had little interest in *echecs* back when I lived here. In fact, the first time I had ever played was with Estelle, when I was recovering from the sickness brought about after my calamitous lighting of the candle and being tossed out of the castle into the snow and cold. The Queen Maraboo piece she had given me back then was now safely in my pocket, my good luck charm.

I made my way to the music room. It was empty, and I felt an irrational sense of disappointment. Somehow I had pictured that this was where I would find Charles, playing his flauto. For a moment I even thought I heard a faint strain of a melody, but knew I must be imagining it.

I went through the entire castle twice and found nothing, no sign of Charles. And I could see nothing that wasn't as I remembered it, with one exception. The red couch in the room where I had eaten most of my meals was missing.

What did it mean? What did any of the troll Jaaloki's words mean? Had I been so completely wrong?

You may not know that place as well as you thought you did.

I had to be missing something. Or was it that the Troll Queen was playing with me, as Jaaloki had said?

I would go through the whole castle again. And again. Until I figured it out.

Doggedly, I returned to the front hall and began again, room by room, holding my torch up, searching each corner and closet and crevice.

And suddenly a thought struck me. Jaaloki was an Under Huldre. What if there were caverns underneath the castle? I was almost positive there hadn't been before. I had never found any trapdoor or stairway down to a cellar or underground caves during the year I lived here. But maybe now there was something down below.

I lifted rugs, looked behind paintings and tapestries,

opened closets, until finally in the kitchen at the back of a cupboard, I found a small door.

I hadn't seen it there before, but the kitchen was one place I had not been allowed to go very often, so it was possible I had overlooked this door.

I opened it and peered through. Dimly I could make out a crude set of stone stairs, leading down. Again there was no light, but there were a few of the oil lamps in sconces, and I lit them with my torch. I began to descend.

At first it felt like an ordinary kitchen cellar with a few rooms holding barrels and shelves for storage. But I came to a tunnel that led beyond those rooms. I followed it and arrived at a place where I could turn left or right. I chose the right turning, and a short while later came to a similar crossroad. I paused, then arbitrarily chose to go left.

It was a rough tunnel but wide and tall enough for me to walk comfortably. There were rooms off the tunnel, and when I illuminated them with my torch, I saw only tumbled rocks and cobwebs in most of them. But occasionally I came to a room with things inside, like piles of old iron bars and broken furniture. At one point I came to one with bleached white bones scattered over its floor. I shuddered, but decided they looked so old and covered with dust that they could not be Charles's bones.

When I came to a fourth turning point, which offered options to go left or right or straight ahead, I stopped.

It was confusing, so many twists and turns. A maze of tunnels. And it struck me.

"It's a labyrinth," I whispered to myself.

I remembered a story Neddy had once told me, an old tale from Gresk. There had been a monster imprisoned at the center of an underground maze of tunnels. The maze had been called a labyrinth, and a hero had come, finding his way through with the help of the king's daughter and a ball of yarn. He had slain the monster and won the kingdom and the princess's hand in marriage.

I was terrified that I might get lost in this labyrinth of troll tunnels. Did I remember the turnings I had taken? I thought there had been four, but maybe it was more. I turned and began to make my way back. Yes, there was the room with the bleached bones. And the broken furniture. But had I passed this room with piles of decaying tapestries? My heart started beating fast. *Slow down,* I told myself. The air was so dead and still. *Four turnings,* I breathed. I should have been back to the beginning by now.

I retreated to the last turning and took a different direction. This time the room on the left with wooden barrels looked familiar. And even better, I thought I saw light ahead.

I breathed a great sigh of relief when I found myself back at the stairs leading up to the kitchen. I ran up them, and headed directly to the weaving room. I found a large spool of pearly white wool and, taking it with me, ran back to the beginning of the maze.

I started again, and this time I laid down a trail of the wool thread behind me.

The farther I went, the colder and deader the air became. I came across more rooms filled with ancient, dusty artifacts, including a pile of rusting swords. In one room I spotted what appeared to be mounds of gold and treasure, topped by a gleaming crown studded with blood-red jewels.

It was like a puzzle, with dead ends, loops, and tunnels that branched out and then rejoined. There were countless times I had to backtrack, rewinding the thread and starting again. I began to worry there was no solution, that it was an infinite maze, with no beginning and no end.

I kept walking, and after a long while, I saw that the yarn was beginning to run out.

I had lost track of time. It had been hours, perhaps even an entire night. I thought of my horse, Ciuin, tethered outside the entrance of the castle, waiting for me. I was confident there were no predators out there, but she must be getting hungry.

The weight of the rock above me began to bear down, making my breath shallow, my legs leaden. I was also getting hungry.

Finally I realized that I must take a break. I sat down on the cold rock and got out a skin bag of water. I drank deeply.

It felt like I was in some underground city, and I was sure

that somewhere down in the streets of this city was my white bear.

And then I heard it. The sound of a flauto.

At first I was sure I was imagining, or wishing, it. I listened closely. Yes, I could just barely hear it. I jumped to my feet and started walking again, with more energy. And the farther I went, the clearer it became.

I stopped abruptly, holding very still, listening. It was a melody I recognized, one that Charles sometimes played. A favorite from his childhood, he had said, though I didn't remember the name. My heart started pounding.

I continued on through the maze of tunnels, listening, letting the sound guide me, continuing to unspool the thread as I went.

There was something odd about the flauto music. I couldn't place it at first, but soon it dawned on me. The playing was rougher, somehow less polished than I was used to hearing from Charles. The notes were more tentative, as if the player was a beginner, unlike Charles, who was an accomplished flautist.

One set of turns seemed to be taking me farther away from the music, so I retraced my steps, rewinding the thread as I went back. I was in an agony of impatience, terrified that suddenly the music would vanish.

But finally I turned a corner and it seemed close at hand.

I spotted a closed door, which was made of a dull gray metal. There was a key in the lock.

I laid my ear to the door and could clearly hear the sound of the flauto. I took a deep breath, my heart beating wildly.

I paused. *This could be some kind of trap,* I thought. Jaaloki's words echoed in my mind.

She plays with you.

I swung my pack from my shoulder and drew my sword.

I took hold of the key and turned it. It moved smoothly in the lock and clicked. The music stopped.

Slowly I opened the door.

MOTHER

ARNE THOUGHT WE SHOULD BE MAKING some kind of written record of this time we were living through, but the thought of forming sentences, much less setting them down on paper, defeated all of us.

We were like shadows of ourselves, moving dreamlike through a landscape of unbearable horror and loss. Every day there was at least one new death, more often as many as ten or even more. And that many bodies to bury.

At first they would toll the bell at Nidaros Cathedral when someone died, but it became too frequent, and the mayor made the decision to silence the bell. I didn't know which was worse, the constant dolorous sound of the bell or the silence.

We in Trondheim had been slow to realize what was happening, despite hearing rumors from sailors who had traveled to Anglia. It was after the death of Havamal's wife that he in particular began to sound the alarm. As a historian, he was keenly aware of the lessons of such quickly spreading diseases in the past, like the Black Death that took so many lives nearly two hundred years ago.

The day we lost our son Willem's wife, Annette, was only the latest in a series of losses. So many friends, so many neighbors had gone before her. Willem was undone but managed to stay strong for the sake of their children. Keeping them safe was the only thing that mattered to him after Annette died.

And then Sara's two-year-old daughter, Lissa, fell ill.

I was there when Lissa first started showing symptoms. She complained of her head hurting and began shivering. We knew the next stage was a high fever followed by the sweating, like nothing any of us had ever seen.

Unlike other influenza epidemics, such as the one that carried off my own parents, the Sweating Sickness didn't seem to target only the most vulnerable—the very young and the very old—but felled the strong among us just as rapidly.

The fear in Trondheim began to escalate. There were edicts by local officials to establish quarantine, to close the ports, to set a curfew. But there were many who were desperate or lawless and didn't heed the rules.

I was most worried about Estelle and Winn, and did not allow them out of the house. I could see Estelle was frightened, but she was also a restless young girl, and she chafed at having to stay indoors all the time. She longed to be with Gudrun and the other children.

Even though I missed Rose and Neddy and Sib sorely and

sometimes had the selfish wish that they were here to provide comfort and aid, overall I was grateful that they were far away and spared this devastation and horror. I prayed that wherever they were, they were safe.

ROSE

I ENTERED. THE ROOM BEFORE ME was barely furnished, and I could see at once it was empty. The music, which had resumed, came from beyond it, and there was a door at the far end, standing ajar. A soft yellow light, and the notes of a flauto, streamed through. Softly I crossed to the second door and peered through the opening.

I saw him immediately. Charles. He was sitting on that old red couch I knew so well, and he was playing the flauto, his eyes closed in concentration.

My heart was flooded with joy. He was alive. My white bear was alive. And he looked well, uninjured. I took a step forward, but stopped. Something wasn't right. At first I could not figure it out, and then I remembered. The music. The music wasn't right.

This wasn't the way my white bear played the flauto. I had heard it from a distance. The notes were hesitant, almost clumsy. I must have made a small noise, because Charles suddenly stopped playing. His eyes opened, and he saw me there in the doorway.

"Charles?" I said. And I took several steps toward him. I

could see his face clearly. It was pale and thin, but it was his face, the face of my white bear.

Yet something else was wrong.

"Charles," I said again, louder.

He was looking at me, straight in the eyes, and I was horrified to see nothing there. His expression was completely blank. There was no joy, no spark of recognition.

"Hello," he said politely. He set his flauto on the couch beside him and stood. He gave a little formal bow, and said, "I was told someone would come for me."

I stared at him, frozen. I didn't understand. For a brief, terrifying moment I wondered if this was a troll shape-shifted to look like Charles. But his voice was my white bear's voice.

"Charles!" I blurted out. "Do you not know me? I'm . . ." But I stopped. I could see in his face a look of deep panic, even terror.

He did not know me, and he was frightened. Had he sustained a head injury during the shipwreck? Was that what had happened? I could see no sign of a wound.

Or, I thought with a shudder, *the Troll Queen has done this to him.*

All at once I could not breathe and there was a roaring in my ears. The room tilted and the sword fell from my hand, clattering onto the stone floor. I sank down, unable to stand. The snake venom, I thought. Or maybe it was shock.

Charles came and knelt beside me.

"Are you unwell?" he asked. His expression again was one of polite concern.

"I'm fine," I said, my voice trembling slightly. "I was bitten by a snake, not very long ago. Sometimes it still affects me."

"I am sorry," said Charles. "I will bring you water. There is wine too," he added, gesturing to a table at the side of the room. It had dishes and goblets and a large pitcher. There was a good deal of food there, as well, bowls of fruit, loaves of bread.

"Wine please," I whispered.

Charles rose and crossed to the table. He poured wine from the pitcher into a goblet and brought it over to me.

I drank. It was a rich, red wine. It cleared my head a little, and I sat up straighter.

"Thank you," I said, then blurted out, "What is your name?"

"I am Charles," he said. "The son of Charles VI of Fransk."

My eyes widened. "King Charles?"

"Yes."

"And how did you come to be here?" I asked.

Charles's face clouded. "I . . . I don't know. I woke up here. On that couch. I have been here some time. I lost count, but many weeks. Food is brought, but only when I am sleeping."

His voice sounded young, and it trembled slightly, as if he was trying to hide the fear I had seen in his face.

"Who told you someone would come for you?" I asked.

"A man. I only saw him once, at the beginning. He was like a skeleton with hard gray skin. I didn't like him."

I drank more from the goblet, trying to keep my breathing slow.

"He gave me the flauto, too. At least I saw him put it on the table in its bag. I was just beginning to learn to play back at the palace." His voice cracked slightly. "It has helped pass the time."

Still holding the goblet, I got to my feet.

"Perhaps you can help me," Charles said. "My thoughts are confused. I cannot remember things. The last I do remember is being home, outside the castle, playing a game with friends, but I lost the ball and . . ." He trailed off.

"That is the last I can remember. Playing with a red ball, with other children. But it is the oddest thing." He gestured at his body. "I can see that I am not a boy."

I let out a muffled cry. Playing with a ball. A red ball.

This man who stood before me, my Charles, my white bear, had the mind and the memory of a nine-year-old boy, Prince of Fransk, 153 years ago.

TROLL QUEEN

I HAVE CHANGED, AND NOT JUST BECAUSE of the scars on my body, those whorls and ridges caused by the burning heat of the sun's power, which I unleashed back when all was lost. Back when the magnificent wedding I had planned to my Myk was ruined. Back when my ice palace splintered and fell. And all because of the softskin girl.

There is one scar that is vast, a long, deep crevice on the right side of my face.

I could have filled it using my arts, returned my appearance to the way it was before, but I chose not to because I wanted the proof of what was done to me. Every time I look in the mirror, or run my finger along the valley in my skin, I am reminded. And I want to be reminded. For it hardens me, each time, a little more.

My skin, too, is harder and stiffer even than before. And when I think back on the lengths to which I once went, the complicated spells I wove to try to soften my skin, I think what a foolish, wasted, blighted misuse of my arts it was. That I did so, that I was reduced to such contemptible behavior, of trying to look like a softskin, kindles the heated rage-wave inside me.

But I am getting better at controlling the rage-wave. I need to control it, focus it.

When I first crawled out of the rubble of my ice palace and Urda was tending to me, the rage-wave was unbridled. I wanted nothing more than to blast everything and everyone into oblivion. But my arts had been damaged. I needed time to heal, with help from Urda and Jaaloki.

I am glad of the hardness in me now, inside and out.

For now I can remember the boy with the red ball, with his melting soft smile. And it no longer affects me. He no longer matters. It is the bairn, and my revenge, and Aagnorak. They are what matter now.

Aagnorak will come. And from the ashes I will rule all.

NEDDY

W HEN SIB AND I ARRIVED IN TRONDHEIM, the streets were deserted. The air was heavy and hot. We could smell smoke and an underlying odor of rot and decay. Sib suggested we put on our muslin masks. I saw an occasional flutter of a curtain being lifted and a neighbor's eyes staring out at us, but no one came out to greet us. I think to steady me, Sib reviewed the precautions we would be taking once we got home. I had an overwhelming feeling of dread as we approached the house.

The door opened, and there stood Mother. She looked exhausted, ravaged. When her eyes lit on us, I could see the different emotions go through her. Happiness that we were there in front of her, but also horror, fear that we were walking into danger.

Sib stepped forward. She hugged Mother to her and said simply, "We are here to help."

First we made sure Winn was safe and well, and then we set to work. Over the next few hours, Sib took charge of the household. She had Mother gather herbs and cook them up on the hearth for a healing concoction. Father was sent to the well to pump buckets full of water, and Estelle was given the task of handing out muslin face coverings to everyone. Sib also taught her how to make more of them so we'd have some in reserve.

Sib instructed everyone on the importance of thoroughly washing hands after being in contact with anyone who had the sickness. She even produced the soap we were all to use, a strong concoction made of lye distilled from the ashes of the barilla plant, as well as animal fat and goat's milk.

Sib, Sara, and I tended to Sara's daughter Lissa, who was dangerously ill.

As we worked, Mother brought us up to date on what had been going on in Trondheim, the death toll so far, the panic and fear, the curfews. She also told us how Willem was coping with the loss of his wife. Everyone was terrified of what might happen next.

Sib and I exchanged a grim look. Things were even darker than we could have imagined.

ROSE

Pulling myself together, I turned to my husband. "I have come here to take you on a journey," I said, keeping my voice as steady as I could.

He nodded. "I will be happy to leave here," he said. "Do you think I might take the flauto with me?"

"Yes," I said. "And we should pack as much food as we can." My provisions had been running low, and it would have been a shame for all the food to go to waste.

"What is your name, if I may ask?" Charles said to me suddenly.

I froze, caught off guard. I felt tears start in my eyes, and I blinked them away angrily.

"My name is . . ." I paused, my head spinning.

Names are odd things, I thought. Charles had desperately needed to know his, after he was no longer a white bear. I had been given a name that was a lie, Ebba Rose, though my father had secretly called me Nyamh in his heart. The name we had given our bairn, Winn, felt like a temporary one, since Charles and I hadn't been able to make up our minds. What name would I tell my white bear who was not my white bear?

"Nyamh," I said impulsively.

"Well met, Lady Nyamh," Charles said, with his princely bow.

I laughed harshly. "No, not a lady. Just Nyamh," I said.

He nodded and went to gather up his flauto, placing it in a velvet pouch.

I stowed as much of the food as I could in my pack. I filled one of my skin bags with wine and another with water.

Why had I told Charles my name was Nyamh? I knew it was partly because I couldn't bear to hear him say Rose in that distant, polite voice. But perhaps it was also because I thought it might help me with what lay ahead, to think of myself as Nyamh, the wild north name Father had originally chosen for me.

For just a moment, I thought about telling Charles everything, that I was Rose, his wife. That we loved each other, that we had a son together. But then I glanced over at him. He was sitting on the red couch watching me, looking lost and young. And all at once I became convinced that if I were to tell this man who believed he was a boy that I was his wife, the panicky, wild-eyed look I had seen before in his eyes would explode into a madness from which there may not be a way back. For now I must keep the truth a secret and find a way to help Charles regain his memory.

When I had packed all I could carry, I gestured to him and we left the room. I looked back once, at the red couch.

The Troll Queen. She had orchestrated this, all of it.

My white bear was gone, but not gone. In some ways it was worse than if he were dead. Here but not here. I shook my head savagely. No. I could not give in to despair. Where there was life, there was also hope.

WHITE BEAR

I WALKED BEHIND THE LADY, marveling at the sure way she followed the white thread. She must have laid it down to guide her back through all these twists and turns. She had come to find me.

I didn't know why, but I trusted her. She wasn't like the skeleton man.

It frightened me to think about all that I did not know or remember. When did I grow into a man's body? How had I come to be in this place, and why?

When I first woke up on the red couch, I was terrified.

I did not know who I was. Or where I was. I couldn't remember anything. And panic had filled me. The place was damp and cool. Was I in some kind of prison? Had I been stolen by some enemy of my father?

Then I realized I had remembered something. I had a father. Who was I? My head hurt. Tears threatened to come, but I wouldn't let them. Someone had told me once that a prince did not cry.

A prince? Was I a prince?

I saw I was lying on a red couch. There was a table against

the wall, and food was on it. If I was in a prison, at least I would not starve. Not right away, anyway.

When the skeleton man put the velvet pouch on the table, my heart leapt. I knew what was inside. A flauto. It was something I knew and loved. It was another clue to who I was.

A boy, a prince perhaps, who had been learning to play a flauto.

After that, I had more memories. Of living in a palace. Of an aunt named Valentina. Of playing with a red ball.

A boy, living in a palace.

But I knew that I was not a boy. My body was larger than a boy's body. I could feel that I had the stubble of a beard on my face.

I snatched my hand from my face, overcome by another wave of fear.

I stood, looking down at myself. I was wearing nice clothing, not sumptuous court clothing as I was used to, but not rough servant's clothing either. Black pants, finely made black leather boots that fit me well, a white shirt, some kind of wool vest, and a jacket. A jacket with pockets.

I reached into the pockets eagerly, hoping to find more clues to who I was. But they were empty.

Panic took hold again. I felt alone and empty and undone. My body began to shake. My head was filled with bursts of light and color.

I remembered my father, the king, once falling to the floor, and they had rushed me away, saying he'd had some kind of fit.

Maybe I was having a fit.

My head pounded. Breathing was hard. As I lay back down on the red couch, hands pressed to my head, I saw the flauto lying on the table.

I lurched over to it and lifted it, feeling its cool metal on my skin. And when I put it to my lips and began to play, the flashes of light and the emptiness and the fear melted away.

I seemed to know one song by heart. I played it.

I lost track of the days. Sometimes when I slept, the food was replenished, freshened. I tried to be brave and to believe the skeleton man when he said someone would be coming for me soon, yet I did not trust him.

But it turned out he was right. For she had come, the lady with purple eyes. And somehow I believed she would help me find my way home.

NEDDY

SIB CAME OUT OF LISSA'S ROOM, untying the strings that held the muslin covering over her face. Her hands were chapped and shook slightly from exhaustion.

"She will live," Sib said in a low voice. "She is weak, but she sleeps now. The crisis is past."

I reached for Sib and pulled her close.

"Thank you," I whispered, lightheaded with relief.

She pulled away. "Wash your hands, Neddy. You cannot be too careful. All of us. And, Neddy"—her voice shook a little—"I fear for Sara. She is exhausted and . . ."

I felt some alarm. "Do you think she has . . ."

Sib shook her head. "No, not yet, anyway. Try not to worry," Sib said. "I have sent her to bed. We just need to keep an eye on her."

We told the news of Lissa's recovery to Mother and Father, who were anxiously waiting in Sara and Harald Soren's great room.

After Sib and I washed up, we went to the kitchen, where I cut some meat and cheese and bread for us, though I hadn't much appetite. We both had little inclination to talk, and I savored those moments, sitting quietly with Sib, the early morning sun gleaming through the window.

Lissa was all right. Sara would be too. I even let myself think that the worst was over.

ROSE

AFTER WE GOT OUT of the underground labyrinth and were up inside the castle, I watched Charles's face closely to see if the sight of all the familiar furnishings might awaken his memory. But his expression remained unchanged. He gazed around as a child would look at a new place he'd come to.

"What is this palace?" he asked. "Who lives here?"

"No one, not anymore," I replied.

"Who used to live here?"

"A prince," I said, thinking, *A prince who was enchanted into a white bear.*

"Like me," he said.

"Yes," I said. Then changed the subject, my voice brisk. "You will need a pack, to carry your flauto and other gear for the journey."

"Will there be danger on the journey?" he asked gravely. I could see his eyes on the sword I had put back in my pack.

"I don't know," I said, but then decided it was best to be honest and went on. "There may be."

"Then I would like a sword," he said.

I told him there was a room on the second floor with several swords in a case. "And take whatever else you want from this castle. We have been given leave to carry away what we need." He nodded understanding.

"There are a few things I must get," I said. "We will meet back here shortly." We were in the great room of the castle. He nodded again.

I had remembered something I wanted to find. It was a book that had been here back when I was living with the white bear. It was in a foreign tongue, one I didn't recognize at the time, and seemed to be a book of maps. It was only later, when I was a servant in Niflheim and saw troll language written down, that I realized it must have been an atlas, a guide to the lands of Huldre. I had thought of it when I realized it might be possible that Charles was hidden at one of the Troll Queen's other dwellings. And even though I had found him, I still had a yearning to see that book, to see if I was right about it.

I found the atlas without much trouble and tucked it under my arm to look at later.

I went back to the weaving room. Even though I had taken a good portion of thread and wool the first time around, there was still much left. I decided to pick three spools of thread, as I had done before. The first was a flame red. I had been wanting to make Estelle a dress, and red was one of her favorite colors.

I was then drawn to a blue-violet color, thinking it a nice blend of my eye color and Charles's. And finally I picked a pale, silvery, almost translucent thread, which reminded me of Sib. It also reminded me of the moon thread I had woven into the dress I had worn to the troll ball back in Niflheim.

After departing the weaving room, I went to a room where I remembered there had been a large box filled with gold coins. When we left the castle for what we thought was the last time, Charles and I had not taken any, not wanting or needing troll riches, but now I thought gold coins might well come in handy for the journey that lay ahead. I found a leather pouch and filled it to the top.

I headed back to the great room and found Charles there, sitting on a large brocaded couch. Next to him were the flauto, a sturdy leather pack, a bedroll, and a sword.

He stood when he saw me, picking up the sword.

"I had been learning swordplay with a tutor back home. But I do not know much about swords. Do you know if this is a good one?"

I wanted to tell him that I knew little of swords myself, but I merely gave an approving nod. "It looks well," I said. "Come, let us see if we can find more skin bags in the kitchen, and then we will be on our way."

Once we were all outfitted and ready to depart, we made our way to the entrance.

It was midmorning when we exited the castle in the

mountain. I immediately went to Ciuin, who was remarkably calm, though clearly in need of food and water.

"There is only Ciuin," I said to Charles after introducing them, "and she is small. We will have to walk. Or take turns riding." He nodded.

Then, pushing away memories of the last time I had done this with my white bear, I instructed this new Charles to help me push the rocks back up against the entrance.

"It is good to be outside," he suddenly said, a pleased smile on his face. "I was in that room for a very long time." The sky was blue and the air fresh. We began to walk.

NEDDY

S ARA FELL ILL THE NEXT MORNING. And by midnight she was gone.

It was a horrible blow, and every one of us reeled from the shock of it. My dear sister Sara, that she could have fallen victim to this cursed sickness seemed unfathomable. Her children left motherless, Harald Soren in a state of grief and shock.

I couldn't help but think back to the time we had come so close to losing Sara before, back when the white bear had come to our door and offered to save her if Rose would come away with him.

Now I feared they were both dead—the white bear and Sara. How cruel life could be.

Sib found me in the back garden, my face wet with tears. She took me in her arms, and we stayed that way for a long time.

MOTHER

I SAT BY LISSA'S BEDSIDE, watching her sleep. The poor bairn was still pale and weak from the Sweating Sickness. She would wake soon, though, and ask for her mama. How was it possible to tell her that her mother was gone?

I felt numb, undone by losing my daughter, too numb even to fear what yet might lie ahead.

Arne came into the room with apple juice for Lissa when she woke. He looked pale too, and after handing me the glass, he sank into a chair and laid his head in his hands.

"Are you well, Arne?" I asked, watching him closely.

"Fine," he said. "'Twas just a bit of dizziness."

Fear rose in me, and I crossed to him, putting my hand on his forehead.

"Don't fuss," he muttered. "I'm just tired."

"Your skin is warm," I said.

"I'm fine," he repeated. "I just need some air. It is close in here."

He stood, but his legs buckled under him, and as he fell, I could see he was trembling.

I quickly went to the door and called, "Sib!"

WHITE BEAR

I T FELT VERY GOOD TO BE OUTDOORS, to feel the sun on my skin. I followed the lady Nyamh, who was leading the horse called Ciuin.

She had warned me about the *hanté* forest, saying that it would be difficult to get through, but she was able to find the way she had traveled before. Since it was mostly cleared, it was not as hard to traverse as she had feared.

We took turns riding Ciuin, and I found that I felt awkward on her. At first I thought it was because there was no saddle, but I got used to that and realized it was more that I couldn't find the rhythm of riding. It puzzled me because I remembered being good on horses before. The stable master once told me I had good form, and unlike others in court, he wasn't one to give false compliments. But I realized that the awkwardness was because of this body I was not used to. My legs and arms were long, and my shoulders broader. Gradually I began to adjust. It helped that the horse was even-tempered and steady.

My thoughts were jumbled. I could not think of the future, and it troubled me to think of the past. I knew I must focus on the present. On what was happening in that very moment. If I didn't, my mind would begin to pop and melt, and the panic would come.

Nyamh had shown me the book of maps she had taken from the castle. I found myself wishing there were a book of maps that would lead me back to my life. Or reveal to me the north, south, east, and west of my life. My tutor always did say that geography was one of my worst subjects. I found it dull, memorizing all those place names.

It was becoming clear to me that I couldn't remember a large chunk of my life. From the point when I was a boy playing with a red ball to waking up in the underground labyrinth with no memory of what lay in between. Boy to man. What had become of my mother and father, my older sisters, my Aunt Valentina? Did they even still live?

The panic rose then, blurring my vision. My mind began to heave and bend, bright colors flashing. The sky was a burning blue; the green of the grass seared my eyes.

I let out a cry, and Ciuin shied.

"Steady," I said in a voice that cracked, and I knew I was saying it to myself as much as to the horse.

I must think only of now.

NEDDY

T HE SWEATING SICKNESS TOOK HOLD of Father quickly and savagely, much the same way it had with Sara. The symptoms raced through Father's body in quick succession. The violent shivering that no number of blankets piled on top of him could relieve, accompanied by severe pain in his neck and shoulders and arms. And then came the sweating. His body became as hot as a blacksmith's furnace, and water poured off him, soaking the sheets and bedding. With Lissa, and even Sara, I hadn't noticed any odor at all, but Father's sweat bore a sickening, unpleasant smell, like that of rotting food.

He cried out in delirium, his hands pressed to his forehead as if the pain there made him want to tear off his own head.

Mother and I took turns ladling water into his mouth as fast as we could, but he still wanted more; his lips cracked with heat and thirst. His pulse raced.

Sib occasionally spooned an elixir she had made of ingredients such as burdock, heartsease, and geranium, as well as a few other herbs I couldn't name. She also brought an unending supply of cool wet cloths to drape on his forehead and chest.

"It is going so fast," Sib whispered as she replaced the wet cloths with fresh cool ones. "I haven't seen it like this before." She looked worried. She also looked exhausted, and would occasionally go to the window of the room as if to breathe in fresh air. But there was none. The weather continued hot and oppressive. Not a breath of wind stirred.

"Is there anything more we can do?" I asked, my heart thudding with dread.

"Don't let him sleep," she said.

I nodded, though Father seemed too agitated and restless for us to be concerned about sleep.

"Rose!" he suddenly cried out. "Where is Rose?"

I sat by him and said, "She is on a journey. But she is safe and will be back with us soon." I prayed this was the truth.

He seemed to hear me and be reassured by my words, for he went back to his previous indistinguishable muttering and thrashing about on the bed.

I continued to hold cups of water to his mouth, but it seemed that as much of it spilled down his chin as got down his throat.

Sib returned with more of her elixir and gave Father several more spoonfuls, followed by another full cup of water. He seemed to settle slightly, though the sweat still poured off him.

Mother took my place, and I watched as she unfolded his

hand, placed a key in his palm, and folded the fingers back over it.

I knew it was a superstition of hers that holding a key would take away a fever. And at this point, I was willing to try anything, even one of Mother's old superstitions.

ROSE

I SAW CIUIN SHY, AND I HURRIED to catch up to them. Charles looked ashen, saying his head hurt. I suggested it was time for a meal break, so we stopped in a meadow a short way down the road.

It was clear that my white bear was in a fragile state. The rift in his memory was deeply troubling to him, and he seemed to be plagued by headaches and strange visions.

I was terrified that the strain would be too great, that he would lose his reason altogether.

The sun had set, and we were both exhausted, so we decided to make camp in the meadow, building a small campfire. The nights were beginning to be cool.

We had stew that night, cooked over the campfire, and though we didn't talk much, it was a companionable meal.

After we said good night and settled into our bedrolls beside the embers of the campfire, I gazed up at the night sky. The truth was I had very little in the way of a plan. The only thing I could think of was to take Charles to the home we had shared, the place where our son was born. I was desperate to see Winn again, to make sure the Troll Queen had not harmed him. But I couldn't bear for Charles to be reunited with Winn and not recognize his son. So I prayed that that seeing our home would wake my white bear's memory.

WHITE BEAR

I WOKE WITH A GASP. The world was spinning. I felt like my bedroll was going to lift off the ground and carry me up to the moon. I was shivering violently.

I heard the sound of bells, like a sleigh. The air was so cold it was freezing inside my mouth. There was ice in my mouth, choking me. I couldn't breathe. I tried crying out, and the ice cracked and slid down my throat like the blade of a sword.

"Charles." A shadow loomed beside me. I couldn't see, my eyes were frozen shut.

"Charles!" The voice came again. I was clawing at my throat, my eyes.

I felt myself being lifted, enfolded in warm arms. The ice in my throat melted. I could breathe. My eyes came unfrozen, and I flicked them open. The lady Nyamh was holding me.

"Charles," she said.

And I said, "Thank you."

ROSE

A FTER HE HAD QUIETED and I returned to my side of the campfire, I was jittery, not able to get the sound of Charles's polite thank-you out of my mind. It had felt so natural, holding him in my arms, only to have it torn apart with those distant careful words.

Charles had withdrawn, in a world of his own after his nightmare.

I knew sleep would not come, so I rekindled the fire and heated water in a pan for tea with chamomile and lemon. Charles's hands were shaking as he drank.

"I just had a nightmare too," I said, trying to keep my voice neutral.

He looked up at me, his face pale. For a moment I thought he was going to speak, but instead shook his head, staring back down into his tea.

I could hear his breathing over the sound of the campfire, and his hand periodically clutched at his throat. I was worried, not knowing how to soothe him. Then I remembered him saying that when the panic came over him in that room down in the labyrinth, he would play the flauto.

"I was wondering," I said softly, "if you would be willing to play me something on your flauto? I don't think I'll be able to sleep, because of the nightmare, and perhaps music will help."

He looked up at me again, and at first I thought he was going to refuse. But he set down his cup. "Yes," he said, his voice strained. "I can do that."

He got his flauto out of its velvet pouch, and tentatively at first, he began to play.

And the sun rose to the sound of the bright notes of a simple Fransk melody played on a flauto.

NEDDY

I WAS SURE WE WERE GOING to lose Father on the second night of his illness. I was sitting by his bedside, and he started gasping, saying he could not breathe. That he was being smothered. His eyes looked terrified. He threw off his coverings and flailed on the bed. Mother came running in and held Father in her arms, speaking calmly to him, telling him to breathe deeply, that he was going to be fine.

Sib joined us with a pile of clean, cool cloths. She sponged Father's face and chest, and suddenly he gave a great shudder and went still. Panic rising in me, I reached for his wrist and was relieved to feel the faint thrumming of his heart against my fingers.

Sib laid her hand on Father's forehead. "I believe the fever has broken," Sib said. "He is not out of danger, but this is a good sign."

Relief flooded through me. I sank into a chair, closing my eyes. I felt that I could sleep for days.

"You two get some rest now," Mother said. "I will stay with Arne."

Sib and I left the room.

"Thank you, Sib," I said to her, pausing in the hallway.

"Have a good long rest, Neddy," she said. "And be sure to wash your hands," she added.

I entered my room, collapsing on the bed, with not even enough energy to lift the covers over me, and fell into a deep sleep.

 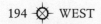

MOTHER

A RNE SLEPT, AND I COULD TELL he was no longer feverish.
I dozed a little, but was awake to see the rays of the rising
sun through the shutters. After checking on Arne, who was
breathing evenly, still in a deep sleep, I went to the kitchen to
prepare breakfast for Estelle and Winn.

During these days of sickness, Estelle had mostly had to
fend for herself, as well as doing much of the looking after of
Winn. Over breakfast I told her how helpful she'd been to all
of us, how proud of her I was, and she beamed at the compliment. She was also very relieved to hear that Arne was better.

Sib came into the kitchen. She asked after Neddy, and I
told her he must still be sleeping. Her brow furrowed a little.

"I'll just check on him," she said.

She returned quickly, and I saw at once she was agitated.

"Water," she said tersely. She grabbed her bag with the
medicines, and hurried back to Neddy's room.

I felt a terrible weakness come over me. Not Neddy.

Estelle looked at me as I got unsteadily to my feet.

"Is Oncle Neddy sick now?" she asked.

"I don't know, child," I said. "Please take some of this apple juice in to your grandfather. Tell him I'll be with him soon."

Estelle nodded gravely. And I went outside to pump more water.

ROSE

NEITHER OF US WAS RIDING the horse as we approached the bend in the road right before it led directly to our house. I walked a little ahead of Charles, wanting to be able to turn and see his face when he saw our home for the first time.

But there was nothing. No flicker of recognition.

Perhaps it will come when we are inside the house, I told myself.

"I know the people who live here," I said, gesturing toward the house and trying to keep my voice neutral. "They are away, traveling, but we can stop here for the night."

I tethered Ciuin, giving her fresh oats, and led Charles into the house. I was barely conscious of anything except watching his face. I had vowed not to be obvious, but it was difficult to mask my emotions.

"It is a pleasant home," Charles said, looking around, seemingly unaware of my avid gaze. "Who lives here?"

I couldn't restrain the sob that burst from me. It was too much, too overwhelming, being here in our own home and him such a stranger to it and to me. I turned away sharply.

"I'm sorry," I said in a strangled voice. "'Tis only something

stuck in my throat. I need water." I hurried back out the front door.

I made my way over to Ciuin, leaning against her warm, solid flank, fighting tears.

I had tried tempering my hopes, but I had become fixated on the belief that when he saw our house, this place where we had lived together as man and wife, where our child was born, he would remember.

But he hadn't. And a horrible possibility crept over me. He might never remember.

When I first found him, I had been so happy. He was alive. But now . . . he was no longer my husband, my white bear. He was a stranger. I didn't know him; he didn't know me.

Perhaps not a stranger. To him I was Nyamh, the lady with violet eyes who had been kind to him.

I would try to be patient. But deep down I was beginning to believe that between my white bear and me there was a door locked tight, with no key.

WHITE BEAR

I STOOD IN THE HOUSE, by myself, not knowing what to do. Nyamh had left in a rush, making a noise that sounded as if she was crying, though she said it was just something caught in her throat.

She had been watching me so closely. This place had to be somewhere I should know, should recognize. I looked around helplessly, willing it to be familiar, desperately hoping it would all come flooding back. I picked up a blue bowl. *I should know this bowl,* I said to myself.

I wanted to know it. I wanted the world to make sense again. I wanted to understand why I saw flashes of pictures in my head, of a seal's whiskers trembling, of swimming in a frigid sea, of rolling in the snow, of the bulge of a setting orange sun resting on the edge of a frozen shoreline.

The house felt comfortable, like someplace I'd like to live.

But I did not know it.

MOTHER

WATCHING THE SWEATING SICKNESS take hold of Neddy was agonizing. Both Arne and I were half out of our minds with fear and grief. And Arne was still so weak from his own recent illness that I worried for him as well.

We had both seen so many die before this. The girl with the red hair who worked in the bakery. The banker with an overfondness for lager. Even the mayor of our town had died just two days before. Willem's wife, Annette, and our own dear Sara. We'd seen whole families taken away in carts to be buried.

But the powerlessness I felt watching Neddy in the throes of this disease that thundered through his body was unbearable. Our son. Just as we had felt with Sara, Arne and I would gladly have given our lives for his, without a second thought.

Sib never left Neddy's side. Her pale, drawn face wore a look of immense and focused determination. It gave me some kind of comfort to think that Sib would do anything in her power to keep him from dying.

At the end of twelve hours, when the sweat had subsided

and the final stages of the illness began to appear, her face grew even more set, fiercer, if that was possible.

Neddy's breath was short, his face the color of bleached bones. Lassitude had come over him, and he lay limp. Sib kept spooning water into his mouth. When she sensed him drifting off to sleep, she spoke his name loudly, firmly. She even shook him to keep him from sleep.

I knew why. It was said that if a patient fell into slumber, they would most surely die.

From across the room I saw Neddy grow still, his eyes shut. Sib shook him hard, then harder, but he didn't stir. She looked up at me.

"Leave, Eugenia," she said.

I looked at her, uncomprehending.

"Leave. Now," she repeated, urgently. "Shut the door."

I left the room.

ROSE

EVEN THOUGH IT FELT AS IF I had been on the road for months and I would gladly have welcomed a warm bath and a comfortable bed, I did not want to stay in my home. It was too painful.

I did not know what to do next. Where to go. My only thought now was to take Charles to Trondheim with me, if he would go. In truth, there was nowhere else in the world he *could* go.

Ever since our arrival at the house, and the emotional outburst I had tried to hide, Charles had been very quiet. He looked drawn and unhappy. I was not much better myself.

When I told him that we would be journeying to La Rochelle, and from there take a ship up to a town in northern Njord, he just nodded.

That night, after making camp, we silently ate a simple meal by the fire.

I could not make small talk. I felt hollowed out, close to hopeless.

"Nyamh," Charles abruptly said. He had a look in his eyes I

could not read in the unsteady flicker of the firelight, but his voice was strained.

"Yes?"

"I have been thinking," he said. "Perhaps it is time I returned to my home, to one of my father's palaces. The Château d'Amboise, or maybe Saumur, where my Aunt Valentina spends a good amount of time. There will be doctors there who could help me . . ."

I stared across the fire at him. My throat was constricted, incapable of speech. Silence lay between us, so dark and heavy I thought it might blot out the flames of the campfire. How was I to tell him that his father and his Aunt Valentina, of whom he seemed very fond, were long dead and buried? That he had no home, at least not one he remembered.

"Yes," I began carefully. "That is something to consider. But there are reasons why it perhaps might not be the best course of action."

"What reasons?" His voice had become high-pitched, and in a sudden flare of firelight, I could see his eyes were wild, his hands clenched.

I opened my mouth and shut it again. I did not know what to do. The truth would terrify him. It might even break him, for good.

He was leaning forward, looking into my face. He suddenly stood.

"No," he said, his tone deliberate. "I do not want to know."

He purposefully crossed to his pack and drew the flauto out of its velvet bag. Returning to his place by the campfire, he began to play.

The playing calmed him, as it had before, and not much later, we both retired to our bedrolls.

I lay wide awake, staring up at the stars. It was time, I thought, for me to face the possibility that the Troll Queen had reached with her pale, ridged fingers into my white bear's mind and removed me from his memory, his heart. Forever.

I didn't think I would sleep at all, but eventually drowsiness overcame me and I fell into a deep slumber.

I was home in Trondheim, and I was looking for Neddy. I couldn't find him anywhere. I searched all the rooms of the house, then went out to the meadow, down by the Nidelva River. But he was nowhere. I had the thought he was hiding from me, to pay me back for all the times I had gone missing as a child and he'd had to come looking for me.

Finally I gave up, exhausted, and made my way back home. I opened the front door, and there he was. But he was lying on his back in the middle of the great room floor. There were puddles of water all around him. His body was very still, and I could not see any sign that he was breathing.

Neddy, I cried out. His eyes didn't open.

Neddy, I cried again, louder. I touched his skin. It was ice-cold.

NEDDY! I cried a third time, so loud that it woke me.

I was trembling violently and could not stop. Charles

appeared beside me. He had a skin bag in hand, the one with the last of the wine from the castle under the mountain.

"Drink," Charles said.

Sitting up, I obeyed. I emptied the small amount that was left.

I lay back down, on my side, wrapping my bedroll around me.

"Who is Neddy?" Charles asked.

"My brother," I said, my voice barely audible.

I was shivering again. I don't know if the nightmare was a lingering effect of the troll-snake venom, but I was filled with dread that something very bad was happening to Neddy. La Rochelle was still days away, and I desperately hoped there would be word from home when we got there.

MOTHER

I LEFT THE ROOM BUT DID NOT SHUT the door all the way, lingering on the threshold. And I saw everything that happened inside the room.

Sib rapidly crossed to the windows and opened them as wide as they would go. She stood there a moment, her body leaning forward, urgent. Then she sat back down beside Neddy, closing her eyes.

And I could have sworn that I heard singing. I couldn't see Sib's lips moving, but the singing must have been coming from her.

The curtains in the windows begin to stir, gently at first, but gradually stronger, until finally they were billowing wildly. I could see Sib's hair blowing about her face. She was standing now, leaning slightly over Neddy, her eyes still closed.

I could feel the wind through the cracked doorway. The air was cool, crisp. It was dry, too, not like the heavy, humid late summer heat we'd been having.

I could almost see this wind as it swept through the room, rustling tablecloths, flicking at Neddy's bed coverings. And I could hear it, like music, like a melody I had heard somewhere before.

It wasn't possible, not any of it. I had to be dreaming, or in some altered state brought on by my fear for Neddy.

But I saw Sib sit beside my son on the bed and take him in her arms. The wind had softened so that it stirred only her silver hair, and now I could see her lips moving, and she was indeed singing.

It was beautiful. I felt tears spring into my eyes, but they were not tears of grief. They were tears of hope.

I thought I saw Neddy's eyes flick open, and the singing stopped, not abruptly but gently, gradually.

And I heard Sib speak. Her voice was low so I could not make out what she said. Except for one word that rang out clear and distinct. *Love.*

ROSE

THE NEXT DAY AS WE JOURNEYED, both of us on foot, I couldn't shake my feeling of unease about Neddy.

When we stopped at midday, Charles sat across from me and I handed him a portion of stale bread and cheese.

"You are worried about your brother?" he asked.

I was tired and wasn't sure I could abide talking about Neddy with this stranger who had once been my white bear. "There might be sickness in the town where he lives," I said.

He nodded. "I lost both an older brother and sister to sickness, but it was before I was born so I never knew them. You are close to your brother." He did not frame it as a question. "Can I ask you something?"

I nodded, a little wary.

"I have been wondering why you came for me, how you knew where I was being held. I think perhaps you and I were . . ." He paused awkwardly, then started again. "In the parts of my life I don't remember, were you and I . . . friends?"

"We were." I tried to keep my tone even.

"Were you in my father's court?"

I shook my head.

"Perhaps we are related?"

I found myself unable to answer. I kept my eyes down, concentrated on chewing the stale bread.

He opened his mouth to say more, but winced, putting his hand to his forehead.

"I have these flashes," he said. "And I don't know if they are memories or dreams or . . ."

"What are they of?"

"They are odd things, like immense looming glaciers. A herd of caribou thundering away from me. The bright red of seal's blood on the snow. Was I perhaps an explorer of some kind? One who traveled in the far north? To the Arktisk, even?"

I was silent. Finally I said, "You did travel the world. And yes, you were in the Arktisk."

His eyes widened. "So they are memories."

"I think they must be."

"I am having them more often. And sometimes they last longer than just a flash."

"That is good," I said.

And finally I felt a thread of hope.

NEDDY

I HAD BEEN DREAMING, AT LEAST I THOUGHT it was a dream, that I was embarking on a journey, a long one, it seemed. In the distance I could see the faces of those who waited for me. Sara, Annette, Havamal's wife. They were watching me come, smiles of welcome on their faces, making sure my journey toward them was safe.

I heard a voice singing, or maybe it was several voices. I wasn't sure whose voices they were at first. I didn't think Sib's was one of them, but then I did hear her voice and she was speaking to me. She sounded annoyed, chiding me for even thinking of going on my journey without her. I wanted to protest, tell her that I would never choose to, but she shushed me. And finally I heard words coming from her lips, words I never thought to hear.

And I decided my journey must wait.

ROSE

B Y MY RECKONING, WE STILL HAD TWO DAYS until we would arrive in La Rochelle. We were walking along a stretch of road I remembered well, and I was thinking of the last time I had traveled it, when Sib, Estelle, Winn, and I were heading to La Rochelle to catch our ship to Trondheim. Winn had been in the sling around my chest and he'd been sleeping, but as we passed this very grove of birch trees with their white trunks, he had opened his eyes and smiled up at me. It was that sweet, glowing smile I could never get enough of. I felt tears come into my eyes as I remembered. I missed my bairn so much, and between the Sweating Sickness and Jaaloki's threat, I was horribly worried for his safety.

To distract myself, I deliberately turned my thoughts to Charles, who was walking beside me, leading Ciuin.

He was having memories. I told myself this was a promising sign. They were from his time as a white bear. I wondered if perhaps his memory was coming back chronologically. Because of the Troll Queen, he had gone from a boy playing with a red ball to a white bear. He was a white bear for close to one hundred and fifty years. That would be a lot of memories.

I took a furtive glance at his profile.

In the past days, I had found myself getting used to things as they were, interacting with him as if he was a distant friend, polite and kind, yet not overly familiar. But there were moments when I would catch a familiar expression on his mouth, or see the dark golden eyelashes on his cheeks when his eyes were closed, and my heart would break all over again.

That night I dreamed of Neddy once more, but this time it was a happy dream, of greeting him at the door after a long journey and him promising me he wouldn't go so far away again.

Another thread of hope.

NEDDY

IT WAS AN ODD COMBINATION, feeling so weak and wrung out and yet so impossibly happy all at the same time. I couldn't even walk, and yet I wanted to run into Trondheim, proclaiming my joy to everyone I met.

Sib's eyes held the same kind of light as mine, though she appeared to be very weary, to the point that she too looked like she had been through the Sweating Sickness.

It was the following morning, and Sib brought me a small bowl of oatmeal and cream Mother had prepared. I didn't have a large appetite yet, but managed a few bites. Sib went to open the windows, letting in sunlight and a fresh breeze.

As I gazed at Sib's face, it looked to me as if she had aged. She was as beautiful as she had always been, but there seemed to be lines in her face I had not noticed before.

"Sib," I said abruptly, setting aside my oatmeal, "how did you heal me?"

She came and sat by me. "It was the elixir; it finally worked," she said. "And the weather changed," she added. "Feel the wind, Neddy. It is a good one."

"I don't think you are telling me everything," I said weakly.

"You need to rest now, Neddy," she said.

And she was right, for I was asleep before she even finished her sentence.

MOTHER

THE SWEATING SICKNESS ALL BUT DISAPPEARED with the change in weather. It was as if the cool, crisp wind washed it away for good.

I didn't say anything to Sib about what I had seen. I didn't know if she knew I had been watching; if so, she too chose not to say anything to me. And I decided not to tell anyone else. I wondered if it was possible I had imagined it all. So much had happened in these past weeks. I had been exhausted.

As Arne said, the weather changed. In the nick of time. It was as simple as that. But sometimes I wondered.

Sib was exhausted, too. I noticed that she slept almost as much as Neddy, and her energy was low. I worried that she was going to fall sick, too, but she assured me she was fine, just tired.

It took time for Neddy to heal, which wasn't surprising, seeing how close he had come to death. But as he healed, it became clear that something had changed between Sib and him. Arne noticed it also, and after we had tucked Estelle and Winn into bed one night and were sitting at the kitchen table drinking tea, I told him I thought it wouldn't be too long before we had a wedding to celebrate.

"There does seem to be something there," Arne said in agreement, "but let's not get ahead of ourselves."

"Oh, I'm sure, Arne," I said. "It is because they almost lost each other."

He nodded again. We had all experienced so much loss these past weeks. All I knew for sure was that Neddy lived and that he and Sib had found their way to each other.

ESTELLE

I T SEEMED THAT THE TIME of the terrible *maladie* was over. The air had changed. People were starting to come out of their houses.

There was still much sadness. So many people had died, and those who hadn't had at least one person they were mourning and often many more than that. I knew it was important to be kind to Gudrun and her brother and sister, who had lost their poor *maman*. I remembered well how sad I was to lose my own *maman* and took special care with them.

I helped too with little Lissa, who had also lost her *maman*. And I thanked the *bon Dieu* that *bébé* Winn had not fallen ill. If something had happened to him, it would have shattered my heart. I had promised Rose to take good care of him, and I was determined to do so, no matter what.

A few days after Oncle Neddy had almost died (I wasn't supposed to know how close he had come to death, but I overheard Grand-mère Eugenia and Grand-père Arne talking about how if it wasn't for Tante Sib, he would surely have died), I asked if I could take Winn for a walk before dinner as we had before the sickness came.

Grand-mère Eugenia looked a little hesitant, but then she smiled and said, "Why not? You have been cooped up for so long. Be sure to go just to the river and back, and do not speak to or get close to anyone. Just as a precaution."

I agreed and bundled Winn up into the sling I wore across my chest. He seemed a little heavier to me. Meals had been more sparse in the past weeks because of the sickness, but Grand-mère Eugenia always made sure there was enough for Winn and me, and he was a growing *bébé*, after all.

There weren't many people out, but the few I saw looked cheerier than I'd seen in a while.

It was a lovely, crisp evening, and it seemed a shame to head straight back once we got to the Nidelva River, so I decided to walk along a little path I had noticed some time ago, one that went beside the river to the north. Just a short way, I told myself.

The river looked *très jolie*, in the late afternoon sun, all sparkly and blue-gray. Winn let out a happy gurgle, and I laughed.

As we rounded a corner, I saw what looked like a white horse standing by the river. I felt a tremor of fear, remembering the stories Gudrun had told me about the Nokken, the white horse who dragged children into the river.

But I realized it wasn't a horse, but a white reindeer, and there were two children with it. It was a beautiful animal, and I wanted to get a closer look. A white reindeer named Vaettur had carried Rose safely away from Niflheim and the evil Troll Queen. I had longed to see one ever since Rose told me the story.

The boy and girl with the reindeer were dressed in white and looked to be my age or a little older. The girl was very pretty, with light yellow hair, and the boy looked nice, with a welcoming smile.

"Hello!" the girl called to me.

I walked toward them. Winn let out another gurgle and wriggled in excitement at seeing the reindeer.

"What a *magnifique* animal!" I said.

"Thank you," said the boy.

"Is it yours?" I asked.

"It is," said the girl. "Would you like a ride?"

I was thrilled, thinking what a great story it would be to tell Gudrun that I rode a white reindeer along the Nidelva River. It wasn't very large, and I was used to riding on horses back in Fransk, so I wasn't afraid.

The girl came up closer to me and held out her arms to take Winn. "I'll watch the sweet bairn while you ride."

"No," I said, pulling away. I suddenly remembered what Grand-mère Eugenia had said about not speaking to strangers.

All at once, I noticed that up close the girl's skin was funny, all ridged and creased. Rose had told me that troll skin was hard and ridged.

I took a few steps back, wrapping my arms protectively around Winn. But then I felt someone grab me from behind. Hard. I was being lifted up onto the back of the reindeer.

I struggled against it, but the grip was too strong. I was on the reindeer, and we were galloping alongside the river.

And then we were up in the air, flying.

I caught my breath, terrified. The ground was swirling away in a dizzying blur. I started to scream, but a hand closed over my mouth.

ROSE

I HAD HOPED THAT PERHAPS after the previous night's happy dream of Neddy, the nightmares were finally over.

But I was wrong. And the one I had that night was the worst of all.

I was in Winn's nursery. I was sitting in a rocking chair near his cradle, sewing, and Estelle sat next to me, reading a book. It was a sunny, hot afternoon, and I was sleepy. I dozed off. A sound woke me, and I opened my eyes to see a large white snake beside the cradle. It had raised itself up and was hovering above it.

I let out a cry and tried to stand, but my arms and legs were frozen. They were not bound by anything, but still I wasn't able to move. I watched in horror as the snake dipped its head down and grabbed the bairn in its mouth.

The bairn looked different, though, smaller, and for a moment I was relieved. It wasn't Winn after all, just a doll that had been lying in the cradle. The snake lifted the doll out of the bed, its mouth clamped on a shoulder, and pivoted, lowering itself to the floor and dropping the doll in front of it. The doll rolled toward me, and I could clearly see that it had Winn's face.

I struggled desperately against the unseen bonds that held me down.

Suddenly the snake began to swallow Winn, first the legs, then the torso, and finally the head. I watched in horror as the snake's mouth closed over Winn's eyes.

I screamed.

Then the snake changed into Jaaloki, and he glided to Estelle, grabbing her by the neck. She let out a strangled cry, and in the flash of a moment, they disappeared.

I woke up trembling violently. No! Not Winn and Estelle.

I was sure I must have screamed out loud and that it would have awakened Charles, but saw he was still fast asleep on his bedroll.

I sat up, my heart pounding.

Jaaloki's words roared in my ears. *It is the bairn who matters now.*

I stood and, pulling my cloak around me, walked away from the now-dead campfire. There was a small stream a stone's throw away, and I found my way to it, still shivering.

I sat beside the stream, listening to the rippling, bubbling sound of the water as it coursed over the stones. Pulling my cloak tighter, I closed my eyes, trying to stop my trembling, concentrating on the soothing sound.

I thought about Neddy, wondering what the dreams I'd had about him meant, if anything. Had he been sick but was now better? Oh, how I missed him. He would have understood, like no one else, the horror of the dream. And the daily nightmare

I was living, having Charles with me but not with me, here but not here.

Neddy, I thought longingly. I would have given anything for him to be with me here, now.

And then he *was* there, beside me. I knew he couldn't be, not really, but I could see the line of his jaw, the dark hair curling at his temples, his clear blue eyes. He was pale, with shadows under his eyes, which I saw now were filled with sorrow. He looked at me, directly into my eyes, and spoke.

"I'm sorry, Rose. They are gone. Winn and Estelle. Vanished. I should have kept them safe. I am sorry, more than I can ever say." Tears came into his blue eyes.

My heart was thudding; my skin prickled with fear.

"Neddy!" I cried, reaching out to him. But he was gone.

"Come back," I whispered. But I knew it was no use. The sound of the gurgling water was all I could hear. "Neddy," I whispered again.

I then remembered him telling me that while I had been on my journey to the land that lay east of the sun and west of the moon, he had once felt me beside him in the reading room of the monastery. I hadn't believed him at first, but we realized it must have been around the time I had been in mortal danger, was about to be attacked by a white bear, not *my* white bear, but the wild one Malmo had saved me from.

When Mother heard Neddy's story, she hadn't been at all surprised, saying that when a bond is strong between a brother and sister, and the circumstances are extraordinary or threatening, one can most assuredly communicate over large distances.

But what did it mean, this "vision," or whatever it was, coming so close after the horrible nightmare about Winn and Estelle? And then I knew what it meant.

The Troll Queen had taken Winn. And perhaps Estelle too.

It is the bairn who matters now.

And it was as I had feared: the bairn was my bairn. My Winn.

BOOK THREE

EST

They drifted rudderless, in raging wind.
—*The Edda*

ESTELLE

I WOKE. AND I WAS FLYING UP HIGH, icy wind on my face. It was so cold.

I wasn't on a reindeer anymore, but in a sleigh. With bells. I could hear the silvery, tinkling sound of them.

The girl, who wasn't a girl anymore but a white-haired, white-skinned, ridge-faced person dressed in black furs, sat next to me. A troll.

On the other side of me was the boy, who, like the girl, had similar features, but was bald, with that same white tree-bark skin. He held a cup to my mouth, and I drank. I didn't want to at first, but I was so cold and the drink was warm and smelled delicious.

It tasted delicious, too, like spicy sweet warm milk.

There was a third troll up at the reins of the sleigh. He turned and smiled at me, and I gasped. The smile was like being kicked in the stomach. He looked like a skeleton. I started shivering again, and the boy troll put the cup back up to my lips.

I was frightened, but mostly I was sleepy. So sleepy. I felt myself drifting off. Then I remembered.

Winn!

My eyes flew open, and I gazed down.

No, he was safe, nestled in the sling at my chest. His eyes were closed. He was sleeping.

Relief flooded through me.

The cup was at my lips again, and I drank more.

MOTHER

I T DID NOT SEEM POSSIBLE, not after all we had been through. But Estelle and Winn had gone, vanished.

I cursed myself for letting her go off with the bairn, by themselves. But I had felt bad for her, all cooped up with nothing but grief and sickness around her for so long.

How could I have known?

But I should have known. I should have read the portents. Yesterday Arne had sneezed to the left, and worse, I had spotted a raven sitting in a tree outside the kitchen window. I had told myself it wasn't gray, but I should have known better.

I had just been so desperate for things to be right again. Safe. I let my guard down.

I didn't know how I would ever forgive myself.

Poor Neddy, still so weak from his sickness. He was beside himself, organizing search parties, questioning anyone who might have seen a girl and a bairn.

The only trace that we found were hoofprints in the muddy bank of the Nidelva. A fisherman had spotted what looked to be a white reindeer, or perhaps it had been a horse. He wasn't sure. And old Widow Lubchek, who lived near the river, swore she had heard a faint tinkling of bells, sleigh bells perhaps. But she was a fanciful sort, and we weren't sure whether to believe her.

Neddy was sure Winn and Estelle had been taken by trolls. He recounted again the story of Rose's encounter with the troll-snake in the underground cavern.

Those words, *it is the bairn who matters now,* had always worried him.

"I should have kept better watch over Winn," Neddy said in anguish.

It didn't make him feel any better when Sib and I both pointed out that he had been very sick and almost died.

I was worried he would become ill again, and so was Sib, I could tell.

None of us knew what to do. How do you search for two children stolen with the aid of the powerful arts of trolls?

Soren would gladly have provided one of his ships, but Neddy didn't know where to go. He considered setting out for La Rochelle, since that was the last place we knew Rose was headed. But Sib convinced him to wait a few days at least, until he got his strength back.

There had been no word from Rose, which wasn't surprising since no ships had been traveling to Trondheim since the outbreak of Sweating Sickness. But we hoped to hear soon.

ROSE

AT DAWN THAT MORNING, I woke and went to my pack. I quietly removed the Huldre book of maps and leafed through it until I came to a page that depicted a map of a mountainous region the trolls called Kaal, with the highest peak named Kaalpok. I compared it to my tattered map of Fransk and found the section that contained the Alpes. The two were almost identical, Mont Blanc being our name for Kaalpok.

Kaalpok, I was convinced, was where Jaaloki said the Troll Queen had taken up residence. *Her favorite aerie at the top of the softskin world.*

And that was where I must go, to the Alpes, to Mont Blanc, to find my son and Estelle.

"Good morning," came Charles's voice. I looked up to see him standing across from me, already getting the campfire started. I had been so absorbed in my maps I had not even noticed.

"Good morning," I replied.

"You are charting our route?" he asked.

"Yes," I said. "But I am charting a new route. Plans have

changed. I must travel east, to the mountainous region called the Alpes."

"Why have the plans changed?" he asked.

I was silent. How could I tell him it was because of a dream? It would sound like madness. But it was the truth.

"I had a dream. It has convinced me we must go to the mountain called Mont Blanc."

He listened, unfazed.

"You see," I went on, "there is someone, who is important to both you and me, who is in danger."

His eyebrows raised at this.

"Someone from my father's court?"

I shook my head, impatient. I wished I could tell him once and for all that there was no such court, that his father was long dead.

He ran a hand over his eyes, then gazed at me directly. "If this person is important to you and me and is in danger, we must go." He smiled, and I got the feeling he was almost happy to have a purpose.

"We need to stop first in La Rochelle as planned," I said. "I have to see if there is any word from my family."

But there was no word. According to the harbormaster, no ships were traveling anywhere near Trondheim, and hadn't been for some time. Northern Njord had been hard hit by the Sweating Sickness.

After speaking to the harbormaster, I had a moment of

doubt. Was I behaving like a madwoman, basing a journey to one of the highest mountain ranges in the world on a dream and my own far-fetched intuition? Perhaps I should instead be trying to get to Trondheim in any way possible, to see my family, make sure they were still alive.

But no. I knew this was what I must do. I didn't know the how or why of it. I just knew I must go to the Huldre dwelling in the Alpes. The Troll Queen's favorite, at the top of the world. Winn and Estelle had been taken there. I was sure of it.

Even though I knew it might not get to him for some time, I wrote a letter to Neddy, telling him of my plan.

Using a portion of the gold coins I had taken from the castle in the mountain, I bought a horse for Charles. We needed to be able to travel faster than we had been, but even with a second horse, it would take us seven days or more to cross Fransk to get to the Alpes, which lay along the border with Sveitsland.

ESTELLE

WHEN I WOKE, I was in a new place, a room.

I was lying in a soft bed.

I was still very sleepy, my head so heavy I could barely lift it.

The ceiling was white. The walls were white. The covers on me were silky white, and there were lots of white pillows.

I felt like something very strange and scary had happened. But I couldn't remember it.

I thought I must be having a dream.

I hoped I would wake up soon.

ROSE

CHARLES TOOK TO THE NEW HORSE with little difficulty, naming her Valentina after that favorite aunt of his.

As we started our trek across Fransk, the weather was unnaturally warm. We encountered a fair number of fellow travelers, and most were friendly, but were inclined, like us, to keep their own company.

On the afternoon of the second day, the weather cooled slightly and it began to rain.

By the time we came to the town of Limoges that evening, we were wet through. Impulsively I suggested we stop at an inn for dinner and a bed. There were still plenty of the gold coins I had taken from the castle, and the prospect of drying off and having a hot meal was appealing. Charles agreed with enthusiasm.

At the beginning of our journey, I had wondered how he was going to handle life on the road, with his most recent memories being those of a pampered prince in the court of Charles VI. But he had been surprisingly adaptable, never complaining, and I wondered if his buried white bear self, who had traveled the world in the roughest of circumstances, was helping him.

There was an inn, with a stable nearby, close to the center of town. The inn was warm and bustling, more than half full, and a fire blazed in the fireplace in the center of the room.

There was one large group around a big table near the fire, and most of the noise came from the folk gathered there. The serving maid who brought us our ale and ham and leek soup said that several were locals and the rest were the party of a friar who was on a pilgrimage to Roncesvalles. It was easy to spot the friar, for he was as large of girth as he was loud of voice.

The serving maid, who told us her name was Marie, was attentive, bringing refills of ale without our asking. I noticed her looking at the two of us in a measuring sort of way, as if trying to figure out how we were related to each other.

If she only knew, I thought.

Her attention was clearly much more directed at Charles than me, and glancing sideways at him, I realized with a little feeling of shock that even in his travel-worn state, with his golden hair and light eyes, he was a very comely man. It may sound odd, but the truth is I had never really thought that much about my husband's looks. After all, I had fallen in love with him as a white bear.

Marie appeared with another refill for Charles's ale.

"I've a message," she said, "from the fat friar over there." She giggled. "He wonders if you would care to join him and his party."

I had noticed the friar glancing our way several times.

"He also offered to pay for your meal," she said, lowering her voice. "He's had a bit more ale than is good for him and is feeling generous, on behalf of the church, of course."

The friar represented much that I disliked about the church in Europa. His robes were of the finest cloth, and his hands sparkled with jeweled rings. But there turned out to be no escaping him, for he was most insistent, and so we found ourselves seated at his table.

Charles at first looked a little uncomfortable, but then he leaned back and drank his ale, listening closely to the conversation. Someone made an off-color joke, poking fun at the Holy Roman Emperor, which the friar found enormously amusing.

Charles glanced over at me, clearly confused at the mention of the Holy Roman Emperor, but he stayed quiet, listening to the jesting banter about Charles V.

We were finally able to get away, pleading an early morning departure, although not before the friar insisted that we join his traveling party the next day, since he too was setting out early and was heading in the same direction.

We agreed, if only to cut the conversation short, but I whispered to Charles as we went up to our room that I'd rather chew nails than travel with the friar, and we agreed that we would try to be up and gone well before him.

When we got up to our small room, I saw that there was just one narrow bed. I flushed, suddenly overcome with the awkwardness of sharing a room with this husband of mine who was there but not there. Charles gazed at the bed, and being a prince with good manners, immediately offered to sleep on the floor. I stiffly accepted his offer, wishing I had never thought of staying at an inn. I slept poorly that night.

Unfortunately the friar was up just as early as we were, and short of being outright rude, we had no choice but to travel with him and his small entourage.

When we stopped for the midday meal, I still had hopes of finding a way to move on without the friar, but he invited us to partake of his provisions, which of course were the finest, and, despite feeling trapped, I did enjoy the roast pheasant and light-as-air pastries.

While we ate, the previously jovial friar took on a serious air, asking if we had heard of the catastrophic events that had recently taken place in the world. And in truth, because of all that had been happening in my own small world, I had to confess that I was ignorant of the series of dire calamities that he proceeded to relate.

It was chilling to hear of the earthquake in Kina, which

had killed hundreds, perhaps thousands of people, as well as flooding in Hollande, which had wiped out entire villages. I did know about the Sweating Sickness, of course, but not about the hundreds of people it had already killed in Anglia and that there were fears it could spiral into something similar to the devastating plague of the 1300s.

"Indeed," said the friar, "there are those who believe the end of the world is upon us."

I had found that there were always those who chose to read portents, my mother being such a person, but she had never taken it so far as to believe the end of the world was approaching.

Because of Neddy, I had learned much of history, and like him, I believed that there were always cycles to life, that terrible things occurred, but that they were followed by periods of peace and healing, and somehow we humans always found a way to rebuild and go on. I would have shared my opinion with the friar, but guessed he would be little interested.

I noticed Charles looking up at the sky and followed his gaze. Abruptly I stood, saying, "I think it best if we continue our travels. It looks as though we are in for a change in the weather."

And indeed banks of gray clouds were piling up from the northeast, while in the southeast there was a blanket of cloud cover that had an odd, almost brown, tinge to it. I paused, feeling slightly uneasy. I didn't recall ever seeing the sky look as it did. I noticed too that the horses were starting to get restless. Charles went over to calm them.

The friar lumbered to his feet. "You're right," he said. "We'd better find a place to shelter." The others in his party followed suit.

There looked to be a large forest not too far in the distance, so we mounted our horses and set out at a brisk trot toward the line of trees.

The wind kicked up and soon was so strong, our horses had to lower their heads and slow their pace so as not to be pushed sideways. I found myself wishing Sib were with us and could tell me the name of this fierce southern wind.

But the wind abruptly shifted, and we were hit by a strong gust from the northeast. Ciuin stood stock-still, trembling. I murmured encouraging words, and she hesitantly moved forward.

The friar's horse had also stopped, and the man let out an exclamation. He began whipping his steed viciously, and the poor horse broke into a trot. The friar's white garments billowed out behind him.

Charles rode up beside me, and I could dimly hear him say something, but there came a great clap of thunder and a bright white flash of light. I could smell rain in the air, and yet it smelled different with a metallic, almost bitter odor.

And then the rain started to fall, in large splashing drops. I felt it on my face and hands. Looking down, I let out a gasp.

The moisture on my hand was a dull red hue. I glanced at Charles, and saw streaks of reddish brown on his face.

The friar let out a terrified cry. "'Tis blood!" he wailed. "The sky is raining blood!" And he whipped his horse harder, urging the terrified animal to move faster. The friar's ivory vestments were stained with red.

Charles and I exchanged looks of amazement and disbelief, and followed the friar.

By the time we reached the wooded area, we were all soaked with the strange red rain. Charles and I wore clothing of a darker hue, so it wasn't as striking as the friar and his white garments splotched with vivid scarlet. But our faces and hands were all a mottled red. The horses, too, were flecked with red, which was the most obvious on Ciuin, who was mostly white.

I didn't know what to make of it, but when I tasted some drops on my hand, it did not taste to me like blood, though it did have a faintly metallic quality.

But the friar was convinced it was Blood Rain. He was trembling with fear, terrified that the god he professed to believe in was filled with wrath and was now preparing to end it all as he had in the day of Noah and the great flood.

"Blood Rain is an evil omen," he said, his teeth chattering. "It is said that there were many sightings of Blood Rain before the Black Death."

I wished more than ever that Neddy were with us. He would have been able to tell me if what the friar said was true.

ESTELLE

I CAME AWAKE SLOWLY. My mouth was dry, and my head hurt. I thought at first I was in Trondheim and that I had fallen ill with the Sweating Sickness. Except I wasn't sweating.

And then I saw the white ceiling and the white walls. And felt the silky white covers over me.

I wasn't at the house in Trondheim. Or in the house in Fransk where I lived with Rose and Charles.

This was a new place, a white place.

I remembered the reindeer and flying through the icy air. I started to sit up. But my head pounded so hard I almost had to lie back down. I managed to stay up, just barely, and looked around me.

It was a white rectangular room. At one end was the bed I lay in and at the other end was another piece of furniture. It wasn't a table, or bookshelf, but it was definitely smaller and higher than a bed. On the wall to my right was a black door. It was shut.

The light was dim, coming mostly from one oil lamp lit by the door. I saw that there was a small window, set up high on the white wall across the room.

My thoughts were fuzzy, but through the pounding in my head, I had an uneasy feeling that something was missing.

I looked down at my chest. I was wearing different clothing, a soft white dress. But more importantly, there was no bairn sling, no Winn.

My heart started racing.

Where was Winn?

I stood then. My knees were weak and my head spun, but I was able to walk.

I moved across the room and, as I came closer, saw that the other piece of furniture was a cradle. It was a large, fancy one, carved of wood and set on rockers. It was mostly painted white, but the slats along the sides were alternately black and white.

I reached the cradle and, my heart hammering, I peered over the side.

Winn was there, fast asleep, lying peacefully on his back, his little hands clenched. I took a deep breath, flooded with relief.

My legs were shaky so I sank to the floor beside the cradle, and I noticed that the slats were carved in the shapes of figures.

I caught my breath. They looked like *echecs* figures, like Queen Maraboo.

My head spun. I didn't think I could make it back to my bed, so I lay down on the floor beside the cradle and fell asleep.

ROSE

I T WAS THANKS TO THE BLOOD RAIN that we were finally able to get away from the friar. He was so shaken by it and by his end-of-the-world fears that he abandoned his pilgrimage to Roncesvalles and decided to go to a much closer monastery that lay to the south.

Charles and I rode on, after stopping at a stream to wash the Blood Rain off ourselves. We were each wrapped in our own thoughts. And when we made camp later that night, we were still quiet.

It was Charles who broke the silence.

"My father is no longer king of Fransk, is he?" he asked.

"No," I said. "He is not."

"Is this Holy Roman Emperor, Charles V, now king of Fransk?"

"No," I answered. "The current ruler of Fransk is Henry II."

Charles looked confused. "I have no brother named Henry. Or uncle." He set down his portion of stew. "I begin to think that a great deal of time has passed, though I do not know how that can be."

I gazed down into my own stew. Abruptly I made up my

mind. The Blood Rain had made things clear. I thought that now I knew what the Troll Queen's Aagnorak was. And it terrified me.

"Charles," I said, "I believe it is time to tell you the truth. Your truth."

His eyes widened.

And without preamble, I launched into the story of the day the Troll Queen had first seen Charles, the day he was playing with a red ball. How she had started wanting him, how her father had been furious when he discovered she had disobeyed all the troll laws and taken him, how he had turned Charles into a white bear. I told him he had been a white bear for one hundred fifty years, had roamed the earth, hoping to be set free of the enchantment.

And then he *had* been set free. I did not tell him how, or the role I had played in it.

But I did say that when he was set free, everyone thought that the Troll Queen had died, that he himself had seen her fall to her death. But she had *not* died. She was very much alive, and she wanted revenge.

It was she who had used fearsome storms to wreck a ship Charles had been on, I said, and imprisoned him underneath the castle in the mountain.

"And it is even worse," I said. "I think it was she who caused the earthquake in Kina, as well as the flooding, the Sweating

Sickness, and the Blood Rain." I took a deep breath. "I believe the Troll Queen wants nothing less than the destruction of all humans, 'softskins' as she calls us."

He stared at me. "This is a great deal to take in." He put a hand to his head, and I could see traces of panic in his eyes.

"I know."

"It sounds like the fairy tales read to me when I was very young."

"I know," I said again. "And there is still more you must know."

He looked apprehensive. "More?"

"Yes," I said. "This Troll Queen has also stolen a child, a bairn. That is where we are going now. To rescue the bairn."

"Whose bairn is it?" His voice was low.

I was silent for a moment. I didn't know if I was going too far, if what I was about to say would cause him harm, in the fragile state he seemed to be in. But I went ahead and said it. "The bairn is yours."

Charles stared straight ahead. I searched his face for signs of distress. Was his mind going to flash colors and heave, the way he'd described before?

"My bairn," he repeated. Then his eyes cleared, and he lowered his hand from his head. Slowly he nodded. "I have had memories of a new-born child. Holding it in my arms. A son, I think?"

I nodded, my breath catching in my throat. He remembered Winn.

"My bairn," he repeated. "And this Troll Queen who stole me, who turned me into a white bear, has now stolen my bairn?"

"Yes."

"What is his name?"

"It hadn't been settled. I believe," I said carefully, "that initially you named it Charles, but you weren't happy with that. So in the meantime, Estelle came up with a nickname, Winn, for the west wind."

"Who is Estelle? Is she my wife?" he asked, his voice matter-of-fact.

My breath caught again, and I was sure my face was flushed. "Uh, no. She is not your wife. She is young, the daughter of a good friend of yours who died. You became her guardian. I believe the Troll Queen has her as well."

"If the girl Estelle and my son are somewhere in the Alpes, we must journey there at once," Charles said, resolute.

It was later as I was refilling our skin bags in a nearby stream that Charles came up to me.

"I have one more question," he said.

"Yes?" I said, looking up at him.

"Nyamh, why do *you* seek this Troll Queen?"

I thought for a moment. "Because she has wronged me as well," I said at last.

"How has she wronged you?"

"She took my husband from me," I said, unblinking.

"Then you seek revenge?"

And I nodded. Yes, in some deep-down part of me, I did seek revenge, for all the Troll Queen had taken from me.

ESTELLE

S OMEONE WAS SHAKING ME.

I looked up and saw a woman with large black eyes and very white skin staring down at me. It was not the troll girl I had traveled in the sleigh with. This woman was older.

She said something in a gravelly, deep voice and, putting her hands under my arms, lifted me to my feet. She was strong.

I couldn't walk very well, but she managed to propel me back to the bed on the other side of the room. She sat me down and handed me a cup of the sweet hot milky drink.

I drank, partly because my mouth was dry and partly because her expression was so severe I was sure she would have forced me to drink it if I hadn't done it on my own.

I stared at her as I drank. She had long white hair, which she wore in a braid down the back of her black dress. Her skin was rough and ridged.

She was a troll. Fear leapt up in me. And I think she could sense it, for she smiled. She gestured at the cup and said that guttural word again, which I guessed meant "drink."

I did. With an approving nod, she rose and walked away

from me. I saw that she had a ring of keys fastened at her waist. They made a faint jingling sound when she walked.

She crossed to the cradle. And bent over it.

I was terrified and started to rise, but my head was too heavy. I sat back down, trying to fight against the sleepiness that was creeping over me.

But as I watched, the troll woman lifted Winn gently out of the bed and rocked him in her arms, gazing down at him. It was hard to tell across the room, but I was almost certain the look on her face was soft, even happy.

I saw her pull a gleaming glass cup out of a pocket on her dress and then she turned so I could not see Winn.

The sleepiness was pulling me down and finally I couldn't fight it anymore. I fell asleep.

WHITE BEAR

A SON.

A Troll Queen who had loved me so much she broke the laws of her world.

Her wrathful father, who had transformed me into a white bear.

A white bear. For one hundred fifty years.

My father, my mother, my brothers and sisters, my Aunt Valentina, all dead, years ago.

These were the pieces of me, of my life. Like a puzzle, the pieces scattered, meaningless until they were whole.

Would I ever be whole again?

Would there be a single moment when it all fell into place, cascading pieces, forming a clear and distinct picture? Of me?

Or would it be a slow thing, a slog, like plowing through waist-deep snow? One piece. Then another. Until, at the end of the journey, they formed a whole.

I wondered suddenly if this had been true of me before. If the reason I had not wanted to name my son Charles was because I did not know who Charles was?

I had been stolen as a nine-year-old boy. Had been a bear

for one hundred fifty years. How could I know myself as a man?

The pain in my head started, along with a shimmer of light at the edge of my eyesight. I put my hands to my temples. No, I would not let the brain fever come. I breathed deeply, telling myself that I did know at least three things: that I loved to play the flauto; that I had once been a white bear who preyed on seals and wandered a beautiful, frozen world; and that I had a son.

I would focus on those and keep moving forward. And maybe there would be more memories, more parts I would be able to fit into the incomplete man that I was now. Become whole again.

I could only try.

ESTELLE

T HIS TIME WHEN I WOKE, I was famished. My stomach was gurgling, loudly. I smelled food and sat up. My head only hurt a little.

I looked around and saw a small table and chair that had not been there before. It had things on it, a covered basket, a goblet, and a plate with steam rising.

I crossed to it quickly. The plate held something that looked like chicken and dumplings. My mouth watered.

But first I went to the cradle. Winn was lying there, contentedly sucking on something that looked like a tall glass cup with a kind of stopper on top, which he was sucking on. It looked like a cow's teat. I had never seen anything like it before. Inside the glass cup was a milky liquid.

The smell of the chicken drew me back to the table. I sat down and began to eat. It was so delicious I didn't even care if the trolls were trying to poison me. I ate and ate until my stomach was full.

Then I rose, stretched, and went back to the cradle.

The glass cup with the funny stopper looked to be empty and was lying beside Winn. He beamed up at me sleepily, lifting his arms to me. I reached down and picked him up out of the cradle.

It felt so good to have his warm, sturdy body next to mine. I realized that he smelled clean and powdery. The troll woman must be changing his cloths, in addition to feeding him.

"*Cher* Winn," I said softly. "I don't know where we are, and I don't know what is going to happen to us, but I promise I will do everything I can to keep you safe."

Winn smiled, gurgling happily.

ROSE

W E ARRIVED IN THE TOWN of Chamonix in the mid-afternoon of our eighth day of travel.

We had been able to see the mountains from afar for some days, but the up-close sight of those snow-covered peaks, stretching well off into the distance, was awe-inspiring.

"That one must be Mont Blanc," said Charles, pointing to the tallest peak in the mountain range.

It dwarfed any of the mountains I had seen before in Njord.

When I was a child, Neddy had told me tales of the frightening creatures that lived up in the tallest peaks of the snow-capped mountains. Ice dragons, ghost wolves, and mountain giants called the Jotun. But never any mention of Huldre.

We were going to need supplies, I realized. Food, as well as equipment that would enable us to tackle the mountain range that lay ahead. There was no Malmo here to help me figure out what I needed, but there must be some similarity between the two worlds. Being in those mountains would be like being in the Arktisk, except that climbing would be involved.

I sent Charles off to buy food to replenish our supply, and I went looking for a place to buy gear.

I finally found a small shop that seemed to have some of the things we needed. I was assisted by a large, talkative man named Ernst, who mostly catered to crystal collectors, mountain men who lived in the nearby village of Tacul. They made their living by climbing up to the glaciers to find crystals to sell.

Ernst sold me a range of climbing equipment—rope, metal spikes, various goatskin garments, as well as some well-crafted snowshoes. He also said that I would need his brand of bedrolls, which were much thicker and more cumbersome than the ones we already had. They were made of rabbit fur, eiderdown, and a thick tightly woven material I couldn't identify but which he said was designed to repel moisture.

Charles and I met in the center of town with our purchases and found what appeared to be a well-run stable, where we arranged to leave our horses, since our journey would now be on foot.

That night we made camp between Chamonix and the village called Tacul, and while we waited for meat pies to warm, Charles and I reviewed each piece of equipment I had gotten for our ascent. I explained that we would attach the spikes to our boots with leather straps, and that the poles tipped with iron would function as both walking sticks and ice picks.

As I filled him in, I had an odd feeling of déjà vu, though in reverse. I was playing the same role to him that Malmo had with me back in Gronland. It was daunting, though, and a bit absurd, considering I knew next to nothing about mountain climbing.

 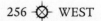

WHITE BEAR

A FTER NYAMH HAD EXPLAINED THE GEAR we would be using to climb the mountains, I asked her about the sword she carried, and if she had received instruction on how to wield it.

She paused, as if not knowing how to answer, then said, "Of a sort. A very long time ago."

"It appears that the same is true of me," I said, with an attempt at a smile. "I was thinking I should practice, since it seems likely there will be danger if we must face the Troll Queen."

Nyamh nodded. "I did the same—practice, I mean—before I came to the castle in the mountain."

"Perhaps we can practice together? I had a tutor back in my father's court . . ." Gesturing at my body, I went on, "But I am different now, bigger, and I think stronger, and I would like to try my hand with this new sword."

"Very well," Nyamh said, smiling. "Let us commence with our swordplay exercise."

ROSE

I T TURNED OUT THAT CHARLES'S KNOWLEDGE of swordplay
was far superior to mine. Even though in truth his lessons
had taken place more than one hundred fifty years ago, they
were much fresher in his memory than mine with Nils Erlend
had been.

Charles knew the names for things, and he was able to
demonstrate various feints and parries, defensive stances and
attacking thrusts. But when we tried to practice together,
it was awkward; our rhythm was not right. And I suddenly
remembered that when I was back in that grove of poplar
trees, swordplay had reminded me of dancing, and I remembered too the memories it had stirred of dancing with my
husband.

I stopped abruptly. Resting my sword against a tree, I
turned to Charles and said, "Did you by chance learn how to
dance in your father's court?"

Charles looked at me in puzzlement, then replied, "I had
started to learn. It is part of a prince's training to be taught
the court dances."

"Let us try," I said, holding out a hand. I told myself it was all part of the swordplay lessons, but I knew it was an excuse to be closer to my husband. And always there was the hope that it would somehow trigger his memory.

Charles moved toward me, tentatively, then reached out his hand. I took it, lightly. And we began to move.

At first our rhythm was as poor as it had been sword fighting. His dancing was more formal than I was used to, there being a difference between court dance and the kind we did at village festivals. But I tried humming and altering the pattern of our steps, and he adapted. We twirled and spun, and I actually began to enjoy it, to forget that this man holding me by the hand had no memory of ever doing this with me before. I smiled at him. He started to smile back, but then his face froze. His eyes went unfocused, his steps faltered. He dropped my hand, letting out a groan.

"Charles?" I said, leaning toward him.

He backed away from me and quickly ran off, wild-eyed, panicky.

I started to follow, but he gestured me away with one hand, the other grasping his forehead.

He went some distance away, sinking to his knees and remaining that way, motionless. I wondered if I should go to him, take him his flauto, comfort him. But I sensed I should keep my distance.

I went and packed up the gear we'd been using. As I sat, waiting, I kept a careful eye on Charles, who still knelt, not moving, both hands pressed to his head. I couldn't help thinking that if dancing with me had such an effect on him—those flashes of color and light and fever in his brain that he'd told me of—the odds of him finding his way back to being my husband seemed very slim indeed.

But after a while, Charles rose and slowly made his way back.

"I'm sorry, Nyamh," he said, his voice low.

"What happened?" I asked.

"It is the brain fever. My head hurts, and my thoughts get confused—it frightens me." He shuddered.

"I understand," I said, though I wasn't telling the truth. Because I didn't think I would ever truly understand how memories of me could have been so completely erased, leaving in their place only pain and colors and the terrible blankness I saw in his eyes.

WHITE BEAR

THE TRUTH IS THAT up until my mind rebelled and over-whelmed me with color and pain and fear, I had enjoyed the dancing.

What had Nyamh been to me, before I lost my memory? I knew she was not my wife, that she was not the mother of my son, because she herself had said she had another husband who was lost because of the Troll Queen. But I felt I should know her, that we were connected somehow.

I pushed all these thoughts away. There were more important things to think about. Like the journey through the mountains that lay ahead.

And finding my son.

ESTELLE

I WOKE UP WITH THAT HEAVY-HEADED FEELING again. My mouth was dry too. I reached for the glass of sweet milk by my bed. But then I stopped.

In the story that Rose told me of her journey to the land that lay east of the sun and west of the moon, there had been a drink the trolls gave their "softskin" servants and the Troll Queen gave Charles. It had an ugly sort of name. What was it? Slank? Yes, I think the drink was called slank. It had something in it that made you sleepy and forgetful. It almost made Charles forget Rose completely. But the little troll Tuki, who died, figured it out and saved the day.

Could this sweet, milky drink be slank? I decided not to drink it anymore. I needed to be awake and have all my wits about me if I was going to keep Winn and me safe.

I crossed over to his crib. Once again he was sucking on that glass cup. But he was almost done, and when he saw me, he lifted both his head and arms in my direction.

"Ooh la, look at you," I said with a smile. "You are raising your head now! What a clever boy."

Winn smiled back, and I pulled him into my arms.

I went to sit in the chair at the table, which I saw had a new basket of bread and a plate of fruit. Settling Winn on my lap, I picked out an apple and bit into it. I started to think over all I could remember about Rose's time with the trolls.

ROSE

Tacul was a tiny town nestled at the base of the first ascent to the Alpes. It consisted of only a couple of small stone buildings huddled together, and we could see no sign of human activity. I was disappointed, since I'd been hoping to find someone there who could perhaps guide us to the best route to Mont Blanc. We even knocked on a couple of the doors, but there was no response.

After passing through Tacul, we came to a long snow-covered trail gradually heading uphill, and we began to follow the path.

The first stretch of the journey took us through a dense forest of high-branching beech trees with silver-gray bark. It was still and oddly dim underneath the canopy of tree branches, but when we came out of the forest, our eyes were dazzled by the smooth, wide expanse of white that spread out before us. It wound upward between craggy outcroppings of rock, looking eerily like an enormous, twisting roadway of snow and ice built by giants.

The man called Ernst, who had sold me our gear, had told me this was a glacier and it was called Glacier des Bois.

Then we noticed something moving on the glacier, small figures making their way toward us. As they came closer, we saw that they were a man accompanied by a large dog and a mule laden with bulging packs.

The man was short and wiry, with a leathery, lined face. I called out a greeting, but the man didn't reply. It wasn't until he and his animals were only a few feet away that he acknowledged our presence, and it was with a scowl. He spoke Fransk, but he spoke quickly and in a dialect that was difficult to understand.

He apparently was asking what we were doing on the Glacier des Bois, and I responded that we were headed for Mont Blanc. The man let fly a torrent of words, spoken so fast I could make out only a few phrases here and there.

"Imbeciles . . . dangerous peaks . . . completely unprepared."

I was startled, but also felt a little irritated, countering that even though it was true we weren't experienced at climbing mountains, we had thoroughly outfitted ourselves in Chamonix.

The man glared at me, but suddenly and unexpectedly invited us to join him for tea. He gestured toward a stand of spruce trees growing along the side of the glacier.

Slightly taken aback, we followed and watched as he deftly set up and lit a small fire. The water was soon boiling, and he poured us cups of a minty herb tea. We perched on rocks and tried to answer the questions he threw at us.

Where did we think we were going?

Mont Blanc.

Why?

Charles and I remained silent. The man frowned and forged on with his questions.

What equipment did we have?

I showed him our gear, and at last we got a few grudging nods. The scowl became less severe.

Were we aware of the dangers ahead? Avalanches? Hidden crevasses? Snow blindness?

I hesitated. "I know a little, but . . ."

The man glared at me. Then he drained his cup of tea, set it down, and said matter-of-factly, "I will guide you to Mont Blanc. Or at least as far as Mont Maudit. After that, you are on your own."

"Thank you!" I said, surprised but very pleased at our good fortune. "We will certainly pay you for your trouble," I added, taking out my leather pouch of gold coins.

But the old man shook his head. "Later," he said, "and then you will pay me what you think I deserve."

He introduced himself, saying his name was Benoitas, but we should call him Ben. His mule was named Molly, and the dog was Pip. I noticed Charles smiling at the dog, holding out his hand in friendship. The dog trotted over and sniffed Charles, presenting his ears for scratching, which Charles was happy to do.

Before we set out again, Ben meticulously checked our gear once more, tightening straps, examining the stitching on the goatskin, making sure the iron tips on our walking sticks were secure. The important things we seemed to be lacking were veil-like coverings for our eyes to combat the glare of sun on snow, but he was able to rig up one for each of us. They reminded me of the ice goggles I had used on my trek to Niflheim. In fact, much of the gear and the snowy terrain we would be covering reminded me of my journey to the top of the world, with the Inuit Malmo as my guide.

Ben gestured at our swords, saying it was a waste of valuable energy to be carrying such things up into the mountains. "No use for swords in the Alpes," he said.

"Perhaps not," I said. "But we will take them just the same."

Ben gave an exasperated shrug, but didn't say any more.

Even though Ben could not have been more different from Malmo, I thought of her often as Ben taught us about mountain trekking. Where Malmo was measured and kind, Ben was voluble and grumpy. Where she was still and spoke simply, almost in the language of poetry, he was in perpetual motion and had a tendency to speak roughly.

He told us he made a living as a crystal collector. He said that at the northeast end of the Glacier des Bois was Col des Cristaux, a place rich with veins of quartz. Crystal collectors, like himself and other men from Tacul, spent the summers at the Jardin de Talèfre, a small island of rock in the midst of the even larger glacier called Glacier de Talèfre. Winters were spent back at the tiny village polishing the crystals they collected, and in spring they took them to the marketplace in Geneva.

We began our journey up the Glacier des Bois. Ben told us stories of ice giants who had built this roadway, though he himself didn't believe in such things. He did however believe the tales of ice dragons living at the highest reaches of Mont Blanc because he himself had seen strange things in the skies above it.

"What sort of strange things?" I asked.

Ben shook his head and said it had almost looked like shimmers of fire.

"The northern lights?" I asked.

Ben shook his head again. "No," he said. "We're too far south here. And, I would swear I saw something flying high in the sky. It was too large and bulky to be a bird. There isn't much I'm afraid of," Ben went on, "but dragons . . . No, I don't like dragons. Which is why I leave you at Mont Maudit."

He cast an appraising glance at our swords. "Perhaps you are wise to bring them, after all."

The walking was smooth at times, arduous at others, especially when large columns of ice thrust up into our path. Ben called them seracs, and they oftentimes bordered deep crevasses that had to be jumped across. We came to one crevasse that was too wide for jumping, and we had to make a long detour around it.

As we walked, Ben kept up a nonstop stream of chatter. He clearly wanted to educate us about this beautiful and dangerous world of the Alpes. He told us the mountains were inhabited by bears, ibex, and wolves but that once we hit the tree line, we would see only a few birds, like snow finches and golden eagles, and an occasional ibex.

He warned us of the dramatic changes in weather we were likely to encounter; a sunny day could transform to low clouds and then to a blizzard of snow or hail in a matter of minutes.

"It does not matter how good a climber you are," he said with a menacing glare at us. "You can never tell when a lightning storm will come. An avalanche fall. A blizzard sweep through. You cannot master these mountains. They will master you."

The higher we got on the Glacier des Bois, the more treacherous it became. Lower down, the crevasses were visible, but higher up, the snow didn't melt, so they were hidden under layers of snow. We had to move slowly, testing the ground ahead with our metal-tipped walking sticks.

The landscape was similar in some ways to the land of ice and snow I had journeyed through before reaching Niflheim— the wind-sculpted ice, the blue of the sky, the sparkling surface of the snow when it was lit by the sun. But the air in the mountains was thinner, and the higher we got, the more labored my breathing became. Looking up at the looming peak of Mont Blanc, still far above us, I wondered how I would be able to breathe at all once we reached it.

We arrived at the crest of the Glacier des Bois just as the sun was hovering at the top of the ridge of mountains ahead. An immense field of snow lay before us.

Ben said this was where we would stop and make camp for the night.

 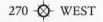

ESTELLE

THINKING ABOUT ROSE MADE ME HOMESICK, and I missed her very much, but it also made me feel braver. I had decided that I would try to be like Rose, that I would think about what she would do if she were in this situation.

And of course what she would do is try to escape from the trolls.

But first I needed to figure out where we were. I had tried the door once, and it had been locked. And the window was high, too high to see out of. *But maybe,* I thought, *if I try standing on Winn's cradle, I'll be tall enough.*

He was napping, so I gently lifted him out of the cradle, taking care not to wake him. I crossed the room and laid him on my bed, surrounding him with soft pillows.

I went back to the cradle, dragged it under the window, and gingerly stepped onto the mattress. The cradle swung from side to side on its rockers, but I steadied myself and stood on my tiptoes. I was just high enough.

At first I didn't know what I was looking at. There was white, only white, as far as I could see. My first thought was that I was in Gronland or up in the Arktisk. Or maybe even Niflheim.

But then I realized how high up I was. And that all those white shapes were mountains, very large mountains, bigger than any in Njord. From the look of it, I was on the tallest peak.

The beauty of it took my breath away. But I also felt very small. And frightened.

Even if I could somehow escape this room with Winn, how would I ever be able to climb down this mountain? And journey through all those other pinnacles of white?

It seemed impossible.

I stepped out of the cradle, pulled it back to its place, went to the bed, and sat beside the sleeping bairn. I almost cried, but told myself that Rose wouldn't cry.

And I must be brave like Rose.

ROSE

THE SNOW FIELDS WERE DOTTED with gnarled dwarf pines, and we set up camp near a small grouping of them.

Ben shared with us his favorite food for mountain trekking, small white round cakes of cheese called *reblochon*. He told us they were rich in fat since they came from the second milking of the cow.

"The wind is changing," said Ben, his head cocked to the side as he passed Charles a second *reblochon*. "Pip doesn't like this wind. It is called *foehn*, blows from north to south and can cause whirlwinds. I don't think this one will. But *foehn* makes Pip uneasy."

I wondered if Sib was familiar with *foehn*. I tried listening to the wind, to its music. I could just make out a faint humming and, like Pip, found myself feeling a little jittery. Charles reached out to scratch Pip's ears, which seemed to calm him.

"*Foehn* often comes before a blizzard," Ben said, and he went on to tell us what to do if we were caught in a blizzard. It was similar to what Malmo and I did in the blizzard we encountered in Gronland, so my thoughts wandered. But I did snap back to attention when he brought up avalanches.

"Have either of you ever been caught in one?" he asked us.

Charles opened his mouth to speak, but changed his mind. I wondered if he had had memories of an avalanche as a white bear, but realized how impossible that would be to explain.

"I haven't," I said, "but have heard about them. They are not uncommon in the higher mountains in Njord."

"They happen here often," Ben said, "and you need to be prepared. I will tell you how to live if you are caught in an avalanche. Pay attention. First, do you know how to swim?" he asked unexpectedly.

Charles and I both nodded.

"When you feel the rumble of an approaching avalanche, you must try to stay high and above it. Use your arms and legs to swim up to the top if possible," Ben said.

He gave a list of other tips on what to do to survive.

Pip became restive, even with Charles's attention, and began to whine.

"Come," said Ben, standing. "Best we move on. Pip and I don't like this wind."

ESTELLE

S INCE I HAD STOPPED DRINKING the sweet, milky slank, I wasn't as tired and could think more clearly. At first the troll woman seemed displeased that I'd stopped drinking it, but she brought me apple cider instead, and there were always a jug of water and a glass left on the table.

I figured out that the troll woman came to the room two times a day, once in the morning and once at night, to change and feed Winn and to bring me meals. She also changed the chamber pot I had found by the bed, and once she brought me hot water, soap, and towels so I could bathe in the copper tub that sat in a corner of the room.

There was a closet in the room, and in it was a change of clothing for me. The clothing I'd been wearing when I was brought here had been washed and was hanging in there too.

It was hard to tell the time of day, except by the darkness of the room at night and by the troll woman's visits.

One evening she brought a beef and carrot stew, and I ate while she changed Winn's cloths. This was a part of being with the trolls I did not mind, since I had never liked that *malodorant* task.

I was surprised to see her sprinkle a fine, almost silvery, powder on Winn's bottom before wrapping it up in the soft white cloths.

She fed him using the glass cup with the teat. I could see her face clearly and realized I had been right before. She looked down at Winn with a nice expression as he ate, almost as if she was fond of him.

"Are you Urda?" I asked suddenly.

She jumped a little, and looked over at me severely. Shifting her position, she deliberately turned her back on me.

"I think you are," I said. "Rose told me about you and your son, Tuki."

Her back stiffened when I said "Tuki," but I went on.

"Rose told me how much she loved your son. She had *un coeur brisé* over his death, very sad. When they couldn't make up their minds about what they were going to name the *bébé*, she said their first choice had been Tuki, but I said he was like the west wind, so they called him Winn."

The troll woman had turned around and was staring at me with an expression I couldn't read, but it was enough to stop me from talking.

She stared at me for a few more moments, then looked down at Winn, her eyes full of tenderness. "Tuki," I thought I heard her whisper.

"You *are* Urda!" I said.

She ignored me. Winn had finished feeding, so she put

him over her shoulder and gently patted his back. A little burp came out, and I could see Urda smile.

She put Winn back in the cradle, laid the soft white blanket over him, and left.

ROSE

W E WERE IN OUR THIRD DAY of climbing when Ben told us we'd be coming to Mont Maudit by the end of the day and he would be leaving us there.

"You should be able to reach the base of Mont Blanc in another half day," he said.

"Has anyone ever scaled Mont Blanc?" Charles asked, his gaze directed at the gleaming spire of the mountain.

"Not as far as I know," Ben replied. He glared at us, then went on. "But fools will always try. Like our king a hundred years ago, who made it a royal dictum that the Aiguille du Dru should be conquered, for the honor of Fransk. As if honor comes from taking needless risks. The Dru is not as tall a mountain as Mont Blanc, but it is equally unscalable, perhaps more so, with a sheer face. It lies that way." He pointed in a southeasterly direction. "Of course our esteemed king didn't climb the Dru himself, but ordered his chamberlain to do it for him." He shook his head. "Such a foolish waste of resources from a foolish leader."

"What king was this?" Charles asked abruptly.

"Charles VII," said Ben.

I watched Charles's face as he took in the meaning of Ben's words. He abruptly rose and, calling Pip to him, walked a distance off.

"What is wrong with him?" asked Ben.

"I'm not sure," I said slowly, "but it is possible he is wondering about King Charles VII, what kind of man he truly was."

ESTELLE

I T WAS THE NIGHTTIME, and I woke up. I didn't usually wake up when it was dark in the room, and I wondered why I did this time. Then I noticed a faint light. It was coming from the direction of Winn's cradle.

I peered closely. It looked like there was a figure standing by the cradle. No, it seemed to be two figures. One was holding a lamp, and the other was holding something larger, something that gleamed gold in the lamplight. *Maybe I am dreaming,* I thought. The one with the lamp handed it to the other, and as she did, I saw it was Urda and I knew I was awake.

Urda leaned down and lifted Winn out of the cradle.

She laid him in the gold thing, which I could see now was a basket or bassinette. She took back the lamp, and the two of them turned toward me.

In the lamplight I could clearly see the other's face. She was a troll woman, and she was beautiful, or would have been beautiful if it weren't for the long, deep scar down one side of her face. She had green eyes and very white ridged skin like Urda. She didn't look in my direction, but carried the gold bassinette to the door.

Urda did look over at me, and I think she saw that my eyes were open. She shook her head at me and moved to open the door for the beautiful woman.

I came wide awake. They were taking Winn away! I jumped up and started to run toward them, but I was too late. Urda swiftly closed the door behind them, and I could hear the key turning in the lock.

I cried out and pounded on the door. "Winn!" I screamed. "Bring him back. Winn!"

WHITE BEAR

M Y MIND REELED. Charles VII would most likely have been my brother. A younger brother, or perhaps a cousin. Who would have been born after I had "died," or rather, after a shape-shifted troll died in my place.

After I was kidnapped by the Troll Queen.

My head was pounding, and I feared that I would have another of those dizzying, color-bursting episodes. I hadn't had one in a while and was hopeful I was done with them.

But it swept over me that if I had not been stolen by the Troll Queen, I would have grown up to be king of Fransk. Not this Charles VII, who drew scorn from a mountain man in the Alpes one hundred fifty years later.

What kind of person had he truly been, this brother or cousin or whoever he was? And what kind of person was I? A king? Hardly. I barely had command over myself. I couldn't imagine being fit to lead a country.

Colors began popping behind my eyes. I couldn't do this anymore. Keep trudging forward through this forgotten life of mine.

I felt someone beside me. The lady Nyamh.

"Are you all right?" she asked.

I shook my head. "I am not."

There was sympathy in her eyes. Kindness.

"I do not know who I am," I said helplessly.

"You are a father," she said.

And she was right. I remembered my son, holding him in my arms.

"And I play the flauto," I said.

She nodded.

The heaving in my mind began to subside. And Nyamh took my arm and gently led me back to where Ben was waiting.

ESTELLE

I DIDN'T SLEEP THE REST OF THE NIGHT, but paced around the room, sometimes crying, sometimes pounding on the door. Where had they taken Winn? Would they bring him back? What were they doing to him?

Hours went by.

It was early morning when suddenly the door opened and Urda entered.

She was alone, and she was carrying Winn in her arms.

I cried out and ran to them.

Urda raised a warning hand, not wanting me to wake the bairn, who was fast asleep.

Silently I watched as she laid Winn in his cradle.

"Where did you take him? What did the beautiful troll woman do to him?"

Urda just glared at me. Turning back to Winn, she straightened his blankets.

"Was she the Troll Queen?" I blurted out. "Did she hurt him? Did she hurt Winn?" I grabbed Urda's arm.

She shook me off, looking flustered, and abruptly left the room. I didn't hear the key turn in the lock.

I gazed down at Winn, who looked just as he always did, sleeping peacefully, a fist pressed against his rosy cheek. I thought to myself that I should seize the opportunity and try to explore this place where Winn and I were prisoners. If I were Rose, I would.

I hesitated, feeling scared. *Maybe I shouldn't leave Winn alone,* I thought, *in case he wakes up.* But I knew I was just making excuses.

So I made myself slip out the door, leaving it open a crack so I could dart back in quickly if I needed to.

I found myself in a hallway lit by lamps. It was grand, much grander than my plain white room. The walls were covered in a velvety gold fabric, and the fixtures holding the oil lamps were a gleaming gold. I listened closely, but all I could hear was the faint guttering of the flames in the lamps. Silently I walked down the hallway toward a closed door at the end of it. When I got there, I slowly turned the knob and discovered that it too was not locked. Cautiously I opened it.

I entered a circular room with a high ceiling like my room but with no windows because it was lined with books from bottom to top. I would have liked to stop and look, but knew I should keep exploring. There was a door at the opposite end of the room, so I crossed to it and cautiously went through, discovering a spiral staircase that led down.

I started descending the staircase, though I wasn't sure I wanted to get too far away from my room. At the bottom was another hallway, and I inched my way forward, listening intently for any sign of life. At the end were two doors. I pressed my ear against one and thought I could hear faint, far-off sounds, but when I tried the other, there was only silence. I opened this door and stepped through. I drew in my breath sharply.

I was in a huge, beautiful room, at least two or three stories high, and it was filled with so much gold and sunlight that it hurt my eyes. At the top, the walls were lined with large windows, which let in the sun. Enormous gold-hued tapestries hung from the walls underneath the windows.

There was a chair at one end that was made entirely of gold and inlaid with glittery precious stones. *This must be a throne room,* I thought.

My eye was drawn to a table in the center of the room. I edged closer, staying alert to any possible noise, and discovered it was an *echecs* set. It was very large and very grand; the pieces on one side were made of white marble, and on the other, black. The carving of the pieces looked like the carving on the slats of Winn's cradle.

Then I heard the faraway sound of a door shutting. I turned and ran. I didn't pause until I was back in my white room. I pulled the door shut and stood there, breathing hard.

I crossed to Winn, who was awake. He smiled at me, and I picked him up, holding him close, my heart still racing. I looked into his face.

"Where did the trolls take you, *cher* Winn?" I whispered.

He looked just the same, but there was something off about him. I couldn't put my finger on it. His eyes seemed different to me. More alert, brighter. He smiled again and all at once let out a string of sounds, almost like he was talking. They weren't words, and I knew it was just bairn talk, but the expression in his eyes was so intent, like he expected me to understand him.

Suddenly the door swung open and Urda walked in. She came over to us and held out her arms to take Winn, but I pulled away, praying she couldn't hear my hammering heart.

Did she see me out of the room? I wondered.

"Why are we here?" I said loudly, my voice shaking. "When can we go home?" I couldn't help it as tears welled up in my eyes.

Urda stared at me, then she abruptly turned and left the room. This time I heard the key click in the lock.

ROSE

S NOW STARTED TO FALL MIDMORNING.

"I must leave you," Ben abruptly announced. He had been eyeing the sky since dawn. "The weather is changing, and I need to return to the snow field before it gets worse."

"You will go straight ahead for a league," he said, pointing, "and soon after, you will be near the bottom of the summit of Mont Blanc. You should make camp there, for I fear a blizzard is coming, and it will be best for you to take shelter until it passes. Look for a small crevice in the rockface. It is not quite a cave, but there is an overhang that will give you some protection."

Ben did not linger over goodbyes and said that we could pay him when we returned. I found myself taking faint cheer from his belief that we would actually be returning from Mont Blanc. But of course he did not know that if I was right and if we even made it that far, we would be confronting an immensely powerful and evil Troll Queen at the top of the peak. If he had known that, perhaps he would have demanded payment upfront.

And then he and Molly and Pip were gone. The falling

snow obscured them from our sight in a matter of moments. Charles and I turned and silently trudged forward.

Some hours later, we made camp at the spot Ben had described, a shallow indentation in the face of the mountain, with a craggy overhang.

After constructing a makeshift tentlike barrier around our crevice, we unpacked our bedrolls and a few other supplies. We even managed to get a small fire going and cooked some frozen rabbit meat.

The snow fell unabated, and the wind began to kick up, fierce and loud. We burrowed into our bedrolls and sat huddled by the fire. The barrier we had created helped, but the wind whistled in at the sides, along with icy pellets of snow.

We were quiet at first, each lost in our own thoughts. I was remembering the last time I had been huddled against a blizzard. It had been with the Inuit Malmo on my journey to Niflheim. Before the blizzard hit, she and I had constructed a sturdy dwelling made of ice blocks, which offered a good deal more protection than the makeshift barrier Charles and I had put together. But that had been against a blizzard that lasted for days and days. Hopefully, this one would be a great deal shorter.

"Can I ask you," I said abruptly, "about the thing that happens in your head, the flashes of color?"

He looked up at me, wary.

"Do you know what brings it on?" I asked.

Shaking his head, he opened his mouth to speak, then closed it again. "The thing is," he finally said, "is that I fear . . ." He paused and took a deep breath. "My father, King Charles VI, was mad, you know. I saw him once, lying on the floor of a palace hallway, crying out that his head was on fire and that someone must get water and put out the flames."

I knew this about my white bear's father, at least the general fact of his madness. Charles had gone to Neddy soon after we were married and said he wanted to know about his father and mother. Neddy had filled him in on what the historical records revealed. We learned that King Charles VI suffered from an intermittent and debilitating madness from the age of twenty-four until he died.

"I also saw him once," Charles went on, "sitting on a chair, not moving. He stayed there for days, and we were all told that he believed himself to be made of glass and that if anyone touched him or made a loud noise, he would shatter."

I shook my head in wonder.

"Nyamh," he said, "sometimes I feel like I am going to shatter, too. And, worse, I fear that I have inherited my father's madness." The words came tumbling out, his eyes bright.

Outside our flimsy tent, the storm raged.

"No," I said, "I do not believe that is true. I think that what happened to you is only to do with the Troll Queen. It was her punishment, either from an injury to your head, during the shipwreck, or through her arts. But you can get better. You will get better. See how far you have come already, the memories that have returned to you."

"You are kind," he said, anguish still in his eyes, "but I fear you are wrong."

I cast about for something that would distract him from his thoughts. And suddenly I remembered the story knife.

"I was caught in a blizzard like this before," I said. "I was in the Arktisk with an Inuit woman named Malmo. It was a blizzard called Negea, and it was worse than this one, lasted for days. To pass the time, Malmo taught me about the story knife."

I burrowed into my pack and drew out the small knife made of ivory. As Malmo had done before me, I used the flat side to level a patch of the snow that lay between us. "She did it like this," I said, using the tip to sketch a picture into the smoothed snow. I drew a very simple picture of a dog. "It is a way to tell stories, to pass the time."

"What is that a picture of?" Charles asked.

"I am not very good at drawing, but that is Pip."

"Of course," he said, smiling. "You said you were in the Arktisk," he went on. "Was I with you? Did I know this Malmo?"

"You did meet her," I said, "but you were not with us during the blizzard Negea."

"I don't remember her," Charles said. "But I have had

memories of a man, a large man with wild hair and a tendency to sing songs about ale. I helped him repair a ship?" he asked uncertainly.

"Yes, that is Thor!" I said. "He is a friend. I miss him," I added. It had been some time since we had been in touch, but the last I'd heard, he seemed to be thriving, living happily with his Inuit wife, Rekko, in Malmo's village of Neyak.

"Thor," said Charles thoughtfully.

"Tell me a story," I said, handing him the story knife. He shook his head, pushing the knife back toward me. "I have no stories," he said. "Stories have a beginning, middle, and end. I have only moments, flashes of pictures in my mind."

"That is what stories are made of," I said. "Moments. One followed by another, by another. Until you have a story."

He shook his head. "I do not believe that. Tell me your stories, Nyamh."

I paused, wondering how far I dared go. Was it the right time to tell the white bear *our* story? Perhaps not. But I could tell him a part of it.

So I told him the story of a maiden who wove three dresses, one silver, one gold, and one the color of the moon. The first she lost to an unscrupulous ship captain, the second she used to bargain passage from a drunken ship captain, and the third she wore to a ball, where she sought to lift the enchantment on a prince.

It was my story of course, and his story. He enjoyed the tale, but he did not recognize it.

Disappointed, I wrapped it up quickly, giving it a simple fairy-tale ending. They lived happily ever after.

Which right now seemed impossible.

WHITE BEAR

WHEN NYAMH FINISHED THE STORY, she laid down the story knife. There was a sad look on her face, and suddenly my heart was pounding and pops of color dotted my eyesight.

I turned away from her, trying to will the feelings away. What if I *was* mad, like my father? And even if I wasn't, how could I be any kind of father, or friend, if I didn't know who I was? With so many pieces of myself missing?

I was immediately struck with a certainty that I had felt exactly this way before. That I had left someone important behind to go look for myself, for my name.

This time I knew my name. But little more.

ESTELLE

U RDA SURPRISED ME THE NEXT DAY by bringing things for Winn and me. Gifts.

For Winn she brought a gold rattle and a gleaming white ring that looked like a teething ring. I had noticed the tiny little white point of a tooth in Winn's mouth, though it didn't seem to be bothering him.

Urda brought books for me, as well as an *echecs* set. It wasn't nearly as fancy as the one I had seen in the throne room, but it was nice. I looked at her in surprise.

"*Merci*," I said, stuttering a little.

Urda nodded, setting the *echecs* pieces up on the table where I usually ate, and went to change Winn.

I looked at the *echecs* and wondered why she had brought it. I had no one to play with, unless . . .

"Do you play *echecs*?" I asked.

She looked at me briefly, then continued changing Winn's cloths.

But when she was done, she crossed to the table and pulled a chair up to one side. She sat down, looking expectant.

I was stunned, but sat down in the chair opposite.

We played three games. She was much better than I was, and she won the first two easily, but in the third game, I made a few bold moves that took her by surprise. For a moment, I thought I might even win, but she came back and beat me decisively.

We didn't speak at all while we played, and at the end of the third game, she just stood up and left.

ROSE

I COULD TELL CHARLES HAD BEEN DISTURBED by my story of the three dresses. He had turned away from me, saying he wanted no more stories, that he needed to rest.

I put away the story knife and burrowed into my bedroll, listening to the blizzard. It seemed to be quieting a little, the winds not as fierce. I think I must have dozed, for abruptly I came awake and heard only silence. The storm was over. Charles was sitting up, watching me.

Silently we packed up our gear, and as I stepped out of the shelter, I caught my breath. Mont Blanc loomed above us, capped by fresh white snow that glittered in the sunlight.

"Magnificent," I said softly.

Strapping on our snowshoes, we began our climb up the mountain.

Charles pointed out a cornice, a heavy, ridged arc of fresh snow up above, and I remembered Ben telling us about cornices, how they could be indicators of the potential for avalanche, and that the threat grew as the day wore on because the heat of the sun loosened the snow.

"Charles," I said intently, grabbing hold of his arm. He

turned to look at me. "I was thinking . . . if by chance we should get separated . . ." I paused, gazing up at the cornice. "If something happens to one of us, I think we should make a pledge that the other will continue on."

Charles was silent.

"The stakes are too high," I went on urgently. "It would be futile to waste time searching. Agreed?"

"We won't get separated," Charles said.

"It is possible. Promise me," I said, holding his gaze. I knew that what I was proposing would be next to impossible for me to honor, that if Charles was swept away from me, I would feel the overwhelming need to search for him. But I also knew I must put Winn and Estelle first, even if it tore my heart in two.

"Very well," said Charles. "I promise."

As we climbed, slowly, cautiously, sounding for crevasses with our alpenstocks, I avidly searched the top of the mountain for any sign of a building or palace, but could see nothing.

What if I'm wrong? I thought to myself. *What if we have come all this way and there is no palace, no Troll Queen, no Winn or Estelle?* I pushed those thoughts away and concentrated instead on breathing. Every step took enormous exertion; my ears had a raspy ringing sound in them, and I battled against nausea.

We both stopped frequently, reminding each other to drink water from our skin bags.

At one of these stops I had to sit, my head spinning.

Charles went on, a little ahead of me. Through the buzzing

in my ears, I heard him call back, "I think I see something just ahead."

I drank, slowly, deeply, my chest heaving.

And then I heard it. A sound like far-off thunder. *Could it be another storm?* I wondered. But no. I knew at once it was not.

"Charles!" I cried out. But it was too late.

Swim! I screamed inside my head.

There was an extraordinary rush of sound, unlike anything I had ever heard. And I saw the wall of white descending, snow shattering and spilling down the mountain, heading directly toward me.

As the snow engulfed me, I desperately moved my arms and legs as if I were in the sea, but within moments, I had no idea which was up and which was down. Snow filled my mouth, and I spat it out. I caromed off things I couldn't see, causing sharp jolts of pain. But I always kept my hands in front of me, always kicked my legs.

I hit something hard, and all went dark.

ESTELLE

A FTER OUR *ECHECS* GAME, I noticed that Urda hadn't locked the door behind her, or at least I didn't remember hearing the click of the lock. I wondered if my coming close to beating her in that third game had distracted her.

I waited a while, until Winn was napping, and tried the door. I was right; it was unlocked.

I slipped out and, following the same pathway I had taken before, soon found myself back in the throne room.

As I was crossing it, to see where the doorway on the other side of the room led, I heard the sound of footsteps. I was too far into the room to escape back the way I had come, so I darted to the nearest wall and slid behind one of the golden tapestries.

I could hear footsteps enter the room. I stayed still, making myself as flat as I could. It was probably Urda, I told myself. But what if it was the beautiful woman, the one I thought was the Troll Queen? My heart pounded.

The footsteps seemed to be heading toward me. But then they stopped, and when I heard the sound of game pieces being lifted and set back down, I realized that the person was near the fancy *echecs* board.

Everything was suddenly silent. For a very long time. I even began to wonder if whoever it was had somehow silently left the room. A place on my back was starting to itch, and it was stuffy and hard to breathe behind the heavy cloth of the tapestry.

Cautiously I peeked out. And there she was, the beautiful troll lady. The Troll Queen. Standing over the *echecs* set. I could see the profile of her face, the side without the scar.

She was holding up one of the game pieces, both hands wrapped around it. I couldn't tell which piece it was.

Her eyes were terrifying. They were wide open and staring, but they weren't the green color I'd noticed before. Instead, they were white-yellow and bright, almost like I was staring directly at the sun. In fact, even though I was not looking straight into her eyes, my own eyes burned, with little pinpricks of black like I got when gazing at the sun too long. I quickly ducked back behind the tapestry and closed my eyes.

The Troll Queen's breathing was loud. I rubbed my prickling eyes and prayed she hadn't seen me.

The deep breathing went on for a while. I decided she must not have seen me and was relieved, but I was getting stiff and desperate for fresh air.

She was quiet again, and I could hear her set down the playing piece with a click on the surface of the board.

I was curious which piece it was, so I risked another peek. It looked to be the queen, which she still had her hand on.

But it was her face that made me catch my breath. The white-yellow light was gone from her eyes, and her expression was full of triumph, like she had just done something she was very proud and pleased about. It scared me a little, and I pulled back behind the tapestry again.

I heard her footsteps as she strode across the room, away from me. And the sound got fainter and fainter until I knew she was gone.

I cautiously moved from behind the tapestry, stretching my arms and shoulders. I crossed to the *echecs* board and reached out to touch the queen, but all of a sudden, I saw Urda. She was standing across the room, shaking her head fiercely at me.

Then she was moving toward me, so fast that she was beside me before I could even breathe. She grabbed my wrist hard.

"Do not ever play with the Morae *echecs*," she said fiercely, "and *never* touch that piece." She leaned even closer and hissed in my ear. "Never touch the queen."

It took me a few moments to realize that she had just spoken to me in Fransk, the first time ever.

She dragged me to my room, so fast I could barely keep my footing, and shoved me inside. I heard the sound of the key turning in the lock.

ROSE

I WAS SWADDLED IN SEALSKIN and completely submerged in the great Njordsjoen, and the white bear had me in his mouth by the nape of my neck. We were swimming in a dim green underwater world.

But abruptly the white bear was gone and I was floating by myself, drifting in the water, without direction. I couldn't breathe, so I wiggled out of the sealskin and kicked my legs hard, swimming up toward the light above. I burst through the surface of the water with a great gasp and gazed around me at the impossible blue of the sky and expanse of sea. I saw someone swimming toward me, and at first I thought it was my white bear, but then I saw it was Winn, my bairn, floating right there in front of me. I was thrilled and relieved, and I reached for him. And it was then that I woke up.

I was buried in snow. The crushing weight of it pressed on my chest so hard I could scarcely breathe, and I could not move my legs. I remembered the long-ago prophecy of the *skjebne-soke* that had so frightened my mother. That I would die a cold and horrible death, suffocating under ice and snow. And in that moment, I was sure I was going to die.

But I could not die. I would not die. I had to live. I had to get to Winn and Estelle.

I breathed, as deeply and deliberately as I could, and my thoughts cleared a little. For now, anyway, I was alive. And I would stay alive. I concentrated my mind on remembering what Ben had told us about surviving an avalanche.

Fortunately my hands had stayed in front of me, and I was able to wiggle them close to my face, cupping my mittened palms in front of my mouth, creating a pocket of air. Ben had warned that my exhaled breath would melt the snow around my face, which would quickly refreeze, creating a barrier of ice. He also said that one should move slowly and methodically, to conserve energy.

I spat out a little saliva and was relieved when it ran down my chin instead of up my nose, which meant that I had landed right side up.

I scooped out the snow around my face to create a larger opening and started to dig upward, praying that indeed I was going up, toward the surface. I had a sense of light above me, though was worried I was confusing it with my dream, but it gave me hope that I wasn't buried too deeply.

I kept punching my hand through the snow above my head. My breathing grew short, and I slowed down. I didn't want to use up the little bit of air I had. Moving slowly, I pressed my hand up and felt the snow loosen, letting my fingers wiggle freely. I was an arm's length from the surface!

I felt a rush of relief. I could do this, I told myself. Even though I felt as if I was encased in stone, I could dig my way out.

Ever since I was a little girl, people always said that I was afraid of nothing, and in fact Mother said many times my fearlessness would be the death of both of us. Neddy continually berated me for my foolhardy bravado. Even Sib had called me *misneachail*, a nickname that in her language meant "without fear." But it was not true, not entirely. There *was* one thing that terrified me. And this was it. Being trapped in a small place where I could not breathe. And it wasn't because of the prophecy of the *skjebne-soke*. I only learned about that when I was older. But I wondered if somehow I had always known it. At any rate, being confined in a tiny space was the one thing that gave me nightmares and made my breath go short.

I needed my breath now, more than I had ever needed it before. I could not panic and remove the little air I had left. If I let terror overtake me, I would die.

I thought fiercely of Winn and Estelle. And even of Charles, though he did not know who I was and perhaps never would. It didn't matter. For him and for our children, I would live.

And so I dug. Holding off the fear with every fiber of my being, I dug and I dug. Slowly, sometimes dislodging only a few granules of snow, I kept chipping and scraping. The moments crawled, and each time I moved my hand, I believed that breath would be my last.

But slowly, agonizingly slowly, the snow above me loosened and shifted, and the light grew brighter. Finally I had created a tunnel to the surface and could breathe more freely.

I stopped for a while to recover my strength. The prospect of extricating my entire body from the rocklike snow that enveloped me seemed almost impossible, but I believed I could do it.

It must have taken me several hours or more to dig myself out of that tomb, but painstakingly, pausing often, I was finally able to pull myself out of the snow.

I lay there a moment, feeling both an overwhelming sense of being alive, but at the same time knowing how close I still was to dying. I had to find shelter and a way to light a fire, or I would freeze to death. And I still had to dig my pack and sword and bedroll out of the place that might have been my grave. It took a long time, perhaps an hour, and by the time I finished, I could not feel my fingers and toes, and I feared I might lose one or more to what Ben had called blackflesh.

I spotted a rocky ledge with a slight overhang, and brushing away snow, I untied the last few pieces of wood that were strapped to the bottom of my pack. Using that long-ago flint with fingers that barely could move, I was able to start a small fire.

The pain that shot through my fingers and toes as they warmed was unbearable, but I gritted my teeth and rubbed and rubbed until finally the pain eased and warmth tingled back into my hands and feet.

I looked around to get my bearings and immediately thought of Charles. All I could see was snow. I traced the path of the avalanche with my eyes. I could see I was not at the bottom of it, but had somehow, miraculously, been swept to the side less than halfway down. I did not recognize the terrain at first, but then spotted a few familiar markers I had noticed on our climb up the mountain.

Gazing up, I could see the peak of Mont Blanc. I had lost a lot of ground, but not as much as I might have.

Where was Charles? Had he survived? He'd gone ahead of me, but had he been swept past me, down to the bottom of the mountain?

I tried calling out his name. The eerie, echoing sound in all that silent whiteness unnerved me. I listened closely, but there was no answering call.

I turned again to my fire, rubbing my hands. Then I leaned back against the rocky surface behind me. We had made a promise to go on without the other. But how could I? What if my white bear was hurt? I couldn't just leave him.

As I sat there, my thoughts whirling around in my head, I noticed something odd about the surface of the cliff face to my right. It was mostly covered with snow, but there were a few spots that were bare, and the rock surface looked strangely smooth. I reached over and brushed away more snow. I discovered that a large area was in fact smooth, or mostly smooth, because I also saw there were carvings on the surface. My heart quickening, I pushed more snow away and saw scrollwork etched into what looked to be greenish marble, and as I dug and swept off the snow, I realized I was looking at the rectangular shape of a doorway. And there was a small handle that gleamed gold.

I reached for it, holding my breath, and turned. It didn't move at first, but when I used more force, it gave a little and I heard a clicking sound. However, when I pulled the door toward me, it did not budge. So I used my dagger, chipping away at the ice and snow encrusted in the door's edges.

After a while, I tried the handle again and this time felt the door give a little. Pulling on the handle and prying with the blade of my knife where it still stuck, I finally got the door open, at least enough so I could squeeze through.

At first it seemed dark inside, especially in contrast to the sun's glare off the white snow outside. But as my eyes adjusted, I became aware of a dim yellowish light, the source of which I could not see, yet it was enough to reveal a small hallway that led to the base of a stairway, a steep staircase that climbed straight up into the mountain.

I hesitated, breathing deeply. I turned and peered back out through the door opening, at the vast whiteness stretching down, the path of the avalanche. We had made a promise to go on, and in that moment I made up my mind.

First I went back to my fire and melted enough snow to fill two skin bags full of water, then I completely doused the fire with snow. I gathered my pack, sword, and bedroll.

I went through the door again and strode up to the stairway. I set my foot on the first step. The stairs were made of polished ivory marble with veins of white swirling through it. And I began to climb, slowly and steadily, my shoes with their metal spikes making a ringing sound on the marble steps.

WHITE BEAR

A S I ROUNDED THE RIDGE, I saw it clearly. A door. It was large and grand, fashioned of some gleaming white material I didn't recognize. From a distance, it would look indistinguishable from the side of the mountain face. But it was a door. I was about to turn back to tell Nyamh what I'd found when I heard the roaring sound. I spun and saw the wall of white hurtling toward me. I had just enough time to grab the handle of the door, open it, and slip through before the onslaught of snow hit.

The door slammed shut, and I could hear the avalanche pounding against it. For I knew that was what it was, an avalanche. I thought desperately of Nyamh, hoping she'd heard it coming and found a safe place to shelter.

The pounding went on and on, until finally it stopped. I went to the door and pushed, but it was shut fast, didn't move even a fraction of an inch. I pictured the snow piled up against it and knew it was futile to try anymore.

What had happened to Nyamh? Was she perhaps lying hurt or broken under that deluge of snow? I closed my eyes, leaning my forehead against the door. I had to believe she was alive, that she didn't need my help. My bairn, my son, was somewhere in this palace and I had to find him. We had agreed to go on if we were separated, and I hoped I was doing the right thing.

I turned and took stock of where I was. It appeared to be the entry hall of a grand dwelling, most likely a palace, though it was very different from the palaces I had lived in as a child in Fransk.

This was loftier, more ornate. And it was full of light. There seemed to be large windows at the front and top of the hall that let in the sun. All the surfaces were either white or gold, so the effect was almost blinding.

There was a grand stairway that curved up high to the next level, but somehow I thought it didn't seem wise to enter the palace that way. There were doorways to both the right and left of the bottom of the stairway so I went to one and opened it. It led me into a hallway, which I followed.

At the end of the hall was another door, and when I opened it, found myself in a large kitchen.

I started to move through it, but suddenly became aware of movement. There were two people, one on either side of me, though I could see at once they were not human. They had white ridged skin like the man who had visited me once in the underground labyrinth. I knew now they were trolls.

One held a large kitchen knife and seemed to be a girl, and the other was a boy who held nothing. But it was he who lunged at me first, his hands closing around my throat. It happened so fast I had no time to react or draw my sword. I reached up and tried to pull his hands away.

He was strong, though, stronger than me, and I felt my breath going. All of a sudden, I was filled with anger, a deep, burning rage, and a surge of energy coursed through my body.

I put my two hands between his grasping ones, and with a roar, I broke them apart. He let out a cry, and I pushed him away. He fell back and I followed, picking him up and throwing him at the wall. I didn't know where all this astonishing strength was coming from. It felt primitive, like it was emerging from somewhere deep inside me. He hit the wall with a thud and crumpled to the ground. And he didn't move again.

The girl with the knife came at me then, and this time I tried to draw my sword. But it stuck in the scabbard. I let out a curse, dodging away from her blade.

She laughed, and I felt the fierce rage again and lunged at her, grabbing her by the legs and tossing her into the air. The knife dropped to the floor with a clang, and she followed, hitting her head hard on the white marble. She too lay unmoving.

I stood there, panting, and gazed in amazement at their two still bodies. I was confused by what had just happened. It was as if some buried part of me had exploded up and out of me.

It must have been my white-bear self. The instinctual drive for survival in a violent, perilous world.

I was so lost in the wonder of it that I didn't see the third troll who had snuck up behind me, with a large cast-iron pan in his hand. I turned to see him swinging it at my head and then I knew no more.

ESTELLE

AFTER LOCKING ME IN MY ROOM, Urda did not come back for a long time. Not with food and not even to change Winn's cloths. I had to do it myself, and he was being fussy, so it was *très désagréable*.

Winn and I both grew very hungry as well. He had long since finished the last cup of the milky drink Urda brought him. I put the rest of the apple cider in the cup, and he seemed to like it. I finished off all the crusts of bread and leftovers from the last meal, but it did little to ease my hunger pangs. At least the water jug was half full.

In spite of the apple cider, Winn continued to be fussy, and I wondered if that tiny tooth was finally bothering him. I urged the teething ring on him, but he kept throwing it at me.

Finally I got him settled down, and he fell asleep in his cradle.

I felt out of sorts, angry at Urda, who had been nice, bringing gifts and playing *echecs*, and then mean, dragging me back to the room and locking me in.

You must be like Rose, I told myself. *You must figure out how to escape.* Maybe there was some way to pry open the lock. I had heard of lock-pickers who broke into people's homes and stole things. I looked all around the room for something I could use. My eye fell on the knife and fork on the table, left over from my last meal.

I took the knife over to the door and knelt down. The blade, which was tapered, fit in the keyhole perfectly, and I tried wiggling it around. I had no idea how the lock worked, so I pulled the knife back out and peered into the keyhole. It made no sense to me, but maybe if I poked around long enough, something would work.

ROSE

THE AIR INSIDE THE TOWER of marble steps was cold, but not as cold as outside. And it was thin, but not quite as thin. The polished surface of the steps was slippery, and I decided to remove the spikes from my boots, realizing they would do me no good on this surface. The walls were made of the same ivory marble, and even in the dim light, there was a glare, like the sun on an expanse of white snow.

At first I told myself this was much easier than climbing a mountain of snow and ice. A stairway. No ledges to haul yourself up. No crevasses to sound. No bitter wind tearing at your skin or ice pelting your face.

But I also knew that when things looked easy, they often turned out to be the opposite. I thought back to the time I was in the castle in the mountain and how I had come to the realization that magic lets you skip over things, in this case dangerous things like crevasses and snow thunder, but you also missed other things like the impossible blue of the sky hanging over undulating white waves of mountains stretching into the distance, or seeing a line of icicles hanging from a jutting ledge glittering in the sun's rays. There was no such variety here in the everlasting stairwell. Just gleaming marble all around me.

And I also knew that this stairway could well be a trap.

It didn't matter, though. If Winn and Estelle were at the top of this tower, and I believed with a certainty that surprised me that they were, then I must climb these stairs.

So I climbed. And I climbed. My legs began to ache, and a stitch developed in my side. My head pounded. And still I climbed. Dizziness feathered red at the sides of my eyesight, and my ears buzzed.

It is the thin air sickness, I reminded myself, and stopped to drink deeply from my skin bag. I chewed some dried rabbit meat.

I began to climb again. Up and up. *Surely the mountain is not this high,* I thought dully, as the stitch in my side returned and I had to labor for every breath. There were pins and needles stabbing my feet and hands. I grew drowsy.

Maybe if I just curled up on the marble steps and took a little rest, I said to myself. But I shook my head, fighting off the drowsiness.

The walls pressed in on me. I longed to be back out on the outside of the mountain, with the crisp cold and blue sky. I began to calculate the time I had spent coming up and wondered if I could make it back to the bottom if I tried. I wasn't sure.

I remembered vividly the days I had spent in the castle in

the mountain, slowly dying of homesickness and despair. I began to feel as though I had been in this tower walking up these stairs as long as I had been trapped in that castle. But in the castle in the mountain, I had been with the white bear, my white bear. Who, even if he had survived the avalanche, was as good as dead to me. He did not know me and never would. And suddenly I was engulfed in grief. Tears rolled down my cheeks.

I stopped again, wiped my face deliberately, and forced myself to drink from my skin bag. I would think only of the stairs that still loomed above me. And of Winn.

ESTELLE

M Y KNEES HURT AND MY FINGERS were numb and I had made no progress on getting the lock to budge. I stood up stiffly, taking a deep breath. I crossed to the table and sat down, pouring myself a small amount of the water from the jug, saving some for Winn.

He had almost finished the apple juice I gave him, but he still slept peacefully.

How I wished I had that ring of Urda's keys, the one she always carried at her waist.

I stared at the *echecs* set in a daze, my stomach rumbling.

"I must be brave like Rose," I said, but tears came to my eyes.

Maybe, I told myself, *Rose will come rescue me and Winn, the way she rescued the white bear.*

ROSE

I T DIDN'T SEEM POSSIBLE that a stairway should rise so
high. I felt as if by now I could have climbed into the highest reaches of the sky and be walking among the stars.

But instead of stars, black spots dappled my vision, along
with the red feathers, and I had to keep blinking them away.
The pain in my side had become almost unbearable. I had
to take each step slowly, crouched over. My feet slipped frequently on the polished marble.

So much for this being the easy way up the mountain, I thought
grimly.

But worst of all was a nearly overwhelming sense of dread
that clenched at my insides. It was like I could feel evil pulsing
above me, around me, threatening my reason. I remembered
kentta murha, the killing fields in Niflheim, and all the frozen,
twisted bodies of discarded softskins. And I thought of the
Blood Rain and of the very earth buckling, killing hundreds,
even thousands of innocent people. Could the Troll Queen
really be capable of such powerful and monstrous magic? I
knew she could. And here I was stumbling up a cursed flight
of marble steps to meet her.

The last time I had faced her, all I had done was wash a shirt. It now seemed like sheer dumb luck and the bravery of the young troll Tuki that had made me able to defeat the Troll Queen and rescue Charles. I had a strong feeling that it was going to take much more than washing a shirt to best her this time.

All I had was a sword I barely knew how to use and my love for Winn and Estelle and my white bear. It would have to be enough.

I stopped and drank deeply from the skin bag, the last of the melted snow water.

I had better reach the top soon, I thought, *or I will perish right here in this tower of marble stairs.*

Hunched over, clutching my side, I began once again to climb.

NEDDY

W E HAD SEARCHED AND SEARCHED for Winn and Estelle, but could find no trace of them. We lost time following a lead on a vagrant, a man who had lost his family, and subsequently his mind, to the Sweating Sickness. There was a rumor that he had been seen near the Nidelva River that day and might have snatched the children.

But he was later found in a run-down ale house and clearly had had nothing to do with the disappearance.

I was going half out of my mind with anguish, and it didn't help my health. I had a relapse of sickness, and Sib forced me to take to my bed for several days.

But finally we received Rose's letter.

It was frustratingly brief, but it conveyed the news that she had found Charles and that he was alive! I was elated to hear that she had been right all along.

I could tell however that there was something wrong, though she was vague in the details. All she said was that she and Charles were setting off on a journey to the mountain in the Alpes called Mont Blanc, where she believed the Troll Queen had taken Winn and Estelle.

So somehow she knew about her bairn, though again she did not say how.

And all I knew was that I must set off as soon as possible for the Alpes.

ROSE

WHEN I CAME TO THE TOP of the stairway, at first it didn't even register. It was all I could do to take the next breath, and the pain in my side felt like a gaping wound. My vision was more black and red than clear, and my legs felt like pillars of stone. I was desperately thirsty, my lips dry and cracked. I suddenly skidded on the polished surface, almost falling flat on my face. And it was then I realized that there were no more stairs.

In the dim yellow light, my blurred eyesight could make out a hallway and, at the end, the shape of a door.

I stood up as straight as I could, rubbed my eyes. I made a few last-minute preparations and said to myself, *Very well. I am here. Time to meet whatever lies behind that door.*

And I opened the door. It swung smoothly on its hinges.

It seemed ridiculous, but for some reason, I had not really thought about what I might find when I reached the top of the stairs, when I actually arrived at the Troll Queen's palace at the peak of Mont Blanc. Three years ago, when I had come to her palace in Niflheim, I had snuck in, disguised as a softskin slave. I suppose I'd had some vague idea that I might be able to sneak in again.

But clearly that was not to be. And what met my faltering vision was a most extraordinary sight. It was almost a tableau, like actors motionless on a stage, waiting for the curtain to rise.

I was in a grand room so glittering with gold and sunlight that my already feeble eyesight was overwhelmed. It had an extraordinarily high ceiling with high windows and was lined with breathtaking gold-hued tapestries and filled with exquisitely carved furniture, much of it golden in color.

But my eyes soon found the Troll Queen, who was placed at the center of the stage, sitting on a throne with a table set before her. She was just as I remembered her, all that immense stone-cold beauty, except for one thing—a deep scar that ran down the right side of her face.

There were two other figures there. Urda, whom I recognized at once, and Jaaloki, who looked the same except for the right side of his nose, which was sunken in and disfigured. Had I done that with my needle?

My knees buckled, and I sank to the floor, licking my cracked lips.

"Get her water," said the Troll Queen in her cold, gravelly voice.

Urda went to a nearby table and poured a goblet of water for me from a golden pitcher.

I took it from her, reaching up with a shaking hand. Her face was expressionless.

I drank, emptying the goblet quickly, and stood again, handing it back to Urda.

"Thank you," I whispered. Then I turned to face the Troll Queen.

"Where is Winn?" I asked, trying to make my voice loud and confident, but it came out only as a pitiful rasping sound.

"He is here," said the Troll Queen, who somehow understood me. "You are alone?"

I nodded. "There was an avalanche," I explained. "Charles and I were separated."

"Of course," she said. "Perhaps it is a relief to you, to be delivered from the pitiable shell of a softskin man who does not know you, who will never know you again." Her eyes taunted me.

I stared back at her. So it was true. She had done this, cruelly and purposefully removed me from my white bear's memory.

"At any rate," the Troll Queen went on, "*he* no longer matters. It is—"

"Yes," I broke in, my voice harsh. "I know. It is the bairn, my bairn, who matters. Where is he?" I repeated.

"You are impatient. First we must have introductions. This is Urda . . . Oh, but you know Urda, don't you?"

Urda and I looked at each other. The last time I had seen her face, it had been a mask of savage grief. Her son, Tuki, had been obliterated right before her eyes. By the Troll Queen, whom she still served, the sorceress who had killed the child she loved. How could she not feel a deep and abiding hatred? But then troll emotions had always been unfathomable to me.

I tried to read Urda's eyes, wondering if it was perhaps *me* she blamed for Tuki's death. But they were blank, unreadable, like two black stones.

"I believe you have also met Jaaloki, prince of the Under Huldre," the Troll Queen continued. Jaaloki smiled at me, laying a finger alongside his now disfigured nose. I was overcome by a chilling feeling of nausea. The snakebite scar on my face burned.

"Jaaloki nearly ruined my little game with his poisoned bite," the Troll Queen said, with an affectionate glance at the skeletal troll beside her, "but you did provoke him."

It was at that point I noticed the table in front of the queen held an *echecs* set. And the Troll Queen saw where I was looking.

"Very good. Yes, this is important. *Skac*," she said. "It is why you are here. At least in part."

I stared, uncomprehending, at her beautiful face, my eyes drawn to the deep scar down the side.

"Where is Winn?" I said again.

"You are tiresome," the Troll Queen said, with an irritated sigh. "Put your things down and come sit." She gestured toward a chair pulled up to the other side of the *echecs* table.

When I didn't move, the Troll Queen nodded to Jaaloki, who was swiftly at my side. He flung my pack and sword to the side of the room and, grabbing me by my upper arms, propelled me to the chair, pushing me into it. His fingers bit into my skin, so hard I was sure they left bruises. *He hates me,* I thought.

"This is how I have amused myself these past three years," the Troll Queen said, her eyes boring into mine. And she hated me too, even more so than Jaaloki did. Her suppressed fury was almost a living, breathing thing between us.

"*Echecs?*" I said softly.

"*Skac,* I call it. And it is my own version," she said with a smile. "Urda and I play. Or I play alone. And if I make this move"—I watched as she moved several pieces about the board, including the white queen, her queen—"the ground in the small province of Armagnac will buckle and break apart.

"And it was this," she went on, moving the game pieces in a different setup, "that caused the Blood Rain in Fransk."

As the meaning of her words sank in, I stared dumbly at the Troll Queen's white hand, with its ridged, whorled skin. She was setting the white queen in its original starting spot, readying the board to begin play. I noticed almost offhandedly that there was an indented line on one side of the face of the playing piece that was the white queen.

"Where is Winn?" I said again. It was all I could think to say.

She closed her eyes, clearly annoyed. "We shall play for the bairn."

The way she said "the bairn" with such indifference shook me. It was the same kind of matter-of-fact indifference she had showed when she spoke of the earth buckling in Armagnac and of the Blood Rain that had so terrified the friar.

"Why?" I asked.

"It is the Huldre way. I am like my father and his father before him. We like games, puzzles, complicated rules to follow. This game of *skac* is simple, really, but I find it entertaining."

And I remembered then the set of conditions that the Troll King had set up, with my white bear's life in the balance, and I understood.

The Troll Queen looked at me, expectantly.

My mind whirled. My knowledge of *echecs* was basic. Back when I first played it with Estelle, I barely knew the game and had improved only slightly over the past few years. Charles enjoyed playing and had taught me to play a passable game, but surely I wasn't good enough to defeat the Troll Queen.

"I need to see Winn," I said. "I need to know that he is alive."

"No," said the Troll Queen.

"Yes," I replied, stubborn.

She shook her head, but turned to Urda. "Bring the girl," she said.

Urda silently left the room.

To my right was a large fire burning in an imposing fireplace with an elaborately carved marble mantelpiece. It flared, letting out a loud crackling sound. I shivered.

I stared down at the board, rubbing my arms to bring warmth into my body.

TROLL QUEEN

THIS SOFTSKIN GIRL, THIS CREATURE before me, with her bloodshot eyes, matted hair, chapped skin, and dirty clothing, is pitiful. Like one of the lowest of my softskin servants back in Niflheim.

She is so beneath me, so unworthy an opponent. She has no power, only a dull persistence. Why have I gone to all this trouble? But I remember all that she stole from me. My ice palace in Niflheim. My people. The boy I was to marry, the one she called Charles but I had named Myk. I run my finger deliberately down the valley in my face.

I could just extinguish her. Have it over with, quickly. But no. I have sought this too long. And it will be right and good and enormously satisfying to watch her as she realizes the fate I have planned for her son.

Then I will be done with her. With all softskins. All except the bairn.

Aagnorak.

ESTELLE

I WAS BACK AT THE KEYHOLE.

One of my fingers was bleeding from all the poking and prying I'd been doing, but I didn't care. And I felt like I was getting close. I was not going to give up until I got the lock open.

Suddenly I heard footsteps approaching.

I had just enough time to remove the knife when a key was thrust into the opposite side of the keyhole. And the door handle in front of my nose turned.

I fell back, and the door swung open. Urda looked down on me sprawled on my back, the knife clutched in my hand.

She took it all in, and I feared for a moment that she would be angry, but she said nothing.

She quickly crossed to Winn, setting a full cup of the milky drink beside him in case he woke. She then turned and beckoned to me.

"Come," she said.

I gaped at her, not moving.

She crossed the room, reached out, and calmly took the

knife from my hand, laying it on the table. Then she grabbed my arm, pulling me to my feet.

"Come," she said again.

Heart pounding, I followed her.

ROSE

WE SAT SILENT for what seemed a long time.

"Are your rules the same as mine?" I asked abruptly, my eyes on the *echecs* board.

She nodded.

"So how will it work?" I asked. "If you capture my king—"

"Your boy is mine."

What did she mean, hers?

"And if I capture yours?"

"He will be restored to you, and you will both leave here unharmed. But of course you will not capture my king." She spoke with a cold-blooded certainty.

"Then why do we play the game?" I asked.

"Because it amuses me. And it gives me the pleasure of destroying several more softskin villages as we play."

"You hate us."

She did not bother to reply. The look in her eyes said it all.

"And once we are done here, I shall begin Aagnorak," she said after a pause.

"What is Aagnorak?" I asked, though I was almost certain I already knew.

"The destruction of the softskin world. Flames will touch the clouds. The sky will turn black, the stars vanish, the earth move. Fire and ice. Aagnorak."

She paused, an imperious, knowing look on her face. "There are Huldre in many hidden corners of this world," she went on, "though not as many as there once were. But when the way has been cleared, the world shall be ours."

"And you will lead it."

"Of course."

I felt like I was in the middle of one of those old Viking tales that Neddy told me when I was a child. And I couldn't believe, or did not want to believe, that what she said was even possible.

And yet three years ago I had seen her power with my own eyes. Had seen her extinguish Tuki in a flash of light. And more recently, I had felt the Blood Rain on my skin and heard the stories of the Sweating Sickness. *Still, perhaps, this is all talk,* I said to myself. *She may indeed be crazed with her rage but hasn't the power to back it up.*

Whether she had read the skepticism in my eyes, or just wanted to be sure I knew her power, I didn't know, but I felt my throat tighten, as if fingers were closing around my neck. I reached up to my throat. Nothing was there. But I felt the pressure as my throat grew tighter and tighter.

The Troll Queen stared at me with narrowed eyes, though I noticed that the green of her irises was tinged with a white-yellow glow. There was a slight smile on her lips, and even though I could see her hands lying on the armrests of her throne, somehow I knew it was her fingers around my throat, squeezing the breath out. I felt my vision begin to grow dark.

Abruptly the invisible hands loosened, and I lay back in my chair, gasping for breath. I could hear something like laughter coming from Jaaloki. It was a jagged, shrill sound that made the hairs on my skin rise.

And then Estelle entered the room with Urda, and my heart leapt up. She looked pale and frightened. But her eyes lit when she saw me, and she straightened her shoulders. I could see Urda's hand on the back of her neck, holding her where she was.

I wanted to run to her, take her in my arms. But the Troll Queen shook her head.

"Tell her that the bairn is alive," she said to Estelle.

The girl's eyes were wide with fear, but she nodded.

"Say it," hissed Urda.

"Winn is alive," Estelle said, her voice trembling. "He has a tooth," she added.

"There," said the Troll Queen. "Now you may make the first move."

Jaaloki went over to Urda and Estelle. And the three of them stood there, a silent audience.

So I did. I moved a pawn two squares ahead. It was a simple, basic beginning move, one Charles had taught me.

The Troll Queen smiled and moved the pawn in front of her queen one space ahead.

I moved a pawn on the other side of the board one space.

The Troll Queen moved her queen one space ahead, behind the pawn she had moved before. I saw with a start that her eyes had changed completely into that white-yellow brightness. I had to turn my own eyes away.

When she removed her hand from the piece, the Troll Queen said with a smile, "A giant wave just washed away a small fishing village in Portugali."

I closed my eyes, picturing the devastation, water crashing in through windows, sweeping terrified people out to sea.

I can't do this anymore, I thought dully. The pain in my side had unaccountably returned. I rested my forehead on my hand. Between my fingers I looked over at Estelle. She was staring at me, an almost urgent expression in her eyes.

"Your move," said the Troll Queen.

I tried to concentrate, removing my hand from my eyes and staring down at the board. And even with my limited knowledge of the game, I saw clearly that in as little as one move, depending on the Troll Queen's whim, my king would be captured. And nothing I could do would change that. I exhaled.

My sword was too far away, but before I entered the throne room I had slipped a dagger in my boot. If I went for the Troll Queen, took her by surprise—

"Your move," she said again.

I looked at Estelle. I knew she knew I had lost. She was being brave, heartbreakingly brave.

I stood.

"Sit," commanded the Troll Queen. "We will finish the game."

I saw Urda's hand tighten on Estelle's shoulder. Jaaloki took several steps toward me.

Still standing, I reached for my knight.

Suddenly Estelle shouted. "Rose! *La reine*. Her queen!"

Jaaloki turned back and lunged toward Estelle. Urda grabbed her, pulling the girl away from the skeleton man.

Without hesitation, without thought, I snatched up the Troll Queen's white queen, the one with the dent along the side of its face. It burned my hand, but I held on. I felt the constriction around my neck again, swifter than before. Vise-like.

And again without thinking, I used all my strength and hurled the queen *echecs* piece into the fire that burned in the great ornate fireplace.

There was a blinding flash of heat and light, along with a thunderous roaring sound. The pressure on my neck vanished, and I spun to look at the Troll Queen.

I gasped when I saw that the top of her head was in flames. She made no sound, but her eyes were bulging out, distended.

The fire flared up high, white-yellow, blinding, and all of a sudden was gone. The Troll Queen's body had turned completely to ash. White-gray ash. It held the shape of a body for a few seconds, then collapsed to the floor, leaving only a pile of light gray.

My mother's dream.

I turned to look for Estelle and saw at once that Jaaloki had her in his grasp, the thin blade of a dagger pressed to her throat. I let out a cry and started toward them.

But Urda sprang first, and I could see the glint of a large kitchen knife in her hand. She plunged it into Jaaloki's side with a shrill cry. Jaaloki staggered back, his skeletal arms releasing Estelle, who twisted away, her neck streaming with blood.

Jaaloki let out a hissing sound, lurched forward, and thrust his knife into Urda's stomach. She fell to the ground, and he toppled backwards, clutching at the wound in his side. I could see his lips working, but he crashed to the floor and lay unmoving.

I ran to Urda and Estelle, who was crouched at the troll woman's side. Red-black blood was everywhere, and I slipped in it as I ran.

I leaned over Urda and saw that she was still alive. I pulled a brocaded cloth from a nearby table and tried pressing it to the wound in her stomach, but it immediately was soaked through with the dark blood. I knew it was a mortal wound.

Still she breathed and with her right hand seemed to be reaching for something at her side. It was her ring of keys she sought, and with a quick, convulsive movement, she wrenched one of the keys off the ring. She turned toward me and said something I couldn't hear, blood bubbling up out of the corner of her mouth. I leaned closer.

"Tuki," she whispered.

"Yes," I said. "I loved him too."

Blood trickled down her chin, but I could see she was smiling.

She reached for my hand and pressed something into it.

"You will find him, your bairn. The Morae," she murmured.

"The what?" I asked, straining to understand her.

"Morae," she repeated. "In Skottland. On an isle in the Western Sea. Beyond Leodhas. You will find him."

Then she closed her eyes and was still.

"Urda?" said Estelle. She stared down at the Troll woman's face, tentatively holding out her hand to touch her white hair.

"She's gone, Estelle," I said. And quickly stuffing what looked to be a small key into my pocket, I laid Urda gently down on the floor. Estelle was crying, and I felt tears come to my eyes, too. Urda.

I pulled Estelle to me and inspected the wound to her neck. It was bloody, but fortunately Jaaloki hadn't cut into a major artery. I found some linen napkins in a nearby dresser and, tearing them into strips, used several to fashion a makeshift bandage. I tied them around her neck, and though I could see it was very painful, Estelle was brave, not letting out a sound.

The burn on the palm of my right hand was uncomfortable, but I quickly wrapped several strips of the cloth around it.

"Come, Estelle," I said. "Take me to Winn."

She nodded, and we started toward the door by which she had entered the throne room with Urda.

But at that moment, we both heard a noise.

It was a whirring, whooshing sound like leaves being blown by a strong wind, and it was coming from the place where the Troll Queen's ashes lay.

Something was moving. I turned and watched in horror. At first I couldn't understand what I was seeing. Then I realized. It was the opposite of Mother's dream about the ashes in the forest. Instead of losing shape and dispersing, these ashes were gaining shape, swirling up into the figure of a creature.

I did not recognize what it was, but it seemed to be part bird, part snake, part lizard, and it was the same white-gray as the ashes.

It was big, twice my size, and had large, powerful wings that were beating rhythmically, though it remained standing on the ground.

It had a curving, cruel-looking beak and a body the shape of a crocodile (which I'd only seen in pictures), but bigger. There were four short, squat legs with gleaming black talons.

"Estelle," I whispered, and she gazed at me, terrified. She too had been watching the ashes form into a creature. "I need you to go to Winn."

The girl seemed frozen, unable to move.

"Please, Estelle," I said urgently. "Go. And take these with you." I handed her my dagger, and, grabbing Urda's keys from her body, pressed them on Estelle. "Just in case. I need you to keep Winn safe, Estelle. Go." I pointed toward the door.

Her head jerked in a nod, and she turned and ran out of the room.

I pivoted, running over to my pack. Drawing out the wind sword, I turned to face the ash creature. *Is it a dragon?* I wondered.

It seemed to be taking shape, solidifying, and had grown larger in the time it had taken me to send Estelle away.

It cocked its head back and opened its sharp beak. A small plume of flame shot up into the air.

Yes, most likely a dragon, I thought. I took a deep breath.

It turned toward me and, beating its wings, rose a few feet off the ground. I could feel the movement of the air across the room.

Trolls could shape-shift. I had seen Jaaloki change into a snake right in front of me. This must be the Troll Queen herself, shifted into the guise of a dragon. And she was heading straight toward me.

I cursed myself for a fool, thinking that somehow the wind sword, which I barely knew how to use, was going to do me any good against this fearsome creature.

What was my mother's dream again? A gray raven turns

me into a million pieces of ash? Was this winged white-gray ash creature going to turn me into a million pieces with that sharp beak and dangerous claws? Or would she merely turn me to ash with a blast of fire from her throat?

I backed away. Her previous burst of flame had not traveled more than a few feet. I could only hope that it had not been merely a tentative exploratory blast.

I scuttled backwards, thinking to circle around the creature's tail. But it moved quickly on its short legs.

I passed Urda's lifeless body and came to the place I had seen Jaaloki fall. He was gone. No body lay there. My heart thundered, my thoughts immediately going to Winn and Estelle.

I was fairly sure the ash creature was too large to fit through the door, unless she could somehow shift herself smaller.

But she must have guessed my thoughts, for in a flash she had swooped around so that she was positioned between me and the door.

ESTELLE

P ART OF ME HADN'T WANTED TO LEAVE ROSE, but most of me did, because the creature that rose up out of the Troll Queen's ashes was *diabolique,* terrifying.

And Rose had insisted. She needed me to go to Winn, make sure he was safe.

I didn't understand what the queen wanted with Winn, but whatever it was, I knew it was evil.

Urda hadn't wanted harm to come to Winn, I could tell that. She had loved him because he reminded her of her own son, Tuki. But Urda was dead now.

I shuddered.

I made my way down the hall. I still didn't know if there were other trolls in the palace, so I was cautious, stepping lightly and listening for any sound.

And, faintly at first, I heard footsteps coming from behind me. My heart pounding, I spotted a door right next to me. I wrenched it open and slipped through, closing it softly behind me. Urda's keys jingled as I moved, but I stilled them.

I heard the footsteps go by, loud, and then recede, until I couldn't hear them anymore. I opened the door and peered out. The hall was empty. In the light from the hall, I could see I was in some kind of closet. It was full of shelves with linens on them. Sheets, table coverings, and even a tall pile of white and black fur skins.

I went back out into the hall and slowly found my way to the white room, praying I wouldn't come across any more trolls. I held tightly to the dagger, but I had never used such a thing before and didn't know if I would be brave enough to try.

Finally I came to the door of the room, but when I went to open it, discovered it was locked.

ROSE

FLAMES SUDDENLY SHOT OUT of the creature's mouth. I could feel the heat, but the fire didn't reach me. I ran in the other direction, colliding with the *echecs* table. Game pieces went flying, and I had to avoid slipping on them.

The creature let out another torrent of flame, and this one felt angry, as if I'd reminded her of the queen I had thrown in the fire. She beat her wings hard and rose up above me.

A tapestry had caught fire, and flames began to spread. The room was getting hot.

My hands were sweating, and I peered up, trying to see what the ash creature was doing.

I saw her glide toward me. Her beak was open, and I could see the fire kindling. I dropped to the floor and rolled, bumping up against the golden throne. Fire swept the floor next to me. I saw there was space beneath the throne, and I wriggled under it. *How hot does flame have to be to melt gold?* I wondered. I heard the sound of her wings beating, felt the rush of air. She was directly above me.

A scratching sound came, of talon on metal, and I realized

she had grabbed the top of the throne in her claws. It began to rise. Soon I would be unprotected.

There was a golden slat connecting the two back legs, and I grabbed hold of it with my free hand.

I was airborne, though only a few feet off the ground so far. The creature started shaking the throne from side to side, trying to dislodge me, yet I held on.

My hand was slippery with sweat, but somehow I managed to maintain my grip. Watching the room lurch wildly beneath me, I saw that on one side we were getting close to the door through which Estelle had gone. We were also getting higher off the ground.

Gauging the timing as best I could, I took a deep breath and let go. I landed hard, pain shooting up my right ankle. I had to roll to avoid the throne, which landed with a crash next to me.

I tried standing, but my ankle gave way, and I fell to the floor again. Air beat on me. She was directly above me and starting to descend.

I sat up, still holding the sword in my sweating palm. *Worse than useless,* I thought. But as I saw the underside of the creature's body hovering above me, I had a sudden preposterous idea.

I got to my knees and took the sword in hand as if it were a spear. Though there was no wind in the throne room, just flame and gold and sunlight, I thought of Sib and tried conjuring up images of a fierce northern wind. Holding my breath, I let the sword fly, aiming straight up.

The wind sword seemed to take on a life of its own, picking up speed as it flew upward, and I watched, stunned, as it pierced through the creature's chin. The blade didn't go in deep, but deep enough to stick there.

The creature swerved to the left, then began to circle down, her body twitching.

She was letting out shrieks of rage and pain. She reached up with her short legs and dislodged the sword, which clattered to the floor not far from me. A shower of dark red blood rained down. *Almost like Blood Rain,* I thought. I grabbed the sword, slick with the dark blood, and backed away.

The creature hit the floor with a thud that shook the room, and in the exact moment she made contact with the ground, she vanished.

I blinked. Had she shifted into another shape? I stared at the spot where she'd landed. All I could see were spatters of dark red blood. There was nothing else.

Uneasy, I gazed around the room. No Troll Queen. No Jaaloki. Just Urda's dead body and me. Where had they gone?

I grabbed a tapestry table runner and used it to wipe off my sword. Stepping around the pools of dark red blood, I ran out the door.

WHITE BEAR

I WOKE UP, MY HEAD THROBBING. I was lying on a white marble floor. And I remembered. I was in the palace at the top of Mont Blanc, in the kitchen.

Slowly I sat up.

There was no one around me. No sign of the troll who had knocked me out, nor of the two I had fought off.

I got to my feet.

It was so quiet. Was my son here somewhere? And Estelle?

I crossed the kitchen and exited a door, making my way down one hallway, then another.

Suddenly I saw her coming toward me. At first I didn't recognize her. But I was immediately flooded with emotions. Hatred, fear, even an unaccountable strange surge of something that felt like affection.

All at once I remembered.

It was the Troll Queen. I knew her cold beautiful face. Except I didn't remember the long scar along one side of it.

She was covered with blood, streaks of it on her white clothing, her arms, even her face. She had a wound under her chin that was running with dark red blood.

But my eye was drawn to something she was carrying in her arms. It was a bairn.

Winn. My son. I remembered my son.

I lunged forward with a shout. "Winn!"

She stared at me, and I could read the hatred in her eyes. But I also saw something softer there. Yearning.

"I go to the Morae. What the softskin girl destroyed shall there be restored." There was fury in her eyes when she said the words *softskin girl*.

"Then I will begin Aagnorak," she continued in the voice of rocks I also remembered well. "And when it is done, I will raise your child to rule Huldre. As once *you* could have." There was taunting, anger in her tone, but there was also still that yearning, for what might have been.

I stared at her, horrified.

And in a moment, she was gone. She and Winn had both disappeared.

"No!"

I heard a far-off scream. Without thinking, I ran toward it.

Estelle

IT TOOK TOO LONG TO FIND THE RIGHT KEY on Urda's ring, but finally I did. The lock clicked, and I opened the door.

I froze. Someone was standing in the middle of the room. It was that skeleton troll the queen had called Jaaloki. The one who had killed Urda. But I'd thought he was dead. He was holding blankets and Winn's glass cup in his hands.

When he saw me, he smiled. Setting down the blankets, he started to blur and shift, and I thought something was wrong with my eyes. I blinked fast and realized: he was turning into a snake. A very large white snake.

There is nothing in the world that frightens me more than snakes. Even small ones. And this snake wasn't small. It was very large, larger than me. I almost fainted dead away.

All I could think of was Winn, who was surely still in the cradle.

"Don't hurt him," I croaked out, still frozen where I was.

The snake began to slide across the room toward me.

I screamed and backed out the door.

The snaked slithered after me, gaining speed. I ran.

But it was too fast, and it caught up to me, winding itself

around my ankles. I fell and tried to crawl away, to twist out of its coils, but the snake tightened its grip and suddenly it was on top of me. I could hear a hissing sound and felt pain sear across my shoulder. I thought I was going to die.

Then I heard footsteps pounding toward me and saw someone come around the corner of the hallway.

It was Charles! He was alive, and he was carrying a sword.

"Help me!" I cried.

He drew his sword and thrust it straight down into the snake's tail.

The snake reared up with an unearthly sort of cry, turning toward Charles. He tried jabbing his sword into the snake again, but the snake was wriggling around too much. I got free and rolled away, huddling by the wall.

WHITE BEAR

I RECOGNIZED THE GIRL, ESTELLE. Another memory returned. But there wasn't time to think about that.

The snake was clearly injured by my blow to its tail; dark blood seeped out of it, leaving a trail on the floor. But otherwise it did not seem fazed.

Had I ever faced a snake as a white bear? I didn't think so. Certainly not one so large. But I still felt that same instinctual rush of adrenaline that I had with the trolls. This snake had bitten Nyamh, I was sure of it, and had been about to crush Estelle.

I wanted to kill it with my bare hands. But I knew its bite was poison. *On the other hand,* I thought grimly, *my sword lessons hadn't covered how to do battle with a large snake.*

It lunged at me, and I had just time to raise my sword, but it was no use. The snake knocked the sword out of my hand with its broad head and, in a flash, had begun to wind itself around me.

Estelle screamed. I tried to push against the snake's body with my hands and was able to keep it from constricting around me too tightly, but I didn't know how long I could hold it off. And the head was coiling around me and soon would be within biting range.

I caught a blur of movement out of the corner of my eye, and Estelle appeared. Her eyes were wide and terrified, but I saw she had a dagger clutched in her hand.

Closing her eyes, she plunged the dagger into the snake's body.

The snake jerked and went slack for a moment, just long enough for me to kick my way free of its coils and grab up my sword.

It whipped its face around toward me, rearing up to strike with its teeth. But before it could, I thrust my sword directly into its open mouth. I pressed forward, putting all my weight behind the weapon. My hand on the hilt was inches from those sharp teeth.

Its eyes widened as if in astonishment, then filmed over, and it crumpled to the floor.

Estelle ran to me and threw her arms around my neck.

"Charles," she cried, tears running down her face.

ROSE

I FOUND ESTELLE AND CHARLES beside the dead troll-snake
that had been Jaaloki. Relief swept through me to see that
my white bear was alive. He had survived the avalanche. And I
thought I saw relief in his eyes as well when I came up to them.

I quickly took in that, in addition to the injury to her neck,
Estelle now had a gash on her shoulder. Charles was comforting her, trying to get a look at the wound, but she was holding
on to him so tightly it was clearly difficult.

"Did the snake bite her?" I asked Charles.

"I think so," he said.

I immediately did what the soldier Julien had done for me,
what seemed a long time ago. I grabbed Estelle by the shoulder
and tried to suck the poison out of the wound. Estelle let out a
scream, but she held still.

When I was done, Charles handed me a cloth to wipe my
mouth, as well as his skin bag of water. I rinsed my mouth and
spat.

"Are you all right?" I asked Estelle. She nodded, though she
looked very pale. "Do you know where Winn is?"

Estelle jumped up, almost falling back down at first, but

she steadied herself. Her legs were shaking as she made her way down the hall toward a door that was standing open. I limped after her. Charles, who stopped only long enough to pull his sword out of the snake's mouth, followed me.

Hearing a shrill cry from Estelle, I hurried into the room.

"He is gone!" Estelle said. "Winn is gone."

"Yes, he is gone," Charles said from behind me. "She has him."

I whirled around. "Who has him?"

"The pale queen," he said. "She was carrying the bairn in her arms. And then she disappeared."

 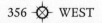

NEDDY

HARALD SOREN HAD AGREED to provide us with a ship, one of his best ships, in fact. He himself was unable to accompany us, feeling he must stay with his children, who had so recently lost their mother, but he said the crew would be made up of his best men.

I was eager to set off, but both Mother and Sib insisted that I wait until I was stronger. Mother even went so far as to say that if I could not climb the stairs of our house without losing my breath, clearly I was not ready to set off on an arduous journey over the sea. I had to admit she was probably right.

It seemed that all I did for the next few days was rest and eat. It was true that I had become unnaturally thin because of my illness. Sib and Mother made it their goal to fatten me up. Finally, after a week, I had begun to fill out and was able to climb the stairs at a fairly brisk pace without having to pause.

The nearest port to Chamonix was Calais, a sea journey that would take five days.

I knew nothing of mountain climbing, and the thought of scaling the Alpes was more than a little daunting, but if that was what it took to find my sister, I was willing to learn.

ROSE

WE ARRIVED AT BEN'S HOUSE in Tacul more dead than
alive.

The journey back from Mont Blanc had been hard. I'm not
sure how Charles, Estelle, and I managed it, but we did.

Much of the palace had been in flames, the throne room
in particular burning fiercely, but Charles somehow found a
pathway through the smoke and falling debris, and we got to
the door that led to the stairs I had climbed up.

I almost tripped over one of the *echecs* pieces, which still
lay scattered on the floor. On an impulse, I reached down and
grabbed it. It was the knight I had last been holding. I thrust
it into the pocket of my cloak, where it joined Queen Maraboo
and the key Urda had given me.

Descending the stairs had been easier than going up,
though with my injured ankle and Estelle's two wounds, especially the snakebite to her shoulder, our progress was still very
slow.

I worried about Estelle and the troll-snake poison, but the
blow he'd struck her seemed more shallow than mine, and I
prayed that less of the toxin had gotten into her blood. She

was brave, though, and even had had the presence of mind to tell us where to find warm furs for us all to wear when we left the palace.

Charles wound up carrying Estelle the last leg of the journey, and we were all exhausted by the time we reached the Glacier des Bois.

Charles managed to kindle a little fire, and we ate the very last of the *reblochon* Ben had given us what seemed a long time ago. Estelle was too feverish and ill to have any appetite.

We spoke little and in fact, since leaving the burning palace, had barely said anything to each other beyond what was necessary to survive the journey. As I chewed the *reblochon*, I was lost in thoughts of the Troll Queen, how angry she must be. The palace at the top of Mont Blanc was the second of her domiciles I had had a hand in destroying. And Jaaloki, to whom she had seemed very attached, was now dead.

"What are you thinking?" asked Charles.

"About her, about the pale queen," I said.

"Where do you think she has taken my son?" he asked.

I felt a stab of pain at the word *my*. Not *our*. It was so unfair, that he should have memories of the Troll Queen. But none of me. I took a deep breath.

"I *know* where she has taken him."

"You do? How?"

"Urda told me, as she was dying."

"Where?"

"To an island off Skottland. In the Western Sea, beyond Leodhas. Urda called it Morae," I said. "I need to look at a map. It is not in the troll atlas, at least as far as I can tell."

"Morae," said Charles. "The queen said something to me about Morae as well. I will go there."

"And so will I," I said.

He gazed at me, searching my face for something.

"Nyamh," he said, "more and more memories have been coming back to me."

"That is a good thing," I said carefully.

"Yes," he agreed. "But the one blank space, the memory that has not returned, is my wife. The mother of my son."

I kept my face still, though my heart was beating fast.

"Does that not seem strange?" he said.

I nodded, not trusting my voice to speak.

"What happened to her? Do you know?"

I nodded again, then said softly, "You lost her."

He shut his eyes as if in pain. "I feared so. You knew her?"

"Yes, very well," I said. Abruptly I stood, muttering something about wanting to check on Estelle and that we should be moving along soon.

I could have told him then, that I was his wife. But something stopped me. It wasn't to protect him anymore, from the madness I had feared would overtake him. It was to protect me. I didn't want him to feel a sense of obligation to me. More than anything in the world, I wanted him to remember me on his own. And to love me as he once had.

Just as we were packing up and making ready to move down the glacier, Ben found us. He had Molly and Pip with him as before, and Pip bounded up to Charles, barking happily.

I could see that Estelle, even in her feverish state, was charmed by the dog. And we were grateful when Ben offered Molly to carry her.

I'm not sure what the mountain man thought of us, with our wounds and burnt clothing, not to mention suddenly having a young Fransk girl with us. He asked me only one question, and that was, "Dragon?"

I nodded and said, "But it is gone now, and I don't believe it will be back."

"Good!" he said emphatically.

He took care of us, turning out to be well versed in dealing with our various injuries and broken bones, my ankle in particular, which he expertly splinted and wrapped. Snakebites, on the other hand, were foreign to him, but he was helpful to me as I tried to recreate the theriac that Sib had made for me back in Etretat. He even had a few of the more obscure herbs on hand.

As I had hoped, her snakebite was not as deep as mine, but

Estelle was smaller, and so the effects were still bad. She lay feverish for several days in the pallet Ben had set up for her.

Charles had told me the rest of what the Troll Queen said to him. That she was going to Morae to complete what she had set in motion. Aagnorak. And that she would raise Winn as *her* son, who would one day rule Huldre.

I shivered. How were Charles and I going to stop her? It was impossible. And yet we must try. We must rescue *our* son.

NEDDY

FINALLY I DEEMED MYSELF ABLE to travel, with Mother's reluctant blessing.

Because of the Sweating Sickness, there had been much disruption in shipping over the past month, so Harald Soren had agreed to help those who needed to journey to points in Njord that lay along our route to Calais. I understood, of course, but couldn't help being impatient at the frequent stops we had to make.

Sib helped keep me calm, and my joy at having her by my side made the delays easier to bear.

I hoped that we would find word from Rose at Calais, as she had said she would try to do in her letter. If not, we would head overland to Chamonix.

ROSE

CHARLES AND I WERE BOTH DESPERATE to go to Skottland, to find Winn and the Troll Queen, but neither of us felt we could leave Estelle behind, and she was clearly too ill to travel.

Much to our surprise, it was Ben who offered a solution.

"I couldn't help but overhear," he said gruffly and without preamble. "Wasn't prying, you know. It is a small house, after all. But I gather you need to get to Calais, as soon as possible?"

We had figured out that Calais was the closest port and the best place to find a ship to Skottland.

"Yes," said Charles.

"And the young miss is too ill to travel, I understand," Ben said. "Well, it just so happens that I need to journey to Calais myself. I have a sister there who is always after me to visit. Long overdue, I am, and Molly, Pip, and I would be happy to help convey the girl. They've both taken a shine to Estelle, and I've done all the crystal gathering I need for the season."

"That is very good of you," said Charles. "But are you sure?"

Ben cut him off with a frown. "Always sure. Wouldn't be offering if I wasn't."

"I think Estelle can make it to Calais," I said, "if she rides on Molly's back. But she may still be too fragile to journey with us to Skottland. She doesn't take well to sea travel," I added.

"As to that, my sister is a kindly sort, much more so than I, and I'm sure you could arrange for the child to stay with her until you are able to come back. Pip and Molly and I might stay for a spell ourselves. Keep her company."

"And I can send word to Neddy, once we get to Calais," I said, thinking out loud. "My brother, that is. He could come get her from Njord."

"Sounds like we've got a plan," said Ben.

We left the next morning. Before departing, I pored over the old tattered map I'd brought along, looking closely at Skottland and its islands. To my disappointment, I could find none named Morae, or anything close. I was sure Urda had said "Morae." Charles had heard the same word from the Troll Queen herself, and in one of her lucid moments during our journey back from Mont Blanc, Estelle had told me about her own incident in the throne room, with the *echecs* queen game piece, and how Urda had told her never to touch the Morae queen.

I was sure I was right about what Urda had said. But why could I not find it on the map? *Perhaps it is too small,* I thought.

I took out the little key Urda had pressed into my hand and looked at it closely for the first time. It was so small, it was hard to imagine what it might unlock. It was pale in color, a grayish white, and more delicate than I had realized. I had assumed it was metal, like most keys, but it felt different, more like ivory.

What did it unlock? And how would it help me rescue Winn from the Troll Queen?

ESTELLE

I DON'T REMEMBER MUCH AFTER LEAVING the troll palace on top of the mountain. I was either very cold or very hot. I had scary dreams of the white troll-snake. I cried out for my *maman*, for Winn, for Rose. I dreamed that Charles was alive, and it turned out that dream was true.

I remembered Urda dying, too. Sometimes I screamed, remembering all the blood. Urda's blood. The snake's blood. *My* blood.

I came to myself more when we were in the little house owned by the frowning man, Ben. There was a dog named Pip, who sometimes licked my face, and a gentle mule named Molly. Even though Ben was grouchy, he was *très gentil* when he ran a cold cloth over my hot face. And he gave me medicine that helped me get better.

When I was feeling a little stronger, Rose came and sat with me, feeding me soup that Ben had made. I found I was a little hungry for the first time, and the soup smelled good.

"Estelle," Rose said, spooning soup into my mouth, "you have been very brave."

"I didn't keep Winn safe," I said, turning away from the spoon, tears coming to my eyes.

"Hush," Rose said. "You did keep him safe, for a long time. You couldn't have stopped what happened. Charles and I couldn't either."

"I'm happy Charles is alive," I said, cheering up a little.

"Yes," she said, but she looked sad.

Then I remembered something. It was when we were coming down the mountain and Charles was carrying me. I was awake for a little while, and I heard him saying something to Rose. Except he called her something else. Namm, or something like that.

"Why did he call you that funny name?" I asked.

She looked surprised. "You mean Nyamh?"

"*Oui*," I said. She offered me another spoonful of soup, but I shook my head. I was feeling tired and not hungry anymore.

"Estelle, Charles was hurt. His head was hurt," she said. "And it took away his memory. Some of it has come back. He remembers you, Estelle. And Winn. But he doesn't remember me. He doesn't know that I am Winn's mother."

I stared at her, in shock. At first I didn't understand what she was saying. But then I did. "That is *triste*, so sad for you, Rose."

"It is," she admitted. "But I am very grateful he is alive. One thing I need to ask of you, Estelle, is not to say anything to him. It is better for him to go on thinking of me as Nyamh."

I said I would do as she asked. Suddenly I was very tired and told Rose I wanted to go to sleep now. Rose helped me lie down and tucked the blankets around me.

She kissed me on the forehead, and I slept.

ROSE

A FTER STOPPING IN CHAMONIX to retrieve our horses, we headed to Calais. The journey took four days and was very taxing on Estelle, who was still weak from the snakebite. Ben guided us to his sister's home, and she turned out to be a cozy, warm woman named Berenice, who was thrilled to see her grumpy brother. She was welcoming to Estelle, making a big fuss over the exhausted girl.

As Ben had predicted, Berenice was happy to have Estelle stay with her. I told her I hoped it wouldn't be for too long, that either we'd be back or my brother Neddy would come for her.

Calais was a bustling port, and a larger town than I had ever been in. It wasn't difficult to find a ship heading to Skottland, and we booked passage on one leaving the next morning.

I composed two letters to Neddy, one to send on to Trondheim and the other to be held here in Calais in case he had received the message I sent from La Rochelle and decided to head straight to Calais, and then on to Mont Blanc.

Because we couldn't take them on the ship to Skottland,

we gave our horses to Berenice and Ben. I was very sad to part from my sweet-natured Ciuin, as was Charles to say goodbye to Valentina, but I was comforted to think they would have a good home.

We set off for the marketplace to buy provisions for the journey ahead. On our way there, I spotted the storefront of a craftsman who specialized in stonework. What caught my eye was an *echecs* set displayed in the window. The pieces appeared to be made of ivory. On an impulse, I told Charles I wanted to stop in the shop, that I would catch up with him at the marketplace. He agreed.

I was greeted by the proprietor, an older gentleman with a quiet manner. He asked what he could help me with. I reached into my pocket and pulled out the two *echecs* pieces—Queen Maraboo and the knight.

The proprietor of the shop smiled when he saw Queen Maraboo, but when he took the knight piece in his hand, his expression grew serious.

"This is very fine workmanship," he said. "How did you come by it?"

I blurted something out about it being the gift of a friend, blushing a little at the lie. But he didn't seem to notice my awkwardness and went back to inspecting it.

"Yes, it is very much like the work of an unknown craftsman who carved *echecs* sets back in the eleven hundreds. It is very fine indeed."

"Is it perhaps from an island in the Western Sea called Morae?" I asked hopefully.

He shook his head. "In truth, I don't know. And I have never heard of such an isle."

I nodded, discouraged, then on an impulse, drew the key out of my pocket.

"I was wondering," I said tentatively, "if you could tell me anything at all about this. It is a key, I think."

He nodded, but I noticed that he flinched a little when he took the key into his callused hands. A frown wrinkled his forehead.

"Yes, it seems to be a key, very small, though . . ." He looked up at me, a strange glint in his eye. "Do you know what it is made of?"

"I thought it to be ivory," I said. "Perhaps walrus tusk?"

He shook his head. "No, it is not ivory. It is bone."

"Bone?"

"Yes," he said, and he set it down and pushed it toward me. "It has the feel of human bone about it. I do not like it."

I stared down at the key. Human bone? I shivered.

I could see he was unsettled by the key, so I took it back and thrust it into my pocket again.

"Thank you for your help," I said. And I left.

It was difficult saying goodbye to Estelle, but I had confidence in Ben and his sister, and Estelle was clearly still too weak to travel. She had gotten very attached to Pip and told me that when we were all back at home, she wanted a puppy of her own, just like Pip. I promised we would try to find one for her.

Charles and I were much together on the ship, and it was a companionable time.

As long as we stayed in the present, it was easy between us. We both accepted that, and it became habit.

I spent some of the time on board ship mending my cloak. Thanks to the Blood Rain, the scorching breath of the dragon, and being buried by an avalanche, it was even more tattered than when I had left for Etretat so many weeks ago. Father's wind rose design was getting harder and harder to make out, but I still loved it well. And I had a strong superstitious feeling about the cloak because, after all, it had gotten me this far.

When I was up on deck, I also tried listening to the winds. I thought I could hear bits of melody here and there, and wished Sib were there with me, to help me make sense of them. I missed Sib and Neddy and the rest of my family. I hoped they were well and safe in Trondheim.

NEDDY

WHEN WE ARRIVED IN CALAIS, I received the letter from Rose. She told me briefly what had befallen, that she and Charles had gone to Skottland in search of Winn, and that Estelle was at the home of a woman named Berenice, with directions on how to find her.

"What is the news, Neddy?" asked Sib, who had watched me read the letter.

"Rose and Charles have gone to Skottland. To the Western Isles."

Sib made a small sound. I glanced at her and thought she looked pale.

"How long ago did they leave?" she asked.

"I'm not sure. I think perhaps a week ago," I said.

We found the home of Berenice with ease and were overjoyed to see Estelle. She looked pale but assured us she was much better. She introduced us to Ben and his dog, Pip. She said too that there was a mule named Molly out back who was *très jolie.*

Sib and I decided to take Estelle into Calais for a treat. Apparently Berenice had introduced her to her own favorite *boulangerie.* While Estelle was making up her mind among all the delicious cakes and pastries, I pulled Sib aside.

"We must go after Rose and Charles," I said.

Sib agreed.

"But it doesn't seem right to drag Estelle along on what could be a dangerous journey," I went on.

"I know," said Sib, "but I believe she is well enough to travel."

We had been so absorbed in our conversation that we hadn't noticed Estelle inching quietly closer.

"I will go with you!" she announced. "I am better now. And Rose said I did a good job of watching over Winn. I want to help find him."

"It is a long sea journey," I said.

I could see the mixed feelings cross her face. Clearly she was remembering the terrible seasickness she had experienced on the passage from Fransk to Trondheim. But abruptly her expression cleared.

"I don't care about the *mal de mer.* I will go," she repeated, her jaw set.

Sib and I exchanged looks. I could not think of any other alternative than to take Estelle with us. We would just have to make sure she was kept out of harm's way.

Rose had said they were going to Leodhas, an isle in the Western Sea, and from there were seeking another isle called Morae. I consulted with the captain of Soren's ship, and he said the main port on Leodhas was a town called Stornoway. He knew of no island called Morae.

"Then we will start in Stornoway," I said.

Estelle was especially sad when it came to parting from Pip and Molly, and I thought I saw tears in the old mountain man's eyes when he bid the Fransk girl a gruff farewell. I made sure they were compensated for taking care of Estelle, even though Ben initially refused any payment.

After replenishing the ship's supplies, we set off for Leodhas.

ROSE

S TORNOWAY WAS ON THE EASTERN COAST of Leodhas, so we hired a cart to take us across the island to Garenin, a town on the west coast. We asked everyone we met on our journey about an isle called Morae, but no one had heard of it. By the time we got to Garenin, we were both tired and discouraged.

Charles suggested that we could use a good meal, so we found the one inn in the small town that served lunch.

We were soon seated at a table. Neither of us felt much like talking. We just sat there glumly and ate the watery onion beef soup we were served, along with some dry brown bread.

"You two look as though you have lost your last farthing," came a voice beside me. I turned to see an older woman wearing a blue scarf, drinking a flagon of ale.

"Something like that," I said.

"Or perhaps a difficult road lies ahead?" she asked, glancing at our swords.

"Yes," I said again. "Or, rather, a difficult task."

"Ah, like making a rope out of ashes," the old woman said.

I flinched. I had had enough of ashes to last me a lifetime.

"Very much like that," said Charles, with a friendly smile.

The woman chuckled.

"I don't suppose you know of a place called Morae around here?" I asked.

"No, no place by that name," she replied. "Unless you're taking about the old tale of the Three Weavers of Mora?"

"I might be," I said, coming alert. Charles, too, leaned closer.

"Aye, it is said there was a wee magic island that lay far off the west coast of Leodhas. In the old tales, it was inhabited by three weavers, who would tell your fortune and grant wishes. The weavers were called the Morae."

"And is there such an island?" I asked.

The woman laughed. "No, dearie. Just in the old tales. If such an isle truly existed, 'twould be a barren, desolate place, fit only for seabirds."

The Three Weavers of Mora. An *echecs* set from the Morae. It couldn't be a coincidence.

"How far was this island said to be from Leodhas?" Charles asked.

"Ah, many leagues, a hundred or more. But there isn't such a place. And if there was, you couldn't land a boat there, according to the old stories."

"Why not?" I queried.

"Protected by a fearsome whirlpool, it is. Like the Corryvreckan, down by Jura, only worse." She went on at some length about the deadly whirlpool surrounding an island she kept insisting didn't exist.

And all I could think about was where we could find a boat to get ourselves there.

NEDDY

EVER SINCE WE HAD MADE THE DECISION to chart our course for Skottland, something in Sib had changed.

She was distant and quiet. She seemed to either prefer to be alone or else with Estelle, who initially had been having a hard time with her seasickness.

I tried to talk to Sib, but she always found an excuse to slip away, usually to be with Estelle. It made me uneasy. I began to worry that our newfound happiness was more uncertain than I had thought.

I was also distracted by a series of events that slowed our progress. First, there was a spell of very bad weather, with winds that drove us off course. Poor Estelle suffered mightily.

And then once the bad weather passed, we had two crew members come down with sickness, not the Sweating Sickness thankfully, but one that involved painful rashes and fever, and which Sib said could be quite contagious, so we had to take a detour to the port of Aberdeen to drop them off. I told them that we would likely be back for them after our journey to Skottland, but I also left them enough gold coins so that they could make their own way back to Njord if for some reason we were diverted or detained.

As a result of these delays, I calculated that we were at least two weeks behind Rose and Charles.

ROSE

T HE CURRACH REMINDED ME of the *kyak* in which Malmo
and I traveled along the coastline of Gronland up to
Tatke Fjord, except that it was larger and it had a small sail
one could use to catch the wind. There were paddles, too, to
use if there was no wind.

It was the woman back at the inn who had directed us to
the boatman, although when I asked where we could find a
currach to rent or buy, she looked at me as if I was deranged.

"You'll not be after trying to find the Weavers of Mora?"
she asked in some alarm.

"Of course not," I said, with a laugh. I went on to make up
a story about how we wanted to do some fishing while we were
in Leodhas.

I'm not sure if she believed me, but she directed us to a
boatman called Macdeag down near the harbor. When we
took our leave, I thanked her and, just before walking away,
she called to me, "If you find a way to make that rope of ashes,
you be sure to come back and tell me the tale."

"We will," Charles said with a smile.

The man Macdeag was willing to rent us a currach for a

reasonable price and didn't seem to mind that we couldn't tell him when we'd be returning it.

There was little wind, and the day was mild. We had provisions enough to last us six days on the water. If we had not found this mythical island in three or four days, we would need to turn back.

At twilight of our first day on the water, Charles suddenly said to me, "Nyamh, if we ever do reach this island of the Morae, what do you think we will find there?"

"I think we will find ou . . . your bairn," I tripped over the word, catching myself just in time. "And the Troll Queen." I shivered, remembering the invisible hands around my throat.

He must have sensed my feeling, because he replied in an encouraging tone, "We have our swords. You have the wind sword."

I had told him of my encounter with the queen when she was a dragon and how I injured her by throwing the sword through the air.

I gave a short laugh. "Somehow I don't think that I'm going to get away with just flinging it at her again."

"No, perhaps not," he answered.

I almost made a joke about how maybe I could wash another shirt, but caught myself in time, realizing he would have no idea what I was talking about.

"Anyway," I said, "I am glad it is the two of us."

"So am I," he replied in a quiet voice.

I smiled, then blushed, looking down.

The weather stayed fair. A light rain fell on the afternoon of the second day, but not enough to require us to bail.

By the third day, we began to get discouraged. The horizon of sea and sky stretched ahead, unbroken by any sign of land. We agreed, one more day. But one day turned into two, then three.

At the beginning of the sixth day, we knew we must turn back. We had already gone too far. Despite being very sparing in what we ate, we knew our provisions wouldn't last us the journey home.

But just when we were on the verge of turning back, I heard a dull roaring sound. Charles heard it too, and the farther west we traveled, the louder it became.

Finally I saw it. An outcropping of land, a dark gray mound rising above the sea.

The sea was getting choppier.

"The whirlpool?" Charles asked, and I nodded, uneasy.

The noise grew louder and louder, and it became harder to paddle, to control the small currach. It was moving fast through the increasingly turbulent waves.

My heart was pounding, and I gripped the paddle tightly. Charles and I exchanged tense glances.

I peered through the spray sent up by the waves, trying to

get a clear view of the island we were fast approaching. There was a low mist over the isle, so it was hard to make out any details, if there were any buildings or trees on it.

The currach was suddenly rocked by a particularly large wave. As we rode it to the top, we saw we were on the very lip of a vast, churning whirlpool.

I let out a cry, paddling backwards as hard as I could, but it was too late. We were caught in the swirling waves and seemed to be on the verge of being sucked downward into the seething maw of water.

The paddle was snatched out of my hands, and the currach began to spin around faster and faster.

All at once, an extraordinary thing happened. It seemed almost as if the waves became a fist that grabbed the currach, raising it up, swirling it around, and tossing it high in the air.

I landed with a crash on a hard surface, and everything went dark for a few seconds.

When I opened my eyes and blinked, I saw that I was lying on a rocky shore. The currach was a few arm's lengths away, and one side of it was smashed in. My head hurt, and my thoughts were fuzzy. I reached up and found that I was bleeding from the right side of my forehead.

And then I realized. I was alone. There was no sign of Charles.

BOOK FOUR

NORD

Wind and water will my witchcraft lull, then fearlessly fare thou forth.
—The Edda

ESTELLE

THE *MAL DE MER* WAS HORRIBLE, worse than I remembered. Like the last time, I was sure I was going to die. Tante Sib said it was partly because of the stormy weather.

And it is true that after a few days, the weather calmed and I didn't feel quite as bad. Tante Sib made me eat biscuits and drink water and suggested I come up on deck with her. At first I said no, shuddering at the thought of looking at all that water, but she insisted, saying the fresh air would do me good.

I didn't feel better right away, but Tante Sib told me to pay attention to the wind on my face, telling me it had a name. I had never heard that winds had names except north, south, east, and west. But she told me there were many different winds, and she started naming them.

The names were so magical, along with the stories that went with them, that I forgot all about feeling sick. Tante Sib said that next time she would tell me about wind music.

After that I felt fine, no *mal de mer* at all, and Oncle Neddy teased Tante Sib about my miraculous cure. She laughed and said that the wind could do all sorts of wonderful things.

I was very grateful to Tante Sib. But I also started to be

worried about her. Once the ship got closer to Skottland, she seemed sad. Different. Except for talking to me about the wind, she didn't talk much at all. I would find her at the railing looking out at the coast of Skottland in the distance, and she looked very unhappy.

I asked her if she had the *mal de mer* now. And she laughed a little, saying no.

"But why do you look so sad?" I asked.

"Do I?" she asked, a little surprised.

"Yes, you do," I said.

She was quiet a few moments, before turning to me, her face serious.

"Don't tell Oncle Neddy this, Estelle," she said, "but it has to do with coming back to Skottland. It is the first time in so long. And not all my memories here are good ones."

"What happened to you in Skottland?" I asked.

"I'm afraid I can't talk about it, Estelle," she said, "but please don't worry. I will do my best to be happier. I have a few favorite winds here in Skottland that always cheer me up."

ROSE

I STOOD UP, SWAYING. I stumbled over to the currach and saw that miraculously both my pack and Charles's, along with our swords, were still nestled in the bottom of the boat.

I pulled my pack out and found a cloth, which I pressed against my forehead. It came away soaked with blood, so I kept it there, applying pressure. Depending on how deep the cut was, I was going to have a whole map of scars on my face.

I stared out at the roiling whirlpool that had just spit me up on shore, looking desperately for some sign of Charles. It seemed impossible that I stood here, still alive, not chewed up into little pieces by that deafening morass, and I shuddered to think that Charles might have been sucked down into it.

I gazed out beyond the maelstrom, searching the horizon. Perhaps Charles had been thrown out of the whirlpool the way I had, in a different direction. But I saw nothing.

I stood there for some time, pressing the cloth to my head. Then I turned and looked at the land I was on. It was a small island, though not as small as I'd initially thought. The thin mist still hovered over it, but I could clearly see a building not far inland.

I had to believe Charles was not dead, that he had some-how escaped the whirlpool. And I knew that he would want me to continue on, to find his son, *our* son.

Leaving Charles's pack and sword in the wrecked currach, I hoisted my pack with the wind sword inside onto my back, and still holding the cloth to my forehead, I started toward the building.

White Bear

WHEN WE HIT THE WHIRLPOOL, it had felt like I was soaring, like a red ball being tossed high into the air. And then I plummeted down, landing hard in cold water. I sank deep beneath the waves, and instinctively pushed myself up, kicking hard with my legs.

I surfaced with a gasp and, seeing a floating piece of wood, which turned out to be one of the currach paddles, I grabbed hold of it. I floated there, getting my breath back.

I looked around and was stunned to see no sign of the island, the whirlpool, the currach, and most importantly, Nyamh. As far as I could see, I was a speck in the midst of a vast open sea.

I looked up and saw the sky was rapidly filling with clouds, dark and ominous. A storm was very close.

ROSE

THE BUILDING LOOKED LIKE A BLACKHOUSE, which I had been told was a common sight in the Western Isles of Skottland. It had thick stone walls and was thatched with a combination of tar and turf.

As I approached the entrance, I slowed. I lowered the cloth from my forehead for a moment and found the bleeding had mostly stopped. I stowed the cloth in my pocket, feeling as I did so for the key Urda had given me. I took a deep breath and walked up to the door.

But there was no lock on the door, nor even a handle, so I pushed on it, and the door swung open easily. I entered.

The light was dim at first, and I held out a hand so I wouldn't bump into anything.

"I win!" called out a silvery voice.

"Ah, but you helped," said another voice, which was also lovely but slightly deeper. "With the whirlpool."

"Only a little," came the first voice, with a high-pitched, melodic laugh at the end.

I peered into the gloom, and as I did, the light brightened

and I could see where I was. It was a large room, very similar to our great room back in Trondheim, with simple furnishings and a hearth at one end. There were many candles, on tables and in wall sconces, which now flickered brightly.

Sitting at a long table, much like the table where my family ate their evening meal, were three women. I stared at them, blinking my eyes a few times, not quite believing what I was seeing. For the three women were exactly identical. Each had smooth, pale skin and pale hair. I had thought Sib's hair to be pale, but the hair of these three women was paler still, almost transparent, as though you should be able to see through it and yet you couldn't. Their eyes were pale too; from a distance, they appeared to be all white, which gave me a shuddery feeling, but as I drew closer, I saw that their irises were translucent, the color of uncooked egg whites.

They watched me, silent now after that first exchange. I gazed around the room and saw the tools of weaving and sewing—spinning wheels, distaffs, baskets of many colors of wool and thread, among other things.

The Three Weavers of Mora.

Something at the back of the room caught my eye. It was an enormous loom that took up the entire wall, and in it was an equally enormous tapestry, which was clearly in the process of being woven.

"Look, she's bleeding!" came the higher lilting voice, and I saw that it belonged to the woman seated on the far right of the table.

I reached up and felt a trickle of blood coming from the cut on my forehead. I found the cloth in my pocket and pressed it to the wound again.

"Come, sit," said the second voice I had heard, which came from the woman in the middle. She gestured at a chair on the other side of the table from them.

"I am Uror," she said. "This is Verendi"—she gestured at the one with the high voice—"and this is Skuld." The third woman gazed at me, unspeaking and unsmiling. I had not heard her voice yet.

"I am Rose," I said.

"Yes, we know," said Verendi, and she laughed again. "We have been looking forward to meeting you. Or at least I have. Uror didn't believe you would make it this far, and Skuld—"

"I had my doubts," Uror interrupted. "But I always knew it was possible."

"You must be hungry!" said Verendi. And she went to the hearth and pulled a loaf of bread from the fire, steam rising off its surface.

"I hope you feel comfortable here. We tried to make it homey and familiar for you. Of course what we are seeing is a bit different from what you see," said Verendi.

And suddenly I was looking at a lush grotto and the three

women were seated in purple velvet chairs pulled up to a gleaming white marble table. Impossibly bright birds darted here and there. The enormous loom with the weaving in it was the same, though it hung between two white marble pillars.

Then just as swiftly, the grotto was gone and the room was as it had been, like my family's great room in Trondheim. I blinked.

"Uh, yes," I said. "It is very homey."

Verendi was now standing at the wooden table, cutting slices of warm bread, one of which she set on a plate, along with grapes and a hunk of yellow cheese. The sight of the food made me feel weak. We had been very sparing with our provisions the past few days in the currach.

Verendi came to me with the plate and was about to hand it to me, but stopped, saying, "Oh, but first . . ."

She lifted her forefinger and ran it over the wound on my forehead. I flinched as her finger approached, but found that instead of hurting, her touch felt warm and comforting, no pain at all.

"There," she said. "All better."

And I reached up and touched where I thought the wound was, but felt nothing, only smooth skin.

"I'm afraid I can't do anything about the other," she said, pointing to my snakebite. "It's already mostly healed."

She handed me the plate, and as I took it, I noticed that part of one of her fingers was missing, the first finger of her left hand went only to the first knuckle. She poured me a cup of an amber-colored drink and handed that to me as well.

The bread was melting soft, the cheese perfectly sour and sweet all at once, and I drank deeply of what turned out to be a fragrant peach-tasting wine. As I ate, my eyes fell on an *echecs* set. It was placed on a table up against the left wall of the room. At a distance, it looked very similar to the one in the Troll Queen's throne room.

"Yes," said Verendi, breaking into my thoughts, which was unnerving to say the least. "That *echecs* set is very like the one the pale queen had. But this is the original. It washed onto our isle about three, or was it four, hundred years ago?" She looked at the other two.

"Three," said Uror.

"Yes, three. And there were several sets. They came in these boxes." She hopped up and showed me one of a few boxes. It was a polished light-colored wood and carved with images of a beast with a ribbon-shaped body and paws that gripped the edges of the box.

"At any rate, we took a fancy to them. So we used our arts to give them power. It makes *echecs* games more amusing, especially for Skuld. When the queen came to find us the first time, we gave her one of the queen pieces. It seemed fitting, you know."

"And when she returned," Uror said, "we gave her a second queen, from one of our other sets."

"That's right," said Verendi. "And with her arts, she made complete sets to go with them."

I looked at the box and the *echecs* set blankly. Two queens. I knew of only the one queen, the one I threw in the fireplace at the top of Mont Blanc.

"It was clever of you to throw it into the fire," said Verendi.

I stared into her pale eyes.

"You're confusing her," said Uror.

"So the Troll Queen came here?" I asked, wanting to understand.

"Oh yes, I thought you knew that already," said Verendi. "She found us, just as you did. And she had a great anger in her, but underneath the anger was a great love."

"Verendi has always had a soft spot for great loves," explained Uror. "Which has been known to cause difficulties."

"You always say that, but I—"

"The Trojan War?" stated Uror.

"All right, yes," said Verendi with the air of one on the losing side of an oft-repeated argument. "Perhaps the Trojan War was a mistake," she added, looking regretful for a moment. But she laughed her sweet laugh.

Uror just shook her head. I noticed as she did so that there was something different about her left eye, a greenish silver glint, almost as if she had a sliver of green glass in the corner of her pale iris.

"This one has no power at all," said the third woman

abruptly, the one called Skuld. Her voice was the deepest of the three, but it was lovely, too, like the sound made by a musical instrument that Charles had once shown me, a basso he had called it.

"We knew that," said Uror.

"Why is she here, then?" asked Skuld.

"It seemed only fair," said Verendi. "You agreed at the time."

Skuld just shook her head, still unsmiling.

"Why did the Troll Queen come to you?" I asked.

"Ah, revenge mostly," answered Uror. "And normally we don't interest ourselves in revenge. But we were bored that day, and Verendi kept going on about the great and beautiful love that burned underneath the anger. She convinced us."

"Convinced you to do what?"

"To give her the first queen," Uror said with a hint of impatience. "And just a small bit of our arts, to augment hers."

"She had been badly hurt, you know," Verendi chimed in. "In body and in spirit. Her arts, too, had suffered."

"I see," I said, though I didn't really. And suddenly I was angry. "So she fashioned a chess set," I said, "and when she played with it, hundreds, perhaps thousands, of people died." I tried to keep my voice neutral, but anger was making my voice brittle.

Uror gazed at me steadily. "We are of the old class of gods, you know. Capricious," she added with a faint smile.

"And what of Aagnorak?" I said. I was shaking now.

"Oh, yes," chimed in Verendi, "there is that. Still a good possibility, I believe."

"You would let that happen? You would allow all the human beings on earth to perish?"

"Occasionally you humans need a sweeping out," said Skuld, implacable.

"That is true, Skuld," said Uror. "But the answer to your question is maybe yes, maybe no. Verendi and I think it is too early. Besides, we aren't terribly keen on trolls ruling the world. Humans are messy, but infinitely more entertaining."

"Trolls aren't really all that powerful, you know," said Verendi. "They are just better than you humans at finding power and using it. Like the sun."

"And us," added Uror.

I stared at them, not able to speak, a chill running through me. They were monstrous, perhaps even more so than the Troll Queen.

"Can we send her away now?" said Skuld. "She is becoming tiresome."

Verendi laughed. "But don't you see?" she said earnestly to the other two, almost as if I wasn't there. "This short, ungainly, rather dirty girl with her squat body and purple eyes may have an even deeper love than the Troll Queen. That is her power."

Skuld made a grating sound like the bow struck hard on a basso string. It could have been a laugh, a derisive laugh.

"I don't understand," I said.

"Did you not journey to Niflheim, or as you and the white bear called it, 'the land that lies east of the sun and west of the moon'? I always thought that sounded so pretty," said Verendi with a happy sigh.

"That was just to make things right, because of the candle —"

"But you crossed the Ice Bridge on your own two feet, the only human to have done so, as far as we know."

"Yes, but —" I started.

"And what about this journey? Why did you come here, to this isle of the Morae?"

"I am looking for my bairn."

"The child born of the love between you and the white bear. You see, that's the mountain-moving, death-defying true love I was talking about," Verendi trilled triumphantly.

"To be accurate, she has never actually moved a mountain," Uror said.

"No, but she helped set one on fire," said Verendi. "And she bested the ash dragon with her wind sword! Not even the Valkyries did that."

I was getting frustrated with these women, with their pale hair and pale eyes and musical voices, calmly talking about me as if I wasn't there.

"You said you gave the pale queen a second *echecs* queen? Recently?"

"Yes," said Uror. "That's when we learned you had bested

her with the wind sword. That was a lucky find, by the way. And when she came this time, Skuld was in a mood to be disruptive. She finds the idea of Aagnorak entertaining," Uror observed with a shrug. "So we gave the Troll Queen the second queen and a bit more of our arts."

"Where is she now?" I asked, my voice shrill.

Verendi suddenly raised her head and said, "Hold!" And she gracefully ran over to one of the windows of the blackhouse.

She stood there, staring out, looking as if she was listening for something.

"Verendi," said Uror in a warning voice.

But Verendi ignored her. Her body went rigid for just a few seconds, then relaxed. She turned around and made her way back to the table, a dreamy smile on her face. "Speaking of true love," she said.

"You are meddling again," said Uror.

And I don't know what put the thought in my head, but I blurted out, "Do you know what has happened to Charles?"

"Funny you should ask," said Verendi. "There was some very bad weather, but he is safe now."

"Then he is alive?" I asked.

Verendi gave her melodic laugh. "Oh, yes, he's alive!" she said.

"You are impossible," muttered Skuld to Verendi.

I looked back and forth between them.

Uror spoke up. "You should know that one thing we have in common with the trolls is that we like games." She gestured at the *echecs* set.

"We always have," agreed Verendi.

My heart sank. Was I to play another losing game of *echecs*?

"Therefore," Uror said, breaking into my thoughts, "we have an agreement with the pale queen that in exchange for giving her the second queen, if you were in fact to turn up on our isle, we would arrange for there to be a task, three tasks actually—"

"Three is our favorite number," said Verendi.

"And if you accomplish these tasks, we will tell you where to find your son. And the queen," finished Uror.

"Who will undoubtedly kill you, and then she will set off Aagnorak," said Skuld. She stood and moved to the *echecs* board. As she moved, I noticed that there was something protruding from the folds of the back of her gown. It moved slightly, and I realized what it was. A tail. Like that of a large cat, long and white and soft-looking.

So it wasn't only their voices that were different. Each had another characteristic that set them apart—the missing half finger of Verendi, the green eye of Uror, and Skuld's tail.

"Oh, Skuld, you are always so sour," trilled Verendi.

"Tell her the tasks," Skuld said, "so we can return to our game." She stood over the *echecs* board, studying it.

"You are a weaver, like us," said Verendi to me.

I watched her pale eyes with a sense of unreality, like I was in a dream or, rather, listening sleepily to one of the old tales Neddy used to tell me as a child at bedtime.

"What am I to weave?" I asked.

"Three cloaks. One made of fire. One made of water. And one made of the wind."

Of course. Impossible, all three. But all I said was "You will supply me with the materials I need?"

Verendi laughed. "Of course. At least, you shall have a place to work, a loom, and all the wool and thread you should require."

"Very well. Show me the loom."

WHITE BEAR

THE STORM CAME UP FAST AND FIERCE. Soon waves the size of houses were coming at me in quick succession, tossing me high, then dropping me low. I clung to the ridiculously puny paddle as if it somehow made a difference, and perhaps it did, at least at first.

I think the buried white bear in me kept me going, too, for a time, but I was tiring, losing strength.

A particularly large wave knocked me down, driving me deep underwater, and it took too long to find the surface. I sputtered, my chest heaving, and realized I had lost my paddle. I saw an enormous wave heading toward me and knew that I wouldn't be able to survive it. I was too weak.

And suddenly an odd sensation took hold of my body. I felt like I was being stretched and torn. Pain shot through me, and it wasn't from the wave.

When the wave crashed down on me, I glided through it with ease, my arms and legs powerful. I didn't know where the surge of energy had come from, but I was relieved. It didn't matter about the paddle anymore. I was somehow buoyant on my own and able to ride the waves much more efficiently. It was even exhilarating.

I was conscious too of feeling immensely hungry.

Gradually the storm died down and I could think straight. Something strange and miraculous had happened, but it was also something that felt like it had happened before. It felt familiar.

I reached forward with my arm, and I immediately saw that my arm was not an arm. It was a paw with white fur and black claws.

I knew then. I was no longer a man. I was a white bear. Again.

NEDDY

W E WERE STILL IN ABERDEEN, having gotten our two ill crew members situated with a local healing woman. We were due to leave that morning, and I was up early, conferring with the captain about the route to Leodhas. All of a sudden, Estelle came running up to me.

"Oncle Neddy," she cried, "I think Sib is leaving us!"

She looked upset.

"What do you mean?" I asked.

And she said that she had been worried about Sib, who had been acting sad and *étrange*. "Last night she told me to be a brave girl and to remember what she had said about the winds. I woke up early this morning, and she was gone. There was a note, addressed to you, left on her bunk. I ran out to look for her, and I thought I saw her leaving the ship."

My heart sank. I had been worried about Sib but hadn't been able to find out what was troubling her.

Estelle handed me the note.

"Thank you," I said, and tore it open in haste. The note wasn't long, and it immediately became clear it was one of farewell.

"Which direction was she going?" I asked Estelle.

"When she left the ship, she went right. That is north, I think. Up the harbor."

I raced off the ship and headed north. There were a handful of vessels docked in that part of the harbor.

I thought I spied Sib's silver hair near one of the ships that was farthest away. I ran faster.

"Sib!" I called.

She turned, an anguished look on her face.

"No, Neddy," she said.

I grabbed her arm.

"Why?" I asked.

"It is in the note."

"No, it isn't. All that is there is goodbye. Tell me." I was angry now. I knew she loved me, she had said so, and I was sure it hadn't been just to keep me from dying.

"Neddy, there are things in my past, I told Rose this, things that make it impossible for me to marry. It wouldn't be fair to you . . ."

I was baffled. "There is nothing that would change how I feel about you, Sib."

"I know that. Nor I you. But—"

"Why now?"

"It is being here," she said. "In Skottland. It is where . . . Painful memories."

"Tell them to me, Sib."

"No."

"What about Rose? Would you leave her and Charles and Winn?"

I could see her hesitate.

"Come back, Sib. I won't press you. If you cannot be with me, I will accept that. But don't sail off to . . ." I stopped, at a loss, gazing up at the ship before us.

"Saint Petersburg," she said, a little embarrassed. "It seemed as far away as I could get."

I shook my head. "Come back," I repeated. "Rose needs you."

She nodded and put her arm through mine. We made our way back to the ship.

ROSE

I T WAS VERENDI WHO LED ME OUTSIDE to a small building
behind theirs. I hadn't noticed it before, but possibly it had
not been there before.

Verendi ushered me through the door. "As I said, you shall
have everything you need, for as long as it takes, and that
includes food and drink, which will replenish itself, so no
need to worry about going hungry. Also, there are three hooks
for you to hang the cloaks on once you are finished," she said,
pointing to an evenly spaced row of gleaming golden hooks
on the wall near the door. "You are free to go outside. But I
would not recommend you come back to our house to ask for
anything more. We will just say no, and it might annoy Skuld."

She gave one of her sweet laughs, wished me luck, and
turned to leave.

But she spun back around. "One last thing about the three
cloaks. In order to pass the test, you must be able to actually
wear each one."

She gave me a little wave and started out the door, but
stopped and turned toward me once again, more deliberately

this time. Her face wore an uncharacteristically serious expression. "I thought I should tell you, dear Rose, that there is a bit of a time pinch. That is, you don't have all the time in the world. The pale queen is doing her own brand of weaving. With her arts. Preparing for Aagnorak. So you mustn't dawdle," Verendi said, and she couldn't resist a little laugh. Then she was gone, her silvery laughter hanging in the air.

So. A weaving time limit. With no less than the fate of the world resting on the outcome. Perfect.

I turned and looked around the room.

Like all things with the Morae, I wasn't sure if what I was seeing was real or not, but the room I found myself in was very similar to my workroom back in Fransk, in the home I had shared with Charles. Of course it didn't really matter if it was real or not, as long as the loom worked and the food filled my belly.

The only thing that did matter now was to find a way to accomplish the tasks they had set me.

As I inspected the materials that were neatly stored on shelves, I knew it was unlikely that I would find a spool of fine thread made of water, a skein of wool made of fire, or a measure of silk made of air. So I would have to figure out another way to weave cloaks of those three materials.

I turned my attention to the loom. It was a beauty, not unlike my favorite loom in the castle in the mountain.

I remembered the dresses of gold, silver, and moon thread I had made on it and wondered if the Morae somehow knew of these. They seemed to know most everything. I also remembered the three spools of thread I had taken away with me from the castle in the mountain, and that I still carried with me. How extraordinary that their colors almost coincided with the colors of these three cloaks I must make. I wondered if it truly was a coincidence. Perhaps it was fate. Or maybe Verendi had found this little way of helping me, in the name of true love.

But I knew I could not get away with merely using thread the colors of flame and seawater and air. The cloaks must be made of actual fire, water, and wind.

Indeed the tasks that lay before me reminded me of finding a land that lay east of the sun and west of the moon, which, no matter how poetic and lovely it sounded, was basically the equivalent of making a rope of ashes. It was nowhere. A place that didn't exist, as I had discovered. I had found Niflheim with help from Thor, and even more, from Malmo. I had no one to help me now.

My mind was blank. It was not possible. None of it was possible. Fire, water, wind. These were the stuff of life, not the material for clothing. I could not build a fire and somehow spin the flames into thread.

I sat down at a broad wooden table, my hand pressed

against my forehead, willing my brain to work. Fire, flame, light. Oil lamps, candles.

Candle!

I jumped to my feet and crossed again to my pack. I quickly found the candle, the one my mother had given me so long ago, the troll candle that had ruined everything. Maybe now . . . ?

Taking the vivid red thread from the castle in the mountain and a spool of a dark orange from the supplies in the house, I sat down at the loom and began casting on. It didn't take long before I was ready, and I began to weave, my fingers flying.

I lost track of time as I always did when I was at the loom. It felt good to be there. I hadn't done any weaving since I'd left home for Trondheim, which felt like a lifetime ago.

The dark orange wool I had chosen was thick and porous, and it blended perfectly with the red. It did not feel like it took a long time before I had woven enough cloth for a cloak.

I cut and sewed, and when it was done, I laid the cloak on the worktable.

I found a small cooking pan, and taking it and the candle, I crossed to the hearth fire, which burned as strongly and steadily as it had since I entered the room.

Methodically, I shaved off pieces of the candle and dropped them into the pan, over and over, until the candle was reduced to a large heap of wax parings.

I set the pan in the fire and watched as the wax slowly melted. I stirred it with a stick until it was completely molten. I carried the pan to the table and, using a long, thin needle to guide me, drizzled candle wax in very fine lines up and down the outside of the cloak, working it into the fabric with my fingers. The hot wax burned my fingertips, but it cooled quickly. I had to return the pan to the fire several times during the process to remelt the wax.

I wasn't sure there would be enough wax to fill the entire cloak, but by apportioning it prudently, I managed to cover most of it.

But I wasn't done. Verendi had told me I was free to move about the island and so, carrying the small pan, I opened the door and went outside. When we had walked from the Morae's blackhouse to the one I was in now, I had noticed a small outcropping of dwarf pine trees a short distance away. I moved among them and, using my dagger, gathered the amber-colored resin and sap that collected in broken knots and fractures of the tree limbs and trunks. I dug and scraped until my small pan was full.

I returned to the house and, as I had done with the candle shavings, placed the pan on the fire. It smoked heavily while I stirred it, but soon I had a pan full of viscous melted pitch. I carried it over to the worktable and, using the stick, laced the pitch throughout the material, making sure to cover spots where there was little wax. When the pan was empty, I returned to the loom and wove material for another cloak, this one made of a dense wool, all black.

Satisfied with my work, I hung both cloaks on one of the three hooks that Verendi had pointed out to me when she showed me my workspace.

Fire. Done. Now to water.

WHITE BEAR

I had been swimming.
A long time.
Such a deep hunger
I ate fish, whole and raw.

I was a white bear again.
Familiar,
like a nightmare,
one that recurs,
over and over.

I remembered well
the struggle
between man and animal.

I needed to hold on to the man.
Everything depended on it.
But it was not easy.

 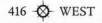

I would have died by now,
had I been a man.
But I was a white bear, strong,
a sure, graceful swimmer.
I could catch fish
(even though I longed for seal!)
and eat them raw.
But the hunger was constant.
Insatiable.

Keep swimming.
Find the lady Nyamh.
And my son.
I must find my son,
save him from the one
who had taken so much already.
The Troll Queen.

ROSE

AFTER EATING BREAD AND CHEESE and meat and washing it down with pear cider from a jug, I went outside, this time taking a large basket with me. I headed down to the shoreline and began walking along it. Immediately I saw what I was looking for and began collecting long tendrils of seaweed. I stowed them carefully in the basket. Every so often, I would spot a seashell in the shape I liked and would scoop that up as well.

When my basket was full, I returned to the blackhouse and emptied it out. I made many such scavenging trips, and the sun had set by the time I was done.

One day gone. I tried to push away thoughts of the Troll Queen and Aagnorak. I needed to concentrate on completing my task.

I had collected one particular type of seaweed. It had long strands with a striking variety of coloration, ranging from purple to yellow to orange to green, and there were clusters of pods along each vine.

I didn't use the loom for this cloak. Instead, I gently laid the long strands of seaweed on the worktable and began to weave them together by hand, going up and over, down and through. It was almost like weaving a basket, except that the material was much more fragile and I had to be very careful and delicate as I worked. And I deliberately wove it so that there were long loops of the seaweed hanging at regular intervals.

I tried to keep the pods intact, but occasionally they would burst open with a watery pop, and often a little phosphorescent sea worm would wriggle out. I left them there in the strands.

I wove in sections and, using the blue-purple thread from the castle in the mountain, bound the sections together. I trimmed as I went so that the edges were uniform.

When I had roughly the shape of a cloak, I took the small shells I had collected and painstakingly made tiny holes in each one with a sharp needle. I sewed them onto the cloak in a wavelike pattern. Then I fashioned ties at the neck with another kind of seaweed, one that was sturdy and pliant.

It was laborious, time-consuming work, though as usual I lost track of time and only my rumbling belly reminded me that I must stop and eat.

But finally I was done.

I held it up and gazed upon my creation. It was beautiful, I decided, with its rippling, glistening texture and all those luminous colors. The shells made satisfying little rhythmic sounds when I moved the material.

I hung the seaweed cloak on the second hook.

Two days gone. Or was it three? My breath went shallow for a moment as I thought about the time slipping away. Aagnorak. Winn.

Steadying myself, I deliberately turned my thoughts to the wind. How I wished I had Sib with me. With all her knowledge of the wind, I was sure she would be able to solve this task.

I cast my mind back to what she had told me, of wind music and of the lists of winds throughout the world. At first my memory was dim, but I closed my eyes and pictured us there on board the ship traveling between Trondheim and La Rochelle, where she had given me my first wind lesson.

I remembered the desert winds first because they were the most colorful. *Bist roz,* which was known to bury villages. *Harmattan,* or sea of darkness, which blew red dust across the Sahara. I remembered too *begiak zabalik*, a persistent fierce wind that roared through the Pyrennes.

There was that Skottish wind she had told me of at the very beginning. In fact, she had introduced me to it, curling it around me and bidding me to listen closely. It had been one of her favorites, she said. A western wind, and I had named my horse after it: *ciuin.*

I also remembered another Skottish wind Sib had told me about that was named for a bird, because when it blew, you felt like you were being caught up in a rush of flying seabirds. *Faoileag*, it was called.

Birds, seabirds. Ideas began to flicker in my mind, but

nothing that took any real shape, so I jumped up and exited the house, making my way to the shoreline. Perhaps if I could feel the sea wind on my skin I would be able to think more clearly.

I found a rock to sit on and closed my eyes, listening to the sound of the waves and the calling of seabirds. I remembered Sib telling me that early people had thought the wind was caused by a giant bird and the flapping of its giant wings. I opened my eyes and saw a bird winging over the water, a petrel, I thought. I watched as it soared high, then dipped down to the water with an easy grace, skimming the surface.

And suddenly I had an idea of how to make a cloak of wind.

WHITE BEAR

I had no direction.
North south east west.
But I pointed my nose
toward the place the sun set.

West,
though I didn't know why.

I swam and
I swam,
riding the ribbons of foam.
Feeling the run of the sea current beneath me.

One night the sky lit up with color.
Green.
Yellow.
Red.
Purple.
Great swaths of color,

pulsing, shimmering across the sky.
Astonishing.

Like the bursts
I had in my mind, before.
Colors instead of memories.

Pulses of purple
reminded me of Nyamh's violet eyes.
Familiar,
but not familiar.

ROSE

A S I HAD DONE WITH THE SEAWEED, so I did with feathers.
I took my basket down to the coast and walked along
the water's edge, searching for the feathers of seabirds.

At first I picked up any I could find, for unlike seaweed,
feathers were not plentiful. I circled the island, which took
several hours, and circled it again, this time zigzagging inland
periodically, and by the end of the day, my basket was half full.

As I searched, I thought about wind, about the wind magic
Sib had taught me. I had not practiced much, but one thing
I had learned from her lesson was to be more attuned to the
wind, like the wild, shifting wind that had preceded the Blood
Rain, and the *foehn* wind in the Alpes that Ben had spoken of.

I concentrated on the wind that blew off the sea, listening
closely to it. At first I heard nothing except the thrumming
of my own heartbeat and the sound of the waves, but over the
time I spent circling the island searching for feathers, I began
to hear some faint sound. Not exactly music, but something
that resembled it.

By the following day, my basket was almost full, but by
then I had decided I wanted only white or very light-colored

feathers. In the castle in the mountain, I had made a shirt for my white bear out of white thread spun from tufts of his fur. That shirt had helped undo the enchantment the Troll King had cast, and I had a superstitious feeling that this cloak should match my white bear. So I had to discard some of the feathers I had already found.

My back hurt and the muscles in my legs ached from bending and crouching to pick up feathers, but on the afternoon of the third day of feather hunting, when I was beginning to fear I would never find enough, I had a stroke of good luck. I came across a wide swath of white feathers on a little hillock overlooking the sea, apparently left by a migrating mass of gannets, a mostly white sea bird. I actually saw a few gannets winging their way on the tail end of the migration, hurrying to catch up.

When my basket could hold no more, I headed back to the workroom. I laid all the white feathers on the worktable to dry and, seeing them spread out, thought I had collected a sufficient amount. I hoped so, anyway, since I didn't think my back or legs could bear any more feather hunting.

I set up the loom with the translucent silvery thread from the castle in the mountain, and I began to weave. More than before, I was reminded of being back in the castle, weaving the cloth that would become the nightshirt for my nightly visitor. I closed my eyes and let myself picture the white bear there before me, and I found myself speaking, as if I was telling him the tale of the Maid of the North. As it had in the castle, the telling of the tale made the time pass faster, and matched the rhythm of my fingers as they moved back and forth.

When I finished the tale, I went to the window of the workroom and threw it open. The wind was cold, but I wanted to listen to it, feel it on my skin, as I wove.

Feeling faintly foolish, I concentrated very hard and tried calling the wind into my fingers. At first I felt nothing, but I kept breathing slowly and listening and concentrating. I may have been imagining it, but it felt like the ends of my fingers vibrated slightly, almost as if they were humming.

Finally I was done. I took the fabric I had woven off the loom and laid it over a chair. I checked on the feathers and found them to be dry. Then I gathered them into a box and laid the translucent cloth out on the table.

I cut and hemmed until I had the shape of the cloak ready.

Using fine white silk thread and a sharp needle, I began sewing the white feathers onto the fabric. As I sewed, I thought of the times I had searched for my white bear after the Troll Queen had taken him from me. There had been so many moments when I thought I would never find him again, or that even if I did, it would be too late.

But not this time. He was alive; Verendi had told me so. He might even have been somewhere near, and perhaps this time he would find me.

There were hundreds of feathers. I didn't count them, I just sewed. The work was even more laborious than the candle wax or the seaweed and shells. I wanted to cover every inch of the fabric with feathers, like it was the body of a living seabird, so they had to be layered densely, overlapping.

By the end of the first day of sewing feathers, I was frazzled, ill-tempered, and beginning to think this was all a ridiculous waste of time. I pricked my finger with the sharp little needle more than once and had to stop and wash the blood from the white feathers it dripped on. At one point, my fingers raw and my head buzzing, I was ready to throw the whole thing out the door. It was taking too long. *Let Aagnorak come,* I thought grimly.

But I summoned the image of my bairn on the day he was born and my white bear standing next to me as I held him, both of us bursting with joy. I kept sewing.

I wasn't sure how much time went by. I took occasional breaks for food and quick dreamless sleeps, but mostly I bent over the cloak, my hands relentlessly threading white feathers into place.

And then I lost myself in the work. I came to a place in my heart, as I have so many times before, where it didn't matter if it was acceptable, if the cloak passed the test and pleased the Morae. Or even whether I succeeded in keeping Aagnorak from coming, from destroying our world. The whole act of creating this cloak—the finding of the feathers, the weaving of the white silk, the painstaking sewing on of the feathers, each one placed just so, exactly where it belonged—filled me with a sense of joy, like when I made the moon dress, as well as the very first cloak I had made. I was creating something beautiful.

When I had sewn the last feather on the cloak and tied off the last knot on the last thread, I set down the needle and gently lifted up my creation. I laughed with pleasure at the sight of the cloak of white feathers, light as air, delicate and strong as the wings of a seabird. I had indeed made something beautiful.

Wind blew in from the window and lifted it slightly, making the feathers rustle. A slanting ray of the just-risen sun shone through the window, and the cloak shimmered.

I took the cloak and hung it on the third hook.

NEDDY

W E ARRIVED IN STORNOWAY, LEODHAS, in the afternoon. At first we could find no trace of Rose and Charles, but finally met a sailor who had noticed a pair answering their description. He said they hired a cart to take them to a town called Garenin, which lay on the west coast of Leodhas. We immediately set sail and arrived at the small town by late evening. There was only one dock, but fortunately it was unoccupied and large enough to accommodate our ship.

The next morning, Sib and I asked around, describing Rose and Charles, and managed to find an old woman in an inn who said she'd spoken with them. They had told her they were going fishing, and she'd sent them to the boatman Macdeag.

As I headed out the door, the old woman called after me, "Will you be wanting to find the Three Weavers of Mora, too?"

I stopped. "Excuse me?" I said, turning back to her.

"The girl in particular was interested in the old tales," the old woman said. And she proceeded to tell me the local legend about the Three Weavers.

As I walked away, I racked my brain. It sounded familiar.

When I rejoined Sib, who had been searching down by the water, I asked her if she knew of these Three Weavers.

She shook her head. "Where I'm from is farther south. I don't know the tales of Leodhas. But it reminds me of something, too. Weavers. Maybe the Fates?"

All at once I knew and kicked myself for not remembering sooner. In Njorden lore, they were called the Norns. Three women who sat at the foot of the tree Yggdrasil and determined the thread of life for all those who inhabited earth, be they animals, humans, or gods.

So Sib and I returned to the inn, and I had the old woman tell us in greater detail about what she had said to Rose about the island to the west, which was surrounded by a dangerous whirlpool.

We made our way back to the ship at once. I wanted to set sail immediately, but a storm had blown in. The captain of our ship was also understandably skeptical about setting sail into uncharted waters to look for an island that existed only in fable.

ROSE

I SANK INTO A CHAIR NEXT TO THE HOOKS with the three finished cloaks and wondered what would happen now. Was I supposed to go to the Morae and tell them the tasks were done? Barely before these thoughts had time to form, the light abruptly changed, and I realized that my workroom no longer had a roof. I rubbed my eyes and, in the next moment, saw that I was now sitting in a lovely walled garden. It looked as if it had been there for centuries with deep green layers of ivy climbing the stone walls, fragrant flowering trees, masses of flowers of all shapes and colors—vivid reds, purples, pinks, and yellows. There was the hum of insects and the melody of birdsong—of trilling songbirds, not the strident calls of seabirds.

I looked and saw that the wall behind me was now made of stone and covered with ivy, complete with the three hooks and my cloaks hanging from them. My pack was nearby as well. And a table stood near the center of the garden, filled with delicious-looking food and drink.

Verendi was unexpectedly at my side, smiling brightly. "You are done!" she said.

And I saw that Skuld and Uror were seated in comfortable

chairs by the table, with an empty one waiting for Verendi, who leaned over and whispered in my ear. "This is one of Skuld's favorite places. We all want her in a good mood, don't we?" She laughed and whispered again, "And I made sure there was a whole basket of ripe figs. Skuld loves figs."

I saw the basket of figs, and my own mouth began to water.

"Now, show us!" Verendi said, crossing to her chair.

I stood and turned to look at my cloaks, neatly hung on their hooks, and suddenly all the joy I had felt before in their making evaporated. How had I thought I could convince the Morae that I had completed their three tasks? The three cloaks looked like ordinary ungainly things hanging there. What had made me think I had created cloaks of fire, water, and wind? I must have been mad.

My legs shook, and I dully wondered when I had last eaten anything. But I straightened my back and took a deep breath.

"I will need a few things," I said.

"You have only to ask," trilled Verendi.

"A bucket of water," I said.

Verendi gestured, and there before me was a bucket filled to the top with water.

"Thank you," I said and crossed to my pack. Removing the flint, I returned to the pegs with the cloaks.

Tying my hair back, I wrapped a dark piece of fabric around my head. I took the black wool cloak that lay underneath the fire cloak and lowered it into the bucket of water, wetting it completely. I lifted the cloak out of the water and wrung it until the cloth no longer dripped.

I pulled the wet fabric around my shoulders, shivering a little as it touched my skin.

Turning to the cloak made of pitch and candle wax, I laid it over a chair. I took the flint and made a spark, holding it to one corner of the cloak, where I had deliberately left a long strand of wax-coated wool protruding. I set it on fire, and right away, the wool caught. I watched as it kindled slowly and began to travel along the warp and weft of the fabric. I picked up the cloak, holding it aloft as it burned.

"It doesn't count just to set a cloak afire," came Skuld's deep voice.

"Wait and see," said Verendi, and I thought I saw her offer Skuld the basket of figs.

When almost the entire cloak was aflame, I draped it around my shoulders, on top of the wet black cloak.

The smell of flame was in my nose, and I could feel the heat through the inner cloak, but my skin did not burn. I raised my arms, holding the cloak aloft. Flames leapt and crackled and danced all across the surface of the cloak.

"See? It is a cloak of fire!" said Verendi. "The flame does not go out."

"I agree," said Uror.

Skuld said nothing, just watched me.

The heat from the fire began to make me sweat, and I could

tell my face was flushed. I became aware of the unmistakable smell of burning hair and realized the hair at the nape of my neck was being singed, despite the head wrap.

"Perhaps," said Skuld with a frown. "Perhaps it could be called a cloak of fire. Let us see the next."

I breathed a sigh of relief and shrugged the burning cloak off my shoulders, stepping quickly away from it. I used the damp inner cloak to smother the flames.

"Show us your cloak of water," said Uror.

I took a deep breath, and after unwinding the damp material from my head and laying it aside, I crossed to the three hooks. I removed the seaweed and shell cloak and carried it over to the bucket of water, which I noticed was once again filled to the brim. Gingerly, I submerged the cloak, pressing lightly so as not to crush or break the vines of seaweed. Water sloshed over the rim of the bucket as I pushed the cloak down.

I let it sit for a few moments, and though it was quiet, except for the occasional warble of birdsong, I could hear Skuld's voice inside my head. *A cloak that is sopping wet isn't the same as a cloak of water.*

I pushed the voice away and drew the cloak from the bucket of water. I quickly draped it over my shoulders and tied it under my chin with the two strands of seaweed. I took hold of the two sides of the cloak and began to undulate the fabric, slowly and rhythmically. Droplets of water rippled off it in iridescent arcs. The loops I had created held on to the water, as did the small shells, which made a whispering, tinkling sound as they came into contact. It was almost like the sound of waves lapping on the shore. The seaweed pods also made squishy, popping noises now and then. The small phosphorescent sea worms began wriggling out of shells and squirmed along the strands of seaweed. The light in the garden suddenly dimmed, as if the sun had been obscured by clouds, which made the phosphorescence gleam all the more brightly. I could hear Verendi's laugh and knew she had caused the light to change. And in the half-light, my cloak indeed looked like a thing of the sea—liquid, silvery, and shimmering with water.

"Beautiful!" called Verendi.

"It is not *made* of water," came Skuld's voice.

"It is lovely," said Uror.

"Yes," said Skuld grudgingly.

The light in the garden returned to normal.

"You are indeed a skilled weaver," said Verendi.

"Yes, as good perhaps as Arachne," agreed Uror.

"Better, I think," said Verendi.

I felt myself blushing a little, pleased at the compliment. I had heard the legends of Arachne, who had angered the goddess Athena with her skill at weaving. Athena ultimately turned Arachne into a spider so she would weave her webs throughout eternity.

The cold water had initially felt good on my skin after the heat of the fire cloak, but now I began to feel chilled. Shivering,

I took the cloak off and hung it on the second hook, where it continued to drip water.

I looked over at the Morae.

"Skuld?" asked Verendi.

"It is *not* a cloak of water," Skuld said, helping herself to another fig. "But if she passes the wind cloak test, I will let this one pass as well."

"Very well. Then it all depends on the cloak of air," said Uror.

I breathed deeply, still shivering.

"Wait," said Verendi. And from somewhere she produced a length of the softest, whitest material I had ever felt, and wrapped it around my shoulders. "Dry yourself first," she added.

Gratefully, I rubbed the impossibly soft cloth over my arms and shoulders.

I set it down, took another deep breath, and lifted the cloak of white feathers off its hook.

NEDDY

S IB, ESTELLE, AND I WERE FINISHING BREAKFAST in the
galley of the ship. I had just asked Sib to pass me a jug of
milk when her face suddenly froze. She sat very still, staring
straight ahead. I turned to see what she was looking at, but
her gaze was directed at the small porthole just opposite her
and the only thing visible was water.

Abruptly she stood. "Excuse me," she said, and quickly left
the galley. Estelle and I looked at each other.

"Is Tante Sib all right?" Estelle asked. "She looked funny."

I stood, feeling alarmed. Was she about to run off again?
"I think I'll just see . . ." I said, and, grabbing up a coat, left the
galley. I went on deck just in time to see Sib on the gangway
departing the ship.

I followed her. She was moving swiftly, through the harbor and out onto the headland, heading north. There was a
cool wind blowing and I noticed Sib didn't have a cloak. She
seemed to be heading toward a sandy beach area some distance north of the harbor.

I wasn't too far behind when I saw her go out onto the sand.
It was a chilly day, and the beach was deserted.

I watched as Sib stopped and removed her leather boots.

"Sib?" I called. But either she did not hear me or was too intent on what she was doing to respond. At any rate she did not turn toward me.

Her boots off, Sib hiked up her skirt, tucking the hem into her belt, and waded into the water. When the water was just above her knees, she stopped and just stood there.

I came up to the shoreline and called to her.

This time she turned. "It's Rose, Neddy," she said. "You were right. She needs me. Go back to the ship. Please." Her voice was urgent.

"But what—"

"Go," she repeated. "And don't worry. It will be fine."

ROSE

I T ALL CAME DOWN TO THE CLOAK OF WIND, and it was of course the hardest, the one I had the least confidence in. I knew it was beautiful. But would they consider it a cloak made of wind? It seemed unlikely.

But I had to try.

Nervously I wrapped it around my shoulders. The feathers rustled gently, gleaming in the late afternoon sunlight.

There wasn't even a breath of wind in that sunny garden. I found myself wondering if the Morae had done that deliberately, Skuld in particular. But in spite of that, I closed my eyes, listening for even the faintest hum of the wind music I had heard when I was making the cloak. As before, I wished that Sib were with me, that she could help me hear it. But what I wished more than anything in this moment was the ability to summon it, as Sib had once summoned the breeze that curled around my body on board the ship to La Rochelle.

As I concentrated, I thought of Charles, or of Charles as he once was. My husband. I thought of the happy times we had had, picnicking by the river, drinking cold cider together, playing his flauto, holding our newborn bairn, the two of us dancing at one of the yearly village fairs. One day we would dance together again. I had to believe that.

I had unconsciously raised my arms as if to dance, and it was at that moment I first heard the music. It started out soft and sweet, but gradually swelled, filling my ears, my veins, my heart.

My eyes still closed, I began to spin, and I could feel the wind twisting around my body, lifting the cloak and breathing its lilting music in my ear. My heart began to pound faster.

The feathers on the cloak fluttered in the wind, and I suddenly felt as if the wind had entered my blood, causing my whole body to thrum with its music.

For a flicker of a moment, I thought I could hear Sib's voice singing, weaving through the music inside me, but thought I must be imagining it.

As I spun, and listened, and thrummed, I felt the strangest sensation, that my body was actually lifting, my feet leaving the ground. And through the music in my ears, I could hear the voice of Uror.

"She has power after all."

"Someone is helping her," came Skuld's voice.

Verendi's laugh trilled. "Nonsense, you can see no one is here."

"Still," Skuld said, implacable.

"Does it matter?" Verendi said. "In truth, Rose has done the task, she has made a cloak of wind."

I was hearing their voices through the swelling music that flowed through my body.

And then the wind began to ebb, and I felt myself gently descending to the ground, the cloak settling in rustling folds around me.

I opened my eyes. Verendi was coming toward me, her arms open, and she drew me into a sweet perfumed hug.

Her pale eyes searched mine. "You have done it, Rose," she said softly. And I was surprised to see what looked like unshed tears glittering in her eyes. "And I think you may be just in time," she added with a whisper.

NEDDY

I DIDN'T LEAVE THE BEACH. I knew I should, but I couldn't. I wanted to be sure Sib was safe. I climbed to a stand of trees not far from where she stood, and stayed there, watching her.

At first she was still, standing knee-deep in the water, facing south and west. But then I saw her arms slowly lifting, and as they did, I saw that the weather was changing. A wind had kicked up. As it grew stronger, whitecaps began to form. The waves grew larger and started splashing Sib. They grew even larger, and I wanted to go to her, fearful that she would be knocked down and pulled out to sea. Indeed she was thoroughly soaked by now, but she stood her ground as the waves buffeted her. And slowly the wind began to diminish, the waves receding to their previous placid state.

Sib's body buckled, and she collapsed into the water. Breaking into a run, I was soon splashing through the water. I scooped Sib up into my arms and carried her to the shoreline, where I gently set her down.

She looked up at me and smiled.

"Neddy," she said, and abruptly spewed a mouthful of seawater onto the sand. Her body was racked by coughing.

I put my arms around her, and the coughing gradually subsided, but I could feel her shivering.

"We need to get you back to the ship," I said.

She nodded and unsteadily rose to her feet. Then she collapsed again. I lifted her into my arms and, carrying her, began to walk toward the harbor.

ROSE

AS I WAS HANGING THE WIND CLOAK on the third hook, a quarrel had broken out between the three Morae. They all agreed that I had completed the tasks, but when Verendi said she thought they should each get one of the cloaks, and that she dearly wanted the cloak made of wind, Skuld had unequivocally said no.

"The girl created them; they are hers."

I started to say that I would be glad to give the cloaks to the Morae, but Skuld would have none of it. Verendi pouted, but all of a sudden, Uror and Skuld were bidding me farewell and the garden vanished. Verendi and I were standing alone on a desolate stretch of shoreline. There was no sign of a whirlpool, the water looking smooth and silvery in the afternoon light.

My currach, which was miraculously whole again, lay by the water. Inside I could see both my pack and Charles's, our two swords, as well as the three cloaks folded neatly in a basket, and next to it another basket, which Verendi said held food for the journey. There were also two paddles.

"You will find your bairn on an even smaller isle than this, due west," said Verendi, pointing out to sea. "It shouldn't take you very long to get there. And of course you know now that appearances are deceptive, that things may look different on the outside to you than they do to us. Or to the Troll Queen."

I nodded. "Will I find her there as well?"

"I cannot tell."

"Or you will not," I said.

Verendi laughed. "But one thing I can tell you, which you may find of interest, is that your love is now a white bear once more."

I stared at her. "What do you mean? How?" I stuttered out.

"I did it," she said, smiling.

"Why?" I asked, my mind reeling.

"Oh, he was drowning. White bears swim better than humans, you know. Much better. And it seemed like symmetry. It was as a white bear that he first loved you, and you him."

"But how?"

"He will be human again, once the pale queen is finished. When I changed him, I wove in that little provision. It seemed only right."

"Finished? Do you mean when she is dead? Or . . . ?"

But Verendi refused to answer any more questions and insisted on helping me launch the currach.

"Time is of the essence, dear Rose," she said.

As I settled into the seat of the currach, paddle in hand,

she called out, "Farewell. We are leaving too. Being in the garden has made Skuld nostalgic for the Hanging Gardens in Babylon."

"Goodbye, Verendi," I said.

She smiled and started to turn away, then turned back.

"Oh, one more thing," she said.

"Yes?" I said, with a stirring of unease.

"The door to the blackhouse where your bairn lies is locked."

I stared back at her. Was this another test or trick?

She just smiled sweetly. "But don't worry. You have the key that will open it."

She waved at me. "*Amor vincit omnia,* she called, and turned to make her way back to the Morae's blackhouse.

NEDDY

Sib was very pale and clearly exhausted, but she looked up at me as I carried her and whispered, "Thank you, Neddy, for not letting me run away. You were right. I couldn't have helped Rose if I was halfway to Saint Petersburg." She gave me a weak smile and closed her eyes.

"I'm glad" was all I said.

I tried to keep her warm, draping my coat over her, but by the time we reached the harbor, she was shivering violently.

I had the ship's cook immediately set a pot of water to boil while I settled Sib in the small cabin that she and Estelle shared.

Estelle asked how Sib had come to be so wet, and I said I would tell her later but that now we needed to get her warm and dry. While I went to get a cup of tea, the young girl helped Sib change into dry clothing and found some extra blankets.

When I came back, I found Sib still shivering, and I sat by her, trying not to look as worried as I felt.

"Will you be all right, Sib?" I asked.

She reached out and took my hand. Her own hand was like

ice. "I have caught a chill is all," she said. "Sleep is what I need. But I can tell you this, Neddy. Rose is safe. For now."

She took several long sips of tea. Then she gave me a sleepy smile, coughed once, and nestled back under the covers. She was asleep in a matter of moments.

I gazed down at that face I loved so well, wondering what it all meant.

Part of me wanted to shake Sib, wake her up, and have her tell me what she knew of Rose. But her face was ashen, her breathing labored, and I knew she needed to sleep. I would have to wait.

 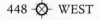

ROSE

A**S I METHODICALLY DUG MY PADDLE** into the placid water, I marveled at how temperate the weather was. It seemed unusual for this time of year, and I wondered if the Morae had something to do with it.

I felt calm, too, like the sea, which surprised me. I was close to finding my bairn, as well as, most likely, to meeting the Troll Queen again. I should have been filled with both excitement and dread. But instead I had a sense of peace. It wasn't an unmindful serenity, lulling myself into a false sense that the hard part was over. It clearly wasn't. But for now I was in a sturdy boat on tranquil waters, and soon I would come to an island with a blackhouse on it. And thanks to Verendi, I knew I had the key to unlock the door, the key Urda had given me. I didn't know what I would find inside. But both Charles and Winn were still alive. And I would do anything in my power to keep them that way.

I stopped at midday to eat. Inside the second basket, I found an array of foods I wasn't familiar with. Among other things, there were pungent green and black olives, a kind of bread that was flat and crusty and very flavorful, a small oblong thing that seemed to be wrapped in seaweed and was filled with rice and meat. I ate happily, the sun warm on my head and arms as I let the currach drift.

While I was eating, I thought back to the extraordinary experience of the white feather cloak and the way the wind had lifted me. Had I really done wind magic? And had Sib somehow heard me and helped, as Skuld had implied? I dreamily tried listening to this gentle wind that rippled around me now. It was coming from the west.

WHITE BEAR

Swimming.
Always swimming.
Losing track of days.
Five? Six? Or more.

Endless hunger.
But then a dead shark,
floating in the water.
Belly full, for once.

My nose
had led me to it.
The smell.

And I remembered.
My white bear nose.

I remembered too
somebody once saying,
about white bears:

A pine needle fell in the forest.
The hawk saw it.
The deer heard it.
The white bear smelled it.

I would use my nose.
It would lead me, guide me.

To Nyamh,
and to my son.

ROSE

THE DAY CONTINUED FAIR as I resumed my paddling. I kept the boat on course, heading due west. My eyes were fixed on the horizon, and by midafternoon, I thought I spotted a small dark shape.

Though my arms were tired, I increased my pace, and the shape got ever bigger. Soon I could make out a small island, with a small building on it.

My heart was pounding now, all that calm and serenity long gone.

The closer I got, the more I could see of the island, which was indeed tiny. All that it seemed to hold was a weathered blackhouse. This one did not have the traditional thatched roof. Instead it was made of the same stone as the rest of the building, and I could even see watermarks on the stones on the very top of the roof, from waves crashing up and over it during stormy weather. There were no windows.

I hopped out of the currach into the cold water at the rocky shoreline. The water was not shallow, and I was submerged up to my waist and nearly went fully underwater at one point, my feet scrabbling for a foothold on the rocks. But I was finally able to pull myself and the currach ashore. Stone steps led up to the door of the blackhouse.

I shouldered my pack and sword and reached into my pocket for the key. It was a familiar feeling, nestled there as it had been ever since Urda gave it to me. I couldn't count how many times I had run my fingers over its ridges. I said a silent thank-you to Urda, wishing she could know that I had found my way here and that soon I would see my bairn.

My heart was racing now. I climbed the steps, key in hand.

I tried the door, even though I knew it would be locked as Verendi had said. It was, so I lifted the key to the lock.

Suddenly a dark shape hurtled down at me. I felt a stabbing pain on my fingers, and at the same time, the key was plucked from my grasp. I saw the beady, glimmering eyes of a bird. It swooped up and away, the key in its beak.

I watched, frozen in shock and disbelief, as the bird circled above me. It looked like a raven, though it wasn't black, but rather a gray color. The gray of ashes.

In horror I saw the bird beat its wings, flying due east at a steady pace. When it was just a dot in the sky, I saw it make a slow circle. Then it was flying back toward me. It glided above me, swooping low enough for me to see there was no key in its beak anymore. It let out a piercing caw and began to fly away again, back toward the east. I watched until it disappeared completely from my sight.

I was numb, undone by shock and a sense of unreality. It

hadn't happened. It could not have happened. Irrationally, I felt in my pocket for the key that had been there for so long. But it was gone. In the blink of an eye, it had been lost to me.

For a moment, I was seized with the desperate urge to plunge into the cold water, swim out to that distant point where the bird must have dropped the key, and dive and dive until I found it. But I knew it was impossible. Even if I could pinpoint where the bird, the Troll Queen as I thought it must be, had dropped it, the waters here were too deep and too cold. I would never find it.

I turned to look at the blackhouse. There were no windows, and the roof was made of stone, but perhaps there was another way in, I thought. Yet even as I halfheartedly circled the building, I knew that too was impossible. It was not just the thick walls of stone that would keep me out. I could almost smell the spells of enchantment that wound around this plain-looking structure.

Only the key would open it. And the key was gone.

I sank to my knees in front of the door. I looked at the lock, felt it with my fingers. Filled with anger, I flung myself at the door, pounding on it, throwing my shoulder against it. Pain shot through my body.

I pounded until my voice and hands were raw. The burn on my palm, which had mostly healed, split open and was oozing blood. Finally I stopped, exhausted, and collapsed onto the stone steps, breathing hard.

Perhaps I could return to the Morae, throw myself on their mercy. Verendi would surely take pity on me. But they were gone, moved on to the gardens in Babylon.

I stared again at the lock. I had been so close. On the other side of this door lay my son. And I could not get to him.

I turned around to look out to sea. Charles. My white bear. Maybe even now he was swimming toward me. Maybe he had found the key. Maybe he could help me get inside this cursed blackhouse. But there was nothing, no sign of any living being as far as my eye could see.

Tears came then.

I'm not sure how long I sat there on those stone steps. I shivered in my wet clothing and stuffed my hands into my pockets, empty now of the small key that had been there for what seemed a long time. Tears pricked my eyes again. But I wearily blinked them back.

I had run my fingers over that key of bone so many times, but now it was gone. The feel of the key was achingly familiar to me, the pattern of indentations along the shaft chiseled into my mind.

I had the thought that maybe if I found a piece of driftwood, I could carve notches into it in the same pattern. But somehow I knew it wouldn't work. It had to be a key of bone. Human bone, as the shopkeeper in Calais had said. I pulled my cold fingers out of my pockets and stared down at them.

The burn wound was still seeping, and I could see faint calluses from my sword fighting lessons.

And an appalling thought came into my head. All the times I had held that bone key in my hand, I remembered thinking that it was the same size as my own little finger.

My mind reeled. No. I couldn't do it. It was too horrifying a thing to consider.

And yet. My sword was sharp. It would take only a moment. The pain would be great, but I had borne pain before. And I had cloth for binding.

But could I do it? And what if it was to no avail? What if the bone key that lay at the bottom of the sea where the raven had dropped it was the only key that would work? And what if my bairn wasn't even inside this blackhouse?

Surely I had done enough. No one would fault me for leaving now. But even as I thought this, I knew I could not do it. Charles was somewhere out there, changed back into a white bear. And he would be freed only if the Troll Queen was "finished," which meant dead, I was sure of it.

And there was Aagnorak. If indeed the queen was about to unleash the end of softskin life, and in its ashes raise my son to rule the Huldre world, clearly there wouldn't be anywhere or anybody for me to return to. I had to get inside this blackhouse. Nothing else mattered.

It was better done quickly. I pulled my dagger out, as well

as my skin bag filled with water and a length of clean cloth, splayed my little finger on the edge of the stone step, and swung the blade.

The next few moments were a blur of pain and blood and revulsion. I must have been in shock, for I felt like I was watching the whole thing from a great distance. I thought I might lose consciousness, but breathed deeply and kept my thoughts steady, focused on my white bear and our child.

Swiftly I poured cold water over the wound and bound the cloth around the place where my finger had been. Blood soaked through the cloth, and I added another layer, still breathing deeply, desperately holding the feeling of dizziness at bay.

I sat still for some time, my eyes closed, pain radiating through my body. Then I put my skin bag to my lips and drank deeply. I couldn't yet look at that which I had cut off my hand, and the thought of what lay ahead made my stomach heave.

But I did it. I took the bone down to the water and cleaned it. Part of me could not believe I had done this thing. And the effort of keeping my thoughts methodical and objective helped to allay the panic, just barely.

Very slowly and meticulously, I carved the pattern of notches I had felt on the bone in my pocket for all that time. Even though a part of me thought the whole thing preposterous and unreal, I felt confident that I had at least done the key right. It matched.

I stood, my legs shaking, and once again climbed the steps to the door.

This time I held the key so tightly my fingers turned white, and I drew my sword just in case. But no gray raven came, and I slipped the bone key, *my* bone key, into the lock. I turned it and heard a click, and miraculously the door opened.

I almost laughed out loud, flooded by a hysterical sense of relief and wonder. It had worked.

My wind sword at the ready, I entered the blackhouse.

WHITE BEAR

I had been swimming
for a lifetime.
Or two.

Hunger was back,
gnawing at me.

But keeping my nose above water,
I let it guide me.

I thought of my son
as a newborn,
cradled in my arms.
The smell of his skin, his hair.

And Nyamh.
The smell of her
as she comforted me
after the nightmare came.

Then I spotted it.
A small island in the distance.
A low building.

Though my legs ached,
I swam faster.

NEDDY

S IB WAS SICK, VERY SICK. I wanted to set off to look for Rose, but I could not leave Sib, and she was far too ill to travel. I found a woman in Garenin who was known for her healing, but nothing she did seemed to help. She said she did not understand this sickness of Sib's. It was more than a chill. It was something deep-rooted and very serious.

I was by her bedside constantly in that cramped little cabin. We had moved Estelle to another room, but the young girl was always at hand, helping bring cool water for the fever and hot tea for the shivering.

On the second day, Sib seemed to come to herself for a moment. She looked up at me, her eyes bright with fever, and said with a strange little smile, "Please don't be sad, Neddy. To die will not be sad. It will be a blessing."

Tears came to my eyes. "Don't talk that way, Sib," I said. "You will get better."

"It is not a bad thing, Neddy, if I don't get better. I can't explain . . ." She closed her eyes.

I didn't understand her words. They terrified me. It was as if she had given up.

ROSE

V ERENDI HAD REMINDED ME that in the world of Morae and trolls, appearances can be misleading. And so it was with the blackhouse.

As soon as I crossed the threshold into the room, everything shifted from dull browns and blacks to crystalline, shimmering ice. In fact, it was a room made entirely of ice—the walls, the ceiling, and even the floor, though it was textured so it wasn't slippery. The few furnishings were all carved from ice. And there were beautiful ice sculptures dotted here and there, with two delicate ice chandeliers hanging from the ceiling. There were round windows set high in the ice walls, which let in sunlight, and one large round window above, directly in the center of the ceiling. The sun that shone through that window was focused on a table below it.

The table held an *echecs* game board, its squares etched in the ice it was made of. But there were no pieces on it.

The other item of furniture that drew my eye immediately was against the far wall, just below one of the round windows. It was a golden cradle, and it rested on a rectangular dais of sheer ice.

I quickly crossed to it, my heart racing. And there was my bairn! He was all bundled up in white furs, looking like a small white bear, fast asleep, his thumb in his mouth. I felt a great rush of love and relief, gazing down on that sweet, rosy face. He looked healthy, unharmed.

"I might have known," came the voice of rocks.

I spun around, and there she was in the doorway. She looked magnificent, more beautiful than ever, despite the scar on her face. She was dressed in a breathtaking white gown, covered by a shimmering white fur cloak. Dazzling translucent jewels sparkled at her throat and wrists.

"How did you manage to get in?" the queen said, but her glance fell on my hand bound with cloth bandages.

I thought I saw a hint of admiration in her eyes. She shook her head and moved toward the table with the *echecs* set in the middle of the room. She was holding something white in her hand, and she set it down in the middle of the board. I could see it was the queen piece, an exact duplicate of the one I had thrown in the fire.

She looked up at me.

"There is no fire here," she said with a smile. "Only ice."

I thought I could hear Winn stirring behind me.

"Here is what is going to happen, softskin girl," the queen said quietly in her jagged voice. "You are going to die. And while you die, slowly, I will tell you of the plans I have for your son. Who will become *my* son. I shall call him Minonn. I will describe to you how I will raise him as a troll and how once the world is rid of softskins, he will help me rule. It will not take him long to forget you and the others of your race. I have already begun giving him arts, you know," she went on with a tone of satisfaction.

I let out a cry.

"Oh, yes, one needs to begin the process young. By the time he is of age, he will be powerful, his arts the equal of any troll's."

Winn let out a little gurgle, and I turned to him protectively, thinking to pull him into my arms.

"No. That I cannot allow . . ."

And I felt the invisible hands, on my throat, on my arms. They were dragging me away from the cradle, across the room to a chair made of ice. I was pushed into a sitting position, and I was bound there, unable to move.

The Troll Queen crossed to the cradle and, lifting Winn out, returned to her spot by the *echecs* table.

I noticed that Winn was now able to hold his head up and move it around, his eyes alert. His gaze fell on me. A smile curled his mouth, and he reached out his arms.

"Maman," I thought I heard him say. I couldn't believe it. Was my bairn already able to talk? Surely he was too young.

"Winn!" I cried.

The queen looked annoyed, and I felt pressure on my neck. My breathing became labored. She gazed up at the round window in the center of the ceiling.

"When the sun is directly above, and it will be soon, I shall finish what I have started. Aagnorak."

Winn began to wriggle in her arms. "Maman!"

I definitely heard it that time.

The grip around my neck grew tighter.

My bairn began to cry. It tore at my heart, and I struggled desperately against the invisible bonds that held me.

Winn was straining to get free of the Troll Queen. She was clearly unused to babies and was awkwardly trying to keep a grip on him.

The pressure on my throat lessened for a moment, and I gasped for air, taking deep breaths. But I still could not move.

I saw Winn turn to look at the person holding him, the person who was keeping him from his mother. And I heard the Troll Queen let out a cry. I could see her body jerk, a look of surprise on her face, and she almost dropped Winn. But she didn't. She straightened, holding him tighter, and let out a laugh.

"Only a bairn, and already your arts are working," she said to my son. "Very good. Still, I can't have you distracting me." She cast a glance up at the round window above her and quickly crossed the room to the cradle. She laid Winn down in it and gave him a glass cup filled with a milky liquid. It had a teat of some kind at the top, and Winn took the cup happily, putting the teat in his mouth.

The queen came to stand in front of me, and this time she put her own hands around my throat. I could see in those beautiful eyes that she wanted to watch me die. Up close. I could feel the ridged skin of her hands as they bit into my throat. I gasped, and my breathing stopped.

"It shall be as I said, softskin girl. Your child is now my child. Your prince, my Myk, is now a shell of a softskin with no memory. And Aagnorak shall destroy your world."

I struggled against the bonds that were holding my body still. Her eyes were a blazing white-yellow, blinding me. I felt myself starting to lose consciousness.

But over the queen's shoulder I saw a blur of white moving rapidly toward us.

I heard a roar, and a large white paw swung at the Troll Queen's head. It knocked her violently to the ground.

I could breathe again, and move. Gasping, I jumped up and darted to where my sword lay. I grabbed it.

My white bear, and he was truly a very large, very angry white bear, loomed over the queen, who lay dazed from the blow to her head. She was looking up at him, in astonishment.

"How . . ." she murmured. "Ah, the Morae," she said with a sigh.

She rolled away from the white bear, scrambling to her feet, and began heading for her *echecs* table. She was looking up at the circle of sunlight coming from the ceiling.

"The *echecs* queen!" I shouted, and the white bear attacked. The Troll Queen spun to face him, and I saw in her hand what at first looked to be a sword but, I realized, was some kind of icicle, or rather an ice sword, sharpened to a deadly point. I watched in horror as she thrust it into the white bear's body. Red blood blossomed from the wound, and he fell with a groan.

I became filled with a fury unlike any I had felt before, and without thought, I charged across the room, and knocking the queen to the ground, I was on top of her. I felt my throat constrict, but I lifted the wind sword up and, with a cry that I didn't even recognize as coming from my own throat, drove it into her.

Time seemed to slow. The Troll Queen stared at the sword buried in her chest, then up at me. Black-red blood was flowing from the wound, soaking her white gown, and a line of it seeped from her nose, trickling down into the valley on the right side of her face. Her eyes locked onto mine, and the squeezing around my throat tightened. Once more, I could no longer breathe. My vision dimmed; the room spun around.

"Charles," I whispered.

The Troll Queen's body gave a great shudder and went still. I gasped. I could breathe again.

My throat burning, I stared into her eyes, and as I watched, they faded from white-yellow to green. And then they emptied. She was dead.

ESTELLE

TANTE SIB HAD FALLEN INTO A SLEEP we could not wake her from. Oncle Neddy said she was still alive. He had me put my fingers to her throat, and I could feel a very faint pulse there.

When Oncle Neddy needed to rest, I sat by her. I told Tante Sib I had been listening to the winds, but I needed her to get better so I could understand their music.

ROSE

I LOOKED OVER AT WHERE THE WHITE BEAR had fallen and saw that he was now a man again. He was Charles. And he was bleeding heavily from his left side.

I went to him quickly, still breathing hard. I looked closely at the wound and thought that, unlike Urda's, it was not a mortal one. But I needed to stanch the bleeding.

His eyes flicked open, and he saw me. A small smile curved his mouth.

"Nyamh," he whispered.

"Yes," I rasped, through my injured throat.

And the hope I'd had without even being aware of it, that once the Troll Queen was dead, he would remember me, died. He would never remember me. I realized that now.

But I saw feeling in his eyes. Relief and joy that I was alive, that Nyamh was alive. And I thought maybe somehow this was destiny, the way it was fated to be. Nyamh had been my first and true name given to me by my father.

These thoughts ran through my mind as I carefully cleaned and bound my white bear's wound.

"Where is Winn? Where is my son?" he asked as I worked.

I had already checked on Winn, knew he was still in the cradle. When I had glanced in, I saw that he was awake, but barely. I guessed that the cup he'd been drinking from was filled with slank.

"He is fine," I said, my voice raw. "Hold still, please."

Suddenly Charles noticed my bandaged hand. "What happened to you, Nyamh?" he asked.

"I will tell you later," I croaked.

When I was satisfied with the binding of his wound, I helped him stand and cross to Winn. Our bairn was fast asleep now. Charles reached over and gently touched his face, his eyes tender. He turned to me.

"Let us leave this place, Nyamh," he said, with a glance over at the lifeless body of the queen.

"Yes," I whispered fervently.

I gathered Winn up, taking the blankets and furs from the cradle with me, and I took him outdoors, away from that room of ice. I settled him in the currach, surrounding him with the bedding. Charles followed me slowly. He was weak from his wound and the loss of blood.

He stopped in the doorway, looking back.

"Should we . . ." he said, trailing off.

"What?"

"Her body," he said.

"Bury her?" I asked.

We were both silent for a few moments.

"No," I finally said, touching my throat.

I went and got my bloody sword and my pack. And, almost as an afterthought, I picked up the queen *echecs* piece from the table.

I shut the door behind me. I could hear a click. Putting my hand on the door handle, I tried turning it, but it did not move.

"It is locked tight," I said in my thick voice to Charles. "And I have the only key." The key made of my bone lay in my pocket.

I looked up at the blackhouse. "Her tomb," I whispered.

Charles went and sat by Winn in the currach, gazing down contentedly at his son.

"Food . . . in the basket," I said, though I was sure I would not be able to swallow anything for a while.

While Charles inspected the contents of the Morae hamper, I took the wind sword down to the water and washed it clean of the Troll Queen's blood. I dried it with a cloth I had taken from the Morae's basket. It was soft, like the cloth Verendi had given me to dry myself.

While I was drying the wind sword, I heard a distant sound, a melody. And I thought I heard Sib, her voice, singing. I knew it was impossible, but it was a mournful song. It sounded like she was saying goodbye.

"No, Sib, no," I whispered, filled with anguish. Something bad was happening, to Sib.

I listened closely to the wind.

NEDDY

S IB HAD BEEN GETTING STEADILY WORSE. The words she had said to me, that seemed to say she welcomed death, tortured me. I couldn't leave her side. I was afraid if I did, she would disappear, die.

She could not die. I would not let her die.

I was sitting by her. It was late afternoon, and I could hear the sound of the wind outside the ship.

Sib's eyes came open, and she saw me. "It is time, Neddy," she said. Her breathing was shallow, but she was smiling.

"No, Sib," I said. I thought of Rose, wishing she were here. Maybe between us we could convince Sib to stay.

And Sib's eyes flickered. "Rose?" she said.

I thought she had become delirious. "Rose will come back to us, soon," I said.

"Rose," Sib said again, and smiled, but it was a different kind of smile. "Open the window, Neddy."

I knew she was delirious then, because the only window in the room was a porthole, and we were below the water line.

"I can't," I said gently.

"Oh, of course," she whispered. "Take me up on deck."

And wordlessly, I gathered her up in my arms, wrapping her in blankets, and carried her up on deck.

I found a fairly sheltered spot on the starboard side and settled her carefully in her blankets. It was a cool autumn afternoon.

"Can you feel it, Neddy?" she said. "It is *ciuin*. Rose is sending it." Her eyes were lit, and I thought I could see color coming into her cheeks.

She laughed. "Rose, what a good student you are," she said softly.

I had no idea what Sib was talking about, but I could feel the wind now, too. It was warmer and softer than the breeze I'd felt when we first came up on deck. And it seemed to be curling around us.

"Very well," Sib said, to no one, as far as I could tell. "If you both insist." And she reached out and took my hand in hers. "I'll stay."

Her hand was no longer icy cold, but warm. I was flooded with relief.

"Welcome back," I said lamely. But she understood.

Estelle found us there, laughing and crying all at once, and she pronounced us a pair of cuckooheads.

WHITE BEAR

I WANTED TO HOLD MY SON, so I picked him up and set him on my lap. He beamed up at me, drowsily.

I looked over at Nyamh, who just a moment ago had been cleaning her sword. Even at a distance, I could see the livid purple bruise marks on her throat. She was sitting very still now, the sword held between her hands. It looked as though her eyes were closed. And I thought I could hear her singing. Slowly she raised the sword up high, in front of her, the song growing louder.

It was lovely. I closed my eyes and listened. Winn seemed to hear it too, and he nestled his head closer to my chest.

I almost dozed off, and it occurred to me I hadn't slept in many days. I had forgotten that white bears didn't need much sleep, especially when they were swimming.

But men do, I thought, yawning.

Nyamh's song ended. She lowered the sword and turned toward us, her cheeks flushed and a look of wonder on her face.

I wanted to ask what had just happened, with the song and the sword, but I was too tired to form words. *Later,* I thought.

BOOK FIVE
OEST

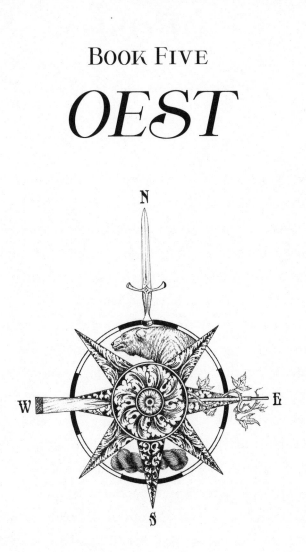

They had a fair wind and came to their father's landing place.
—The Edda

ROSE

C HARLES FELL ASLEEP SHORTLY after we launched the currach, Winn snug in his lap.

I was tired, too, very tired, but I wanted to get away from the island. There was a fresh wind, and it was that friendly western wind, *ciuin,* that I now loved better than any other. I raised the sail and pointed the tiller east.

As Charles and Winn slept, I thought about what had happened when I was cleaning the wind sword. I had felt the music suddenly and the sword lifted up in my hands of its own volition. It had been a similar feeling to when I was demonstrating the wind cloak for the three Morae. I had felt as if the wind had entered me, making my body thrum with its music. And also, as before, I thought I felt Sib's answer, and this time she was telling me that she wasn't going to say goodbye after all.

When we came to the island of the Morae, I was careful to give the whirlpool a wide berth. Charles had awakened by then, and it was he who noticed the box floating in the sea.

I recognized it at once as one of the boxes Verendi had shown me that held the *echecs* sets. They must have decided to be done with them. I was tempted to try to retrieve the box and take it home with us, but it bobbed away, and pursuing it would have meant getting too close to the whirlpool.

So I let it go, wondering idly where it might wash up one day.

One astonishing thing that occurred was that the Morae hamper of food never seemed to empty. No matter how much we ate, and Charles ate a great deal, it replenished itself. He liked the food, which he thought was the kind you might find in Gresk. He grew particularly fond of a pie he found at the bottom, made of spinach, creamy white cheese, and flaky pastry. As I watched him eat, I was very grateful to the Morae for this parting gift.

It grew cold out on the sea. I was glad of the white furs for Winn, and I had Charles put on the black cloak that I had made to go under the fire cloak. It was small for him and he said it smelled of smoke, but he was grateful for the warmth.

Charles was curious about the three cloaks I had made for the Morae, so in my raspy, whispery voice, I managed to tell him the whole story. I left out Verendi's "great love" bit, but he marveled at my ingenuity, especially when it came to the wind cloak.

I told him I thought Sib had had something to do with that.

Then he wanted to know about my bound hand. I hadn't dared look at it since, and the cloths binding it were dirty and stained with dried blood. Silently I unwound them.

Charles was horrified. "Nyamh! How?"

And even though it hurt to talk, I told him as best I could, about the bird and the lost key, and all that followed.

He was silent for a long time after that, looking up at me in wonder every now and then. I busied myself with cleaning the place where my finger had been and carefully rebinding it with fresh soft cloth, again from the Morae hamper.

Winn awoke, and we discovered that his cloths were very smelly. We found that, like the basket of food, the cloths from the Morae magically replenished themselves, which came in very handy.

It was Charles who came up with the plan of dipping the bairn's bottom in the sea to rinse him off, and washing his cloths in the same way.

The water was cold, and Winn let out a squeal at first, but he seemed to enjoy kicking his feet in the sea waves. I watched a little nervously at first, but I needn't have worried. Charles kept a tight hold of his son.

NEDDY

ONCE SIB HAD RECOVERED, we immediately set sail. Our captain was still leery of this search for a mythical island not on the map, but I insisted.

That night was a fine autumn evening with a bright half-moon above. Sib came and joined me on deck. There was color back in her face, and once she had settled beside me, I took hold of her hand.

"Just tell me, Sib, that you are not planning on going anywhere anytime soon?"

She smiled, squeezing my hand. "No, Neddy, I'm not going anywhere."

"And how do you feel about the possibility of *never* leaving me?"

She turned and gazed at me. I waited anxiously for her reply, but she said nothing.

"I'm asking you to marry me, Sib."

"I know."

"And?"

"Yes," she said. And I grabbed her to me in an unbelieving, ecstatic embrace.

"But first," she said, pulling away, "I need to tell you."

I gazed at her, feeling a flicker of alarm at the solemn expression on her face. "Tell me what?"

"Everything. The reason I was not sad at the thought of dying. Why I felt I could never marry. It is a strange tale, Neddy, one that most would have trouble believing. But with the things you and your family have witnessed and lived through, I'm hoping you will understand."

She took a deep breath and began.

"When I was a bairn, less than a year old, I was stolen away from my mother and taken to live with people who were not my own."

"What people?" I asked.

"The Sidhe, they call themselves. In other parts of the world, they are known as fairies or elves or fee, and like trolls, they live hidden from human eyes, mostly underground. They are not evil like the Troll Queen, but they are not good, either. They are selfish and cold and indifferent to anyone's needs but their own.

"They stole me because I was a pretty wee child with blond curls who would entertain them for a time."

I gazed at Sib, my eyes wide. I had heard of fairies, but thought they were made-up creatures from children's stories, which of course was what I had once believed about trolls.

"My mother finally found a way to rescue me, but I lived

with the Sidhe for five years. And in those years, several things happened to me. First, I learned about the wind."

"The wind?"

She nodded. "The Sidhe woman I lived with had that as her skill, and she taught it to me. I told Rose about this. I even taught her wind music, as I call it. It is a kind of arts or magic, and it is what saved me. Or Rose saved me. But I am getting ahead of myself."

She gazed off over the river. "The wind music is how I healed you, Neddy," she said, turning back to me. "I had never done anything like it before. I wasn't even sure that I could. But I called on *airde gaoth,* a bracing fresh wind from the west. It is said to have healing in it."

I squeezed her hand, not able to find the words to express how grateful I was, but she knew. "Sib, did the calling of *airde gaoth* harm you?"

She paused before replying. "When I call on the wind, like I did the time we needed to cross Halsfjord, it depletes me, takes much out of me. And healing you, and later, when I helped Rose, those nearly broke me."

She took a deep breath. "But there is more, Neddy. Something else happened to me when I was with the Sidhe. You see, I took on some of their qualities, one in particular that sets me apart from other human beings." She paused again. "This thing is the reason I did not want to get close to you, Neddy. In truth, it still worries me."

I could not imagine what she was leading to.

"You see, the Sidhe live much longer lives than we do. They are not immortal exactly, but they age very, very slowly. And by living among them, in their world, some of that rubbed off onto me. I didn't realize it right away, but as the years went on, my mother saw it. She prepared me as best she could, knowing I'd still be young when she died."

And suddenly so many little things I had wondered about Sib came together in my head. The ageless way she had about her. The many places she had traveled to. The experiences she'd lived through, like the Sweating Sickness, which hadn't occurred in Europa for a hundred years.

I must have been gaping at her, for she shook her head, giving a wistful laugh.

"That is just the expression I never wanted to see on your face," she said.

"I'm sorry," I said, squeezing her hand again. "It is a lot to take in."

"Of course it is," she replied. "You'll want to know how old I am, and I can't tell you that, not exactly. But I believe I have lived close to two hundred years."

I shook my head in wonder, trying to absorb all the ramifications.

"As I said, I am not immortal. And if someone should thrust a dagger into my heart, I would die. But I seem to be immune to most of the sicknesses of our world."

We were silent a few moments.

"Have you . . ." I started, but stopped, feeling awkward all of a sudden.

"I have not had a husband, or children," Sib said, her eyes on the horizon. A gull swooped down and glided over the surface of the water, wings not moving.

"Early on, I had friends, people I grew close to, but when they aged and I did not, it was hard, even frightening for them. So I always traveled on. And I stopped getting close to people. It was too painful. I felt very different, outside of life somehow. I was not Sidhe, but I was not human anymore either. I belonged nowhere." Her eyes were bright with tears. "So I lived a wandering life, never staying in one place for very long.

"When I was stolen by the trolls, it was almost a relief. I also thought it possible I might finally die, since they were so brutal with their slaves. But Rose and Charles rescued me and took me in. I couldn't help but love them."

She paused, wiping a tear from her cheek.

"Even now I don't know, Neddy," she said. "I'm still trying to figure out this strange, overlong life of mine."

"But you are now willing to let me try to help you sort it out?" I asked.

She nodded, and I pulled her into my arms, my heart brimming. I would not have thought it possible to love Sib more than before, but I did.

Then she pulled away. "I do wonder, though, if something

has changed," Sib said softly. "Ever since I called on the *airde gaoth*, I have felt different. Would it not be ironic if I started to age, and it is you who buries me?"

"How about this, Sib," I said with a smile. "Let's not think about our dying time just now, but concentrate on the time we have ahead of us, together."

She smiled back. "I can do that," she said.

ROSE

W E WERE IN THE THIRD DAY of our journey back to
Leodhas. Winn was showing signs of wanting to crawl,
which wasn't good timing, given that we three were confined
to the small currach.

I was relieved, though, that he only called me Maman once.
Charles thought he'd said, *Nyamh* and was impressed that
Winn somehow had picked up my name.

"Although he is showing no sign of saying Papa or Dada,"
he said wistfully.

"He will," I replied.

By the fourth day, we were beginning to be sick of even the
flaky cheese and spinach pie, though Charles's hunger seemed
unabated. "Still a little of the white bear hanging on," he said,
ruefully, "though I have to say that even one thousand serv-
ings of spinach pie would be a great deal better than eating
dead raw shark in the middle of the sea."

He went on to describe the northern lights he had seen,
how immense and beautiful they were. But out of the corner
of my eye, I saw Winn had managed to let himself down into

the bottom of the currach and was about to grab hold of my wind sword.

Charles got to him just in time, snatching the sword away, and Winn let out a howl of disappointment. Charles's nose wrinkled.

"Time for a change," he said, and grabbing Winn up, he unwrapped his cloths, handing them to me.

"Thank you," I said dryly, and turned to rinse them over the side of the currach.

Charles did his bottom-dipping routine, and Winn continued to cry and sputter. I handed Charles a clean cloth from the Morae hamper.

"Nyamh," Charles suddenly blurted out as he wrapped the fresh cloth on Winn's bottom, "You have never spoken to me of the husband you lost. I wondered if you . . . if you perhaps still have feelings for him?"

"I do," I said. My throat was better, though still purple with bruising, so my voice only cracked a little.

"Oh," Charles answered, looking a little crestfallen. "But maybe . . ." he went on, then stopped. He abruptly started up again, his voice rushed, "I know this is the worst possible moment I could pick, and I am still a puzzle of a man, with too many missing pieces. But I was wondering, would you ever consider, I mean, do you think it even remotely possible that you might one day consider taking me as . . . as husband? Nyamh?"

Winn had stopped crying and let out a chortle, reaching for Charles's ear.

Nyamh. I gazed at him silently.

And I decided that it was enough.

In some unexpected astonishing way we had found our way back to each other. And in truth, I had fallen in love all over again, but this time with the man, not the white bear.

"Yes," I said. "I do. I would. I will."

NEDDY

I T WAS ESTELLE WHO SPOTTED THE LITTLE BOAT. She had been determined to be the first to spy the isle we were hoping to find and had been fastened to the prow, watching the horizon avidly.

"*Regardez!*" she shouted out, and turned toward me. "It is them, Oncle Neddy. I know it is!"

I peered in the direction she was pointing.

"Rose," I whispered. Then louder, I called out, "Rose!"

MOTHER

SOON AFTER THEIR RETURN, Rose sat us down and explained all about Charles's lost memory of her and how we were supposed to keep quiet about it. She said she was planning on telling him, but not until after they were wed. For the second time.

I told her it was *extremely* unlucky to wed the same person twice, and Rose and I had a quarrel that went on for some time. But she wouldn't change her mind. And Arne told me I needed to respect her decision.

I tried hard, but the name Nyamh stuck in my throat. It had always bothered me that Arne had secretly named her that, entirely against my wishes. So I just avoided calling Rose anything at all.

Winn was more endearing than ever, with his sweet nature and winsome smile. He had grown so much, was already talking and of course crawling everywhere. He loved splashing in any kind of water, had a dreamy, farseeing look in his eyes, and loved to laugh. A west-born child if ever I'd seen one.

It was a busy time, planning not just one but two weddings, Sib and Neddy first and then Rose and Charles. Fortunately

 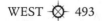

both couples wanted small celebrations. Especially Rose and Charles. Which was understandable. A second wedding!

The whole notion made me shudder. I told Rose more than once, with all the ill fortune they'd already faced, why tempt fate? A second wedding. It was madness.

ROSE

WE ALL BORE SCARS from our brush with the pale queen. Some visible, some not.

My ankle had long since healed, and the purple bruises at my neck had mostly faded, but I still took the prize for the most impressive tapestry of scars, the lost finger being the most eye-catching. It had healed cleanly, with the help of an herbal concoction of Sib's. And I found it took little time to get used to being without it. The only thing that gave me trouble at first was weaving, but that soon came easily once again.

Estelle took great pride in her scars, especially the troll-snake bite on her shoulder, which her "cousins" were in awe of.

The wound to Charles's side had also healed cleanly. It was a white jagged ridge that sometimes ached on cold nights. It also reminded us both a little of troll skin.

Sib had developed a tendency to catch cold easily, but this actually pleased her, since it proved to her that she had indeed become more "human." She and Neddy had told Charles and me of her history soon after we returned to Trondheim. I could not even fathom that Sib had been alive so long. But it struck me that she and Charles bore that in common, and in truth, I do think they became closer as a result.

Neddy was somewhat embarrassed to have acquired no scars at all, and in fact, had come out of the whole thing with the greatest piece of luck he could imagine, Sib as his soon-to-be wife.

And Winn, well, that remained to be seen. Since that moment in the blackhouse that turned into an icehouse, when the Troll Queen had been holding Winn, neither Charles nor I had noticed any sign of the arts she claimed to have given him. It was true he was a very alert child, talking far sooner than any bairn I'd ever heard tell of. But Neddy reminded me that I too had been an unusual bairn, walking much earlier than most bairns.

One rather unfortunate outcome of what had occurred was that Mother got it into her head that because of the dream of the ash raven and the extraordinary accuracy of its prophecy, she had the makings of a *skjebne-soke*. She even suggested that she and I join forces, as a sort of mother-daughter fortune-telling team, and that we should offer our services far and wide.

I told her that under no circumstances would I consider such a thing. She wasn't deterred, of course, until Father pointed out that she'd had only one dream since the raven dream. It had been about the lingonberry plants in the woods beyond our meadow all withering and dying out, when in point of fact, we had the best crop of lingonberries ever that fall.

Fortunately Mother continued her previous non-dreaming ways and was forced to reconsider her *skjebne-soke* ambitions.

NEDDY

S IB AND I GOT MARRIED the week before winter solstice in the barn behind our family house. Rose, Estelle, and Gudrun had set dozens of candles all around, as well as garlands of Njorden spruce tied up with red ribbons. Sib looked radiant in a simple white dress and a circlet of white holly berries in her silver hair. I felt like the luckiest man alive.

Just as we were ready to begin the ceremony of binding, I stepped up to Sib, saying I had something I wanted to read out loud. Sib was surprised, but happily agreed. I felt a little nervous as I drew out my paper with the writing on it.

"It's a poem," I said. "And it is short, I promise," I added, catching Rose's eye. She grinned.

"To Sib," I read.

> *You are my west wind,*
> *my east, north, and south.*
> *And you have blown open*
> *the door to my heart.*
> *Forever.*

Everyone clapped, at first politely, but then with more enthusiasm. I noticed that Rose clapped the loudest. But most important, Sib hugged me tight, her eyes glistening, and whispered in my ear, "It was beautiful, Neddy. Thank you."

And as we were putting the rings on each other's fingers, I felt a gentle wind curling around us, and could have sworn I heard a faint melody. I saw a quick knowing look pass between Sib and Rose and I smiled. I guessed that the wind was *ciuin* and knew that it was a lucky one.

Father told me later that once again Mother had deliberately not brought a handkerchief to the wedding, but this time Father had assigned Estelle the job of loaning her one, only to discover that it was bad luck for a girl from Fransk, wearing a red dress, to loan anybody anything on someone's wedding day.

"Such nonsense," Father had grumbled, but, resigned, handed over his handkerchief to Mother.

ROSE

M Y SECOND WEDDING TO THE WHITE BEAR took place on the winter solstice itself.

We gathered in the great room, just as we had almost four years before.

I well knew Mother believed that marrying the same person twice was exceedingly unlucky and that she had tied little sprigs of dried bayberry all over the room for luck, as well as loading herself down with good luck charms. Estelle said the odor was far superior to the garlic that had been ever present during the Sweating Sickness.

Mother had also insisted that Charles put three grains of coarse salt in the left-hand pocket of his jacket. I told him to ignore her, but he said there was no harm and gamely went along with it.

And then came the moment when Charles turned to me, preparing to put the silver Valois ring on my left ring finger. But suddenly he froze.

Something flared in his eyes; they almost seemed to change color, as if he was being lit from within. His mouth curved into a wide smile, and reaching over, he deliberately slid the ring onto my thumb, saying, "I take you, *Rose*, for wife."

I stared at him in shock.

"Did he say Rose?" I heard Mother say.

And Father whispered loudly, "Yes, he said Rose. Now, hush, Eugenia."

But Mother called out in a triumphant voice, "Just in the nick of time. Why, that is the best luck of all!"

And at that moment, my white bear kissed me, over and over and over again.

After the wedding celebration was finished, after we raised the last toast, ate the last bite of the traditional wedding cake, *kransekake,* and washed the last dish, Charles and I slipped away to our favorite spot by Trondheim harbor. We were bundled up in furs and scarves and mittens, but just as we had four years ago, we sat side by side on a blanket, sipping cold apple juice and eating brown bread. We could see a handful of Yule bonfires off on Munkholmen Island to celebrate the solstice. And instead of looking up into a pale midnight sun sky, we were treated to a display of northern lights that seemed to have been put on especially for us.

"Rose," Charles said, "I have a confession to make."

I turned to look at him.

"It is true that I had come to care about you as Nyamh. But

when you told me that you had cut off your finger to make a key to get into the blackhouse, well, it crossed my mind . . . I mean, I wondered, because who but a mother would do such a thing? A mother for her child. You had said you had a husband who was lost—"

"Which was the truth," I said.

"I know. But still I wondered."

A swath of dazzling purple pulsed across the sky.

"Why do you think you finally remembered?" I asked. "Why did it happen then, putting the ring on my finger? Why not when the pale queen died?"

"I have wondered that myself," he replied. "And I cannot tell you the why of it, only the how. How for the longest time, there was this hole, a blank space, where the memory of a wife should be. I desperately wanted to fill it, see a face, which I believed wasn't yours. But then I came to a point when I didn't want to remember, because of the feelings I was beginning to have for you, for Nyamh. But when we were standing there, with the rings, in front of all the people we love, it came flooding back. Like a blazing sun bursting through pitch-dark clouds. The blank spot was gone. The one I loved then was the one I loved now. Or is it the other way around?" He smiled broadly.

I laughed. "And it was just in the nick of time, according to Mother. Apparently your remembering me at that crucial moment removed all the bad luck of a second marriage," I said. Giving a mock shudder, I added. "Think of the doom we narrowly averted."

"A close call indeed," he said, grinning.

I took a sip of apple juice, dreamily watching the vivid plumes of green and purple and blue billow across the sky.

"There's something else I've been thinking," Charles said.

"Yes?" I asked.

"About Winn, about our son," he said. "His name."

I came alert, for I had been thinking of that as well. "What about his name?"

"That it should be Tuki. It was our first thought, when he was born. And . . ."

I nodded. "Urda," I said. "It is because of her he is alive."

"Yes," said Charles.

"It would please her," I said.

"We can go on calling him Winn," Charles said. "It does suit him."

"But *not* because Mother says he is west-born," I said vehemently.

"No, not because of that," Charles said, smiling.

We heard the distant strains of musical notes, no doubt from the winter solstice celebration over on Munkholmen. I recognized the instrument being played as a *harpeleik*, a handheld stringed instrument like a zither that was a favorite of Charles's. The haunting melody wafted around us like one of Sib's winds.

Charles got to his feet. "Rose?" he said, holding out his hand.

I stood, taking his hand, and under the solstice moon, bundled up in our furs and scarves and mittens, we danced. Slowly at first, then whirling and spinning, until finally, out of breath, laughing, we collapsed onto the snowy ground.

And I knew then as I had known from the beginning. It didn't matter whether or not we lived happily ever after. We were where we truly belonged. My white bear and I. Together.

WHITE BEAR

WOULD YOU LIKE TO PLAY? I had once asked the strange, beautiful girl with a voice like rocks.

I looked back over all those years. And realized once and for all that those words had been both my undoing *and* my salvation.

I had lost a kingdom, but gained a life.

A life with Rose.

Estelle

ROSE AND CHARLES DECIDED to officially give Winn the name Tuki. Because of Urda, which seemed right. They said I could go on calling him Winn, and I thought I probably would, especially when he scrunched his face up and howled like the *vent de l'ouest*. They also said that when Winn got old enough, he could decide himself what name he wanted to be called.

Rose made me a beautiful cloak using the wind rose design that Grand-père Arne drew for me, and she gave it to me as a Yule gift, along with the most adorable puppy in the whole wide world. I named him Pip. Gudrun was very envious.

Rose and Charles also decided that we would all stay in Trondheim, make our home here, which made me very happy. I liked it in Njord, where there were cloudberries and *kjottboller*, aunts and uncles, grandparents and cousins.

And there were also far fewer snakes.

Glossary

Alpes—Alps mountain range

Anglia—England

Arktisk—the Arctic

Armagnac—a province in France

echecs—chess (in Fransk)

Europa—Europe

Fransk—France, also French

Gresk—Greece, also Greek

Gronland—Greenland

Hollande—Holland

Huldre—the troll kingdom (also its people)

Inuit—a people who live in the far north of Greenland and Canada

kentta murha—killing fields in Niflheim

Kina—China

leidarstein—lodestone

Leodhas—Isle of Lewis, Scotland

Niflheim—frozen land of the dead

Njord—Norway

Njordsjoen—North Sea

Nokken—a shape-shifting water monster that often takes the form of a white horse

Portugali—Portugal

Pyrennes—the Pyrenees mountains

skac—chess (in Huldre)

skjebne-soke—fortuneteller

Skottland—Scotland

Spania—Spain

Sveitsland—Switzerland

Sverige—Sweden

Under Huldre—a race of trolls that lives underground

ACKNOWLEDGMENTS

When I finished *East* all those years ago, I never dreamed I would set out on another journey with Rose and her white bear. But my indefatigable homegirl tugged and tugged on my sleeve, telling me her adventuring wasn't done. Not by a long shot.

And I was lucky to have an equally indefatigable assortment of comrades on my journey who provided much-needed navigation, support, wisdom, and tactical advice.

Thank you:

To Rubin Pfeffer, who is rock-steady, creative, and shrewd, the best agent a girl could ever have.

To Nicole Sclama, my remarkable editor. Even though you officially took the reins mid-journey, I quickly realized you'd been there all along, loving Rose and her white bear. Thank you for your tireless heart and talent.

To Jeannette Larson, with whom I only got to travel for a short spell but whose insight and grace were invaluable. And Elizabeth Bewley, who was along for an even shorter stretch, but who was an enthusiastic caretaker.

To the team at HMH, who shepherded this new journey

with creativity and care, especially copyeditor Ana Deboo, who had a laser eye for all my modern slang, French malapropisms, and historical inaccuracies. And someday I promise I'll finally figure out the difference between *further* and *farther.*

To Michael Stearns, my editor and spirit guide on *East,* who still makes me laugh.

To *all* librarians/Havamals, and especially Mark, Erin, Megan, and Bev at UAPL for tracking down answers to all my unusual, sometimes preposterous, questions.

To David Diaz, who motivated me to finally come up with a birth direction chart and whose resulting wind rose inspired me during the last leg of the journey.

To Jody Casella and Natalie Richards, my early readers, who keep me grounded and helped me find that artist within. And to Cecil Castellucci, who met me once at a panel in LA and over Thai food agreed to read a first draft.

To the rest of OHYA—Erin McCahan (who gets the very first ARC!), Lisa Klein, Margaret Peterson Haddix, Julia DeVillers, Linda Gerber (welcome back!), Rae Carson (we still miss you!)—because the truth is I never really had a tribe until I found you.

To Allyn Johnston, just because you believed in me from the *very* beginning and were willing to take a chance on me when others weren't so sure.

To my TROLs—Beth, Claudia, Carol, Edie G., Lori, Kristen, Sandy, Sally, Arlene, and Susan—who are not in fact trolls, but instead the most excellent group of children's lit champions in the universe.

To my mom, for your enduring support and love, and for teaching me early on to love books.

To Vita, my rock-star philosopher daughter, who stepped up at a crucial moment to be my first reader. Love you to the moon and back and then some.

To Charles, as always, who makes what I do possible. You are patient and wise and good, and I would gladly suffer altitude sickness for you. And in fact, I have.

And lastly a special thank-you to all the young women who grew up with *East,* and who still write me amazing letters that make me cry. You are all Rose, each in your own way, and you are all wonderful.